DESPERATE REM

THOMAS HARDY was born in Higher Bockhampton, Dorset, on 2 June 1840; his father was a builder in a small way of business, and he was educated locally and in Dorchester before being articled to an architect. After sixteen years in that profession and the publication of his earliest novel *Desperate Remedies* (1871), he determined to make his career in literature; not, however, before his work as an architect had led to his meeting, at St Juliot in Cornwall, Emma Gifford, who became his first wife in 1874.

In the 1860s Hardy had written a substantial amount of unpublished verse, but during the next twenty years almost all his creative effort went into novels and short stories. *Jude the Obscure*, the last written of his novels, came out in 1895, closing a sequence of fiction that includes *Far from the Madding Crowd* (1874), *The Return of the Native* (1878), *Two on a Tower* (1882), *The Mayor of Casterbridge* (1886), and *Tess of the d'Urbervilles* (1891).

Hardy maintained in later life that only in poetry could he truly express his ideas; and the more than nine hundred poems in his collected verse (almost all published after 1898) possess great individuality and power.

In 1910 Hardy was awarded the Order of Merit; in 1912 Emma died and two years later he married Florence Dugdale. Thomas Hardy died in January 1928; the work he left behind—the novels, the poetry, and the epic drama *The Dynasts*—forms one of the supreme achievements in English imaginative literature.

PATRICIA INGHAM is Senior Research Fellow and Reader in English at St Anne's College, Oxford. She has edited texts by Hardy, Dickens, Gaskell, and Gissing, as well as writing widely on the Victorian novel. Her work includes *Thomas Hardy: A Feminist Reading* (1989), *Dickens, Women and Language* (1992), *The Language of Gender and Class: Transformation in the Victorian Novel* (1996), *Invisible Writing and the Victorian Novel* (2001), and *The Brontës: A Critical Reader* (2002). She is the General Editor of the Authors in Context series in Oxford World's Classics, for which she has written the volume on Thomas Hardy (2003).

OXFORD WORLD'S CLASSICS

For over 100 years Oxford World's Classics have brought readers closer to the world's great literature. Now with over 700 titles—from the 4,000-year-old myths of Mesopotamia to the twentieth century's greatest novels—the series makes available lesser-known as well as celebrated writing.

The pocket-sized hardbacks of the early years contained introductions by Virginia Woolf, T. S. Eliot, Graham Greene, and other literary figures which enriched the experience of reading.

Today the series is recognized for its fine scholarship and reliability in texts that span world literature, drama and poetry, religion, philosophy and politics. Each edition includes perceptive commentary and essential background information to meet the changing needs of readers.

OXFORD WORLD'S CLASSICS

═══

THOMAS HARDY

Desperate Remedies

═══

Edited with an Introduction and Notes by
PATRICIA INGHAM

OXFORD
UNIVERSITY PRESS

OXFORD

UNIVERSITY PRESS

Great Clarendon Street, Oxford OX2 6DP

Oxford University Press is a department of the University of Oxford.
It furthers the University's objective of excellence in research, scholarship,
and education by publishing worldwide in

Oxford New York

Auckland Bangkok Buenos Aires Cape Town Chennai
Dar es Salaam Delhi Hong Kong Istanbul Karachi Kolkata
Kuala Lumpur Madrid Melbourne Mexico City Mumbai Nairobi
São Paulo Shanghai Taipei Tokyo Toronto

Oxford is a registered trade mark of Oxford University Press
in the UK and in certain other countries

Published in the United States
by Oxford University Press Inc., New York

Editorial matter © Patricia Ingham 2003

The moral rights of the author have been asserted
Database right Oxford University Press (maker)

First published as an Oxford World's Classics paperback 2003
Reissued 2009

British Library Cataloguing in Publication Data

Data available

Library of Congress Cataloging in Publication Data

Data available

ISBN 978–0–19–955482–9

12

Typeset in Ehrhardt
by RefineCatch Limited, Bungay, Suffolk
Printed and bound in Great Britain
by Clays Ltd, Elcograf S.p.A.

For Mary, Tony, and Michael Dixon

For Max, Tom, and Michael Dixon

CONTENTS

ACKNOWLEDGEMENTS

I should like to thank Jenny Harrington for her generous help in preparing this edition. I am also grateful to Emma Plaskitt and the News International Research Fund.

INTRODUCTION

Readers who do not wish to learn details of the plot will prefer to treat the Introducion as an Epilogue

When *Desperate Remedies* became Hardy's first published novel in 1871, one reviewer suggested that it was a desperate remedy 'for an emaciated purse'.[1] This is an allusion to its use of a genre that was hugely popular in the 1860s, the sensation novel—now most familiar in the works of Wilkie Collins. Hardy had been advised by George Meredith to write a narrative with 'more plot' than his earlier attempt, *The Poor Man and the Lady*, and this was his response. His novel certainly did not lack plot, and perhaps had an excess of it. The villainous central figure, Aeneas Manston, is the illegitimate son (as well as the steward) of his employer, Miss Cytherea Aldclyffe. Although married, he becomes infatuated with Cytherea Graye, a girl who has been reduced to serving as Miss Aldclyffe's maid but who is, as becomes evident, the daughter of the man who was the love of Miss Aldclyffe's life, whom she rejected from shame at her pregnancy by another man. Manston is a ruthless manipulator, and having disposed of his wife and hidden her corpse, he succeeds in persuading Cytherea to marry him. This involves playing on her affection for her ailing brother, Owen Graye. Before the marriage can be consummated, however, suspicions are aroused. Cytherea is separated from her putative husband by friends. The body of Manston's wife is discovered and he is arrested after attempting to rape Cytherea. He commits suicide, leaving a full confession. The girl is now free to marry Edward Springrove, the impoverished man she really loves. Miss Aldclyffe dies, apparently of a broken heart in the form of a burst blood vessel. Such a melodramatic story led later critics to regard *Desperate Remedies* as a youthful pot-boiler far removed from the major works of Hardy in the 1880s and 1890s. In fact it laid the foundation for such texts: both in its engagement with the issues of class and gender and in the emergence of the wider question of what Hardy was to call 'the Whence and

[1] R. G. Cox, *Thomas Hardy: The Critical Heritage* (New York: Barnes & Noble, 1970), 4.

the Wherefore of things'. These were to become his permanent preoccupations.

The earlier unpublished novel had been refused by no fewer than three publishers. Though it was never printed in its original form, Hardy used it as a basis for his novella, *An Indiscretion in the Life of an Heiress*, in 1878. From this work, the title of the original text, surviving comments from the publishers who were approached, and an account by Edmund Gosse of what Hardy recalled in 1915 about his first novel, it is possible to reconstruct it in some detail.[2] And if *Desperate Remedies* is the foundation of later novels, it already owes much to *The Poor Man and the Lady*. Certainly Hardy plundered the latter for his first published novel as well as for *An Indiscretion*. For it is evident from the sources listed that Hardy's first attempt at narrative focused on a figure who was to become a prototype for many of his central male characters. This figure is a man of humble origins whose intellectual or artistic talents lead him to expect upward mobility but whose move across the social divide is thwarted by the class above him. Such men include Stephen Smith in *A Pair of Blue Eyes*, Swithin St Clair in *Two on a Tower*, Jude Fawley in *Jude the Obscure*, as well as related figures like George Somerset in *A Laodicean* and Christopher Julian in *The Hand of Ethelberta*.

The Poor Man *and Social Class*

At the beginning of his career Hardy's focus was on social class, with marriage of a lower-class man to a superior woman as a test of acceptability. Obviously there is a parallel with his own life, for he was the son of a working builder as well as being an exceptionally talented man. Like the hero of *The Poor Man*, Hardy fell in love with the daughter of a higher-class family, that of John Gifford, a solicitor who rejected him as a son-in-law. Gifford wrote of Hardy as a 'low-born churl who has presumed to marry into my family'.[3] In *The Poor Man*, Will Strong is a professional success but frustrated in his love for Miss Allenville (the Lady) by her wealthy family, who prefer a superior suitor. The issue, however, is not so much thwarted love as

    [2] Pamela Dalziel, 'Exploiting *The Poor Man*: The Genesis of Hardy's *Desperate Remedies*', *Journal of English and Germanic Philology*, 94: 2 (1995), 220–32.
    [3] M. Millgate, *Thomas Hardy: A Biography* (Oxford: Oxford University Press, 1982), 143.

the injustice inherent in the family's refusal to accept a man who is in all respects suitable as a husband for Geraldine except for his humble origins. Geraldine is a subsidiary figure, and indeed shows the family awareness of Strong's social inferiority even though she loves him. The lovers are consequently not equally represented as victims: it is Strong who is the martyr to social pressures. The idea of women as victimized, whatever their class, was to come later, as Hardy gradually recognized the two forms of discrimination as equivalent. The beginning of this recognition is found in *Desperate Remedies*, as will appear. But evidently in *The Poor Man* social satire on the failings of the upper classes was the central subject. As one of the rejecting publishers, Alexander Macmillan, put it, Hardy went in for the 'wholesale blackening of a class' which was inappropriate for a writer who lacked 'large & intimate knowledge of it'.[4] Macmillan felt that, unlike Thackeray in his social satire, 'you mean *mischief*'.

From what is known of *The Poor Man*, it is clear that the title captures the whole of the plot and there are no further complications to deflect attention from it. In *Desperate Remedies* a similar plot is there in the struggles of Edward Springrove to rise from his humble origins. From the beginning Springrove is represented (like his predecessors, Will Strong and Egbert Mayne) as victimized by the class system/machine. He is the son of a mere tenant farmer, educated, as others see it, beyond his true social position. Consequently he is not accepted by his social superiors, no matter what his talents. His first aspiration to become a successful poet is eroded by the sense that 'worldly advantage from an art doesn't depend upon mastering it. I used to think it did; but it doesn't. Those who get rich need have no skill at all as artists.' All they need is 'an earnestness in making acquaintances, and a love for using them'. He believes that 'they give their whole attention to the art of dining out' (p. 44).

There is a parallel here with the narrator who makes clear—by his comments on how the upper classes deal with the lower—that he speaks from a social position that matches Springrove's. He too demonstrates his literary aspirations by the use of multiple allusions to canonical works of literature. Springrove connects himself with great poets such as Milton by relating his fate to Edward King, the dead poet mourned in 'Lycidas' as ill-treated by fate. The narrator

⁴ Ibid. 110.

does the same with his many poetic quotations, strewn obtrusively throughout the text, typically in contexts quite alien to their original sense. For instance, a gleam of light is said with no relevance to remind Cytherea of 'the well-known good deed in a naughty world' (p. 53) which Portia refers to in *The Merchant of Venice* (V. i. 90) to describe her lighted house. Or the narrator throws in a Latin tag, *Talibus incusat* ('in such terms he complained') (p. 187) à propos Manston to his mother in the scene where he blackmails her into forcing Springrove to marry his cousin Adelaide, and not Cytherea. A biblical phrase, 'fishers of men', referring to the apostles drawing men into the Christian fold, is applied to Cytherea to indicate her ability to 'catch men'.

These allusions and others assert a claim by the narrator to belong to the cultural elite. The source for many of the quotations is Palgrave's anthology *The Golden Treasury of the Best Songs and Lyrical Poems in the English Language* (1861), a copy of which was given to Hardy in 1862 by his friend Horace Moule. He kept it throughout his life, and it became a tool for self-education; its use in the novel lends the narrator a distinct air of the autodidact. In a notebook Hardy kept headed 'Studies and Specimens &c' he copied quotations from which he drew vocabulary or produced variations on familar phrases. As the editors of the notebook point out, Hardy 'was seeking to provide himself with a poetic background, educate himself in poetic techniques, and initiate a process from which he might just possibly emerge as a practising, perhaps even a publishing, poet'.[5] The use of allusions in *Desperate Remedies* indicates an aspiration to the intellectual and socially superior classes on the part of the narrator; but it became a permanent tool for Hardy. Its use developed in subtlety and sophistication to culminate in *Jude the Obscure*, where Jude's frustrated educational ambition leads him to wrench quotations to his own ironic use.

Certainly the narrator's sensitivity to social snubs in *Desperate Remedies* indicates an empathy with Springrove's own, and is aroused in various contexts. Apparently randomly, during Miss Aldclyffe's visit to her solicitor in London, the narrator refers to the inhabitants of London's clubland as 'the usual well-dressed clubbists—rubicund with alcohol' (p. 104); presumably they are busily

[5] Pamela Dalziel and M. Millgate (eds.), *Thomas Hardy's 'Studies, Specimens &c' Notebook* (Oxford: Clarendon Press, 1994), p. x.

engaged in the kind of networking that Springrove despises in would-be authors. He observes that Miss Aldclyffe's haughtiness 'resented a criticism of her conduct' (p. 193). He describes Owen Graye's 'morbid horror of giving trouble to people above him in rank, and especially to their men-servants, who looked down upon him as a hybrid monster from regions far below the touch-my-hat stage of supremacy' (pp. 144–5). But the narrator most clearly aligns himself with Springrove in his generalization deriving from the latter's interview with Miss Aldclyffe when she coerces him into marrying his cousin: 'Miss Aldclyffe, like a good many others in her position, had plainly not realised that a son of her tenant and inferior, could have become an educated man, who had learnt to feel his individuality, to view society from a Bohemian stand-point far outside the farming grade in Carriford parish' (pp. 192–3).

The Sensation Novel

But there are many complicating factors in *Desperate Remedies* surrounding the story lifted from *The Poor Man*. Hardy, in his Preface to the 1889 edition of the novel, described the book's components as 'mystery, entanglement, surprise, and moral obliquity'. The last of these is a generalized description of illicit passion of various kinds, leading to adultery and bigamy as well as blackmail, theft, and murder. Not all of these appear in every sensation novel, but all are present in *Desperate Remedies*. Similar events are to be found in earlier Gothic novels, where they are given exotic or fantastic settings, but by framing them in solidly domestic surroundings, the sensation novel brings them into contemporary life in a way that makes social issues relevant. They appear more like the lurid newspaper reports of violent crimes which made popular reading, then and later. In a censorious moral climate such novels were licensed for publication and popularity by the narratorial condemnation of the shocking goings-on. As one reviewer put it, either naively or ironically: 'All the crime is done under proper reprobation and yet the writers and the readers have all the benefit of the crime.'[6] The formula is not unfamiliar from today's tabloid newspapers.

The sensation novel, however, planted a bridgehead on the very

[6] E. K. Helsinger *et al.* (eds.), *The Woman Question: Society and Literature in Britain and America 1837–1883* (Manchester: Manchester University Press, 1983), iii. 131.

territory that Hardy wished to explore: relationships between the sexes in a realistic domestic setting that related to conventional social mores. As he was to put it much later in an article of 1890, 'Candour in English Fiction', 'conscientious fiction alone it is which can excite a reflective and abiding interest in the minds of thoughtful readers of mature age . . . who consider that, in representations of the world, the passions ought to be proportioned as in the world itself'. What he has in mind is made clear: 'Life being a physiological fact, its honest portrayal must be largely concerned with . . . the relations of the sexes, and the substitution for such catastrophes as favour the false colouring best expressed by the regulation finish that "they married and were happy ever after" of catastrophes based upon sexual relations as it is.'[7] The sensation novel with the emphasis on illicit passions provided the opportunity to challenge conventional ideas about gender and sexuality. In *Desperate Remedies* Hardy took full advantage of it.

Though the genre provided nothing like the freedom of the graphic underground pornography of the time, it could represent sexually passionate heroines. Such women could elope with a stable-boy, or succumb to an adulterous relationship or wish to do so. The treatment, however, was indirect, not graphic, and physical details were replaced by verbal protestations. Hardy was one of the first writers to engage in a more direct treatment, though it is still mild by modern standards. By the 1890s he and other writers, like George Gissing (1857–1903) and George Moore (1852–1933), had thoroughly colonized this new area. In his first novel, as he handled his subject of the man in love with a woman of a higher class, Hardy developed an interest in the woman not evident in what we know as *The Poor Man*. This grew as he opened up the area of gender and sexuality in a way that challenges the conventional definitions.

In a typical and very popular sensation novel, *Lady Audley's Secret* (1862) by Mary Elizabeth Braddon, the unscrupulous central character has all the angelic beauty of a conventional heroine. But a skilful portrait of her reveals her inner darkness as would-be murderer and reckless bigamist. The painting gives 'a lurid lightness to the blonde complexion, and a strange sinister light to the deep blue eyes . . . [and] a hard and almost wicked look' to her 'pretty pouting

---

[7] H. Orel (ed.), *Thomas Hardy's Personal Writings* (London: Macmillan, 1967), 127–8.

mouth' (Vol. I, ch. 8). This 'unwomanly' combination of feminine beauty and evil forms one of the central attractions of the narrative at a time when blonde beauty is typically associated with womanly innocence (witness Lucy Deane in George Eliot's *The Mill on the Floss* of 1860). Lady Audley, however, is not motivated by sexual passion any more than Lucy. Her aims are luxury and social position, and she merely uses her beauty as the purchase price for what she ruthlessly pursues.

Shocking though such a figure must have been, it is superficial when compared with Hardy's representation of a similarly vicious character in *Desperate Remedies*. His evildoer is a translation of Lady Audley into masculine form in the 'beautiful' Aeneas Manston. Like hers, his beauty tells a story. For the contemporary reader it could be read off as a psychiatric report:

The most striking point in his appearance was the wonderful, almost preternatural, clearness of his complexion. There was not a blemish or speck of any kind to mar the smoothness of its surface or the beauty of its hue. Next, his forehead was square and broad, his brows straight and firm . . . Eyes and forehead both would have expressed keenness of intellect too severely to be pleasing, had their force not been counteracted by the lines and tone of the lips. These were full and luscious to a surprising degree, possessing a woman-like softness of curve, and a ruby redness so intense, as to testify strongly to much susceptibility of heart. (pp. 127–8)

This must have been more disturbing to the early readers than the account of Lady Audley's portrait since, aside from the pronouns, it reads like a description of a beautiful woman. Furthermore, as decoded by a Victorian reader, it would speak tellingly of sexual ambiguity. In the contemporary pseudo-science of physiognomy, the upper part of the human head, and particularly the eyes, represents the 'intellectual organs'. The lower part, including nose and mouth, are 'animal organs'. According to the theory, women and non-white races were closer to animals, and so their mouths typically indicate susceptibility to irrational emotions while their eyes and foreheads show weak intellectual qualities. Men, by contrast, have a firmness about eyes and brows indicating intellectual strength, while the lower part of their faces reveal less emotionalism. So, written into Manston's red and 'luscious' mouth is a marked femininity. This reading of him is made also by Miss Aldclyffe's solicitor, who interprets him as a voluptuary.

Manston's sexual allure is frequently referred to but, unlike Lady Audley's, it is shown in action, in the episode describing his first meeting with Cytherea in the thunderstorm which drives her to shelter in his house. In what becomes a displaced seduction, he works on her feelings by his organ-playing. The music becomes the surrogate for a physical embrace as the varying strains 'shook and bent her to themselves, as a gushing brook shakes and bends a shadow cast across the surface'. Her response is specific and phys-ical: 'She was swayed into emotional opinions concerning the strange man before her; new impulses of thought came with new harmonies, and entered into her with a gnawing thrill.' She suc-cumbs to the attraction, 'involuntarily shrinking up beside him, and looking with parted lips at his face' (p. 132).

In this trance-like state she agrees to meet Manston the next day. But once the magnetism exerted by his physical presence is removed, her feelings subside. She is horrified to realize how he has 'fascinated' her, and cancels the arrangement to meet. She returns to and persists in her love for Edward Springrove, feeling no more for Manston than she would for 'some fascinating panther or leopard' (p. 139). None the less, the organ-playing scene makes clear (as did the one in *An Indiscretion* from which it derives) the capacity of an unmarried woman to find herself physically attracted by a man of 'marvellous beauty'. This aligns the text with a medical minority at the time who thought women capable of sexual feeling.

The unease generated by this episode is compounded by the fact that it takes place after Cytherea's first night at Miss Aldclyffe's house. Consequently mother and son appear to be in competition for the single object of their desires. Miss Aldclyffe, like Manston, has sexual ambiguity inscribed in her appearance. Though a handsome woman, she has 'clear steady eyes' indicating a manly intellect and determination, as well as 'a severity about the lower outlines of her face which gave a masculine cast to this portion of her countenance'. Yet there is said to be a degree of 'Womanly weakness . . . [in] the curve of her forehead and brows'. Her mouth too expresses 'a cap-ability for and tendency to strong emotion' (p. 54). She is, then, a mixture of masculine and feminine, but Hardy takes this idea to extremes in what has come to be called 'the lesbian scene' in *Desper-ate Remedies*. In this episode, unparalleled elsewhere in Hardy, Miss

Aldclyffe shows an apparently sexual passion for another woman (a point evidently not understood at the time).

Miss Aldclyffe herself attributes her passionate feelings for the girl to her discovery that, if she had not separated from Cytherea's father, she might have been her mother. But the physical attraction to Cytherea pre-dates her knowledge of this connection. Already, when interviewing her for the post of lady's maid, she reverses a decision to reject her at the sight of the girl's beauty. It would, she thinks, be worth some trouble 'to have a creature who could glide round my luxurious indolent body in that manner, and look at me in that way' (p. 56).

Physical affection between women was of course acceptable at this period as natural to such soft-hearted creatures. But the episode in which she insists on the night of Cytherea's arrival on joining the girl in her bed has overtones unsuited to motherly affection. Instead, the older woman behaves like a lover. She feels herself freed 'from the last remnant of restraint', flings her arms round Cytherea and, pressing her to her heart, begs a kiss. When the kiss is somewhat cool, she pleads to be kissed 'more earnestly'. She herself kisses the girl 'as if in the outburst of strong feeling, long checked, and yearning for something to love and be loved by in return'. It is Miss Aldclyffe's sense that she is in competition with a man for Cytherea that gives the scene its lesbian colouring. On learning that the girl has been kissed by a lover she becomes 'jealous and gloomy'. Like Edward Knight in *A Pair of Blue Eyes*, she feels that Cytherea has been sullied by already having been kissed by a man. She chides the girl almost as though she had prostituted herself and begs: 'Cytherea, try to love me more than you love him—do. I love you better than any man can. Do, Cythie, don't let any man stand between us.' The narrator reiterates the idea that Miss Aldclyffe herself has expressed when he describes her as being 'jealous as any man could have been' (p. 84).

Cytherea's own response reinforces the idea that she finds the older woman's behaviour alarming because of 'This vehement imperious affection ... too rank, sensuous, and capricious for endurance'. It is striking that in toning down the scene in later editions of *Desperate Remedies*, Hardy removed the word 'sensuous'. Miss Aldclyffe is said finally 'to give herself over to a luxurious sense of content and quiet', while Cytherea tosses restlessly and wishes the other woman would leave her. As Patrick Roberts puts it, this seems like a post-orgasmic calm for Miss Aldclyffe: 'It is as though the passion she has felt for Cytherea has metaphorically followed the familiar pattern of the arousal of sexual desire and its release in fulfilment and not all that metaphorically either.'[8] On this reading, if the organ scene is metaphorical seduction, this scene is metaphorical rape. Hardy later and ineffectively toned down the lesbian implications, possibly because, as the century wore on, a knowledge of the existence of lesbianism became more widespread; but the result is to make such implications more obtrusive.

Women and Inferiority

Having given Cytherea a sexual dimension in the scenes with Manston and his mother, Hardy seems gradually to look at her in a new light. Originally Cytherea is merely a foil for the sufferings of her brother, and the narrator explains the differences between them as they react to poverty in terms of conventional generalizations about the inferiority of women. On their father's death their responses are quite different. Owen is embittered but Cytherea accepts their position: 'We can put up with being poor . . . if they only give us work to do . . . Yes, we desire as a blessing what was given us as a curse, and even that is denied. However, be cheerful.' Yet her resilience here is disparaged as a weakness caused by the natural inferiority of women: 'In justice to desponding men, it is as well to remember that the brighter endurance of women at these epochs—invaluable, sweet, angelic, as it is—owes more of its origin to a narrower vision that shuts out many of the leaden-eyed despairs in the van, than to a hopefulness intense enough to quell them' (p. 51). Similarly, Cytherea is undervalued for her restraint in preparing herself uncomplainingly for a marriage she is undertaking largely for her brother's benefit. Her mechanical attention to her clothes is read as a typically feminine concern with such trivialities. She is even said to feel, like all women, that her clothes are 'part of her body'. A man, on the other hand—the narrator asserts—may spend more time on his clothes than a woman, 'but even then there is no fetishism in his idea of them' (p. 233).

[8] P. Roberts, 'Patterns of Relationship in *Desperate Remedies*', *Thomas Hardy Journal*, 8: 2 (1992), 52.

Some early feminist critics, alert to such generalizations, found other examples in *Under the Greenwood Tree, A Pair of Blue Eyes, Far From the Madding Crowd, A Laodicean,* and *The Trumpet Major.* They failed to notice, however, a different assessment creeping into all these novels and beginning even in *Desperate Remedies.* This discourse emerges slowly, and its first appearance is unobtrusive. When Cytherea restrains herself from public distress at the sight of her lover Springrove in church with the woman he is engaged to marry, the narrator is stung to comment. This behaviour of Cytherea, he believes, is a result of 'an illogical power entirely denied to men in general—the power not only of kissing, but of delighting to kiss the rod by a punctilious observance of the self-immolating doctrines in the Sermon on the Mount' (p. 205). This is a curious assertion from a narrator whose apparent acceptance of current accounts of femininity has been recorded in his balance-sheet of male and female characteristics. In such accounts the primary characteristic of womanhood at its most perfect is selflessness. As one popular conduct book puts it: 'With regard of the women of England, I have already ventured to assert that the quality for which, above all others, they are esteemed and valued, is their disinterested kindness. A selfish woman may not improperly be regarded as a monster.'[9] Since a woman in her best and most natural form is, as Ellis says, an agent for the good of others, it is startling that this supremely feminine selflessness is described as an 'illogical power' of 'self-immolation'. The explanation appears to be that by this stage in the narrative, as her wedding to Manston approaches, Cytherea's position is increasingly seen to resemble and be equatable with that of her lover, the 'poor man' Springrove. As he has been left open to pressure and manipulation by his inferior origins, she has been exposed to the same pressures by her gender.

It is the erasure of individual identity by the upper classes, when dealing with members of the lower classes such as Springrove and the narrator, that connects the latter to women whose individuality is erased by their gender. As Cytherea, through pressure exerted by Manston via her brother, succumbs to an unwanted marriage for money, she begins to appear the same kind of victim as Springrove, pressurized by his superiors into a similarly loveless marriage. This realization is present in the narrator's hostility to Cytherea

[9] Sarah Stickney Ellis, *The Women of England: Their Social Duties and Domestic Habits* (London: Fisher, 1839), 73.

'kissing the rod'. It emerges fully developed when she speaks to her brother after the wedding ceremony and wishes she were dead at the thought of what comes next. Owen embraces her but rebukes her in conduct-book terms that allude to the usual theology of femininity: 'Many a woman has gone to ruin herself . . . and brought those who love her into disgrace, by acting upon such impulses as possess you now.' It is her 'duty to society' (p. 236) to kiss the rod and live with 'all the appearance of a good wife'.

This conventionally impeccable advice is met with an answer that results from the narrator's recognition of the crushing of identity inflicted on both Cytherea and Springrove:

Yes—my duty to society . . . But ah, Owen, it is difficult to adjust our outer and inner life with perfect honesty to all! Though it may be right to care more for the benefit of the many than for the indulgence of your own single self, when you consider that the many, and duty to them, only exist to you through your own existence, what can be said?

She goes on to speak of her inner self which creates her sense of individual identity, that individual identity which his superiors also fail to recognize in Springrove. How, she wonders, does the society which imposes the duty of a loveless marriage on her regard her? They may pity her:

But they will never, never realize that it was my single opportunity of existence, as well as of doing my duty, which they are regarding; they will not feel that what to them is but a thought, easily held in those two words of pity, 'Poor girl', was a whole life to me; as full of hours, minutes, and peculiar minutes, of hopes and dreads, smiles, whisperings, tears, as theirs (p. 236).

This passage is a turning-point in Hardy's view of women. Here in *Desperate Remedies* he comes to see the mismatch between the outer life imposed on women and the inner life they experience: he has found what was to become the main focus of his novels. Subsequently in the treatment of Elfride in *A Pair of Blue Eyes*, Bathsheba in *Far From the Madding Crowd*, Eustacea Vye in *The Return of the Native*, and Viviette in *Two on a Tower*, he addresses the same issue. After the latter novel was published in 1887 he set to work to get rid of 'the doll of English fiction', an essential change 'if England is to have a school of fiction at all'.[10] From that date he again took up

---

[10] R. L. Purdy and M. Millgate (eds.), *The Collected Letters of Thomas Hardy*, 7 vols. (Oxford: Clarendon Press, 1978–88), i. 250.

topics familiarized by the sensation novels but dropped after *Desperate Remedies*: marital breakdown, adultery, seduction, bigamy, and murder as a crime of passion. In addition he dealt with one consequence of illicit passion—divorce. One or more of these themes were handled in *The Woodlanders*, *Tess of the d'Urbervilles*, *Jude the Obscure*, and *The Well-Beloved*. In his novels he expresses the idea that, as in *Jude the Obscure*, the woman usually gets the worst of it in the long run. In a letter he examines the ramification of society's treatment of women and challenges 'the present pernicious conventions' relating to 'illegitimacy, the stereotyped household (that it must be the unit of society), the father of a woman's child (that it is anybody's business but the woman's own)'.[11]

In *The Woodlanders* Hardy records the fact that, as neither wife nor widow, and unable to sue for divorce, Grace Fitzpiers is obliged to return to a husband who will continue his infidelities. In *Tess* he reassesses the question of what constitutes rape and the nature of the stigma attaching to illegitimacy and the unmarried mother. In *Jude the Obscure* he scrutinizes different kinds of unhappy marriage and the social impact on a woman of an extramarital relationship. In all of these he transforms the sub-erotic register of *Desperate Remedies* into a more directly erotic one: dealing openly with Fitzpiers's physical magnetism to which Grace responds; challenging the idea that Tess's final acquiescence makes Alec's actions any less rape; and describing Sue Bridehead's aversion to sexual relations with her husband. The focus of moral outrage has shifted irreversibly. The basis for these social issues is laid down in *Desperate Remedies* as an extension of the purely sensational treatment of illicit passion and its consequences.

So too is concern with the wider questions that Hardy perceives as lying behind these stories of individual relationships in the late novels. The effects of an insistence on the inferiority of women in a society that is also class-ridden are always compounded for him by the randomness of events which work to further disastrous outcomes. But from his earliest days as a novelist Hardy could not simply rest on an acceptance of such randomness. For him it always raised questions. Though in the period from 1869 he had not yet totally abandoned his religious beliefs, he was already questioning

[11] Ibid., iii. 238.

the idea of a benign God or even of a plausible one. Causality became an obsession for him, which the sensation novel offered suitable material to explore. Such exploration led naturally to the framing of the problem of 'the Whence and the Wherefore of things',[12] of ultimate causes.

The Role of Chance

Hardy's first attempt to make sense of the role of chance coincidences in human lives is to be found in the chapter divisions which structure *Desperate Remedies*. Surprisingly, as one reviewer noticed, he abandoned the practice of using quotations to head chapters and supplies each with a title on a similar pattern. These headings give the length of time and frequently the date when the events of the chapters take place. They vary from 'the Events of Thirty Years' (starting years before the births of Cytherea and Owen Graye) to 'The Events of Three Hours' (starting at midday on 23 March). These titles, like the ticking of a clock, serve superficially to mark the passing of time, as though in an attempt to impose some order on extraordinary events which, by chance, bring confusion and disaster.

More significantly these headings make a statement about the perception of the passage of time for the characters involved. Cytherea and her brother are only retrospectively involved in the events of the early years in their father's life, which can therefore be summarized as a starting-point for the events of thirty years. By contrast, 'The Events of One Day', which happens to be the first that Cytherea spends at Knapwater House enduring Miss Aldclyffe's volatile treatment, is extended painfully for her. Manston's escape from his police pursuers, attempted rape of Cytherea, struggle with her, and his final capture are 'The Events of Three Hours', which becomes a prolonged period of time for those anxious to capture him.

These changes in the tempo of *Desperate Remedies* signal that what determines the duration of time is not the hands on a clock but the intensity and significance of the events for participants. One critic has called this measuring time by red-letter days for individuals.[13] As Hardy puts it in the earliest novel, such red-letter episodes may be

[12] Orel, *Personal Writings*, 48.
[13] Rebecca Steinitz, 'Diaries and Displacements in *Wuthering Heights*', *Studies in the Novel*, 2: 4 (2000), 407–18. This article uses these two accounts of time.

'slight' in themselves, but characteristically they take up 'a relevant and important position between the past and the future of the persons herein concerned' (p. 34). In other words, they are significant as causes of what is to follow, forming links in a mysterious causal chain. This is a premise with which *Desperate Remedies* opens: 'In the long and intricately inwrought chain of circumstances which renders worthy of record some experiences of Cytherea Graye, Edward Springrove, and others, the first event directly influencing the issue was a Christmas visit' (p. 7). This opening certainly implies that the narrator is not devising but merely recording a causal pattern; yet it is quite unclear who 'wrought' it. Later the same point is made as to the picking up of an existing sequence: 'The sole object of this narration being to present in a regular series the several episodes and incidents which directly helped forward the end ... every contiguous scene without this qualification is necessarily passed over' (p. 69).

A similar focus on causally important events is found in *Tess of the d'Urbervilles* which is divided into 'Phases'. Each Phase belongs only to Tess and marks a major change in her life, as the titles indicate: 'The Maiden', 'Maiden No More', 'The Rally', 'The Woman Pays', 'The Convert', and 'Fulfilment'. Each episode—the rape/seduction, the baby's death, desertion by Angel, the return to Alec, the murder and return to Angel—is a link in a chain of events and depends on a string of coincidences. In *Jude the Obscure* the elements of 'intricately wrought chain which accidentally provides repetitions and parallels' are associated with the names of the towns to which Jude is successively driven to move. His final return to die in Christminster, where his hopes were first destroyed, locks the chain into a vicious circle.

The paradox of these patterns is that they are represented as the result of chance coincidences and at the same time as predetermined. Strikingly, in *Desperate Remedies* the presence of frequent coincidences is foregrounded as a 'strange concurrence of phenomena' (p. 165). This specifically refers to the construction of a dangerous bonfire outside the inn at Carriford, coinciding with the unexpected arrival of Manston's wife Eunice, the razing at the crucial moment of the inn by fire, and the assumption that she has been burnt to death. By chance the only person who knows that Eunice did not die in the fire reveals the fact on the very day of Manston's wedding to Cytherea.

This prevents the consummation of the marriage by separating the newly married couple. More coincidences follow, until the truth is unearthed that Manston killed his wife and Cytherea is saved in the nick of time from being raped by him.

Some critics in the twentieth century argued that Hardy was unable to construct a plot without clumsy use of coincidences. But this early novel makes it clear that he deliberately chooses them and positively draws attention to them. Cytherea, in a conversation with her brother about her apparently chance meeting with the only other Cytherea in the country (Miss Aldclyffe), remarks on this and related coincidences. She argues that they occur often enough to be a normal feature of life and multiply mysteriously:

two disconnected events will fall strangely together by chance, and people scarcely notice the fact beyond saying, 'Oddly enough it happened that so and so were the same,' and so on. But when three such events coincide without any apparent reason for the coincidence, it seems as if there must be invisible means at work. You see, three things falling together in that manner are ten times as singular as two cases of coincidence which are distinct. (p. 146)

The same arguments for some force that causes the string of linked events is made by the narrator in commenting on the combination of the location of Farmer Springrove's bonfire and a sudden change in wind direction which leads to the destruction of the inn and its consequences: 'It seemed as if the treacherous element knew that there had arisen an opportunity for devastation.' The 'invisible means' and 'the treacherous element' represent Hardy's first attempt to give a name to a force or a cause in which already he only half believed.

The state of half-belief persisted to the end of his novel-writing career, although by then he might be expected to regard the chance linking of events as a random pattern bound to crop up when large numbers are involved. But the idea of causality as an enigma is evidenced by the variety of names he gives to this force behind events. In the later novels he sometimes indicates that a sequence of improbable events leading to disaster can be attributed to 'destiny' or 'fate'. The narrator in *The Mayor of Casterbridge* refers to 'the ingenious machinery contrived by the gods for reducing human possibilities of amelioration to a minimum' (ch. 44). Occasionally a narrator implies that some individuals attract such incidents, and once (famously but provisionally) Hardy names the cause as 'The President of the Immortals'.

Perhaps his paradoxical views are best expressed in his poem on the sinking of the *Titanic*, 'The Convergence of the Twain'. It does not focus on the great loss of life but on the fact of the 'unsinkable' ship meeting the invincible iceberg, in a collision that is at once random and yet obscurely willed:

> Alien they seemed to be:
>   No mortal eye could see
> The intimate welding of their later history,
>   Or sign that they were bent
>   By paths coincident
> On being anon twin halves of one august event.[14]

In *Desperate Remedies* the agent of many chance events is the written word, which proves so slippery. Miss Aldclyffe sends Manston a letter purporting to come from the Society of Architects to lure him into her employ, which brings him into dangerous contact with Cytherea. The older woman also uses a casual note from Cytherea to Manston which is so phrased that it persuades Springrove that the girl is in love with the steward. Manston himself advertises for his 'missing' wife whom he has killed, and induces Anne Seaway, a prostitute, to write a letter claiming that she is Eunice Manston. He tampers with a letter to Owen Graye which might reveal that Anne is not his wife. A similar role, though a more infrequent one, is given to the written word in Hardy's late novels. The misuse of Lucetta's love-letters to Henchard in *The Mayor of Casterbridge* leads to the mocking skimmity ride and her death because she chances to be pregnant. In *The Woodlanders* Grace changes 'lose' to 'keep' in Marty's graffiti on Giles's house to make it read 'O Giles, you've lost your dwelling place, And therefore, Giles, you'll keep your Grace' (ch. 15). When Giles assumes the change was made by some idler, Grace assumes he has ignored her. Tess's letter to Angel before their wedding, confessing her affair with Alec, fails to reach him and precipitates what happens when she confesses too late. Jude has illusions about what he will find in the Latin textbooks that he laboriously acquires. Hardy's attitude to the written word in the first

---

[14] S. Hynes (ed.), *The Complete Poetical Works of Thomas Hardy* (Oxford: Clarendon Press, 1987), ii. 11.

and last of his novels seems to be crystallized in the epigraph to *Jude the Obscure*: 'The letter killeth.'

   Desperate Remedies is not a deviation from Hardy's natural narrative mode, a detour on the way to his mature novels. As the connections outlined above have shown, *The Woodlanders*, *Tess*, *Jude the Obscure*, and *The Well-Beloved* all represent the apotheosis of the sensation novel. In writing his own first version of the genre, Hardy finds the medium that became uniquely his.

NOTE ON THE TEXT

Desperate Remedies was published anonymously by Tinsley Brothers in 1871, stretched to three volumes as publishing conditions required at the time. No manuscript survives, but there is other documentary evidence which gives some clues as to its contents. All editions subsequent to the first were in one volume. These were:

1874: an American edition by Henry Holt & Co. in their Leisure Hour series;

1889: the 'New Edition' by Ward and Downey (reprinted in 1892 by I. Heinemann as the 'Popular Edition';

1896: as Volume XII of the first collection of Hardy's novels, the 'Wessex Novels', published by Osgood, McIlvaine;

1912: in the last revised collected edition, as Volume XV of the 'Wessex Edition'.

Of these only the 1889, 1896, and 1912 versions are considered here, since the American edition included changes not passed on to later editions.

Before publication of what is now regarded as the original text, there had been external advice and editorial interference which afford glimpses of the original manuscript. The text had already been rejected by Macmillan, and in advising this, their reader, John Morley, spoke of 'the violation of a young lady at an evening party, and the subsequent birth of a child' as virtually unprintable.[1] Though Hardy then passed the manuscript on to Tinsley Brothers, he took Morley's advice and deleted the incident. This left vague the question of quite how Miss Aldclyffe became pregnant, but the fact that Manston is her illegitimate son was not erasable from the plot. A similarly superficial prudery is evident in Tinsley's comment that 'the woman who is Mrs Manston's *substitute* need not be put forward quite so prominently as his *mistress*'.[2] Again Hardy deleted the word,

---

[1] Charles Morgan, *The House of Macmillan 1843–1943* (London: Macmillan, 1943), 93–4.
[2] R. L. Purdy, *Thomas Hardy: A Bibliographical Study* (Oxford: Clarendon Press, 1968), 5.

though the fact of the relationship remains clear. What Hardy himself said in mitigation of his sensationalism was that he had made 'too crude an interpretation'[3] of George Meredith's advice when rejecting *The Poor Man and the Lady* to 'write a story with a plot'.[4]

An examination of the changes in the editions of 1871, 1889, 1896, and 1912 reveals four main areas of interest: social class; sexual matters; 'Wessex' (or topography); and dialect. These topics will be dealt with separately and traced through the versions listed, with major alterations also recorded in the Explanatory Notes.

The subject of class remained always a sensitive one for Hardy, particularly as he was one of the many whose self-education and professional success moved him up the social ladder. There are several references in the 1871 edition which suggest a narratorial hostility to the middle classes because of their patronizing or indifferent attitude to the 'inferiors'. By 1889, when Hardy had published several more novels, including *A Pair of Blue Eyes*, *Far From the Madding Crowd*, *The Return of the Native*, *The Mayor of Casterbridge*, and *The Woodlanders*, his social position had changed and the bitter references of 1871 are toned down. In the first edition the narrator refers to 'that inquisitiveness towards inferiors which passes for high-breeding amongst the pinchbeck aristocracy of country villages'. In 1889 this becomes 'that inquisitiveness into the private affairs of the natives which passes for high breeding in country villages'. In 1871 Owen feels that Miss Aldclyffe's servants regard him as 'a hybrid monster from regions far below the touch-my-hat stage of supremacy'. By 1889 this becomes the less bitter 'a hybrid monster as to social position'. In the first edition the coffin prepared for Manston elicits a comment on death from Farmer Springrove: 'I have often thought how far the richer class sink into insignificance beside the poor on extreme occasions like this.' This is toned down in 1896: to 'I have often thought how much smaller the richer classes are made to look than the poor at last pinches like this'.

The question of the social standing of Owen Graye and Edward Springrove is evidently a sensitive one. Both, like Hardy, are training as architects and are referred to as 'clerk' in 1871. This is a very general term used of any minor office-worker. An original reference

[3] M. Millgate (ed.), *The Life and Work of Thomas Hardy by Thomas Hardy* (London: Macmillan, 1984), 87.
[4] Ibid. 66.

to Owen as an 'under-clerk' in an architect's office is changed in 1896 to the more skilled 'under-draughtsman'. Similarly, Edward in 1871 is referred to in one place as 'head clerk' and in another as an 'architect's clerk'. In 1889 his position is upgraded by the text to 'head draughtsman' and 'an architect'.

In the handling of sexual matters, as already indicated, the prudery of publishers like Macmillan and Tinsley (as well as pressure from the circulating libraries such as Mudies) produced some early tinkering by Hardy. There was some uncertainty as to the propriety of using the word 'bosom', as well as to showing even accidental physical contact between a man and woman. By 1896 most changes relating to such matters (and more explicit ones) were in the direction of greater frankness, as Hardy's standing as a novelist allowed him more freedom and the power of Mudies and other lending libraries declined. There is one striking exception to this trend toward sexual explicitness: the scene in which Miss Aldclyffe gets into Cytherea's bed and embraces her.

Some forty-one years after the original version of the scene was published, significant changes were made to the episode in 1912. The sexual overtones in the incident in the 1871 edition are readily apparent to the modern reader, but they caused no stir at the time. The alterations in 1912 are striking because they attempt to weaken the suggestion that the older woman's strangely passionate feelings are sexual. Rather, it is more forcibly implied that they are maternal. So in 1871 Miss Aldclyffe's first utterance after flinging her arms round the girl is 'Now kiss me'. In 1912 she immediately adds a reason for this: 'You seem as if you were my own, own child!' This refers to her enduring passion for Cytherea's father, from whom she parted long ago. Similarly, her bare statement, 'But I can't help loving you', is given a justificatory gloss in 1912: 'But I am a lonely woman, and I want the sympathy of a pure girl like you, and so I can't help loving you.' Her declaration in 1871, 'I love you better than any man can', suggests the same kind of love as a man's. The 1912 version, 'I love you more sincerely than any man can', suggests something less heated. The same effect is achieved by the change in the narratorial comment that Miss Aldclyffe yearns 'for something to love and be loved by in return'. In 1912 this is weakened to 'for something to care for and be cared for by in return'. Mary Rimmer makes the illuminating suggestion that these changes are 'made because in the 1870s many people were unaware of the existence of lesbian or Sapphic passion and so were untroubled by the episode. Thus this aspect of the scene remained "unintelligible" to most readers at the time.'[5] By 1912 such knowledge was widespread, and consequently so too was intolerance of any reference to lesbianism in fiction.

The history of the topography of the novel is less than straightforward in respect of the changes made to place-names in 1896 and 1912. *Desperate Remedies* was published well before the use of the name 'Wessex' in *Far From the Madding Crowd* (1874), let alone before the concept of such a region. Places mentioned in the novel, Creston, Froominster, and Carriford, are loosely based on Weymouth, Dorchester, and Stinsford respectively. In later novels such as *The Return of the Native* (1878) and *The Mayor of Casterbridge* (1886) there was some attempt at a degree of consistency in the correspondences between actual locations and fictional names. Accordingly, in 1888 Hardy wrote to the publisher, Edward Marston:

Could you, whenever advertising my books, use the words 'Wessex novels' at the head of the list? I mean, instead of 'By T. H.', 'T. H.'s Wessex novels', or something of the sort? I find that the name *Wessex* wh. I was the first to use in fiction, is getting to be taken up everywhere: & it would be a pity for us to lose the right to it for want of asserting it.[6]

It was in the following year, in the 1889 edition, that changes were made to place-names in *Desperate Remedies*. Significantly these did not draw the novel into the now developing concept of 'Wessex' found in the novels of the 1880s. Casterbridge by 1889 was the permanent form that Hardy now regularly used for the fictional equivalent of Dorchester. Yet in the Ward and Downey edition of *Desperate Remedies* in that year he changed 1871's Froominster into Troominster, not Casterbridge. Other names were also changed in a way not consistent with 'Wessex' in its final form. The obvious explanation is that Hardy did not regard *Desperate Remedies* as integral to his 'Wessex' novels. Simon Gatrell makes the ingenious suggestion that 'Hardy's sense of Wessex and its importance to him as an idea that would unite all his work had reached just the stage that a

[5] Mary Rimmer (ed.), *Desperate Remedies* (Harmondsworth: Penguin, 1998), 451.
[6] R. L. Purdy and M. Millgate (eds.), *The Collected Letters of Thomas Hardy* (Oxford: Clarendon Press, 1978), i. 171.

new edition of *Desperate Remedies* might have undermined; he had neither the time nor the energy to rewrite the topography of the novel to accord with other novels that have their action in approximately the same area; so he decided to push it further away'.[7]

It was not until the Osgood, McIlvaine collected edition of 1896 that a comprehensive revision of the novels in the interests of 'Wessex' meant that considerable consistency in the use of names and distances was introduced. It extended even to *Desperate Remedies*, which was accepted as part of a 'Wessex' now extending far beyond Dorset. Troominster is replaced by Casterbridge (for Dorchester), and Creston by the now familiar Budmouth for a location based on Weymouth. It would be a mistake to assume that this increase in internal consistency (by no means complete) as to place-names and distances transformed 'Wessex' into a 'realistic' picture of Dorset and adjacent counties. Though Hardy himself produced a map of the area for the 1896 'Wessex Novels', he always insisted that this place was partly imaginary. In the 1896 edition of *Desperate Remedies* he writes off-handedly in the Prefatory Note:

To the foregoing note I have only to add that, in the present edition of 'Desperate Remedies', some Wessex towns and other places that are common to the scenes of several of these stories have been called for the first time by the names under which they appear elsewhere, for the satisfaction of any reader who may care for consistency in such matters.

'Wessex' is a complex matter of time as well as place, and even with the changed names *Desperate Remedies* lacks much that goes to make up the nostalgia of the other novels' recreation of a past time with its merits and drawbacks.

In the collected editions of 1896 and 1912 changes were also made across the novels, including *Desperate Remedies*, to the use of dialect by rustic speakers. Markers of dialect appear to be sometimes increased in 1896 but decreased in 1912. These changes can be easily misunderstood if there is no attempt to recognize their basis. Hardy himself wrote in 1878: 'Hardly any phonetic principle at all is observed; and if a writer attempts to exhibit on paper the precise accents of a rustic speaker, he disturbs the proper balance of a true

---

[7] S. Gatrell, *Hardy, the Creator, and Textual Biography* (Oxford: Clarendon Press, 1988), 125.

representation.'[8] So, from his earliest novels he aimed at an impressionistic effect. This did not require consistency in the usages of individual speakers nor an accurate representation of all dialectal forms. The adjustments he made to dialect in *Desperate Remedies* all relate to marginal characters, unlike some of the later novels. By 1912 the toning down of dialect in such speakers lessens its obtrusive effect. So, for instance, forms like *zid* 'said', *naibour*, *hev*, *been* 'being', *'ithout*, give way to *sid*, *neighbour*, *have*, *being*, and *without*. Also the frequent use of *-en* for standard *-ing* in 1871 is restricted to present participles like *sayen* 'saying', while other words ending in *-ing* such as *nothen* 'nothing' are restored to the latter form. Dialect forms of pronoun (which are particularly obtrusive), such as *'a* 'he' or *en* 'him', are found less frequently by 1912. Some of this diminution has the effect of suggesting that a speaker is slightly higher up the social scale than those who use dialect markers more frequently.

It is the text of the first three-volume edition of 1871 that is used here, presenting the novel as it appeared to its first readers, the distinctive product of a struggling young novelist at a time of three-deckers and sensation novels. Only obvious errors are removed. The present volume also includes the three pieces of prefatory material that Hardy wrote in 1889, 1896, and 1912.

[8] *Athenaeum* 30 (Nov. 1878), 688.

SELECT BIBLIOGRAPHY

Biography

Michael Millgate, *Thomas Hardy: A Biography* (Oxford: Oxford University Press, 1982): the definitive biography.
—— (ed.), *The Life and Work of Thomas Hardy by Thomas Hardy* (London: Macmillan, 1984): Hardy's own account of his life, published after his death under his wife's name.

Hardy's Non-fictional Writing

Harold Orel (ed.), *Thomas Hardy's Personal Writings: Literary Opinions, Reminiscences* (London: Macmillan, 1967).
R. L. Purdy and Michael Millgate (eds.), *The Collected Letters of Thomas Hardy*, 7 vols. (Oxford: Clarendon Press, 1978–88).

Critical Studies

Richard D. Altick, *The English Common Reader: A Social History of the Mass Reading Public 1800–1900* (Chicago: University of Chicago Press, 1967).
Penny Boumelha, *Thomas Hardy and Women: Sexual Ideology and Narrative Form* (Brighton: Harvester, 1982).
J. B. Bullen, *The Expressive Eye: Fiction and Perception in the Work of Thomas Hardy* (Oxford: Clarendon Press, 1986).
Joe Fisher, *The Hidden Hardy* (London: Macmillan, 1992).
Annette Frederico, *Masculine Identity in Hardy and Gissing* (London and Toronto: Associated University Presses, 1991).
John Goode, *Thomas Hardy: The Offensive Truth* (Oxford, Blackwell, 1988).
Ian Gregor, *The Great Web: The Form of Hardy's Major Fiction* (London: Faber & Faber, 1974).
Guinevere L. Griest, *Mudie's Circulating Library and the Victorian Novel* (Indiana: Indiana University Press, 1970).
Winifred Hughes, *The Maniac in the Cellar: Sensation Novels of the 1860s* (Princeton: Princeton University Press, 1980).
Patricia Ingham, *Thomas Hardy: A Feminist Reading* (Hemel Hempstead: Harvester, 1989).
Michael Millgate, *Thomas Hardy: His Career as a Novelist* (London: Bodley Head, 1971; rev. edn. Macmillan, 1994).
Lyn Pykett, *The Sensation Novel* (Northcote House Educational Publishers, 1994).

John Sutherland, *Stanford Companion to Victorian Fiction* (Stanford: Stanford University Press, 1989).

Peter Widdowson, *Hardy in History: A Study in Literary Sociology* (London and New York: Routledge 1989).

Desperate Remedies

David Ball, 'Hardy's Experimental Fiction', *Journal of the English Association*, 35: 151 (1986), 27–36.

Pamela Dalziel, 'Exploiting *The Poor Man*: The Genesis of Hardy's *Desperate Remedies*', *Journal of English and Germanic Philology*, 94: 2 (1995), 220–32.

Lawrence Jones, 'The Music Scenes in *The Poor Man and the Lady*, *Desperate Remedies*, and *An Indiscretion in the Life of an Heiress*', *Notes and Queries*, 24 (1977) 32–4.

Catherine Neale, '*Desperate Remedies*: The Merits and Demerits of Popular Fiction', *Critical Survey*, 5: 2 (1993), 117–22.

Ian Ousby, 'Class in *Desperate Remedies*', *Durham University Journal*, 76: 2 (1984), 217–22.

Norman Page, 'Visual Techniques in Hardy's *Desperate Remedies*', *Ariel*, 4: 1 (1973), 65–71.

Patrick Roberts, 'Patterns of Relationship in *Desperate Remedies*', *Thomas Hardy Journal*, 8: 2 (1992), 50–7.

Richard Sylvia, 'Thomas Hardy's *Desperate Remedies*: "All My Sin Has Been Because I Love You So" ', *Colby Quarterly* 35: 2 (1999), 102–16.

G. Glen Wickens, 'Romantic Myth and Victorian Nature in *Desperate Remedies*', *English Studies in Canada*, 8: 2 (1982), 154–73.

George Wing, '*Edwin Drood* and *Desperate Remedies*: Prototypes of Detective Fiction in 1870', *Studies in English Literature*, 13 (1973), 677–87.

Judith B. Wittenburg, 'Early Hardy Novels and the Fictional Eye', *Forum on Fiction*, 16 (1983), 151–64.

—— 'Thomas Hardy's First Novel: Women and the Quest for Autonomy', *Colby Library Quarterly*, 18 (1982), 47–54.

Further Reading in Oxford World's Classics

Mary Elizabeth Braddon, *Aurora Floyd*, ed. P. D. Edwards.

—— *Lady Audley's Secret*, ed. David Skilton.

Wilkie Collins, *Armadale*, ed. Catherine Peters.

—— *The Law and the Lady*, ed. Jenny Bourne Taylor.

—— *Miss or Mrs?*, *The Haunted Hotel*, *The Guilty River*, ed. Norman Page and Toru Sasaki.

—— *The Moonstone*, ed. John Sutherland.

—— *The Woman in White*, ed. John Sutherland.

Thomas Hardy, *Far From the Madding Crowd*, ed. Suzanne B. Falck-Yi.
—— *An Indiscretion in the Life of an Heiress and Other Stories*, ed. Pamela Dalziel.
—— *Jude the Obscure*, ed. Patricia Ingham.
—— *Life's Little Ironies*, ed. Alan Manford and Norman Page.
—— *The Mayor of Casterbridge*, ed. Dale Kramer.
—— *A Pair of Blue Eyes*, ed. Alan Manford.
—— *The Return of the Native*, ed. Simon Gatrell.
—— *Selected Poetry*, ed. Samuel Hynes.
—— *Tess of the d'Urbervilles*, ed. Juliet Grindle and Simon Gatrell.
—— *The Trumpet-Major*, ed. Richard Nemesvari.
—— *Two on a Tower*, ed. Suleiman M. Ahmad.
—— *Under the Greenwood Tree*, ed. Simon Gatrell.
—— *The Well-Beloved*, ed. Tom Hetherington.
—— *Wessex Tales*, ed. Kathryn R. King.
—— *The Woodlanders*, ed. Dale Kramer.
Patricia Ingham, *Thomas Hardy* (Authors in Context).

A CHRONOLOGY OF THOMAS HARDY

	Life	Historical and Cultural Background
1835		Telegraph comes into use.
1837		William IV dies and is succeeded by Victoria.
1838		Anti-Corn Law League set up.
1839		Chartist riots.
1840	2 June: Thomas Hardy born, Higher Bockhampton, Dorset, eldest child of a builder, Thomas Hardy, and Jemima Hand, who have been married for less than six months. Younger siblings: Mary (b. 1841), Henry (b. 1851), Katharine (Kate) (b. 1856).	Victoria marries the German prince, Albert. Penny postage instituted. Charles Dickens, *The Old Curiosity Shop* serialized Charles Darwin, *The Voyage of HMS Beagle*
1842		Underground labour banned for women and children. Robert Browning, *Dramatic Lyrics* Alfred Tennyson, *Poems*
1843		Dickens, *A Christmas Carol* John Ruskin, *Modern Painters*
1844		Factory Act limiting working hours for women and children. Robert Chambers, *Vestiges of the Natural History of Creation* (popularizing an evolutionary view)
1845		John Henry Newman joins the Roman Catholic Church. Benjamin Disraeli, *Sybil* F. Engels, *Condition of the Working Classes in England in 1844*
1846		'Railway Mania' year: 272 Railway Acts passed. Repeal of the Corn Laws which have protected farm prices. Irish potato famine (1845–9) kills over a million people.
1847		Ten Hour Factory Act (limiting working hours). Charlotte Brontë, *Jane Eyre* Emily Brontë, *Wuthering Heights*

Life	*Historical and Cultural Background*
1848–56 Schooling in Dorset.	
1848	Chartist Petition to Parliament and end of Chartism. Year of revolutions in Europe. Public Health Act (inspired by Edwin Chadwick's Report into the Sanitary Conditions of the Working Classes). Pre-Raphaelite Brotherhood founded. Dickens, *Dombey and Son* Elizabeth Gaskell, *Mary Barton* Anne Brontë, *The Tenant of Wildfell Hall* William Makepeace Thackeray, *Vanity Fair* Marx and Engels, *The Communist Manifesto*
1850	Public Libraries Act. Dickens, *David Copperfield* Tennyson, *In Memoriam*
1851	The Great Exhibition at the Crystal Palace in Hyde Park, supported by Prince Albert, a great success. Ruskin, *The Stones of Venice*
1852	Thackeray, *Henry Esmond*
1853	Vaccination against smallpox becomes compulsory. Dickens, *Bleak House* Charlotte Brontë, *Villette* Gaskell, *Cranford* Matthew Arnold, *Poems*
1854	Outbreak of the Crimean War: Britain and France defend European interests in the Middle East against Russia; Florence Nightingale goes out to Scutari in the Crimea. Dickens, *Hard Times*
1855	Gaskell, *North and South* Anthony Trollope, *The Warden* (first of the Barchester novels)
1856 Hardy watches the hanging of Martha Browne for the murder of her husband (thought to be remembered in the death of Tess Durbeyfield on the gallows).	Crimean War ends; Victoria Cross for bravery instituted. Elizabeth Barrett Browning, *Aurora Leigh* (lengthy and melodramatic verse narrative of a woman writer's life)

Life	*Historical and Cultural Background*
1856–62 Articled to Dorchester architect John Hicks; later his assistant; late 1850s, important friendship with Horace Moule (eight years older, middle class, and Cambridge educated) who becomes his intellectual mentor and encourages his self-education in the classics.	
1857	Matrimonial Causes Act makes divorce possible without an Act of Parliament, but on unequal terms for men and women. Dickens, *Little Dorrit* Trollope, *Barchester Towers* Gustave Flaubert, *Madame Bovary*
1858	Indian Mutiny crushed. George Eliot, *Scenes of Clerical Life*
1859	Darwin, *The Origin of Species* Samuel Smiles, *Self-Help* J. S. Mill, *Liberty* Dickens, *A Tale of Two Cities* Eliot, *Adam Bede* Tennyson, *Idylls of the King*
1860	Cobden Act extends free trade. Eliot, *The Mill on the Floss* Wilkie Collins, *The Woman in White*
1861	Death of Prince Albert: Victoria goes into seclusion. Outbreak of American Civil War. Dickens, *Great Expectations* Eliot, *Silas Marner* Francis Palgrave, *Golden Treasury* (much quoted by Hardy) Isabella Beeton, *Book of Household Management* (sells over 60,000 copies in one year)
1862 Employed as a draughtsman by London architect, Arthur Blomfield. Self-education continues, including earlier English writers.	Mary Elizabeth Braddon, *Lady Audley's Secret* (the best known of the lurid sensational novels of the 1860s)
1863	Work begins on first London underground (steam) railway. Football Association founded as professional sport. The Metropolitan Line is developed. Thackeray dies. Eliot, *Romola* Mill, *Utilitarianism* in book form

	Life	*Historical and Cultural Background*
1864		Albert Memorial is constructed. Newman, *Apologia Pro Vita Sua* Trollope, *Can You Forgive Her?* (the first of the political series, the Palliser novels)
1865		Founding by William Booth of what becomes the Salvation Army. End of American Civil War. Dickens, *Our Mutual Friend*
1866		After the defeat of the Reform Bill to extend the vote: rioting in Hyde Park. Eliot, *Felix Holt, the Radical* Gaskell, *Wives and Daughters*, left unfinished at her death
1867	Returns to Dorset as a jobbing architect. He works for Hicks on church restoration.	Second Reform Act increases voters to two million; Mill tries to include women in the Bill but fails. Paris Exhibition. Trollope, *The Last Chronicle of Barset* (last of the Barchester novels) Marx, *Das Kapital*
1868	Completes his first novel *The Poor Man and the Lady* but it is rejected for publication (see 1878).	Founding of the Trades Union Congress. Collins, *The Moonstone* Browning, *The Ring and the Book*
1869	Works for the architect Crickmay in Weymouth, again on church restoration.	Suez Canal opened. Founding of Girton College. Arnold, *Culture and Anarchy* Mill, *The Subjection of Women*
1870	After many youthful infatuations thought to be referred to in early poems, he meets Emma Lavinia Gifford, his future wife, on a professional visit to St Juliot in north Cornwall.	Married Women's Property Act gives wives the right to keep their earnings. Elementary Education Act enabling local authorities to set up schools. Dickens dies, leaving *The Mystery of Edwin Drood* unfinished. D. G. Rossetti, *Poems*
1871	*Desperate Remedies* published in volume form by Tinsley Brothers.	Legalizing of trade unions. First Impressionist Exhibition in Paris. Religious tests abolished at Oxford, Cambridge, and Durham universities. Eliot, *Middlemarch* Darwin, *The Descent of Man*
1872	*Under the Greenwood Tree* published in volume form by Tinsley Brothers.	

	Life	*Historical and Cultural Background*
1873	*A Pair of Blue Eyes* (based on his meeting with Emma) and previously serialized in *Tinsleys' Magazine*. Horace Moule commits suicide in Cambridge.	Mill, *Autobiography* Walter Pater, *Studies in the History of the Renaissance* (encouraging 'Art for Art's sake' and an impetus towards the later Aesthetic Movement)
1874	*Far from the Madding Crowd* (previously serialized in the *Cornhill Magazine*). Hardy marries Emma and sets up house in Surbiton, London. (They have no children, to Hardy's regret, and she never gets on with his family.)	Factory Act.
1875	Emma and Hardy return to Swanage in Dorset.	Artisans' Dwellings Act (providing housing for the 'respectable poor' or 'artisans'). Efficient system of compulsory vaccination of children against smallpox introduced. Trollope, *The Way We Live Now* (fierce satire on contemporary society and its greed)
1876	*The Hand of Ethelberta* (previously serialized in the *Cornhill Magazine*) published in volume form.	Disraeli creates Victoria Empress of India. Alexander Graham Bell patents the telephone. Invention of the phonograph. Eliot, *Daniel Deronda* Henry James, *Roderick Hudson*
1878	*The Return of the Native* (previously serialized in *Belgravia*) published in volume form. The Hardys move back to London (Tooting). Serialized version of part of the unpublished first novel appears in *Harper's Weekly* in New York as *An Indiscretion in the Life of an Heiress* (never included in his collected works).	London University grants degrees to women for the first time. G. H. Lewes dies.
1879		Beginning of a long though intermittent economic depression in Britain, lasting into the 1890s. William Morris's lecture, *The Art of the People*, explaining ideas which led later to the Arts and Crafts Movement in the latter part of the century. Henrik Ibsen, *A Doll's House* James, *Daisy Miller*

	Life	*Historical and Cultural Background*
1880	*The Trumpet-Major* (previously serialized in *Good Words*) published in volume form. Hardy is ill for many months.	Gladstone becomes Prime Minister for the second time. George Eliot and Gustave Flaubert die. Education Act makes elementary education compulsory. Charles Parnell demands home rule for Ireland. George Gissing, *Workers in the Dawn* Tennyson, *Ballads and Other Poems* Trollope, *The Duke's Children* (last of the Palliser novels)
1881	*A Laodicean* (previously serialized in *Harper's New Monthly Magazine*) published in volume form. The Hardys return to Dorset, living at first in Wimborne.	Death of Carlyle. 'Otto' safety bicycle patented: Hardy and Emma become keen cyclists. By the 1890s many have succumbed to 'bicycle mania'. Ibsen, *Ghosts* (involving syphilis but later seen by Queen Victoria) James, *Portrait of a Lady*
1882	*Two on a Tower* (previously serialized in the *Atlantic Monthly*) published in volume form.	
1882–90		Parliament repeatedly vetoes votes for women.
1883		Andrew Mearns, *The Bitter Cry of Outcast London* (exposé of poverty)
1884	Hardy becomes a Justice of the Peace and serves as a magistrate in Dorchester.	Third Reform Bill. Founding of the Fabian Society.
1885	The Hardys move for the last time: to a house, Max Gate, outside Dorchester, designed by Hardy and built by his brother.	Death of General Gordon at Khartoum. Criminal Law Amendment Act (raises age of consent to 16).
1886	*The Mayor of Casterbridge* (previously serialized in the *Graphic*) published in volume form.	Repeal of the Contagious Diseases Act. Irish Home Rule Act.
1887	*The Woodlanders* (previously serialized in *Macmillan's Magazine*) published in volume form. Hardy begins to visit London for 'the Season'. Visit to Italy.	Victoria's Golden Jubilee.
1888	*Wessex Tales*. Visit to Paris.	Matthew Arnold dies.

Life	*Historical and Cultural Background*
1889	London dock strike.
	Robert Browning dies.
	William Booth, *Life and Labour of the People in London* (exhaustive documentary account) starts publication
	G. B. Shaw, *Fabian Essays on Socialism*
	Ibsen, *A Doll's House* staged in London
	Gissing, *The Nether World*
1890	Decline of the circulating libraries and the death of the three-volume novel. William Morris founds the Kelmscott Press. Housing of the Working Classes Act. Oscar Wilde, *The Picture of Dorian Gray* Ibsen, *Hedda Gabler*
1891	*Tess of the d'Urbervilles* (previously serialized in censored form in the *Graphic*) published in volume form. It simultaneously enhances his reputation as a novelist and causes a scandal because of its advanced views on sexual conduct. *A Group of Noble Dames* (tales) also published.	
1892	Hardy's father, Thomas, dies. Serialized version of *The Well-Beloved*, entitled *The Pursuit of the Well-Beloved*—virtually a different novel from the later book version—published in the *Illustrated London News*. Hardy's estrangement from Emma increases.	Death of Alfred Tennyson. Wilde, *Lady Windermere's Fan* Rudyard Kipling, *Barrack-Room Ballads*
1892–3	*Our Exploits at West Poley*, a long tale for boys, published in an American periodical, *The Household*.	
1893	Meets Florence Henniker, one of several society women with whom he had intense friendships. Collaborates with her on *The Spectre of the Real* (published 1894).	Keir Hardie sets up the Independent Labour Party. Wilde, *A Woman of No Importance*

	Life	*Historical and Cultural Background*
1894	*Life's Little Ironies* (tales)	Kipling, *The Jungle Book*
1895	*Jude the Obscure* appears in volume form: a savage attack on marriage which worsens relations with Emma. Serialized previously in *Harper's New Monthly Magazine* in bowdlerized form. It receives both eulogistic and vitriolic reviews. The latter are a factor in his ceasing to write novels.	Oscar Wilde jailed for homosexual offences; serves three years. The first Bristol electric tramway. Wilde, *The Importance of Being Earnest* H. G. Wells, *The Time-Machine*
1895–6	First collected edition: the Wessex Novels (16 volumes). This includes the first book edition of *Jude the Obscure*.	
1896		Locomotive on the Highways Act (car speed maximum 14 m.p.h.). Death of William Morris. Wells, *The Island of Dr Moreau*
1897	*The Well-Beloved*, a newly rewritten version of the 1892 serial, added to the Wessex Novels as volume XVII. From now on he only publishes the poetry he has been writing since the 1860s.	Queen Victoria's Diamond Jubilee. Existing suffrage organizations unite as National Union of Women's Suffrage Societies. Havelock Ellis, *Sexual Inversion*
1898	*Wessex Poems and Other Verses*. Hardy and Emma continue to live at Max Gate but are now estranged and 'kept separate'.	Germany begins the building of a large battle fleet. Britain responds by doing the same. Wilde released from prison. Wilde, *The Ballad of Reading Gaol*
1899–1902		Boer War in South Africa over the Transvaal gold mines; Britain crushes the Boers.
1900		Labour Representation Committee set up to get Labour candidates into Parliament. Wilde and Ruskin die.
1901	*Poems of the Past and the Present* (post-dated 1902)	Victoria dies and is succeeded by Edward VII.
1902	Macmillan becomes his publisher.	James, *The Wings of the Dove*
1903		First manned flight by Wright brothers in the USA. Motor Car Act raises speed limit to 20 m.p.h. James, *The Ambassadors*

	Life	*Historical and Cultural Background*
1904	Hardy's mother Jemima, the single most important influence in his life, dies. Part 1 of *The Dynasts* (epic drama in verse on Napoleon) published.	Anglo–French Entente. James, *The Golden Bowl*
1905	At about this time Hardy meets Florence Emily Dugdale, his future second wife, then aged 26. She is soon a friend of Hardy and Emma, and his part-time secretary.	Increased trade-union activity. E. M. Forster, *Where Angels Fear to Tread*
1906	Part 2 of *The Dynasts*.	Thirty Labour MPs are elected in General Election.
1907		Anglo–Russian Entente. Act allowing marriage with deceased wife's sister. First London cinema. Forster, *The Longest Journey*
1908	Part 3 of *The Dynasts* completes the work.	Non-contributory state pension is set up. Forster, *A Room with a View*
1909	*Time's Laughingstocks and Other Verses*.	Housing and Town Planning Act (to help provide working-class housing). Labour Exchanges Act (seeking employment previously difficult).
1910	Is awarded the Order of Merit, having previously refused a knighthood. Also receives the Freedom of Dorchester.	Edward VII dies and is succeeded by George V.
1911		National Insurance Act. D. H. Lawrence, *The White Peacock*
1912	27 November: Emma dies, still estranged. Her death triggers the writing of Hardy's finest love lyrics, *Poems of 1912–1913*, about their early time together in Cornwall which he now revisits.	William Morris produces first cheap Morris Oxford car. George V attends first Royal Command Variety Performance.
1912–13	Publication of a major collected edition of novels and verse by Hardy: the Wessex Edition (24 volumes).	
1913	*A Changed Man and Other Tales*.	A suffragette throws herself under the King's horse at the Derby. Lawrence, *Sons and Lovers*

	Life	*Historical and Cultural Background*
1914	10 February: Hardy marries Florence Dugdale (who was hurt by the poems written about Emma after her death). *Satires of Circumstance*; *The Dynasts: Prologue and Epilogue*	Start of First World War. A million copies of books now available in free public libraries. James Joyce, *Dubliners*
1914–15		Joyce, *A Portrait of the Artist as a Young Man*
1915	Mary, Hardy's sister, dies. His distant relative, Frank George, is killed at Gallipoli.	Virginia Woolf, *The Voyage Out* Lawrence, *The Rainbow*
1916	*Selected Poems*	Self-proclamation of an independent Irish Republic.
1917	*Moments of Vision and Miscellaneous Verses*	T. S. Eliot, *Prufrock and Other Observations*
1918		First World War ends. Vote extended to men over 21 and some women over 30. Those Irish who want independence set up their own parliament, the Dáil, and the Irish 'troubles' begin. British troops ruthlessly repress the rebels. Education Act raises the school-leaving age to 14 and extends education for some to 16.
1919		Russian Revolution helps stir up working-class militancy. First satisfactory contraceptive for women is devised.
1919–20	Mellstock Edition of novels and verse (37 volumes).	
1920		Increased social awareness is indicated by extension of National Insurance against unemployment. Lawrence, *Women in Love*
1921		Ireland splits into new republic and the North, which remains part of the United Kingdom.
1922	*Late Lyrics and Earlier with Many Other Verses*	BBC is set up. Joyce, *Ulysses* Woolf, *Jacob's Room* T. S. Eliot, *The Waste Land*
1923	*The Famous Tragedy of the Queen of Cornwall* (drama). Florence Henniker dies. The Prince of Wales, the future Edward VIII (later the Duke of Windsor), visits Max Gate.	

Life	Historical and Cultural Background
1924	Dramatized version of *Tess* performed at Dorchester. Hardy is infatuated with the local woman, Gertrude Bugler, who plays Tess.	First Labour Government formed by Ramsay MacDonald. Forster, *A Passage to India*
1925	*Human Shows, Far Phantasies, Songs and Trifles*	Woolf, *Mrs Dalloway* and *The Common Reader* (essays)
1926		May: General Strike, lasting 9 days. James Ramsay MacDonald forms a coalition government which he leads until 1935 but is expelled from the Labour Party who refuse to support it.
1927		Invention of talking pictures. Woolf, *To the Lighthouse*
1928	11 January: Hardy dies. His heart is buried in Emma's grave at Stinsford, his ashes in Westminster Abbey. *Winter Words in Various Moods and Metres* published post-humously. Hardy's brother, Henry, dies.	Vote is extended to women over 21. Lawrence, *Lady Chatterley's Lover* Woolf, *Orlando*
1928–30	Hardy's autobiography is completed by his second wife and published on his instructions under her name.	
1937	Florence, Hardy's second wife, dies.	
1940	Hardy's last sibling, Kate, dies.	

DESPERATE REMEDIES

A Novel

"Though a course of adventures which are only connected with each other by having happened to the same individual is what most frequently occurs in nature, yet the province of the romance-writer being artificial, there is more required from him than a mere compliance with the simplicity of reality."

SIR W. SCOTT*

CONTENTS

CONTENTS

VOLUME I

VOLUME I

CHAPTER I

THE EVENTS OF THIRTY YEARS

§ 1. *December and January, 1835–36*

In the long and intricately inwrought chain of circumstance which renders worthy of record some experiences of Cytherea* Graye, Edward Springrove, and others, the first event directly influencing the issue was a Christmas visit.

In the above-mentioned year eighteen hundred and thirty-five, Ambrose Graye, a young architect* who had just commenced the practice of his profession in the midland town of Hocbridge, went to London to spend the Christmas holidays with a friend who lived in Bloomsbury. They had gone up to Cambridge in the same year, and, after graduating together, Huntway, the friend, had entered orders.*

Graye was handsome, frank, and gentle. He had a volatility of thought which, exercised on homeliness, was humour; on nature, picturesqueness; on abstractions, poetry. Being, as a rule, broadcast, it was all three.

Of the wickedness of the world he was too forgetful. To discover evil in a new friend is to most people only an additional experience: to him it was ever a surprise.

While in London he became acquainted with a retired officer in the navy named Bradleigh, who, with his wife and their daughter, lived in a small street not far from Russell Square. Though they were in no more than comfortable circumstances, the captain's wife came of an ancient family whose genealogical tree was interlaced with some of the most illustrious and well-known in the kingdom.

The young lady, their daughter, seemed to Graye by far the most beautiful and queenly* being he had ever beheld. She was about nineteen or twenty, and her name was Cytherea. In truth she was not so very unlike country girls of that type of beauty, except in one respect. She was perfect in her manner and bearing, and they were not. A mere distinguishing peculiarity, by catching the eye, is often read as the pervading characteristic, and she appeared to him no less than perfection throughout—transcending her rural rivals in very nature. Graye did a thing the blissfulness of which was only eclipsed by its hazardousness. He loved her at first sight.

His introductions had led him into contact with Cytherea and her parents two or three times on the first week of his arrival in London, and accident and a lover's contrivance brought them together as frequently the week following. The parents liked young Graye, and having few friends (for their equals in blood were their superiors in position), he was received on very generous terms. His passion for Cytherea grew not only strong, but ineffably strong: she, without positively encouraging him, tacitly assented to his schemes for being near her. Her father and mother seemed to have lost all confidence in nobility of birth, without money to give effect to its presence, and looked upon the budding consequence of the young people's reciprocal glances with placidity, if not actual favour.

Graye's whole delicious dream terminated in a sad and unaccountable episode. After passing through three weeks of sweet experience, he had arrived at the last stage—a kind of moral Gaza*—before plunging into an emotional desert. The second week in January had come round, and it was necessary for the young architect to leave town.

Throughout his acquaintanceship with the lady of his heart there had been this marked peculiarity in her love: she had delighted in his presence as a sweetheart should, yet from first to last she had repressed all recognition of the true nature of the thread which drew them together, blinding herself to its meaning and only natural tendency, and appearing to dread his announcement of them. The present seemed enough for her without cumulative hope: usually, even if love is in itself an end, it must be regarded as a beginning to be enjoyed.

In spite of evasions as an obstacle, and in consequence of them as a spur, he would put the matter off no longer. It was evening. He took her into a little conservatory on the landing, and there among the evergreens, by the light of a few tiny lamps, infinitely enhancing the freshness and beauty of the leaves, he made the declaration of a love as fresh and beautiful as they.

"My love—my darling, be my wife!"

"We must part now," said she, in a voice of agony. "I will write to you." She loosened her hand and rushed away.

In a wild fever Graye went home and watched for the next morning. Who shall express his misery and wonder when a note containing these words was put into his hand?

"Good-bye; good-bye for ever. As recognised lovers something divides us eternally. Forgive me—I should have told you before; but your love was sweet! Never mention me."

That very day, and as it seemed, to put an end to a painful condition of things, daughter and parents left London to pay off a promised visit to a relative in a western county. No message or letter of entreaty could wring from her any explanation. She begged him not to follow her, and the most bewildering point was that her father and mother appeared, from the tone of a letter Graye received from them, as vexed and sad as he at this sudden renunciation. One thing was plain: without admitting her reason as valid, they knew what that reason was, and did not intend to reveal it.

A week from that day Ambrose Graye left his friend Huntway's house and saw no more of the Love he mourned. From time to time his friend answered any inquiry Graye made by letter respecting her. But very poor food to a lover is intelligence of a mistress filtered through a friend. Huntway could tell nothing definitely. He said he believed there had been some prior flirtation between Cytherea and her cousin, an officer of the line, two or three years before Graye met her, which had suddenly been terminated by the cousin's departure for India, and the young lady's travelling on the continent with her parents the whole of the ensuing summer, on account of delicate health.* Eventually Huntway said that circumstances had rendered Graye's attachment more hopeless still. Cytherea's mother had unexpectedly inherited a large fortune and estates in the west of England by the rapid fall of some intervening lives. This had caused their removal from the small house by Gower Street, and, as it appeared, a renunciation of their old friends in that quarter.

Young Graye concluded that his Cytherea had forgotten him and his love. But he could not forget her.

§2. *From 1843 to 1861*

Eight years later, feeling lonely and depressed—a man without relatives, with many acquaintances but no friends,—Ambrose Graye met a young lady of a different kind, fairly endowed with money and good gifts. As to caring very deeply for another woman after the loss of Cytherea, it was an absolute impossibility with him. With all, the beautiful things of the earth become more dear as they elude pursuit; but with some natures utter elusion is the one special event which will make a passing love permanent for ever.

This second young lady and Graye were married. That he did not, first or last, love his wife as he should have done, was known to all; but few knew that his unmanageable heart could never be weaned from useless repining at the loss of its first idol.

His character to some extent deteriorated, as emotional constitutions will under the long sense of disappointment at having missed their imagined destiny. And thus, though naturally of a gentle and pleasant disposition, he grew to be not so tenderly regarded by his acquaintances as it is the lot of some of those persons to be. The winning and sanguine impressibility of his early life developed by degrees a moody nervousness, and when not picturing prospects drawn from baseless hope he was the victim of indescribable depression. The practical issue of such a condition was improvidence, originally almost an unconscious improvidence, for every debt incurred had been mentally paid off with a religious exactness from the treasures of expectation before mentioned. But as years revolved, the same course was continued, from the lack of spirit sufficient for shifting out of an old groove when it has been found to lead to disaster.

In the year eighteen hundred and sixty-one his wife died, leaving him a widower with two children. The elder, a son named Owen, now just turned seventeen, was taken from school, and initiated as pupil to the profession of architect in his father's office. The remaining child was a daughter, and Owen's junior by a year.

Her christian name was Cytherea, and it is easy to guess why.

§ 3. *October the twelfth, 1863*

We pass over two years in order to reach the next cardinal event of the story. The scene is still the Grayes' native town of Hocbridge, but as it appeared on a Monday afternoon in the month of October.

The weather was sunny and dry, but the ancient borough was to be seen wearing one of its least attractive aspects. First on account of the time. It was that stagnant hour of the twenty-four when the practical garishness of Day, having escaped from the fresh long shadows and enlivening newness of the morning, has not yet made any perceptible advance towards acquiring those mellow and soothing tones which grace its decline. Next, it was that stage in the progress of the week when business—which, carried on under the gables of an old country place, is not devoid of a romantic sparkle—was well-nigh extinguished. Lastly, the town was intentionally bent upon being attractive by exhibiting to an influx of visitors the local talent for dramatic recitation, and provincial towns trying to be lively are the dullest of dull things.

Provincial towns are like little children in this respect, that they interest most when they are enacting native peculiarities unconscious of beholders. Discovering themselves to be watched they attempt to be entertaining by putting on an antic,* and produce disagreeable caricatures which spoil them.

The weather-stained clock face in the low church tower standing at the intersection of the three chief streets was expressing half-past two to the Town-Hall opposite, where the much talked-of reading from Shakespeare was about to be commenced. The doors were open, and those persons who had already assembled within the building were noticing the entrance of the new-comers—silently criticising their dresses—questioning the genuineness of their teeth and hair—estimating their private means.

Among these later ones came an exceptional young maiden who glowed amid the dulness like a single bright-red poppy in a field of brown stubble. She wore an elegant dark jacket, lavender dress, hat with grey strings and trimmings, and gloves of a colour to harmonize. She lightly walked up the side passage of the room, cast a slight glance around, and entered the seat pointed out to her.

The young girl was Cytherea Graye, her age was now about eighteen. During her entry, and at various times whilst sitting in her seat and listening to the reader on the platform, her personal appearance formed an interesting subject of study for several neighbouring eyes.

Her face was exceedingly attractive, though artistically less perfect than her figure, which approached unusually near to the standard of faultlessness. But even this feature of hers yielded the palm to the gracefulness of her movement, which was fascinating and delightful to an extreme degree.

Indeed, motion was her speciality, whether shown on its most

extended scale of bodily progression, or minutely, as in the uplifting
of her eyelids, the bending of her fingers, the pouting of her lip. The
carriage of her head—motion within motion—a glide upon a
glide—was as delicate as that of a magnetic needle. And this flexibil-
ity and elasticity had never been taught her by rule, nor even been
acquired by observation, but, *nullo cultu,** had naturally developed
itself with her years. In childhood, a stone or stalk in the way, which
had been the inevitable occasion of a fall to her playmates, had usually left her safe and upright on her feet after the narrowest escape by
oscillations and whirls for the preservation of her balance. At mixed
Christmas parties, when she numbered but twelve or thirteen years,
and was heartily despised on that account by lads who deemed themselves men, her apt lightness in the dance covered this incomplete-
ness in her womanhood, and compelled the self-same youths in spite
of resolutions to seize upon her childish figure as a partner whom
they could not afford to contemn. And in later years, when the
instincts of her sex had shown her this point as the best and rarest
feature in her external self, she was not found wanting in attention to
the cultivation of finish in its details.

Her hair rested gaily upon her shoulders in curls, and was of a
shining corn yellow in the high lights, deepening to a definite nut
brown as each curl wound round into the shade. She had eyes of a
sapphire hue, though rather darker than the gem ordinarily appears;
they possessed the affectionate and liquid sparkle of loyalty and good
faith as distinguishable from that harder brightness which seems to
express faithfulness only to the object confronting them.

But to attempt to gain a view of her—or indeed of any fascinating
woman—from a measured category, is as difficult as to appreciate the
effect of a landscape by exploring it at night with a lantern—or of a
full chord of music by piping the notes in succession. Nevertheless it
may readily be believed from the description here ventured, that
among the many winning phases of her aspect, these were particularly striking:—

1. During pleasant doubt, when her eyes brightened stealthily
and smiled (as eyes will smile) as distinctly as her lips, and in the
space of a single instant expressed clearly the whole round of degrees
of expectancy which lie over the wide expanse between Yea and Nay.

2. During the telling of a secret, which was involuntarily accompanied by a sudden minute start, and ecstatic pressure of the

listener's arm, side, or neck, as the position and degree of intimacy dictated.

3. When anxiously regarding one who possessed her affections.

She suddenly assumed the last-mentioned bearing during the progress of the present entertainment. Her glance was directed out of the window.

Why the particulars of a young lady's presence at a very mediocre performance were prevented from dropping into the oblivion which their intrinsic insignificance would naturally have involved— why they were remembered and individualised by herself and others through after years—was simply that she unknowingly stood, as it were, upon the extreme posterior edge of a tract in her life, in which the real meaning of Taking Thought had never been known. It was the last hour of experience she ever enjoyed with a mind entirely free from a knowledge of that labyrinth into which she stepped immediately afterwards—to continue a perplexed course along its mazes for the greater portion of twenty-nine subsequent months.

The Town Hall, in which Cytherea sat, was an Elizabethan building of brown stone, and the windows were divided into an upper and a lower half by a transom of masonry.* Through one opening of the upper half could be seen from the interior of the room the housetops and chimneys of the adjacent street, and also the upper part of a neighbouring church spire, now in course of completion under the superintendence of Miss Graye's father, the architect to the work.

That the top of this spire should be visible from her position in the room was a fact which Cytherea's idling eyes had discovered with some interest, and she was now engaged in watching the scene that was being enacted about its airy summit. Round the conical stonework rose a cage of scaffolding against the white sky; and upon this stood five men—four in clothes as white as the new erection close beneath their hands, the fifth in the ordinary dark suit of a gentleman.

The four working-men in white were three masons and a mason's labourer. The fifth man was the architect, Mr. Graye. He had been giving directions as it seemed, and now, retiring as far as the narrow footway allowed, stood perfectly still.

The picture thus presented to a spectator in the Town Hall was curious and striking. It was an illuminated miniature, framed in by the dark margin of the window, the keen-edged shadiness of which emphasised by contrast the softness of the objects enclosed.

The height of the spire was about one hundred and twenty feet, and the five men engaged thereon seemed entirely removed from the sphere and experiences of ordinary human beings. They appeared little larger than pigeons, and made their tiny movements with a soft, spirit-like silentness. One idea above all others was conveyed to the mind of a person on the ground by their aspect, namely, concentration of purpose: that they were indifferent to—even unconscious of—the distracted world beneath them, and all that moved upon it. They never looked off the scaffolding.

Then one of them turned; it was Mr. Graye. Again he stood motionless, with attention to the operations of the others. He appeared to be lost in reflection, and had directed his face towards a new stone they were lifting.

"Why does he stand like that?" the young lady thought at length—up to that moment as listless and careless as one of the ancient Tarentines, who, on such an afternoon as this, watched from the Theatre the entry into their Harbour of a power that overturned the State.*

She moved herself uneasily. "I wish he would come down," she whispered, still gazing at the sky-backed picture. "It is so dangerous to be absent-minded up there."

When she had done murmuring the words her father indecisively laid hold of one of the scaffold-poles, as if to test its strength, then let it go and stepped back. In stepping, his foot slipped. An instant of doubling forward and sideways, and he reeled off into the air, immediately disappearing downwards.

His agonised daughter rose to her feet by a convulsive movement. Her lips parted, and she gasped for breath. She could utter no sound. One by one the people about her, unconscious of what had happened, turned their heads, and inquiry and alarm became visible upon their faces at the sight of the poor child. A moment longer, and she fell to the floor.

The next impression of which Cytherea had any consciousness was of being carried from a strange vehicle across the pavement to the steps of her own house by her brother and an older man. Recollection of what had passed evolved itself an instant later, and just as

they entered the door—through which another and sadder burden
had been carried but a few instants before—her eyes caught sight of
the south-western sky, and, without heeding, saw white sunlight
shining in shaft-like lines from a rift in a slaty cloud. Emotions will
attach themselves to scenes that are simultaneous—however foreign
in essence these scenes may be—as chemical waters will crystallise
on twigs and wires. Ever after that time any mental agony brought
less vividly to Cytherea's mind the scene from the Town Hall
windows than sunlight streaming in shaft-like lines.

§ 4. *October the nineteenth*

When death enters a house, an element of sadness and an element of
horror accompany it. Sadness, from the death itself; horror, from the
clouds of blackness we designedly labour to introduce.

The funeral had taken place. Depressed, yet resolved in his
demeanour, Owen Graye sat before his father's private escritoire,*
engaged in turning out and unfolding a heterogeneous collection of
papers—forbidding and inharmonious to the eye at all times—most
of all to one under the influence of a great grief. Laminæ* of white
paper tied with twine were indiscriminately intermixed with other
white papers bounded by black edges—these with blue foolscap
wrapped round with crude red tape.

The bulk of these letters, bills, and other documents were submitted to a careful examination, by which the appended particulars were
ascertained:—

First, that their father's income from professional sources had
been very small, amounting to not more than half their expenditure;
and that his own and his wife's property, upon which he had relied
for the balance, had been sunk and lost in unwise loans to
unscrupulous men, who had traded upon their father's too open-
hearted trustfulness.

Second, that finding his mistake, he had endeavoured to regain his
standing by the illusory path of speculation. The most notable
instance of this was the following. He had been induced, when at
Plymouth in the autumn of the previous year, to venture all his
spare capital on the bottomry security* of an Italian brig* which had
put into the harbour in distress. The profit was to be considerable, so
was the risk. There turned out to be no security whatever. The

circumstances of the case rendered it the most unfortunate speculation that a man like himself—ignorant of all such matters—could
possibly engage in. The vessel went down, and all Mr. Graye's
money with it.

Third, that these failures had left him burdened with debts he
knew not how to meet; so that at the time of his death even the few
pounds lying to his account at the bank were his only in name.

Fourth, that the loss of his wife two years earlier had awakened
him to a keen sense of his blindness, and of his duty by his children.
He had then resolved to reinstate by unflagging zeal in the pursuit of
his profession, and by no speculation, at least a portion of the little
fortune he had let go.

Cytherea was frequently at her brother's elbow during these
examinations. She often remarked sadly,

"Poor papa failed to fulfil his good intention for want of time,
didn't he, Owen? And there was an excuse for his past, though he
never would claim it. I never forget that original disheartening blow,
and how that from it sprang all the ills of his life—everything connected with his gloom, and the lassitude in business we used so often
to see about him."

"I remember what he said once," returned the brother, "when I
sat up late with him. He said, 'Owen, don't love too blindly: blindly
you will love if you love at all, but a little care is still possible to a
well-disciplined heart.* May that heart be yours as it was not mine,'
father said. 'Cultivate the art of renunciation.' And I am going to,
Cytherea."

"And once mamma said that an excellent woman was papa's
ruin, because he did not know the way to give her up when he
had lost her. I wonder where she is now, Owen? We were told not to
try to find out anything about her. Papa never told us her name,
did he?"

"That was by her own request, I believe. But never mind her; she
was not our mother."

The love affair which had been Ambrose Graye's disheartening
blow was precisely of that nature which lads take little account of,
but girls ponder in their hearts.

§ 5. *From October the nineteenth to July the ninth*

Thus Ambrose Graye's good intentions with regard to the reintegration of his property had scarcely taken tangible form when his sudden death put them for ever out of his power.

Heavy bills, showing the extent of his obligations, tumbled in immediately upon the heels of the funeral from quarters previously unheard and unthought of. Thus pressed, a bill was filed in Chancery* to have the assets, such as they were, administered by the Court.

"What will become of us now?" thought Owen continually.

There is in us an unquenchable expectation, which at the gloomiest time persists in inferring that because we are *ourselves*, there must be a special future in store for us, though our nature and antecedents to the remotest particular have been common to thousands.

Thus to Cytherea and Owen Graye the question how their lives would end seemed the deepest of possible enigmas. To others who knew their position equally well with themselves the question was the easiest that could be asked.—"Like those of other people similarly circumstanced."

Then Owen held a consultation with his sister to come to some decision on their future course, and a month was passed in waiting for answers to letters, and in the examination of schemes more or less futile. Sudden hopes that were rainbows to the sight proved but mists to the touch. In the meantime, unpleasant remarks, disguise them as some well-meaning people might, were floating around them every day. The undoubted truth, that they were the children of a dreamer who let slip away every farthing of his money and ran into debt with his neighbours—that the daughter had been brought up to no profession—that the son who had, had made no progress in it, and might come to the dogs—could not from the nature of things be wrapped up in silence in order that it might not hurt their feelings; and as a matter of fact, it greeted their ears in some form or other wherever they went. Their few acquaintances passed them hurriedly. Ancient pot-wallopers,* and thriving shopkeepers, in their intervals of leisure, stood at their shop doors—their toes hanging over the edge of the step, and their obese waists hanging over their toes—and in discourses with friends on the pavement, formulated the course of the improvident, and reduced the children's prospects to a shadow-like attenuation. The sons of these men (who wore breast-pins of a sarcastic kind,* and smoked humorous pipes) stared at Cytherea with a stare unmitigated by any of the respect that had formerly softened it.

Now it is a noticeable fact that we do not much mind what men think of us, or what humiliating secret they discover of our means, parentage, or object, provided that each thinks and acts thereupon in isolation. It is the exchange of ideas about us that we dread most; and the possession by a hundred acquaintances, severally insulated, of the knowledge of our skeleton-closet's whereabouts, is not so distressing to the nerves as a chat over it by a party of half a dozen—exclusive depositaries though these may be.

Perhaps, though Hocbridge watched and whispered, its animus would have been little more than a trifle to persons in thriving circumstances. But unfortunately, poverty, whilst it is new, and before the skin has had time to thicken, makes people susceptible inversely to their opportunities for shielding themselves. In Owen was found, in place of his father's impressibility, a larger share of his father's pride, and a squareness of idea which, if coupled with a little more blindness, would have amounted to positive prejudice. To him humanity, so far as he had thought of it at all, was rather divided into distinct classes than blended from extreme to extreme. Hence by a sequence of ideas which might be traced if it were worth while, he either detested or respected opinion, and instinctively sought to escape a cold shade that mere sensitiveness would have endured. He could have submitted to separation, sickness, exile, drudgery, hunger and thirst, with stoical indifference, but superciliousness was too incisive.

After living on for nine months in attempts to make an income as his father's successor in the profession—attempts which were utterly fruitless by reason of his inexperience—Graye came to a simple and sweeping resolution. They would privately leave that part of England, drop from the sight of acquaintances, gossips, harsh critics, and bitter creditors of whose misfortune he was not the cause, and escape the position which galled him by the only road their great poverty left open to them—that of his obtaining some employment in a distant place by following his profession as a humble under-clerk.*

He thought over his capabilities with the sensations of a soldier grinding his sword at the opening of a campaign. What with lack of employment, owing to the decrease of his late father's practice, and the absence of direct and uncompromising pressure towards monetary results from a pupil's labour (which seems to be always the case when a professional man's pupil is also his son), Owen's progress in the art and science of architecture had been very insignificant indeed. Though anything but an idle young man, he had hardly reached the age at which industrious men who lack an external whip to send them on in the world, are induced by their own common sense to whip on themselves. Hence his knowledge of plans, elevations, sections, and specifications, was not greater at the end of two years of probation than might easily have been acquired in six months by a youth of average ability—himself, for instance,—amid a bustling London practice.

But at any rate he could make himself handy to one of the profession—some man in a remote town—and there fulfil his indentures. A tangible inducement lay in this direction of survey. He had a slight conception of such a man—a Mr. Gradfield—who was in practice in Creston, a seaport town and watering-place in the west of England.

After some doubts, Graye ventured to write to this gentleman, asking the necessary question, shortly alluding to his father's death, and stating that his term of apprenticeship had only half expired. He would be glad to complete his articles* at a very low salary for the whole remaining two years, provided payment could begin at once.

The answer from Mr. Gradfield stated that he was not in want of a pupil who would serve the remainder of his time on the terms Mr. Graye mentioned. But he would just add one remark. He chanced to be in want of some young man in his office—for a short time only, probably about two months—to trace drawings, and attend to other subsidiary work of the kind. If Mr. Graye did not object to occupy such an inferior position as these duties would entail, and to accept weekly wages which to one with his expectations would be considered merely nominal, the post would give him an opportunity for learning a few more details of the profession.

"It is a beginning, and above all, an abiding place, away from the shadow of the cloud which hangs over us here—I will go," said Owen.

Cytherea's plan for her future, an intensely simple one, owing to the even greater narrowness of her resources, was already marked

out. One advantage had accrued to her through her mother's possession of a fair share of personal property, and perhaps only one. She
had been carefully educated. Upon this consideration her plan was
based. She was to take up her abode in her brother's lodging at
Creston, when she would immediately advertise for a situation as
governess, having obtained the consent of a lawyer at Reading who
was winding up her father's affairs, and who knew the history of her
position, to allow himself to be referred to in the matter of her past
life and respectability.

Early one morning they departed from their native town, leaving
behind them scarcely a trace of their footsteps.

Then the town pitied their want of wisdom in taking such a step.
"Rashness; they would have done better in Hocbridge."

But what is Wisdom really? A steady handling of any means to
bring about any end necessary to happiness.

Yet whether one's end be the usual end—a wealthy position in
life—or no, the name of wisdom is never applied but to the means to
that usual end.

CHAPTER II

THE EVENTS OF A FORTNIGHT

§ 1. *The ninth of July*

The day of their departure was one of the most glowing that the climax of a long series of summer heats could evolve. The wide expanse of landscape quivered up and down like the flame of a taper, as they steamed along through the midst of it. Placid flocks of sheep reclining under trees a little way off appeared of a pale blue colour. Clover fields were livid with the brightness of the sun upon their deep red flowers. All waggons and carts were moved to the shade by their careful owners; rain-water butts fell to pieces; well-buckets were lowered inside the covers of the well-hole, to preserve them from the fate of the butts, and generally, water seemed scarcer in the country than the beer and cider of the peasantry* who toiled or idled there.

To see persons looking with children's eyes at any ordinary scenery, is a proof that they possess the charming faculty of drawing new sensations from an old experience—a healthy sign, rare in these feverish days—the mark of an imperishable brightness of nature.

Both brother and sister could do this; Cytherea more noticeably. They watched the undulating corn-lands, monotonous to all their companions; the stony and clayey prospect succeeding those, with its angular and abrupt hills. Boggy moors came next, now withered and dry—the spots upon which pools usually spread their waters, showing themselves as circles of smooth bare soil, over-run by a net-work of innumerable little fissures. Then arose plantations of firs, abruptly terminating beside meadows cleanly mown, in which high-hipped, rich-coloured cows, with backs horizontal and straight as the ridge of a house, stood motionless or lazily fed. Glimpses of the sea now interested them, which became more and more frequent till the train finally drew up beside the platform at Creston.*

"The whole town is looking out for us," had been Graye's impression throughout the day. He called upon Mr. Gradfield—the only man who had been directly informed of his coming—and found that Mr. Gradfield had forgotten it.

However, arrangements were made with this gentleman—a stout, active, grey-bearded burgher of sixty—by which Owen was to commence work in his office the following week.

The same day Cytherea drew up and sent off the advertisement appended:—

"A YOUNG LADY is desirous of meeting with an ENGAGEMENT as GOVERNESS or COMPANION. She is competent to teach English, French, and Music. Satisfactory references.
"Address, C. G., Post Office, Creston."

It seemed a more material existence than her own that she saw thus delineated on the paper. "That can't be myself; how odd I look," she said, and smiled.

§ 2. *July the eleventh*

On the Monday subsequent to their arrival in Creston, Owen Graye attended at Mr. Gradfield's office to enter upon his duties, and his sister was left in their lodgings alone for the first time.

Despite the sad occurrences of the preceding autumn, an unwonted cheerfulness pervaded her spirit throughout the day. Change of scene—and that to untravelled eyes—conjoined with the sensation of freedom from supervision, revived the sparkle of a warm young nature ready enough to take advantage of any adventitious restoratives. Point-blank grief* tends rather to seal up happiness for a time than to produce that attrition which results from griefs of anticipation that move onward with the days: these may be said to furrow away the capacity for pleasure.

Her expectations from the advertisement began to be extravagant. A thriving family, who had always sadly needed her, was already definitely pictured in her fancy, which, in its exuberance, led her on to picturing its individual members, their possible peculiarities, virtues, and vices, and obliterated for a time the recollection that she would be separated from her brother.

Thus musing, as she waited for his return in the evening, her eyes fell on her left hand. The contemplation of her own left fourth finger by symbol-loving girlhood of this age is, it seems, very frequently, if not always, followed by a peculiar train of romantic ideas. Cytherea's thoughts, still playing about her future became directed into this romantic groove. She leant back in her chair, and taking hold of the fourth finger,* which had attracted her attention, she lifted it with the tips of the others, and looked at the smooth and tapering member for a long time,

She whispered idly, "I wonder, who and what He will be?"

"If he's a gentleman of fashion, he will take my finger so, just with the tips of his own, and with some fluttering of the heart, and the least trembling of his lip, slip the ring so lightly on that I shall hardly know it is there—looking delightfully into my eyes all the time.

"If he's a bold, dashing soldier, I expect he will proudly turn round, take the ring as if it equalled Her Majesty's crown in value, and desperately set it on my finger thus. He will fix his eyes unflinchingly upon what he is doing—just as if he stood in battle before the enemy (though, in reality, very fond of me, of course), and blush as much as I shall.

"If he's a sailor, he will take my finger and the ring in this way, and deck it out with a housewifely touch and a tenderness of expression about his mouth, as sailors do: kiss it, perhaps, with a simple air, as if we were children playing an idle game, and not at the very height of observation and envy by a great crowd saying 'Ah! they are happy now!'

"If he should be rather a poor man—noble-minded and affectionate, but still poor*——"

Owen's footsteps rapidly ascending the stairs, interrupted this fancy-free meditation. Reproaching herself, even angry with herself for allowing her mind to stray upon such subjects in the face of their present desperate condition, she rose to meet him, and make tea.

Cytherea's interest to know how her brother had been received at Mr. Gradfield's broke forth into words at once. Almost before they had sat down to table, she began cross-examining him in the regular sisterly way.

"Well, Owen, how has it been with you today? What is the place like—do you think you will like Mr. Gradfield?"

"Oh, yes. But he has not been there today; I have only had the head clerk* with me."

Young women have a habit, not noticeable in men, of putting on at a moment's notice the drama of whomsoever's life they choose. Cytherea's interest was transferred from Mr. Gradfield to his representative.

"What sort of a man is he?"

"He seems a very nice fellow indeed; though of course I can hardly tell to a certainty as yet. But I think he's a very worthy fellow; there's no nonsense in him, and though he is not a public school man he has read widely, and has a sharp appreciation of what's good in books and art. In fact, his knowledge isn't nearly so exclusive as most professional men's."

"That's a great deal to say of an architect, for of all professional men they are, as a rule, the most professional."

"Yes; perhaps they are. This man is rather of a melancholy turn of mind, I think."

"Has the managing clerk any family?" she mildly asked, after a while, pouring out some more tea.

"Family; no!"

"Well, dear Owen, how should I know?"

"Why, of course he isn't married. But there happened to be a conversation about women going on in the office, and I heard him say what he should wish his wife to be like."

"What would he wish his wife to be like?" she said, with great apparent lack of interest.

"Oh, he says she must be girlish and artless: yet he would be loth to do without a dash of womanly subtlety, 'tis so piquant. Yes, he said, that must be in her; she must have womanly cleverness. 'And yet I should like her to blush if only a cock-sparrow* were to look at her hard,' he said, 'which brings me back to the girl again: and so I flit backwards and forwards. I must have what comes, I suppose,' he said, 'and whatever she may be, thank God she's no worse. However, if he might give a final hint to Providence,' he said, 'a child among pleasures, and a woman among pains was the rough outline of his requirement.' "

"Did he say that? What a musing creature he must be."

"He did, indeed."

§ 3. *From the twelfth to the fifteenth of July*

As is well known, ideas are so elastic in a human brain, that they have no constant measure which may be called their actual bulk. Any important idea may be compressed to a molecule by an unwonted crowding of others; and any small idea will expand to whatever length and breadth of vacuum the mind may be able to make over to it. Cytherea's world was tolerably vacant at this time, and the head clerk became factitiously pervasive. The very next evening this subject was again renewed.

"His name is Springrove," said Owen, in reply to her. "He is a man of very humble origin,* it seems, who has made himself so far. I think he is the son of a farmer, or something of the kind."

"Well, he's none the worse for that, I suppose."

"None the worse. As we come down the hill, we shall be continually meeting people going up." But Owen had felt that Springrove was a little the worse, nevertheless.

"Of course he's rather old by this time."

"Oh, no. He's about six-and-twenty—not more."

"Ah, I see . . . What is he like, Owen?"

"I can't exactly tell you his appearance: 'tis always such a difficult thing to do."

"A man you would describe as short. Most men are those we should describe as short, I fancy."

"I should call him, I think, of the middle height; but as I only see him sitting in the office, of course I am not certain about his form and figure."

"I wish you were, then."

"Perhaps you do. But I am not, you see."

"Of course not, you are always so provoking. Owen, I saw a man in the street to-day whom I fancied was he—and yet, I don't see how it could be, either. He had light brown hair, a snub nose, very round face, and a peculiar habit of reducing his eyes to straight lines when he looked narrowly at anything."

"Oh no. That was not he, Cytherea."

"Not a bit like him in all probability."

"Not a bit. He has dark hair—almost a Grecian nose,* regular teeth, and an intellectual face, as nearly as I can recall to mind."

"Ah, there now, Owen, you *have* described him. But I suppose he's not generally called pleasing, or—"

"Handsome?"

"I scarcely meant that. But since you have said it, is he handsome?"

"Rather."

"His *tout ensemble** is striking?"

"Yes—Oh no, no—I forgot: it is not. He is rather untidy in his waistcoat, and neck-ties, and hair."

"How vexing! . . . . it must be to himself, poor thing."

"He's a thorough bookworm—despises the pap-and-daisy school of verse*—knows Shakespeare to the very dregs of the footnotes. Indeed he's a poet himself in a small way."

"How delicious!" she said, "I have never known a poet."

"And you don't know him," said Owen, drily.

She reddened. "Of course I don't. I know that."

"Have you received any answer to your advertisement?" he inquired.

"Ah—no!" she said, and the forgotten disappointment which had showed itself in her face at different times during the day, became visible again.

Another day passed away. On Thursday, without inquiry, she learnt more of the head clerk. He and Graye had become very friendly, and he had been tempted to show her brother a copy of some poems of his—some serious and sad—some humorous—which had appeared in the poets' corner of a magazine from time to time. Owen showed them now to Cytherea, who instantly began to read them carefully and to think them very beautiful.

"Yes—Springrove's no fool," said Owen didactically.

"No fool!—I should think he isn't, indeed," said Cytherea, look-ing up from the paper in quite an excitement: "To write such verses as these!"

"What logic are you chopping, Cytherea. Well, I don't mean on account of the verses, because I haven't read them; but for what he said when the fellows were talking about falling in love."

"Which you will tell me?"

"He says that your true lover breathlessly finds himself engaged to a sweetheart, like a man who has caught something in the dark. He doesn't know whether it is a bat or a bird, and takes it to the light when he is cool to learn what it is. He looks to see if she is the right age, but right age or wrong age, he must consider her a prize. Some-time later he ponders whether she is the right kind of prize for him. Right kind or wrong kind—he has called her his, and must abide by it. After a time he asks himself, 'Has she the temper, hair, and eyes I meant to have,* and was firmly resolved not to do without?' He finds it is all wrong, and then comes the tussle—"

"Do they marry and live happily?"

"Who? Oh, the supposed pair. I think he said—well, I really forget what he said."

"That *is* stupid of you!" said the young lady with dismay.

"Yes."

"But he's a satirist—I don't think I care about him now."

"There you are just wrong. He is not. He is, as I believe, an impulsive fellow who has been made to pay the penalty of his rashness in some love affair."

Thus ended the dialogue of Thursday, but Cytherea read the verses again in private. On Friday her brother remarked that Springrove had informed him he was going to leave Mr. Gradfield's in a fortnight to push his fortunes in London.

An indescribable feeling of sadness shot through Cytherea's heart. Why should she be sad at such an announcement as that, she thought, concerning a man she had never seen, when her spirits were elastic enough to rebound after hard blows from deep and real troubles as if she had scarcely known them? Though she could not answer this question she knew one thing, she was saddened by Owen's news.

Ideal conception, necessitated by ignorance of the person so imagined, often results in an incipient love, which otherwise would never have existed.

§ 4. *July the twenty-first*

A very homely and rustic excursion by steamboat to Lewborne Bay, forms the framework of the next incident in the chain. The trip was announced through the streets on Thursday morning by the weak-voiced town crier, to be at six o'clock the same evening. The weather was lovely, and the opportunity being the first of the kind offered to them, Owen and Cytherea went with the rest.

They had reached the bay, and had lingered together for nearly an hour on the shore and up the hill which rose beside the cove, when Graye recollected that a mile or two inland from this spot was an interesting mediæval ruin. He was already familiar with its characteristics through the medium of an archæological work, and now finding himself so close to the reality, felt inclined to verify some theory he had formed respecting it. Concluding that there would be

just sufficient time for him to go there and return before the boat had
left the cove, he parted from Cytherea on the hill, struck downwards,
and then up a heathery valley.

She remained where he had left her till the time of his expected
return, scanning the details of the prospect around. Placidly spread
out before her on the south was the open Channel, reflecting a blue
intenser by many shades than that of the sky overhead, and dotted in
the foreground by half-a-dozen small craft of contrasting rig, their
sails graduating in hue from extreme whiteness to reddish brown,
the varying actual colours varied again in a double degree by the rays
of the declining sun.

Presently the first bell from the boat was heard, warning the passengers to embark. This was followed by a lively air from the harps
and violins on board, their tones, as they arose, becoming intermingled with, though not marred by, the brush of the waves when
their crests rolled over—at the point where the check of the shore
shallows was first felt—and then thinned away up the slope of
pebbles and sand.

She turned her face landward, and strained her eyes to discern, if
possible, some sign of Owen's return. Nothing was visible save the
strikingly brilliant, still landscape. The wide concave which lay at the
back of the cliff in this direction was blazing with the western light,
adding an orange tint to the vivid purple of the heather, now at the
very climax of bloom, and free from the slightest touch of the invidious brown that so soon creeps into its shades. The light so intensified
the colours that they seemed to stand above the surface of the earth
and float in mid-air like an exhalation of red. In the minor valleys,
between the hillocks and ridges which diversified the contour of the
basin, but did not disturb its general sweep, she marked brakes of
tall, heavy-stemmed ferns, five or six feet high, in a brilliant light-
green dress—a broad riband of them with the path in their midst
winding like a stream along the little ravine that reached to the foot
of the hill, and delivered up the path to its grassy area. Among the
ferns grew holly bushes deeper in tint than any shadow about them
whilst the whole surface of the scene was dimpled with small conical
pits, and here and there were round ponds, now dry, and half
overgrown with rushes.

The last bell of the steamer rang. Cytherea had forgotten herself,
and what she was looking for. In a fever of distress lest Owen should

be left behind, she gathered up in her hand the corners of her hand-kerchief, containing specimens of the shells, seaweed and fossils with which the locality abounded, descended to the beach, and mingled with the knots of visitors there congregated from other interesting points around; from the inn, the cottages, and hired conveyances that had returned from short drives inland. They all went aboard by the primitive plan of a narrow plank on two wheels—the women being assisted by a rope. Cytherea lingered till the very last, reluctant to follow, and looking alternately at the boat and the valley behind. Her delay provoked a remark from Captain Jacobs, a thickset man of hybrid stains, resulting from the mixed effects of fire and water, peculiar to sailors where engines are the propelling power.

"Now then, missie, if you please. I am sorry to tell 'ee our time's up. Who are you looking for, miss?"

"My brother—he has walked a short distance inland; he must be here directly. Could you wait for him—just a minute?"

"Really, I am afraid not, m'm." Cytherea looked at the stout, round-faced man, and at the vessel, with a light in her eyes so expressive of her own opinion being the same on reflection, and with such resignation, too, that, from an instinctive feeling of pride at being able to prove himself more humane than he was thought to be—works of supererogation are the only sacrifices that entice in this way—and that at a very small cost, he delayed the boat till some elderly unmarried girls* among the passengers began to murmur.

"There, never mind," said Cytherea, decisively. "Go on without me—I shall wait for him."

"Well, 'tis a very awkward thing to leave you here all alone," said the captain. "I certainly advise you not to wait."

"He's gone across to the railway station, for certain," said another passenger.

"No—here he is!" Cytherea said, regarding, as she spoke, the half-hidden figure of a man who was seen advancing at a headlong pace down the ravine which lay between the heath and the shore.

"He can't get here in less than five minutes," the passenger said. "People should know what they are about, and keep time. Really, if——"

"You see, sir," said the captain, in an apologetic undertone, "since 'tis her brother, and she's all alone, 'tis only nater to wait a minute now he's in sight. Suppose now you were a young woman, as might be, and had a brother, like this one, and you stood of an evening upon this here wild lonely shore, like her, why you'd want us to wait, too, wouldn't you, sir? I think you would."

The person so hastily approaching had been lost to view during this remark by reason of a hollow in the ground, and the projecting cliff immediately at hand covered the path in its rise. His footsteps were now heard striking sharply upon the stony road at a distance of about twenty or thirty yards, but still behind the escarpment. To save time, Cytherea prepared to ascend the plank.

"Let me give you my hand, miss," said Captain Jacobs.

"No—please don't touch me," said she, ascending cautiously by sliding one foot forward two or three inches, bringing up the other behind it, and so on alternately—her lips compressed by concentration on the feat, her eyes glued to the plank, her hand to the rope, and her immediate thought to the fact of the distressing narrowness of her footing. Footsteps now shook the lower end of the board, and in an instant were up to her heels with a bound.

"O Owen, I am so glad you are come!" she said, without turning. "Don't, don't shake the plank or touch me, whatever you do. . . . . There, I am up. Where have you been so long?" she continued, in a lower tone, turning round to him as she reached the top.

Raising her eyes from her feet, which, standing on the firm deck, demanded her attention no longer, she acquired perceptions of the new-comer in the following order:—unknown trousers; unknown waistcoat; unknown face. The man was not her brother, but a total stranger.

Off went the plank; the paddles started, stopped, backed, pattered in confusion, then revolved decisively, and the boat passed out into deep water.

One or two persons had said, "How d'ye do, Mr. Springrove?" and looked at Cytherea, to see how she bore her disappointment. Her ears had but just caught the name of the head clerk, when she saw him advancing directly to address her.

"Miss Graye, I believe?" he said, lifting his hat.

"Yes," said Cytherea, colouring, and trying not to look guilty of a surreptitious knowledge of him.

"I am Mr. Springrove. I passed Humdon Castle about half an hour ago, and soon afterwards met your brother going that way. He had been deceived in the distance, and was about to turn without seeing the ruin, on account of a lameness that had come on in his leg or foot. I proposed that he should go on, since he had got so near; and afterwards, instead of walking back to the boat, get across to Galworth Station—a shorter walk for him—where he could catch the late train, and go directly home. I could let you know what he had done, and allay any uneasiness."

"Is the lameness serious, do you know?"

"Oh, no; simply from over-walking himself. Still, it was just as well to ride home."

Relieved from her apprehensions on Owen's score, she was able slightly to examine the appearance of her informant—Edward Springrove—who now removed his hat for a while, to cool himself. He was rather above her brother's height. Although the upper part of his face and head was handsomely formed, and bounded by lines of sufficiently masculine regularity, his brows were somewhat too softly arched, and finely pencilled for one of his sex; without prejudice, however, to the belief which the sum total of his features inspired—that though they did not prove that the man who thought inside them would do much in the world, men who had done most of all had had no better ones. Across his forehead, otherwise perfectly smooth, ran one thin line, the healthy freshness of his remaining features expressing that it had come there prematurely.

Though some years short of the age at which the clear spirit bids good-bye to the last infirmity of noble mind,* and takes to house-hunting and consols,* he had reached the period in a young man's life when episodic pasts, with a hopeful birth and a disappointing death, have begun to accumulate, and to bear a fruit of generalities; his glance sometimes seeming to state, "I have already thought out the issue of such conditions as these we are experiencing." At other times he wore an abstracted look: "I seem to have lived through this moment before."

He was carelessly dressed in dark grey, wearing a narrow bit of black ribbon as a neck-tie; the bow of which was disarranged, and stood obliquely—a deposit of white dust having lodged in the creases.

"I am sorry for your disappointment," he continued, keeping at her side. As he spoke the words, he glanced into her face—then fixed his eyes firmly, though but for a moment, in hers, which, at the same instant, were regarding him. Their eyes having met, became, as it were, mutually locked together, and the single instant only which good breeding allows as the length of such a glance, became trebled: a clear penetrating ray of intelligence had shot from each into each, giving birth to one of those unaccountable sensations which carry home to the heart before the hand has been touched or the merest compliment passed, by something stronger than mathematical proof, the conviction, "A tie has begun to unite us."*

Both faces also unconsciously stated that their owners had been much in each other's thoughts of late. Owen had talked to the head clerk of his sister as freely as to Cytherea of the head clerk.

A conversation began, which was none the less interesting to the parties engaged because it consisted only of the most trivial and commonplace remarks. Then the band of harps and violins struck up a lively melody, and the deck was cleared for dancing; the sun dipping beneath the horizon during the proceeding, and the moon showing herself at their stern. The sea was so calm, that the soft hiss produced by the bursting of the innumerable bubbles of foam behind the paddles could be distinctly heard. The passengers who did not dance, including Cytherea and Springrove, lapsed into silence, leaning against the paddle-boxes,* or standing aloof— noticing the trembling of the deck to the steps of the dance— watching the waves from the paddles as they slid thinly and easily under each other's bosom.

Night had quite closed in by the time they reached Creston harbour, sparkling with its white, red, and green lights in opposition to the shimmering path of the moon's reflection on the other side, which reached away to the horizon till the flecked ripples reduced themselves to sparkles as fine to the eye as gold dust.

"I will walk to the station and find out the exact time the train arrives," said Springrove, rather eagerly, when they had landed.

She thanked him much.

"Perhaps we might walk together," he suggested, hesitatingly. She looked as if she did not quite know, and he settled the question by showing the way.

They found, on arriving there, that on the first day of that month the particular train selected for Graye's return had ceased to stop at Galworth station.

"I am very sorry I misled him," said Springrove.

"Oh, I am not alarmed at all," replied Cytherea.

"Well, it's sure to be all right—he will sleep there, and come by the first in the morning. But what will you do, alone?"

"I am quite easy on that point; the landlady is very friendly. I must go indoors now. Good-night, Mr. Springrove."

"Let me go round to your door with you?" he pleaded.

"No, thank you; we live close by."

He looked at her as a waiter looks at the change he brings back. But she was inexorable.

"Don't—forget me," he murmured. She did not answer.

"Let me see you sometimes," he said.

"Perhaps you never will again—I am going away," she replied, in lingering tones; and turning into Cross Street, ran indoors and upstairs.

The sudden withdrawal of what was superfluous when first given, is often felt as an essential loss. It was felt now with regard to the maiden. More, too, after a first meeting, so pleasant and so enkindling, she had seemed to imply that they would never come together again. The young man softly followed her, stood opposite the house and watched her come into the upper room with the light. Presently his gaze was cut short by her approaching the window and pulling down the blind—Edward dwelling upon her vanishing figure with a hopeless sense of loss akin to that which Adam is said by logicians to have felt when he first saw the sun set, and thought, in his inexperience, that it would return no more.*

He waited till her shadow had twice crossed the window, when, finding the charming outline was not to be expected again, he left the street, crossed the harbour-bridge, and entered his own solitary chamber on the other side, vaguely thinking as he went (for unnamed reasons),

> "One hope is too like despair
> For prudence to smother."*

CHAPTER III

THE EVENTS OF EIGHT DAYS

§ 1. *From the twenty-second to the twenty-seventh of July*

But things are not what they seem. A responsive love for Edward Springrove had made its appearance in Cytherea's bosom with all the fascinating attributes of a first experience—not succeeding to or displacing other emotions, as in older hearts, but taking up entirely new ground; as when gazing just after sunset at the pale blue sky we see a star come into existence where nothing was before.

His parting words, "Don't forget me," she repeated to herself a hundred times, and though she thought their import was probably commonplace, she could not help toying with them,—looking at them from all points, and investing them with meanings of love and faithfulness,—ostensibly entertaining such meanings only as fables wherewith to pass the time, yet in her heart admitting, for detached instants, a possibility of their deeper truth. And thus, for hours after he had left her, her reason flirted with her fancy as a kitten will sport with a dove, pleasantly and smoothly through easy attitudes, but disclosing its cruel and unyielding nature at crises.

To turn now to the more material media through which this story moves, it so happened that the very next morning brought round a circumstance which, slight in itself, took up a relevant and important position between the past and the future of the persons herein concerned.

At breakfast time, just as Cytherea had again seen the postman pass without bringing her an answer to the advertisement, as she had fully expected he would, Owen entered the room.

"Well," he said, kissing her, "you have not been alarmed of course. Springrove told you what I had done, and you found there was no train?"

"Yes, it was all clear. But what is the lameness owing to?"

"I don't know—nothing. It has quite gone off now . . . . Cytherea, I hope you like Springrove.—Springrove's a nice fellow, you know."

"Yes. I think he is, except that——"

"It happened just to the purpose that I should meet him there, didn't it? And when I reached the station and learnt that I could not get on by train my foot seemed better. I started off to walk home, and went about five miles along a path beside the railway. It then struck me that I might not be fit for anything to day if I walked and aggravated the bothering foot, so I looked for a place to sleep at. There was no available village or inn, and I eventually got the keeper of a gate-house,* where a lane crossed the line, to take me in."

They proceeded with their breakfast. Owen yawned.

"You didn't get much sleep at the gate-house last night, I'm afraid, Owen," said his sister.

"To tell the truth, I didn't. I was in such very close and narrow quarters. Those gate-houses are such small places, and the man had only his own bed to offer me. Ah, by-the-bye, Cythie, I have such an extraordinary thing to tell you in connection with this man!—by Jove, I had nearly forgotten it! But I'll go straight on. As I was saying, he had only his own bed to offer me, but I could not afford to be fastidious, and as he had a hearty manner, though a very queer one, I agreed to accept it, and he made a rough pallet* for himself on the floor close beside me. Well, I could not sleep for my life, and I wished I had not stayed there, though I was so tired. For one thing, there were the luggage trains rattling by at my elbow the early part of the night. But worse than this, he talked continually in his sleep, and occasionally struck out with his limbs at something or another, knocking against the post of the bedstead and making it tremble. My condition was altogether so unsatisfactory that at last I awoke him, and asked him what he had been dreaming about for the previous hour, for I could get no sleep at all. He begged my pardon for disturbing me, but a name I had casually let fall that evening had led him to think of another stranger he had once had visit him, who had also accidentally mentioned the same name, and some very strange incidents connected with that meeting. The affair had occurred years and years ago; but what I had said had made him think and dream about it as if it were but yesterday. What was the word? I said. 'Cytherea,' he said. What was the story? I asked then. He then told me that when he was a young man in London he borrowed a few pounds to add to a few he had saved up, and opened a little inn at Hammersmith. One evening, after the inn had been open about a couple of months, every idler in the neighbourhood ran off to Westminster. The Houses of Parliament were on fire.*

"Not a soul remained in his parlour besides himself, and he began picking up the pipes and glasses his customers had hastily relinquished. At length a young lady about seventeen or eighteen came in. She asked if a woman was there waiting for herself—Miss Jane Taylor. He said no; asked the young woman if she would wait, and showed her into the small inner room. There was a glass pane in the partition dividing this room from the bar to enable the landlord to see if his visitors, who sat there, wanted anything. A curious awkwardness and melancholy about the behaviour of the girl who called, caused my informant to look frequently at her through the partition. She seemed weary of her life, and sat with her face buried in her hands, evidently quite out of her element in such a house. Then a woman much older came in and greeted Miss Taylor by name. The man distinctly heard the following words pass between them.

" 'Why have you not brought him?'

" 'He is ill: he is not likely to live through the night.'

"At this announcement from the elderly woman, the younger one fell to the floor in a swoon, apparently overcome by the news. The landlord ran in and lifted her up. Well, do what they would they could not for a long time bring her back to consciousness, and began to be much alarmed. 'Who is she?' the innkeeper said to the other woman. 'I know her,' the other said, with deep meaning in her tone. The elderly and young women seemed allied, and yet strangers.

"She now showed signs of life, and it struck him (he was plainly of an inquisitive turn,) that in her half-bewildered state he might get some information from her. He stooped over her, put his mouth to her ear, and said sharply, 'What's your name?' 'Catch a woman napping if you can, even when she's asleep or half dead,' says the gatekeeper. When he asked her her name, she said immediately,—

" 'Cytherea'—and stopped suddenly."

"My own name!" said Cytherea.

"Yes—your name. Well, the gateman thought at the time it might be equally with Jane a name she had invented for the occasion, that they might not trace her; but I think it was truth unconsciously uttered, for she added directly afterwards, 'O what have I said!' and was quite overcome again—this time with fright. Her vexation that the woman now doubted the genuineness of her other name, was very much greater than that the innkeeper did, and it is evident that to blind the woman was her main object. He also learnt, from words this other woman casually dropped, that meetings of the same kind had been held before, and that the falseness of the *soi-disant** Miss Jane Taylor's name had never been suspected by this companion or confederate till then.

"She recovered, rested there for an hour, and first sending off her companion peremptorily (which was another odd thing), she left the house, offering the landlord all the money she had to say nothing about the circumstance. He has never seen her since, according to his own account. I said to him again and again, 'Did you find out any more particulars afterwards?' 'Not a syllable,' he said. O he should never hear any more of that—too many years had passed since it happened. 'At any rate you found out her surname?' I said. 'Well, well, that's my secret,' he went on. 'Perhaps I should never have been in this part of the world if it hadn't been for that. I failed as a publican, you know.' I imagine the situation of gateman was given him and his debts paid off as a bribe to silence; but I can't say. 'Ah, yes,' he said, with a long breath. 'I have never heard that name mentioned since that time till to night, and then there instantly rose to my eyes the vision of that young lady lying in a fainting fit.' He then stopped talking and fell asleep. Telling the story must have relieved him as it did the Ancient Mariner,* for he did not move a muscle or make another sound for the remainder of the night. Now, isn't that an odd story!"

"It is, indeed," Cytherea murmured. "Very, very strange."

"Why should she have said your most uncommon name?" continued Owen. "The man was evidently truthful, for there was not motive sufficient for his invention of such a tale, and he could not have done it either."

Cytherea looked long at her brother. "Don't you recognise anything else in connection with the story?" she said.

"What?" he asked.

"Do you remember what poor papa once let drop—that Cytherea was the name of his first sweetheart in Bloomsbury, who so mysteriously renounced him? A sort of intuition tells me that this was the same woman."

"O no—not likely," said her brother sceptically.

"How not likely, Owen? There's not another woman of the name in England. In what year used papa to say the event took place?"

"Eighteen hundred and thirty-five."

"And when were the Houses of Parliament burnt?—stop, I can tell you." She searched their little stock of books for a list of dates, and found one in an old school history.

"The Houses of Parliament were burnt down in the evening of the sixteenth of October, eighteen hundred and thirty-four."

"Nearly a year and a quarter before she met father," remarked Owen.

They were silent. "If papa had been alive, what a wonderful absorbing interest this story would have had for him," said Cytherea by-and-by. "And how strangely knowledge comes to us. We might have searched for a clue to her secret half the world over, and never found one. If we had really had any motive for trying to discover more of the sad history than papa told us, we should have gone to Bloomsbury; but not caring to do so, we go two hundred miles in the opposite direction, and there find information waiting to be told us. What could have been the secret, Owen?"

"Heaven knows. But our having heard a little more of her in this way (if she is the same woman) is a mere coincidence after all—a family story to tell our friends if we ever have any. But we shall never know any more of the episode now—trust our fates for that."

Cytherea sat silently thinking.

"There was no answer this morning to your advertisement, Cytherea," he continued.

"None."

"I could see that by your looks when I came in."

"Fancy not getting a single one," she said, sadly. "Surely there must be people somewhere who want governesses?"

"Yes; but those who want them, and can afford to have them, get them mostly by friends' recommendations; whilst those who want them, and can't afford to have them, do without them."*

"What shall I do?"

"Never mind it. Go on living with me. Don't let the difficulty trouble your mind so; you think about it all day. I can keep you Cythie, in a plain way of living. Twenty-five shillings a week* do not amount to much, truly; but then many mechanics have no more, and we live quite as sparingly as journeymen mechanics.* . . . . 'Tis a meagre narrow life we are drifting into," he added, gloomily, "but it is a degree more tolerable than the worrying sensation of all the world being ashamed of you, which we experienced at Hocbridge."

"I couldn't go back there again," she said.

"Nor I. O, I don't regret our course for a moment. We did quite right in dropping out of the world." The sneering tones of the remark were almost too laboured to be real. "Besides," he continued, "something better for me is sure to turn up soon. I wish my engagement here was a permanent one instead of for only two months. It may, certainly, be for a longer time, but all is uncertain."

"I wish I could get something to do, and I must too," she said firmly. "Suppose, as is very probable, you are not wanted after the beginning of October—the time Mr. Gradfield mentioned—what should we do if I were dependent on you only throughout the winter?"

They pondered on numerous schemes by which a young lady might be supposed to earn a decent livelihood—more or less convenient and feasible in imagination, but relinquished them all until advertising had been once more tried, this time taking lower ground. Cytherea was vexed at her temerity in having represented to the world that so inexperienced a being as herself was a qualified governess; and had a fancy that this presumption of hers might be one reason why no ladies applied.

The new and humbler attempt appeared in the following form:—

"NURSERY GOVERNESS OR USEFUL COMPANION. A young person wishes to hear of a situation in either of the above capacities. Salary very moderate. She is a good needlewoman. Address C., 3, Cross Street, Creston."

In the evening they went to post the letter, and then walked up and down the esplanade for a while. Soon they met Springrove, said a few words to him, and passed on. Owen noticed that his sister's face had become crimson. Rather oddly they met Springrove again in a few minutes.

This time the three walked a little way together, Edward ostensibly talking to Owen, though with a single thought to the reception of his words by the maiden at the farther side, upon whom his gaze was mostly resting, and who was attentively listening—looking fixedly upon the pavement the while. It has been said that men love with their eyes; women with their ears.

As Owen and himself were little more than acquaintances as yet, and as Springrove was wanting in the assurance of many men of his age, it now became necessary to wish his friends good evening, or to find a reason for continuing near Cytherea by saying some nice new thing. He thought of a new thing; he proposed a pull across the bay. This was assented to. They went to the pier; stepped into one of the gaily painted boats moored alongside, and sheered off. Cytherea sat in the stern steering.

They rowed that evening; the next came, and with it the necessity of rowing again. Then the next, and the next, Cytherea always sitting in the stern with the tiller ropes in her hand. The curves of her figure welded with those of the fragile boat in perfect continuation, as she girlishly yielded herself to its heaving and sinking, seeming to form with it an organic whole.

Then Owen was inclined to test his skill in paddling a canoe. Edward did not like canoes, and the issue was, that, having seen Owen on board, Springrove proposed to pull off after him with a pair of sculls; but not considering himself sufficiently accomplished to do finished rowing before an esplanade full of promenaders when there was a little swell on, and with the rudder unshipped* in addition, he begged that Cytherea might come with him and steer as before. She stepped in, and they floated along in the wake of her brother. Thus passed the fifth evening on the water.

But the consonant pair were thrown into still closer companionship, and much more exclusive connexion.

§ 2. *July the twenty-ninth*

It was a sad time for Cytherea—the last day of Springrove's management at Gradfield's, and the last evening before his return from Creston to his father's house, previous to his departure for London.

Graye had been requested by the architect to survey a plot of land nearly twenty miles off, which, with the journey to and fro, would occupy him the whole day, and prevent his returning till late in the evening. Cytherea made a companion of her landlady to the extent of sharing meals and sitting with her during the morning of her brother's absence. Mid-day found her restless and miserable under this arrangement. All the afternoon she sat alone, looking out of the window for she scarcely knew whom, and hoping she scarcely knew what. Half past five o'clock came—the end of Springrove's official day. Two minutes later Springrove walked by.

She endured her solitude for another half-hour, and then could endure no longer. She had hoped—under the title of feared—that Edward would have found some reason or other for calling, but it seemed that he had not. Hastily dressing herself she went out, when the farce of an accidental meeting was repeated. Edward came upon her in the street at the first turning.

> "He looked at her as a lover can;
> She looked at him as one who awakes—
> The past was a sleep, and her life began."*

"Shall we have a boat?" he said, impulsively.

How exquisite a sweetheart is at first! Perhaps, indeed, the only bliss in the course of love which can truly be called Eden-like is that which prevails immediately after doubt has ended and before reflection has set in—at the dawn of the emotion, when it is not recognised by name, and before the consideration of what this love is, has given birth to the consideration of what difficulties it tends to create; when on the man's part, the mistress appears to the mind's eye in picturesque, hazy, and fresh morning lights, and soft morning shadows; when, as yet, she is known only as the wearer of one dress, which shares her own personality; as the stander in one special position, the giver of one bright particular glance, and the speaker of one tender sentence; when, on her part, she is timidly careful over what she says and does, lest she should be misconstrued or under-rated to the breadth of a shadow of a hair.

"Shall we have a boat?" he said again, more softly, seeing that at his first question she had not answered, but looked uncertainly at the ground, then almost, but not quite, in his face, blushed a series of minute blushes, left off in the midst of them, and showed the usual signs of perplexity in a matter of the emotions.

Owen had always been with her before, but there was now a force of habit in the proceeding, and with Arcadian innocence* she assumed that a row on the water was, under any circumstances, a natural thing. Without another word being spoken on either side, they went down the steps. He carefully handed her in, took his seat, slid noiselessly off the sand, and away from the shore.

They thus sat facing each other in the graceful yellow cockle-shell,* and his eyes frequently found a resting place in the depths of hers. The boat was so small that at each return of the sculls, when his hands came forward to begin the pull, they approached so near to her bosom that her vivid imagination began to thrill her with a fancy that he was going to clasp his arms round her. The sensation grew so strong that she could not run the risk of again meeting his eyes at those critical moments, and turned aside to inspect the distant horizon; then she grew weary of looking sideways and was driven to return to her natural position again. At this instant he again lent forward to begin, and met her glance by an ardent fixed gaze. An involuntary impulse of girlish embarrassment caused her to give a vehement pull at the tiller-rope, which brought the boat's head round till they stood directly for shore.

His eyes, which had dwelt upon her form during the whole time of her look askance, now left her; he perceived the direction in which they were going.

"Why you have completely turned the boat, Miss Graye?" he said, looking over his shoulder. "Look at our track on the water—a great semicircle, preceded by a series of zigzags as far as we can see."

She looked attentively. "Is it my fault or yours?" she inquired. "Mine, I suppose?"

"I can't help saying that it is yours."

She dropped the ropes decisively, feeling the slightest twinge of vexation at the answer.

"Why do you let go?"

"I do it so badly."

"O no; you turned about for shore in a masterly way. Do you wish to return?"

"Yes, if you please."

"Of course, then, I will at once."

"I fear what the people will think of us—going in such absurd directions, and all through my wretched steering."

"Never mind what the people think." A pause. "You surely are not so weak as to mind what the people think on such a matter as that?"

That answer might almost be called too firm and hard to be given by him to her, but never mind. For almost the first time in her life she felt the delicious sensation, although on such an insignificant subject, of being compelled into an opinion by a man she loved. Owen, though less yielding physically, and more practical, would not have had the intellectual independence to answer a woman thus. She replied quietly and honestly—as honestly as when she had stated the contrary fact a minute earlier—

"I don't mind."

"I'll unship the tiller that you may have nothing to do going back but to hold your parasol," he continued, and arose to perform the operation, necessarily leaning closely against her, to guard against the risk of capsizing the boat as he reached his hands astern. His warm breath touched and crept round her face like a caress; but he was apparently only concerned with his task. She looked guilty of something when he seated himself. He read in her face what that something was—she had experienced a pleasure from his touch. But he flung a practical glance over his shoulder, seized the oars, and they sped in a straight line towards the shore.

Cytherea saw that he read in her face what had passed in her heart, and that reading it, he continued as decided as before. She was inwardly distressed. She had not meant him to translate her words about returning home so literally at the first; she had not intended him to learn her secret; but more than all she was not able to endure the perception of his learning it and continuing unmoved.

There was nothing but misery to come now. They would step ashore; he would say good-night, go to London to-morrow, and the miserable she would lose him for ever. She did not quite suppose, what was the fact, that a parallel thought was simultaneously passing through his mind.

They were now within ten yards, now within five; he was only now waiting for a "smooth"* to bring the boat in. Sweet, sweet Love must not be slain thus,* was the fair maid's reasoning. She was equal to the occasion—ladies are—and delivered the god:—*

"Do you want very much to land, Mr. Springrove?" she said letting her young violet eyes pine at him* a very, very little.

"I? Not at all," said he, looking an astonishment at her enquiry which a slight twinkle of his eye half belied. "But you do?"

"I think that now we have come out, and it is such a pleasant evening," she said, gently and sweetly, "I should like a little longer row if you don't mind? I'll try to steer better than before if it makes it easier for you. I'll try very hard."

It was the turn of his face to tell a tale now. He looked, "We understand each other—Ah, we do, darling!" turned the boat, and pulled back into the Bay once more.

"Now steer me wherever you will," he said, in a low voice. "Never mind the directness of the course—wherever you will."

"Shall it be Laystead shore?" she said, pointing in that direction.

"Laystead shore," he said, grasping the sculls. She took the strings daintily, and they wended away to the left.

For a long time nothing was audible in the boat but the regular dip of the oars, and their movement in the rowlocks. Springrove at length spoke:—

"I must go away to-morrow," he said, tentatively.

"Yes," she replied, faintly.

"To endeavour to advance a little in my profession in London."

"Yes," she said again, with the same preoccupied softness.

"But I shan't advance."

"Why not? Architecture is a bewitching profession. They say that an architect's work is another man's play."

"Yes. But worldly advantage from an art doesn't depend upon mastering it. I used to think it did; but it doesn't. Those who get rich need have no skill at all as artists."

"What need they have?"

"A certain kind of energy which men with any fondness for art possess very seldom indeed—an earnestness in making acquaintances, and a love for using them. They give their whole attention to the art of dining out, after mastering a few rudimentary facts to serve up in conversation.* Now after saying that, do I seem a man likely to make a name?"

"You seem a man likely to make a mistake."

"What's that?"

"To give too much room to the latent feeling which is rather common in these days among the unappreciated, that because some markedly successful men are fools, all markedly unsuccessful men are geniuses."

"Pretty subtle for a young lady," he said, slowly. "From that remark I should fancy you had bought experience."

She passed over the idea. "Do try to succeed," she said, with wistful thoughtfulness, leaving her eyes on him.

Springrove flushed a little at the earnestness of her words, and mused. "Then, like Cato the Censor, I shall do what I despise to be in the fashion,"* he said at last . . . "Well, when I found all this out that I was speaking of, whatever do you think I did? From having already loved verse passionately, I went on to read it continually; then I went rhyming myself. If anything on earth ruins a man for useful occupation, and for content with reasonable success in a profession or trade, it is the habit of writing verses on emotional subjects, which had much better be left to die from want of nourishment."

"Do you write poems now?" she said.

"None. Poetical days are getting past with me,* according to the usual rule. Writing rhymes is a stage people of my sort pass through, as they pass through the stage of shaving for a beard, or thinking they are ill-used, or saying there's nothing in the world worth living for."

"Then the difference between a common man and a recognised poet is, that one has been deluded, and cured of his delusion, and the other continues deluded all his days."

"Well, there's just enough truth in what you say, to make the remark unbearable. However, it doesn't matter to me now that I 'meditate the thankless Muse' no longer,* but . . ." He paused as if endeavouring to think what better thing he did.

Cytherea's mind ran on to the succeeding lines of the poem, and their startling harmony with the present situation suggested the fancy that he was "*sporting*" with her,* and brought an awkward contemplativeness to her face.

Springrove guessed her thoughts, and in answer to them simply said, "Yes." Then they were silent again.

"If I had known an Amaryllis was coming here, I should not have made arrangements for leaving," he resumed.

Such levity, superimposed on the notion of *sport*, was intolerable to Cytherea; for a woman seems never to see any but the serious side of her attachment, though the most devoted lover has all the time a vague and dim perception that he is losing his old dignity and frittering away his time.

"But will you not try again to get on in your profession? Try once more; do try once more," she murmured. "I am going to try again. I have advertised for something to do."

"Of course I will," he said, with an eager gesture and smile. "But we must remember that the fame of Christopher Wren himself depended upon the accident of a fire in Pudding Lane.* My successes seem to come very slowly. I often think, that before I am ready to live, it will be time for me to die. However, I am trying—not for fame now, but for an easy life of reasonable comfort."

It is a melancholy truth for the middle classes, that in proportion as they develop, by the study of poetry and art, their capacity for conjugal love of the highest and purest kind, they limit the possibility of their being able to exercise it—the very act putting out of their power the attainment of means sufficient for marriage. The man who works up a good income has had no time to learn love to its exquisite extreme; the man who has learnt that has had no time to get rich.

"And if you should fail—utterly fail to get that reasonable wealth," she said, earnestly, "don't be perturbed. The truly great stand upon no middle ledge; they are either famous or unknown."*

"Unknown," he said, "if their ideas have been allowed to flow with a sympathetic breadth. Famous only if they have been convergent and exclusive."

"Yes; and I am afraid from that, that my remark was but discouragement, wearing the dress of comfort. Perhaps I was not quite right in——"

"It depends entirely upon what is meant by being truly great. But the long and the short of the matter is, that men must stick to a thing if they want to succeed in it—not giving way to over-much admiration for the flowers they see growing in other people's borders; which I am afraid has been my case." He looked into the far distance and paused.

Adherence to a course with persistence sufficient to ensure success is possible to widely appreciative minds only when there is also found in them a power—commonplace in its nature, but rare in such combination—the power of assuming to conviction that in the outlying paths which appear so much more brilliant than their own, there are bitternesses equally great—unperceived simply on account of their remoteness.

They were opposite Laystead shore. The cliffs here were formed of strata completely contrasting with those of the farther side of the Bay, whilst in and beneath the water hard boulders had taken the place of sand and shingle, between which, however, the sea glided noiselessly, without breaking the crest of a single wave, so strikingly calm was the air. The breeze had entirely died away, leaving the water of that rare glassy smoothness which is unmarked even by the small dimples of the least aërial movement. Purples and blues of divers shades were reflected from this mirror accordingly as each undulation sloped east or west. They could see the rocky bottom some twenty feet beneath them, luxuriant with weeds of various growths, and dotted with pulpy creatures reflecting a silvery and spangled radiance upwards to their eyes.

At length she looked at him to learn the effect of her words of encouragement. He had let the oars drift alongside, and the boat had come to a standstill. Everything on earth seemed taking a contemplative rest, as if waiting to hear the avowal of something from his lips. At that instant he appeared to break a resolution hitherto zealously kept. Leaving his seat amidships he came and gently edged himself down beside her upon the narrow seat at the stern.

She breathed quicker, and warmer: he took her right hand in his own right: it was not withdrawn. He put his left hand behind her neck till it came round upon her left cheek: it was not thrust away. Lightly pressing her, he brought her face and mouth towards his own; when, at this the very brink, some unaccountable thought or spell within him suddenly made him halt—even now, and as it seemed as much to himself as to her, he timidly whispered, "May I?"

Her endeavour was to say No so denuded of its flesh and sinews that its nature would hardly be recognised, or in other words a No from so near the positive frontier as to be affected with the Yes accent. It was thus a whispered No, drawn out to nearly a quarter of a minute's length, the O making itself audible as a sound like the spring coo of a pigeon on unusually friendly terms with his mate. Though conscious of her success in producing the kind of word she had wished to produce, she at the same time trembled in suspense as to how it would be taken. But the time available for doubt was so short as to admit of scarcely more than half-a-dozen vibrations: pressing closer he kissed her. Then he kissed her again with a longer kiss.

It was the supremely happy moment of their experience. The bloom and the purple light* were strong on the lineaments of both. Their hearts could hardly believe the evidence of their lips.

"I love you, and you love me, Cytherea!" he whispered.

She did not deny it; and all seemed well. The gentle sounds around them from the hills, the plains, the distant town, the adjacent shore, the water heaving at their side, the kiss, and the long kiss, were all "many a voice of one delight,"* and in unison with each other.

But his mind flew back to the same unpleasant thought which had been connected with the resolution he had broken a minute or two earlier. "I could be a slave at my profession to win you, Cytherea; I would work at the meanest honest trade to be near you—much less claim you as mine; I would—anything. But I have not told you all; it is not this; you don't know what there is yet to tell. Could you forgive as you can love?" She was alarmed to see that he had become pale with the question.

"No—do not speak," he said. "I have kept something from you, which has now become the cause of a great uneasiness. I had no right—to love you; but I did it. Something forbade—"

"What?" she exclaimed.

"Something forbade me—till the kiss—yes, till the kiss came; and now nothing shall forbid it! We'll hope in spite of all . . . . I must however, speak of this love of ours to your brother. Dearest, you had better go indoors whilst I meet him at the station, and explain everything."

Cytherea's short-lived bliss was dead and gone. O, if she had known of this sequel would she have allowed him to break down the barrier of mere acquaintanceship—never, never!

"Will you not explain to me?" she faintly urged. Doubt—indefinite, carking doubt had taken possession of her.

"Not now. You alarm yourself unnecessarily," he said, tenderly. "My only reason for keeping silence is that with my present knowledge I may tell an untrue story. It may be that there is nothing to tell. I am to blame for haste in alluding to any such thing. Forgive me, sweet—forgive me." Her heart was ready to burst, and she could not answer him. He returned to his place and took to the oars.

They again made for the distant Esplanade, now, with its line of houses, lying like a dark grey band against the light western sky. The sun had set, and a star or two began to peep out. They drew nearer their destination, Edward as he pulled tracing listlessly with his eyes the red stripes upon her scarf, which grew to appear as black ones in the increasing dusk of evening. She surveyed the long line of lamps on the sea wall of the town, now looking small and yellow, and seeming to send long taper roots of fire quivering down deep into the sea. By-and-by they reached the landing steps. He took her hand as before, and found it as cold as the water about them. It was not relinquished till he reached her door. His assurance had not removed the constraint of her manner: he saw that she blamed him mutely and with her eyes, like a captured sparrow. Left alone, he went and seated himself in a chair on the Esplanade.

Neither could she go indoors to her solitary room, feeling as she did in such a state of desperate heaviness. When Springrove was out of sight she turned back, and arrived at the corner just in time to see him sit down. Then she glided pensively along the pavement behind him, forgetting herself to marble like Melancholy herself,* and mused in his company unseen. She heard, without heeding, the notes of pianos and singing voices from the fashionable houses at her back, from the open windows of which the lamp-light streamed to meet that of the orange-hued full moon, newly risen over the Bay in front. Then Edward began to pace up and down, and Cytherea, fearing that he would notice her, doubled behind and across the road, flinging him a last wistful look as she passed out of sight. No promise from him to write: no request that she herself would do so—nothing but an indefinite expression of hope in the face of some fear unknown to her. Alas, alas!

When Owen returned he found she was not in the small sitting-room, and creeping up stairs into her bed-room with a light, he discovered her there lying asleep upon the coverlet of the bed, still with her hat and jacket on. She had flung herself down on entering, and succumbed to the unwonted oppressiveness that ever attends full-blown love. The wet traces of tears were yet visible upon her long drooping lashes.

> "Love is a sowre delight, and sugred griefe,
> A living death, and ever-dying life."*

"Cytherea," he whispered, kissing her. She awoke with a start and vented an exclamation before recovering her judgment. "He's gone!" she said.

"He has told me all," said Graye, soothingly. "He is going off early to-morrow morning. 'Twas a shame of him to win you away from me, and cruel of you to keep the growth of this attachment a secret."

"We couldn't help it," she said, and then jumping up—"Owen, has he told you *all?*"

"All of your love from beginning to end," he said simply.

Edward then had not told more—as he ought to have done: yet she could not convict him. But she would struggle against his fetters. She tingled to the very soles of her feet at the very possibility that he might be deluding her.

"Owen," she continued, with dignity, "what is he to me? Nothing. I must dismiss such weakness as this—believe me, I will. Something far more pressing must drive it away. I have been looking my position steadily in the face, and I must get a living somehow. I mean to advertise once more."

"Advertising is no use."

"This one will be." He looked surprised at the sanguine tone of her answer, till she took a piece of paper from the table and showed it him. "See what I am going to do," she said, sadly, almost bitterly. This was her third effort.

"LADY'S MAID. Inexperienced. Age eighteen. G., 3, Cross Street, Creston."

Owen—Owen the respectable—looked blank astonishment. He repeated in a nameless, varying tone, the two words,

"Lady's maid!"

"Yes; lady's maid. 'Tis an honest profession," said Cytherea, bravely.

"But *you*, Cytherea?"

"Yes, I—who am I?"

"You will never be a lady's maid—never, I am quite sure."

"I shall try to be, at any rate."

"Such a disgrace—"

"Nonsense! I maintain that it is no disgrace!" she said, rather warmly. "You know very well—"

"Well, since you will, you must," he interrupted. "Why do you put 'inexperienced'?"

"Because I am."

"Never mind that—scratch out 'inexperienced.' We are poor, Cytherea, aren't we?" he murmured, after a silence, "and it seems that the two months will close my engagement here."

"We can put up with being poor," she said, "if they only give us work to do . . . . . . Yes, we desire as a blessing what was given us as a curse,* and even that is denied. However, be cheerful, Owen, and never mind!"

In justice to desponding men, it is as well to remember that the brighter endurance of women at these epochs—invaluable, sweet, angelic, as it is—owes more of its origin to a narrower vision that shuts out many of the leaden-eyed despairs* in the van, than to a hopefulness intense enough to quell them.

CHAPTER IV

THE EVENTS OF ONE DAY

§ 1. *August the fourth. Till four o'clock*

The early part of the next week brought an answer to Cytherea's last note of hope in the way of advertisement—not from a distance of hundreds of miles, London, Scotland, Ireland, the Continent—as Cytherea seemed to think it must, to be in keeping with the means adopted for obtaining it, but from a place in the neighbourhood of that in which she was living—a country mansion about fifteen miles off. The reply ran thus:—

"KNAPWATER HOUSE,
"*August 3rd*, 1864.

"Miss Aldclyffe is in want of a young person as lady's maid. The duties of the place are light. Miss Aldclyffe will be in Creston on Thursday, when (should G. still not have heard of a situation) she would like to see her at the Belvedere Hotel, Esplanade, at four o'clock. No answer need be returned to this note."

A little earlier than the time named, Cytherea, clothed in a modest bonnet, and a black silk jacket, turned down to the hotel. Expectation, the fresh air from the water, the bright, far-extending outlook, raised the most delicate of pink colours to her cheeks, and restored to her tread a portion of that elasticity which her past troubles, and thoughts of Edward, had well-nigh taken away.

She entered the vestibule, and went to the window of the bar.

"Is Miss Aldclyffe here?" she said, to a nicely-dressed barmaid in the foreground, who was talking to a landlady covered with chains, knobs, and clamps of gold, in the background.

"No, she isn't," said the barmaid, not very civilly. Cytherea looked a shade too pretty for a plain dresser.

"Miss Aldclyffe is expected here," the landlady said to a third person, out of sight, in the tone of one who had known for several days the fact newly-discovered from Cytherea. "Get ready her room—be quick." From the alacrity with which the order was given and taken, it seemed to Cytherea that Miss Aldclyffe must be a woman of considerable importance.

"You are to have an interview with Miss Aldclyffe here?" the landlady enquired.

"Yes."

"The young person had better wait," continued the landlady, didactically. With a money-taker's intuition, she had rightly divined that Cytherea would bring no profit to the house.

Cytherea was shown into a nondescript chamber, on the shady side of the building, which appeared to be either bedroom or day room, as occasion necessitated, and was one of a suite at the end of the first-floor corridor. The prevailing colour of the walls, curtains, carpet, and coverings of furniture, was more or less blue, to which the cold light coming from the north-easterly sky, and falling on a wide roof of new slates—the only object the small window commanded—imparted a more striking paleness. But underneath the door, communicating with the next room of the suite, gleamed an infinitesimally small, yet very powerful, fraction of contrast—a very thin line of ruddy light, showing that the sun beamed strongly into this room adjoining. The line of radiance was the only cheering thing visible in the place.

People give way to very infantine thoughts and actions when they wait; the battle-field of life is temporarily fenced off by a hard and fast line—the interview. Cytherea fixed her eyes idly upon the streak, and began picturing a wonderful paradise on the other side as the source of such a beam—reminding her of the well-known good deed in a naughty world.*

Whilst she watched the particles of dust floating before the brilliant chink she heard a carriage and horses stop opposite the front of the house. Afterwards came the rustle of a lady's dress down the corridor, and into the room communicating with the one Cytherea occupied.

The golden line vanished in parts like the phosphorescent streak caused by the striking of a match; there was the fall of a light footstep on the floor just behind it; then a pause. Then the foot tapped impatiently, and "There's no one here!" was spoken imperiously by a lady's tongue.

"No, madam: in the next room. I am going to fetch her," said the attendant.

"That will do, or you needn't go in: I will call her."

Cytherea had risen, and she advanced to the middle door with the chink under it as the servant retired. She had just laid her hand on the knob, when it slipped round within her fingers, and the door was pulled open from the other side.

§ 2. *Four o'clock*

The direct blaze of the afternoon sun, partly refracted through the crimson curtains of the window, and heightened by reflection from the crimson-flock paper* which covered the walls, and a carpet on the floor of the same tint, shone with a burning glow round the form of a lady standing close to Cytherea's front with the door in her hand. The stranger appeared to the maiden's eyes—fresh from the blue gloom, and assisted by an imagination fresh from nature—like a tall black figure standing in the midst of fire. It was the figure of a finely-built woman, of spare though not angular proportions.

Cytherea involuntarily shaded her eyes with her hand, retreated a step or two, and then she could for the first time see Miss Aldclyffe's face in addition to her outline, lit up by the secondary and softer light that was reflected from the varnished panels of the door. She was not a very young woman, but could boast of much beauty of the majestic autumnal phase.

"Oh," said the lady, "come this way." Cytherea followed her to the embrasure of the window.*

Both the women showed off themselves to advantage as they walked forward in the orange light; and each showed too in her face that she had been struck with her companion's appearance. The warm tint added to Cytherea's face a voluptuousness which youth and a simple life had not yet allowed to express itself there ordinarily; whilst in the elder lady's face it reduced the customary expression, which might have been called sternness, if not harshness, to grandeur, and warmed her decaying complexion with much of the youthful richness it plainly had once possessed.

She appeared now no more than five and thirty, though she might easily have been ten or a dozen years older. She had clear steady eyes, a Roman nose* in its purest form, and also the round prominent chin with which the Cæsars are represented in ancient marbles; a mouth expressing a capability for and tendency to strong emotion, habitually controlled by pride. There was a severity about the lower outlines of the face which gave a masculine cast to this portion of her countenance. Womanly weakness was nowhere visible save in one part—the curve of her forehead and brows—there it was clear and emphatic. She wore a lace shawl over a brown silk dress, and a net bonnet set with a few blue cornflowers.

"You inserted the advertisement for a situation as lady's-maid giving the address, G., Cross Street?"

"Yes, madam. Graye."

"Yes. I have heard your name—Mrs. Morris, my housekeeper, mentioned you, and pointed out your advertisement."

This was puzzling intelligence, but there was not time enough to consider it.

"Where did you live last?" continued Miss Aldclyffe.

"I have never been a servant before. I lived at home."

"Never been out? I thought too at sight of you that you were too girlish-looking to have done much. But why did you advertise with such assurance? It misleads people."

"I am very sorry: I put 'inexperienced' at first, but my brother said it is absurd to trumpet your own weakness to the world, and would not let it remain."

"But your mother knew what was right, I suppose?"

"I have no mother, madam."

"Your father, then?"

"I have no father."

"Well," she said, more softly, "Your sisters, aunts, or cousins."

"They didn't think anything about it."

"You didn't ask them, I suppose."

"No."

"You should have, then. Why didn't you?"

"Because I haven't any of them, either."

Miss Aldclyffe showed her surprise. "You deserve forgiveness then at any rate, child," she said, in a sort of dryly-kind tone. "However, I am afraid you do not suit me, as I am looking for an elderly person. You see, I want an experienced maid who knows all the usual duties of the office." She was going to add, "Though I like your appearance," but the words seemed offensive to apply to the lady-like girl before her, and she modified them to, "though I like you much."

"I am sorry I misled you, madam," said Cytherea.

Miss Aldclyffe stood in a reverie, without replying.

"Good afternoon," continued Cytherea.

"Good-bye, Miss Graye—I hope you will succeed."

Cytherea turned away towards the door. The movement chanced to be one of her masterpieces. It was precise: it had as much beauty as was compatible with precision, and as little coquettishness as was compatible with beauty.

And she had in turning looked over her shoulder at the other lady with a faint accent of reproach in her face. Those who remember Greuze's "Head of a Girl"* in one of the public picture-galleries, have an idea of Cytherea's look askance at the turning. It is not for a man to tell fishers of men* how to set out their fascinations so as to bring about the highest possible average of takes within the year; but the action that tugs the hardest of all at an emotional beholder is this sweet method of turning which steals the bosom away and leaves the eyes behind.

Now Miss Aldclyffe herself was no tyro at wheeling.* When Cytherea had closed the door upon her, she remained for some time in her motionless attitude, listening to the gradually dying sound of the maiden's retreating footsteps. She murmured to herself, "It is almost worth while to be bored with instructing her in order to have a creature who could glide round my luxurious indolent body in that manner, and look at me in that way—I warrant how light her fingers are upon one's head and neck. . . . . What a silly modest young thing she is, to go away so suddenly as that!" She rang the bell.

"Ask the young lady who has just left me to step back again," she said to the attendant. "Quick! or she will be gone."

Cytherea was now in the vestibule, thinking that if she had told her history, Miss Aldclyffe might perhaps have taken her into the household; yet her history she particularly wished to conceal from a stranger. When she was recalled she turned back without feeling much surprise. Something, she knew not what, told her she had not seen the last of Miss Aldclyffe.

"You have somebody to refer me to, of course," the lady said when Cytherea had re-entered the room.

"Yes: Mr. Thorn, a solicitor at Reading."

"And are you a clever needlewoman?"

"I am considered to be."

"Then I think that at any rate I will write to Mr. Thorn," said Miss Aldclyffe, with a little smile. "It is true, the whole proceeding is very irregular; but my present maid leaves next Monday, and neither of the five I have already seen seem to do for me. . . . . Well, I will write to Mr. Thorn, and if his reply is satisfactory, you shall hear from me. It will be as well to set yourself in readiness to come on Monday."

When Cytherea had again been watched out of the room, Miss Aldclyffe asked for writing materials that she might at once communicate with Mr. Thorn. She indecisively played with the pen. "Suppose Mr. Thorn's reply to be in any way disheartening—and even if so from his own imperfect acquaintance with the young creature more than from circumstantial knowledge—I shall feel obliged to give her up. Then I shall regret that I did not give her one trial in spite of other people's prejudices. All her account of herself is reliable enough—yes, I can see that by her face. I like that face of hers."

Miss Aldclyffe put down the pen and left the hotel without writing to Mr. Thorn.

CHAPTER V

THE EVENTS OF ONE DAY

§ 1. *August the eighth. Morning and afternoon*

At post time on that following Monday morning, Cytherea watched so anxiously for the postman, that as the time which must bring him narrowed less and less her vivid expectation had only a degree less tangibility than his presence itself. In another second his form came into view. He brought two letters for Cytherea.

One from Miss Aldclyffe, simply stating that she wished Cytherea to come on trial: that she would require her to be at Knapwater House by Monday evening.

The other was from Edward Springrove. He told her that she was the bright spot of his life: that her existence was far dearer to him than his own: that he had never known what it was to love till he had met her. True, he had felt passing attachments to other faces from time to time; but they all had been weak inclinations towards those faces as they then appeared. He loved her past and future, as well as her present. He pictured her as a child: he loved her. He pictured her of sage years: he loved her. He pictured her in trouble: he loved her. Homely friendship entered into his love for her, without which all love was evanescent.

He would make one depressing statement. Uncontrollable circumstances (a long history, with which it was impossible to acquaint her at present) operated to a certain extent as a drag upon his wishes. He had felt this more strongly at the time of their parting than he did now—and it was the cause of his abrupt behaviour, for which he begged her to forgive him. He saw now an honourable way of freeing himself, and the perception had prompted him to write. In the meantime might he indulge in the hope of possessing her on some bright future day, when by hard labour generated from her own encouraging words, he had placed himself in a position she would think worthy to be shared with him?

Dear little letter: she huddled it up. How much more important a love-letter seems to a girl than to a man! Springrove was unconsciously clever in his letters, and a man with a talent of that kind may write himself up to a hero in the mind of a young woman who loves him without knowing much about him. Springrove already stood a cubit higher* in her imagination than he did in his shoes.

During the day she flitted about the room in an ecstasy of pleasure, packing the things and thinking of an answer which should be worthy of the tender tone of the question, her love bubbling from her involuntarily, like prophesyings from a prophet.

In the afternoon Owen went with her to the railway station, and put her in the train for Carriford Road, the station nearest to Knapwater House.

Half an hour later she stepped out upon the platform, and found nobody there to receive her—though a pony-carriage was waiting outside. In two minutes she saw a melancholy man in cheerful livery running towards her from a public-house close adjoining, who proved to be the servant sent to fetch her. There are two ways of getting rid of sorrows: one by living them down, the other by drowning them. The coachman drowned his.

He informed her that her luggage would be fetched by a spring-waggon in about half-an-hour; then helped her into the chaise* and drove off.

Her lover's letter lying close against her neck, fortified her against the restless timidity she had previously felt concerning this new undertaking, and completely furnished her with the confident ease of mind which is required for the critical observation of surrounding objects. It was just that stage in the slow decline of the summer days, when the deep, dark, and vacuous hot-weather-shadows are beginning to be replaced by blue ones that have a surface and substance to the eye. They trotted along the turnpike road* for a distance of about a mile, which brought them just outside the village of Carriford, and then turned through large lodge-gates, on the heavy stone piers of which stood a pair of bitterns cast in bronze. They then entered the park and wound along a drive shaded by old and drooping lime-trees, not arranged in the form of an avenue, but standing irregularly, sometimes leaving the track completely exposed to the sky, at other times casting a shade over it, which almost approached gloom—the under surface of the lowest boughs hanging at a uniform level of six feet above the grass—the extreme height to which the nibbling mouths of the cattle could reach.

"Is that the house?" said Cytherea, expectantly, catching sight of a grey gable between the trees, and losing it again.

"No; that's the old manor house—or rather all that's left of it. The Aldclyffes used to let it sometimes, but it was oftener empty. 'Tis now divided into three cottages. Respectable people didn't care to live there."

"Why didn't they?"

"Well 'tis so awkward and unhandy. You see so much of it has been pulled down, and the rooms that are left won't do very well for a small residence. 'Tis so dismal, too, and like most old houses stands too low down in the hollow to be healthy."

"Do they tell any horrid stories about it?"

"No, not a single one."

"Ah, that's a pity."

"Yes, that's what I say. 'Tis just the house for a nice ghastly hair-on-end story, that would make the parish religious. Perhaps it will have one some day to make it complete; but there's not a word of the kind now. There, I wouldn't live there for all that. In fact I couldn't. Oh, no, I couldn't."

"Why couldn't you?"

"The sounds."

"What are they?"

"One is the waterfall, which stands so close by that you can hear that there waterfall in every room of the house, night or day, ill or well. 'Tis enough to drive anybody mad: now listen."

He stopped the horse. Above the slight common sounds in the air came the unvarying steady rush of falling water from some spot unseen on account of the thick foliage of the grove.

"There's something awful in the regularity of that sound, is there not, Miss?"

"When you say there is, there really seems to be. You said there were two—what is the other horrid sound?"

"The pumping engine. That's close by the Old House, and sends water up the hill and all over the Great House. We shall hear that directly . . . . There, now listen."

From the same direction down the dell they could now hear the whistling creak of cranks, repeated at intervals of half a minute, with a sousing noise between each: a creak, a souse, then another creak, and so on continually.

"Now if anybody could make shift to live through the other sounds, these would finish him off, don't you think so, Miss? That machine goes on night and day, summer and winter, and is hardly ever greased or visited. Ah, it tries the nerves at night, especially if you are not very well; though we don't often hear it at the Great House."

"That sound is certainly very dismal. They might have the wheel greased. Does Miss Aldclyffe take any interest in these things?"

"Well, scarcely; you see her father doesn't attend to that sort of thing as he used to. The engine was once quite his hobby. But now he's getten old and very seldom goes there."

"How many are there in family?"

"Only her father and herself. He's an old man of seventy."

"I had thought that Miss Aldclyffe was sole mistress of the property, and lived here alone."

"No, M—." The coachman was continually checking himself thus, being about to style her Miss* involuntarily, and then recollecting that he was only speaking to the new lady's maid.

"She will soon be mistress, however, I am afraid," he continued, as if speaking by a spirit of prophecy denied to ordinary humanity. "The poor old gentleman has decayed very fast lately." The man then drew a long breath.

"Why did you breathe sadly like that?" said Cytherea.

"Ah! . . . . When he's dead peace will be all over with us old servants. I expect to see the whole house turned inside out."

"She will marry, do you mean?"

"Marry—not she! I wish she would. No, in her soul she's as solitary as Robinson Crusoe,* though she has acquaintances in plenty, if not relations. There's the rector, Mr. Raunham—he's a relation by marriage,—yet she's quite distant towards him. And people say that if she keeps single there will be hardly a life between Mr. Raunham and the heirship of the estate. Dang it,* she don't care. She's an extraordinary picture of womankind—very extraordinary."

"In what way besides?"

"You'll know soon enough, Miss. She has had seven lady's-maids this last twelvemonth. I assure you 'tis one body's work to fetch 'em from the station and take 'em back again. The Lord must be a Tory at heart,* or he'd never permit such overbearen goings on."

"Does she dismiss them directly they come?"

"Not at all—she never dismisses them—they go themselves. You see 'tis like this. She's got a very quick temper; she flies in a passion with them for nothing at all; next mornen they come up and say they are going; she's sorry for it and wishes they'd stay, but she's as proud as a lucifer,* and her pride won't let her say 'Stay,' and away they go. 'Tis like this in fact. If you say to her about anybody, 'Ah, poor thing!' she says, 'Pish! indeed!' If you say, 'Pish, indeed!' 'Ah, poor thing!' she says directly. She hangs the chief baker, and restores the chief butler, though the devil but Pharaoh herself can see the difference between 'em.''*

Cytherea was silent. She feared she might be again a burden to her brother.

"However, you stand a very good chance," the man went on; "for I think she likes you more than common. I have never known her send the pony-carriage to meet one before; 'tis always the trap, but this time she said, in a very particular ladylike tone, 'Roobert, gaow with the pony-kerriage.' . . . There, 'tis true, pony and carriage too are getten rather shabby now," he added, looking round upon the vehicle as if to keep Cytherea's pride within reasonable limits.

" 'Tis to be hoped you'll please in dressen her to-night."

"Why to-night?"

"There's a dinner-party of seventeen; 'tis her father's birthday, and she's very particular about her appearance at such times. Now look; this is the house. Livelier up here, isn't it, Miss?"

They were now on rising ground, and had just emerged from a clump of trees. Still a little higher than where they stood was situated the mansion, called Knapwater House,* the offices gradually losing themselves among the trees behind.

§ 2. *Evening*

The house was regularly and substantially built of clean grey freestone* throughout, in that plainer fashion of Greek classicism that prevailed at the latter end of the last century, when the copyists called designers had grown weary of fantastic variations in the Roman orders.* The main block approximated to a square on the ground plan, having a projection in the centre of each side, surmounted by a pediment.* From each angle of the east side ran a line of buildings lower than the rest, turning inwards again at their farther end and forming within them a spacious open court, within which resounded an echo of astonishing clearness. These erections were in their turn backed by ivy-covered ice-houses,* laundries, and stables, the whole mass of subsidiary buildings being half buried beneath close-set shrubs and trees.

There was opening sufficient through the foliage on the right hand to enable her on nearer approach to form an idea of the arrangement of the remoter or south front also. The natural features and contour of this quarter of the site had evidently dictated the position of the house primarily, and were of the ordinary, and upon the whole, most satisfactory kind, namely, a broad, graceful slope running from the terrace beneath the walls to the margin of a placid lake lying below, upon the surface of which a dozen swans and a green punt floated at leisure. An irregular wooded island stood in the midst of the lake; beyond this and the further margin of the water were plantations and greensward of varied outlines, the trees, heightening, by half veiling, the softness of the exquisite landscape stretching behind.

The glimpses she had obtained of this portion were now checked by the angle of the building. In a minute or two they reached the side door, at which Cytherea alighted. She was welcomed by an elderly woman of lengthy smiles and general pleasantness, who announced herself to be Mrs. Morris, the housekeeper.

"Mrs. Graye, I believe?" she said.

"I am not—O yes, yes, we are all mistresses,"* said Cytherea, smiling, but forcedly. The title accorded her seemed disagreeably like the first slight scar of a brand, and she thought of Owen's prophecy.

Mrs. Morris led her into a comfortable parlour called The Room. Here tea was made ready, and Cytherea sat down, looking whenever occasion allowed, at Mrs. Morris with great interest and curiosity to discover if possible, something in her which should give a clue to the secret of her knowledge of herself, and the recommendation based upon it. But nothing was to be learnt, at any rate just then. Mrs. Morris was perpetually getting up, feeling in her pockets, going to cupboards, leaving the room for two or three minutes, and trotting back again.

"You'll excuse me, Mrs. Graye," she said. "But 'tis the old gentleman's birthday, and they always have a lot of people to dinner on that day, though he's getting up in years now. However, none of them are sleepers*—she generally keeps the house pretty clear of lodgers (being a lady with no intimate friends, though many acquaintances), which, though it gives us less to do, makes it all the duller for the younger maids in the house." Mrs. Morris then proceeded to give in fragmentary speeches an outline of the constitution and government of the estate.

"Now are you sure you have quite done tea? Not a bit or drop more? Why you've eaten nothing, I'm sure. . . . Well, now, it is rather inconvenient that the other maid is not here to show you the ways of the house a little, but she left last Saturday, and Miss Aldclyffe has been making shift with poor old clumsy me for a maid all yesterday and this morning. She is not come in yet. I expect she will ask for you, Mrs. Graye, the first thing. . . . . I was going to say that if you have really done tea, I will take you up-stairs, and show you through the wardrobes—Miss Aldclyffe's things are not laid out for to-night yet."

She preceded Cytherea up-stairs, pointed out her own room, and then took her into Miss Aldclyffe's dressing-room, on the first floor; where, after explaining the whereabouts of various articles of apparel, the housekeeper left her, telling her that she had an hour yet upon her hands before dressing time. Cytherea laid out upon the bed in the next room all that she had been told would be required that evening, and then went again to the little room which had been appropriated to herself.

Here she sat down by the open window, leant out upon the sill like another Blessed Damozel,* and listlessly looked down upon the brilliant pattern of colours formed by the flower-beds on the lawn—now richly crowded with late summer blossom. But the vivacity of spirit which had hitherto enlivened her, was fast ebbing under the pressure of prosaic realities, and the warm scarlet of the geraniums, glowing most conspicuously, and mingling with the vivid cold red and green of the verbenas, the rich depth of the dahlia, and the ripe mellowness of the calceolaria, backed by the pale hue of a flock of meek sheep, feeding in the open park, close to the other side of the fence, were, to a great extent, lost upon her eyes. She was thinking that nothing seemed worth while; that it was possible she might die in a workhouse; and what did it matter? The petty, vulgar, details of servitude that she had just passed through, her dependence upon the whims of a strange woman, the necessity of quenching all individuality of character in herself, and relinquishing her own peculiar tastes to help on the wheel of this alien establishment, made her sick and sad, and she almost longed to pursue some free, out-of-doors employment, sleep under trees or a hut, and know no enemy but winter and cold weather,* like shepherds and cowkeepers, and birds and animals—ay, like the sheep she saw there under her window. She looked sympathizingly at them for several minutes, imagining their enjoyment of the rich grass.

"Yes—like those sheep," she said, aloud; and her face reddened with surprise at a discovery she made that very instant.

The flock consisted of some ninety or a hundred young stock ewes: the surface of their fleece was as rounded and even as a cushion, and white as milk. Now she had just observed that on the left buttock of every one of them were marked in distinct red letters the initials "E. S."

"E. S.," could bring to Cytherea's mind only one thought; but that immediately and for ever—the name of her lover, Edward Springrove.

"Oh, if it should be . . . . !" She interrupted her words by a resolve. Miss Aldclyffe's carriage at the same moment made its appearance in the drive; but Miss Aldclyffe was not her object now. It was to ascertain to whom the sheep belonged, and to set her surmise at rest one way or the other. She flew down-stairs to Mrs. Morris.

"Whose sheep are those in the park, Mrs. Morris?"

"Farmer Springrove's."

"What farmer Springrove is that?" she said, quickly.

"Why, surely you know? Your friend Farmer Springrove, the cider maker, and who keeps the Three Tranters Inn;* who recommended you to me when he came in to see me the other day?"

Cytherea's mother-wit suddenly warned her in the midst of her excitement that it was necessary not to betray the secret of her love. "Oh, yes," she said, "of course." Her thoughts had run as follows in that short interval:—

"Farmer Springrove is Edward's father, and his name is Edward, too.

"Edward knew I was going to advertise for a situation of some kind.

"He watched the *Times*, and saw it, my address being attached.

"He thought it would be excellent for me to be here that we might meet whenever he came home.

"He told his father that I might be recommended as a lady's maid; that he knew my brother and myself.

"His father told Mrs. Morris; Mrs. Morris told Miss Aldclyffe."

The whole chain of incidents that drew her there was plain, and there was no such thing as chance in the matter. It was all Edward's doing.

The sound of a bell was heard. Cytherea did not heed it, and still continued in her reverie.

"That's Miss Aldclyffe's bell," said Mrs. Morris.

"I suppose it is," said the young woman, placidly.

"Well, it means that you must go up to her," the matron continued, in a tone of surprise.

Cytherea felt a burning heat come over her, mingled with a sudden irritation at Mrs. Morris's hint. But the good sense which had recognised stern necessity prevailed over rebellious independence; the flush passed, and she said, hastily,

"Yes, yes; of course, I must go to her when she pulls the bell—whether I want to or no."

However, in spite of this painful reminder of her new position in life, Cytherea left the apartment in a mood far different from the gloomy sadness of ten minutes previous. The place felt like home to her now; she did not mind the pettiness of her occupation, because Edward evidently did not mind it; and this was Edward's own spot. She found time on her way to Miss Aldclyffe's dressing-room to hurriedly glide out by a side door, and look for a moment at the unconscious sheep bearing the friendly initials. She went up to them to try to touch one of the flock, and felt vexed that they all stared sceptically at her kind advances and then ran pell-mell down the hill. Then, fearing anyone should discover her childish movements, she slipped indoors again, and ascended the staircase, catching glimpses, as she passed, of silver-buttoned footmen, who flashed about the passages like lightning.

Miss Aldclyffe's dressing-room was an apartment which, on a casual survey, conveyed an impression that it was available for almost any purpose save the adornment of the feminine person. In its hours of perfect order nothing pertaining to the toilet was visible; even the inevitable mirrors with their accessories were arranged in a roomy recess not noticeable from the door, lighted by a window of its own, called the dressing window.

The washing-stand figured as a vast oak chest, carved with grotesque Renaissance ornament. The dressing-table was in appearance something between a high altar and a cabinet piano,* the surface being richly worked in the same style of semi-classic decoration, but the extraordinary outline having been arrived at by Mr. James Sparkman, an ingenious joiner* and decorator from the neighbouring town, after months of painful toil in cutting and fitting, under Miss Aldclyffe's immediate eye, the materials being the remains of two or three old cabinets the lady had found in the lumber room. About two-thirds of the floor was carpeted, the remaining portion being laid with parquetry of light and dark woods.

Miss Aldclyffe was standing at the larger window, away from the dressing-niche. She bowed and said pleasantly, "I am glad you have come. We shall get on capitally, I dare say."

Her bonnet was off. Cytherea did not think her so handsome as on the earlier day; the queenliness of her beauty was harder and less warm. But a worse discovery than this was that Miss Aldclyffe, with the usual obliviousness of rich people to their dependents' specialities, seemed to have quite forgotten Cytherea's inexperience, and mechanically delivered up her body to her handmaid without a thought of details, and with a mild yawn.

Everything went well at first. The dress was removed, stockings and black boots were taken off, and silk stockings and white shoes were put on. Miss Aldclyffe then retired to bathe her hands and face, and Cytherea drew breath. If she could get through this first evening, all would be right. She felt that it was unfortunate that such a crucial test for her powers as a birthday dinner should have been applied on the threshold of her arrival, but *n'importe*.*

Miss Aldclyffe was now arrayed in a white dressing-gown, and dropped languidly into an easy chair, pushed up before the glass. The instincts of her sex and her own practice told Cytherea the next movement. She let Miss Aldclyffe's hair fall down about her shoulders, and began to arrange it. It proved to be all real; a satisfaction.

Miss Aldclyffe was musingly looking on the floor, and the operation went on for some minutes in silence. At length her thoughts seemed to return to the present, and she lifted her eyes to the glass.

"Why, what on earth are you doing with my head?" she exclaimed, with widely opened eyes. At the words she felt the back of Cytherea's little hand tremble against her neck.

"Perhaps you prefer it done the other fashion, madam?" said the maiden.

"No, no; that's the fashion right enough, but you must make more show of my hair than that, or I shall have to buy some, which God forbid!"

"It is how I do my own," said Cytherea, naively, and with a sweetness of tone that would have pleased the most acrimonious under favourable circumstances; but tyranny was in the ascendant with Miss Aldclyffe at this moment, and she was assured of palatable food for her vice by having felt the trembling of Cytherea's hand.

"Yours, indeed! *Your* hair! come, go on." Considering that Cytherea possessed at least five times as much of that valuable auxiliary to woman's beauty as the lady before her, there was at the same time some excuse for Miss Aldclyffe's outburst. She remembered herself, however, and said more quietly, "Now then, Graye . . . . By the bye, what do they call you downstairs?"

"Mrs. Graye," said the handmaid.

"Then, tell them not to do any such absurd thing—not but that it is quite according to usage; but you are too young yet."

This dialogue tided Cytherea safely onward through the hair-dressing till the flowers and diamonds were to be placed upon the lady's brow. Cytherea began arranging them tastefully, and to the very best of her judgment.

"That won't do," said Miss Aldclyffe, harshly.

"Why?"

"I look too young—an old dressed doll."

"Will that, madam?"

"No. I look a fright—a perfect fright!"

"This way, perhaps?"

"Heavens! Don't worry me so." She shut her lips like a trap.

Having once worked herself up to the belief that her head-dress was to be a failure that evening, no cleverness of Cytherea's in arranging it could please her. She continued in a smouldering passion during the remainder of the performance, keeping her lips firmly closed, and the muscles of her body rigid. Finally, snatching up her gloves, and taking her handkerchief and fan in her hand, she silently sailed out of the room, without betraying the least consciousness of another woman's presence behind her.

Cytherea's fears that at the undressing this suppressed anger would find a vent, kept her on thorns throughout the evening. She tried to read; she could not. She tried to sew; she could not. She tried to muse; she could not do that connectedly. "If this is the beginning, what will the end be!" she said in a whisper, and felt many misgivings as to the policy of being overhasty in establishing an independence at the expense of congruity with a cherished past.

§ 3. *Midnight*

The sole object of this narration being to present in a regular series the several episodes and incidents which directly helped forward the end, and only these, every contiguous scene without this qualification is necessarily passed over,* and as one, the Aldclyffe state dinner.

The clock struck twelve. The company had all gone, and Miss Aldclyffe's bell rang loudly and jerkingly.

Cytherea started to her feet at the sound, which broke in upon a fitful sleep that had overtaken her. She had been sitting drearily in her chair waiting minute after minute for the signal, her brain in that state of intentness which takes cognizance of the passage of Time as a real motion—motion without matter—the instants throbbing past in the company of a feverish pulse. She hastened to the room, to find the lady sitting before the dressing shrine, illuminated on both sides, and looking so queenly in her attitude of absolute repose, that the younger woman felt the awfullest sense of responsibility at her Vandalism in having undertaken to demolish so imposing a pile.

The lady's jewelled ornaments were taken off in silence—some by her own listless hands, some by Cytherea's. Then followed the outer stratum of clothing. The dress being removed, Cytherea took it in her hand and went with it into the bedroom adjoining, intending to hang it in the wardrobe. But on second thoughts, in order that she might not keep Miss Aldclyffe waiting a moment longer than necessary, she flung it down on the first resting-place that came to hand, which happened to be the bed, and re-entered the dressing-room with the noiseless footfall of a kitten. She paused in the middle of the room.

She was unnoticed, and her sudden return had plainly not been

expected. During the short time of Cytherea's absence, Miss Aldclyffe had pulled off a kind of chemisette* of Brussels net,* drawn high
above the throat, which she had worn with her evening dress as a
semiopaque covering to her shoulders, and in its place had put her
night-dress round her. Her right hand was lifted to her neck, as if
engaged in fastening her night-dress.

But on a second glance Miss Aldclyffe's proceeding was clearer to
Cytherea. She was not fastening her night-dress; it had been carelessly thrown round her, and Miss Aldclyffe was really occupied in
holding up to her eyes some small object that she was keenly scrutin-
ising. And now on suddenly discovering the presence of Cytherea at
the back of the apartment, instead of naturally continuing or concluding her inspection, she desisted hurriedly; the tiny snap of a
spring was heard, her hand was removed, and she began adjusting
her robes.

Modesty might have directed her hasty action of enwrapping her
shoulders, but it was scarcely likely, considering Miss Aldclyffe's
temperament, that she had all her life been used to a maid,
Cytherea's youth, and the elder lady's marked treatment of her as if
she were a mere child or plaything. The matter was too slight to
reason about, and yet upon the whole it seemed that Miss Aldclyffe
must have a practical reason for concealing her neck.

With a timid sense of being an intruder Cytherea was about to
step back and out of the room; but at the same moment Miss Aldclyffe turned, saw the impulse, and told her companion to stay, looking into her eyes as if she had half an intention to explain something.
Cytherea felt certain it was the little mystery of her late movements.
The lady withdrew her eyes; Cytherea went to fetch the dressing-
gown, and wheeled round again to bring it up to Miss Aldclyffe, who
had now partly removed her night-dress to put it on the proper way,
and still sat with her back towards Cytherea.

Her neck was again quite open and uncovered, and though hidden
from the direct line of Cytherea's vision, she saw it reflected in the
glass—the fair white surface and the inimitable combination of
curves between throat and bosom which artists adore being brightly
lit up by the light burning on either side.

And the lady's prior proceedings were now explained in the simplest manner. In the midst of her breast, like an island in a sea of
pearl, reclined an exquisite little gold locket, embellished with

arabesque work* of blue, red, and white enamel. That was undoubtedly what Miss Aldclyffe had been contemplating and, moreover, not having been put off with her other ornaments, it was to be retained during the night—a slight departure from the custom of ladies which Miss Aldclyffe had at first not cared to exhibit to her new assistant, though now, on further thought, she seemed to have become indifferent on the matter.

"My dressing-gown," she said, quietly fastening her night-dress as she spoke.

Cytherea came forward with it. Miss Aldclyffe did not turn her head, but looked enquiringly at her maid in the glass.

"You saw what I wear on my neck, I suppose?" she said to Cytherea's reflected face.

"Yes, madam, I did," said Cytherea to Miss Aldclyffe's reflected face.

Miss Aldclyffe again looked at Cytherea's reflection as if she were on the point of explaining. Again she checked her resolve and said lightly.

"Few of my maids discover that I wear it always. I generally keep it a secret—not that it matters much. But I was careless with you, and seemed to want to tell you. You win me to make confidences that . . . . . ."

She ceased, took Cytherea's hand in her own, lifted the locket with the other, touched the spring and disclosed a miniature.

"It is a handsome face, is it not?" she whispered, mournfully, and even timidly.

"It is."

But the sight had gone through Cytherea like an electric shock, and there was an instantaneous awakening of perception in her, so thrilling in its presence as to be well-nigh insupportable. The face in the miniature was the face of her own father—younger and fresher than she had ever known him—but her father!

Was this the woman of his wild and unquenchable early love? And was this the woman who had figured in the gate-man's story as answering the name of Cytherea before her judgment was awake? Surely it was. And if so, here was the tangible outcrop of a romantic and hidden stratum of the past hitherto seen only in her imagination; but as far as her scope allowed, clearly defined therein by reason of its strangeness.

Miss Aldclyffe's eyes and thoughts were so intent upon the miniature that she had not been conscious of Cytherea's start of surprise. She went on speaking in a low and abstracted tone.

"Yes, I lost him." She interrupted her words by a short meditation, and went on again. "I lost him by excess of honesty as regarded my past. But it was best that it should be so . . . . . . I was led to think rather more than usual of the circumstances to-night because of your name. It is pronounced the same way, though differently spelt."

The only means by which Cytherea's surname could have been spelt to Miss Aldclyffe must have been by Mrs. Morris or Farmer Springrove. She fancied Farmer Springrove would have spelt it properly if Edward was his informant, which made Miss Aldclyffe's remark obscure.

Women make confidences and then regret them.

The impulsive rush of feeling which had led Miss Aldclyffe to indulge in this revelation, trifling, as it was, died out immediately her words were beyond recall; and the turmoil, occasioned in her by dwelling upon that chapter of her life, found vent in another kind of emotion—the result of a trivial accident.

Cytherea, after letting down Miss Aldclyffe's hair, adopted some plan with it to which the lady had not been accustomed. A rapid revulsion to irritation ensued. The maiden's mere touch seemed to discharge the pent-up regret of the lady as if she had been a jar of electricity.*

"How strangely you treat my hair!" she exclaimed.

A silence.

"I have told you what I never tell my maids as a rule; of course *nothing* that I say in this room is to be mentioned outside it." She spoke crossly no less than emphatically.

"It shall not be, madam," said Cytherea, agitated and vexed that the woman of her romantic wonderings should be so disagreeable to her.

"Why on earth did I tell you of my love?" she went on.

Cytherea made no answer.

The lady's vexation with herself, and the accident which had led to the disclosure swelled little by little till it knew no bounds. But what was done could not be undone, and though Cytherea had shown a most winning responsiveness, quarrel Miss Aldclyffe must. She recurred to the subject of Cytherea's want of expertness, like a bitter reviewer, who finding the sentiments of a poet unimpeachable, quarrels with his rhymes.

"Never, never before did I serve myself such a trick as this in engaging a maid." She waited for an expostulation: none came. Miss Aldclyffe tried again.

"The idea of my taking a girl without asking her more than three questions, or having a single reference, all because of her good l——, the shape of her face and body! It *was* a fool's trick. There, I am served right—quite right, by being deceived in such a way."

"I didn't deceive you," said Cytherea. The speech was an unfortunate one, and was the very "fuel to maintain its fires"* that the other's petulance desired.

"You did," she said, hotly.

"I told you I couldn't promise to be acquainted with every detail of routine just at first."

"Will you contradict me in this way! You are telling untruths, I say."

Cytherea's lip quivered. "I would answer that remark if—if—."

"If what?"

"If it were a lady's!"*

"You girl of impudence—what do you say? Leave the room this instant, I tell you."

"And I tell you that a person who speaks to a lady as you do to me, is no lady herself!"

"To a lady? A lady's maid speaks in this way. The idea!"

"Don't 'lady's maid' me: nobody is my mistress. I won't have it!"

"Good Heavens!"

"I wouldn't have come—No—I wouldn't! if I had known!"

"What?"

"That you were such an ill tempered unjust woman!"

Possess beyond the Muse's painting,* Miss Aldclyffe exclaimed,—

"A Woman, am I! I'll teach you if I am a Woman!" and lifted her hand as if she would have liked to strike her companion. This stung the maiden into absolute defiance.

"I dare you to touch me!" she cried. "Strike me if you dare, madam! I am not afraid of you—what do you mean by such an action as that!"

Miss Aldclyffe was disconcerted at this unexpected show of spirit, and ashamed of her unladylike impulse now it was put into words.

She sank back in the chair. "I was not going to strike you—go to your room—I beg you to go to your room," she repeated in a husky whisper.

Cytherea, red and panting, took up her candlestick and advanced to the table to get a light. Standing close to them the rays from the candles struck sharply on her face. She usually bore a much stronger likeness to her mother than to her father, but now, looking with a grave, reckless, and angered expression of countenance at the kindling wick as she held it slanting into the other flame, her father's features were distinct in her. It was the first time Miss Aldclyffe had seen her in a passionate mood, and wearing that expression which was invariably its concomitant. It was Miss Aldclyffe's turn to start now; and the remark she made was an instance of that sudden change of tone from high-flown invective to the pettiness of curiosity which so often makes women's quarrels ridiculous. Even Miss Aldclyffe's dignity had not sufficient power to postpone the absorbing desire she now felt to settle the strange suspicion that had entered her head.

"You spell your name the common way, G, R, E, Y, don't you?" she said with assumed indifference.

"No," said Cytherea, poised on the side of her foot, and still looking into the flame.

"Yes, surely? The name was spelt that way on your boxes: I looked and saw it myself.

The enigma of Miss Aldclyffe's mistake was solved. "O was it?" said Cytherea. "Ah I remember Mrs Jackson, the lodging-house keeper at Creston, labelled them. We spell our name G, R, A, Y, E."

"What was your father's trade?"

Cytherea thought it would be useless to attempt to conceal facts any longer. "He was not a trade," she said. "He was an architect."

"The idea of your being an architect's daughter!"

"There's nothing to offend you in that I hope?"

"O no."

"Why did you say 'the idea'?"

"Leave that alone. Did he ever visit in Gower Street one Christmas, many years ago?—but you would not know that."

"I have heard him say that Mr. Huntway, a curate somewhere in that part of London, and who died there, was an old college friend of his."

"What is your Christian name?"

"Cytherea."

"No! And is it really? And you knew that face I showed you? Yes, I see you did."

Miss Aldclyffe stopped, and closed her lips impassibly. She was a little agitated.

"Do you want me any longer?" said Cytherea, standing candle in hand and looking quietly in Miss Aldclyffe's face.

"Well—no: no longer," said the lady, lingeringly.

"With your permission, I will leave the house tomorrow morning, madam."

"Ah." Miss Aldclyffe had no notion of what she was saying.

"And I know you will be so good as not to intrude upon me during the short remainder of my stay?"

Saying this Cytherea left the room before her companion had answered. Miss Aldclyffe, then, had recognised her at last, and had been curious about her name from the beginning.

The other members of the household had retired to rest. As Cytherea went along the passage leading to her room her dress rustled against the partition. A door on her left opened, and Mrs. Morris looked out.

"I waited out of bed till you came up," she said, "it being your first night, in case you should be at a loss for anything. How have you got on with Miss Aldclyffe?"

"Pretty well—though not so well as I could have wished."

"Has she been scolding?"

"A little."

"She's a very odd lady—'tis all one way or the other with her. She's not bad at heart, but unbearable in close quarters. Those of us who don't have much to do with her personally, stay on for years and years."

"Has Miss Aldclyffe's family always been rich?" said Cytherea.

"O no. The property, with the name, came from her mother's uncle. Her family is a branch of the old Aldclyffe family on the maternal side. Her mother married a Bradleigh—a mere nobody at that time—and was on that account cut by her relations. But very singularly the other branch of the family died out one by one—three of them, and Miss Aldclyffe's great uncle then left all his property, including this estate, to Captain Bradleigh and his wife—Miss

Aldclyffe's father and mother—on condition that they took the old family name as well. There's all about it in the *Landed Gentry*.* 'Tis a thing very often done."

"O, I see. Thank you. Well, now I am going. Good night."

CHAPTER VI

THE EVENTS OF TWELVE HOURS

§ 1. *August the ninth. One to two o'clock, a.m.*

Cytherea entered her bedroom, and flung herself on the bed, bewildered by a whirl of thought. Only one subject was clear in her mind, and it was that in spite of family discoveries, that day was to be the first and last of her experience as a lady's maid. Starvation itself should not compel her to hold such a humiliating post for another instant. "Ah," she thought, with a sigh, at the martyrdom of her last little fragment of self-conceit, "Owen knows everything better than I."

She jumped up and began making ready for her departure in the morning, the tears streaming down when she grieved and wondered what practical matter on earth she could turn her hand to next. All these preparations completed, she began to undress, her mind unconsciously drifting away to the contemplation of her late surprises. To look in the glass for an instant at the reflection of her own magnificent resources in face and bosom, and to mark their attractiveness unadorned, was perhaps but the natural action of a young woman who had so lately been chidden whilst passing through the harassing experience of decorating an older beauty of Miss Aldclyffe's temper.

But she directly checked her weakness by sympathising reflections on the hidden troubles which must have thronged the past years of the solitary lady, to keep her, though so rich and courted, in a mood so repellent and gloomy as that in which Cytherea found her; and then the young girl marvelled again and again, as she had marvelled before, at the strange confluence of circumstances which had brought herself into contact with the one woman in the world whose history was so romantically intertwined with her own. She almost began to wish she were not obliged to go away and leave the lonely being to loneliness still.

In bed and in the dark, Miss Aldclyffe haunted her mind more persistently than ever. Instead of sleeping, she called up staring visions of the possible past of this queenly lady, her mother's rival.

Up the long vista of bygone years she saw, behind all, the young girl's flirtation, little or much, with the cousin, that seemed to have been nipped in the bud, or to have terminated hastily in some way. Then the secret meetings between Miss Aldclyffe and the other woman at the little inn at Hammersmith and other places: the commonplace sobriquet she adopted: her swoon at some painful news, and the very slight knowledge the elder female had of her partner in mystery. Then, more than a year afterwards, the acquaintanceship of her own father with this his first love; the awakening of the passion, his acts of devotion, the unreasoning heat of his rapture, her tacit acceptance of it, and yet her uneasiness under the delight. Then his declaration amid the evergreens: the utter change produced in her manner thereby, seemingly the result of a rigid determination: and the total concealment of her reason by herself and her parents, whatever it was. Then the lady's course dropped into darkness, and nothing more was visible till she was discovered here at Knapwater, nearly fifty years old, still unmarried and still beautiful, but lonely, embittered, and haughty. Cytherea imagined that her father's image was still warmly cherished in Miss Aldclyffe's heart, and was thankful that she herself had not been betrayed into announcing that she knew many particulars of this page of her father's history, and the chief one, the lady's unaccountable renunciation of him. It would have made her bearing towards the mistress of the mansion more awkward, and would have been no benefit to either.

Thus conjuring up the past, and theorising on the present, she lay restless, changing her posture from one side to the other and back again. Finally, when courting sleep with all her art, she heard a clock strike two. A minute later, and she fancied she could distinguish a soft rustle in the passage outside her room.

To bury her head in the sheets was her first impulse; then to uncover it, raise herself on her elbow, and stretch her eyes wide open in the darkness; her lips being parted with the intentness of her listening. Whatever the noise was, it had ceased for the time.

It began again and came close to her door, lightly touching the panels. Then there was another stillness; Cytherea made a movement which caused a faint rustling of the bedclothes.

Before she had time to think another thought a light tap was given. Cytherea breathed: the person outside was evidently bent upon finding her awake, and the rustle she had made had encouraged the hope.

The maiden's physical condition shifted from one pole to its opposite. The cold sweat of terror forsook her, and modesty took the alarm. She became hot and red; her door was not locked.

A distinct woman's whisper came to her through the keyhole: "Cytherea!"

Only one being in the house knew her Christian name, and that was Miss Aldclyffe. Cytherea stepped out of bed, went to the door, and whispered back, "Yes?"

"Let me come in, darling."

The young woman paused in a conflict between judgment and emotion. It was now mistress and maid no longer; woman and woman only. Yes, she must let her come in, poor thing.

She got a light in an instant, opened the door, and raising her eyes and the candle, saw Miss Aldclyffe standing outside in her dressing-gown.

"Now you see that it is really myself, put out the light," said the visitor. "I want to stay here with you, Cythie. I came to ask you to come down into my bed, but it is snugger here. But remember that you are mistress in this room, and that I have no business here, and that you may send me away if you choose. Shall I go?"

"O no; you shan't indeed if you don't want to," said Cythie, generously.

The instant they were in bed Miss Aldclyffe freed herself from the last remnant of restraint. She flung her arms round the young girl, and pressed her gently to her heart.

"Now kiss me," she said.*

Cytherea upon the whole, was rather discomposed at this change of treatment; and, discomposed or no, her passions were not so impetuous as Miss Aldclyffe's. She could not bring her soul to her lips for a moment, try how she would.

"Come kiss me," repeated Miss Aldclyffe.

Cytherea gave her a very small one, as soft in touch and in sound as the bursting of a bubble.

"More earnestly than that—come."

She gave another, a little but not much more expressively.

"I don't deserve a more feeling one, I suppose," said Miss Aldclyffe, with an emphasis of sad bitterness in her tone. "I am an ill-tempered woman, you think; half out of my mind. Well, perhaps I am; but I have had grief more than you can think or dream of. But I can't help loving you*—your name is the same as mine—isn't it strange?"

Cytherea was inclined to say no, but remained silent.

"Now, don't you think I must love you?" continued the other.

"Yes," said Cytherea, absently. She was still thinking whether duty to Owen and her father, which asked for silence on her knowledge of her father's unfortunate love, or duty to the woman embracing her, which seemed to ask for confidence, ought to predominate. Here was a solution. She would wait till Miss Aldclyffe referred to her acquaintanceship and attachment to Cytherea's father in past times: then she would tell her all she knew: that would be honour.

"Why can't you kiss me as I can kiss you? Why can't you!" She impressed upon Cytherea's lips a warm motherly salute, given as if in the outburst of strong feeling, long checked, and yearning for something to love and be loved by* in return.

"Do you think badly of me for my behaviour this evening, child? I don't know why I am so foolish as to speak to you in this way. I am a very fool, I believe. Yes. How old are you?"

"Eighteen."

"Eighteen . . . . . Well, why don't you ask me how old I am?"

"Because I don't want to know."

"Never mind if you don't. I am forty-six; and it gives me greater pleasure to tell you this than it does to you to listen. I have not told my age truly for the last twenty years till now."

"Why haven't you?"

"I have met deceit by deceit, till I am weary of it—weary, weary—and I long to be what I shall never be again—artless and innocent, like you. But I suppose that you, too, will prove to be not worth a thought, as every new friend does on more intimate knowledge. Come, why don't you talk to me, child? Have you said your prayers?"

"Yes—no! I forgot them to-night."

"I suppose you say them every night as a rule?"

"Yes."

"Why do you do that?"

"Because I always have, and it would seem strange if I were not to. Do you?"

"I? A wicked old sinner like me! No, I never do. I have thought all such matters humbug for years—thought so so long that I should be glad to think otherwise from very weariness; and yet, such is the code of the polite world that I subscribe regularly to Missionary Societies and others of the sort . . . Well, say your prayers, dear,—you won't omit them now you recollect it. I should like to hear you very much. Will you?"

"It seems hardly—"

"It would seem so like old times to me—when I was young, and nearer—far nearer Heaven than I am now. Do, sweet one."

Cytherea was embarrassed; and her embarrassment arose from the following conjuncture of affairs. Since she had loved Edward Springrove, she had linked his name with her brother Owen's in her nightly supplications to the Almighty. She wished to keep her love for him a secret, and above all a secret from a woman like Miss Aldclyffe; yet her conscience and the honesty of her love would not for an instant allow her to think of omitting his dear name, and so endanger the efficacy of all her previous prayers for his success by an unworthy shame now: it would be wicked of her, she thought, and a grievous wrong to him. Under any worldly circumstances she might have thought the position justified a little finesse, and have skipped him for once; but prayer was too solemn a thing for such trifling.

"I would rather not say them," she murmured first. It struck her then that this declining altogether was the same cowardice in another dress, and was delivering her poor Edward over to Satan just as unceremoniously as before. "Yes; I will say my prayers, and you shall hear me," she added, firmly.

She turned her face to the pillow and repeated in low soft tones the simple words she had used from childhood on such occasions. Owen's name was mentioned without faltering, but in the other case, maidenly shyness was too strong even for religion, and that when supported by excellent intentions. At the name of Edward she stammered, and her voice sank to the faintest whisper in spite of her.

"Thank you, dearest," said Miss Aldclyffe. "I have prayed too, I verily believe. You are a good girl, I think." Then the expected question came.

" 'Bless Owen,' and who, did you say?"

There was no help for it now, and out it came. "Owen and Edward," said Cytherea.

"Who are Owen and Edward?"

"Owen is my brother, madam," faltered the maid.

"Ah, I remember. Who is Edward?"

A silence.

"Your brother, too?" continued Miss Aldclyffe.

"No."

Miss Aldclyffe reflected a moment. "Don't you want to tell me who Edward is?" she said at last, in a tone of meaning.

"I don't mind telling; only . . . ."

"You would rather not, I suppose?"

"Yes."

Miss Aldclyffe shifted her ground. "Were you ever in love?" she inquired, suddenly.

Cytherea was surprised to hear how quickly the voice had altered from tenderness to harshness, vexation, and disappointment.

"Yes—I think I was—once," she murmured.

"Aha: and were you ever kissed by a man?"*

A pause.

"Well, were you?" said Miss Aldclyffe, rather sharply.

"Don't press me to tell—I can't—indeed, I won't, madam."

Miss Aldclyffe removed her arms from Cytherea's neck. " 'Tis now with you as it is always with all girls," she said, in jealous and gloomy accents. "You are not, after all, the innocent I took you for. No, no." She then changed her tone with fitful rapidity.

"Cytherea, try to love me more than you love him—do. I love you better* than any man can. Do, Cythie; don't let any man stand between us. Oh, I can't bear that!" She clasped Cytherea's neck again.

"I must love him now I have begun," replied the other.

"Must—yes—must," said the elder lady, reproachfully. "Yes, women are all alike. I thought I had at last found an artless woman who had not been sullied by a man's lips, and who had not practised or been practised upon by the arts which ruin all the truth and sweetness and goodness in us. Find a girl, if you can, whose mouth and ears have not been made a regular highway of by some man or another! Leave the admittedly notorious spots—the drawing-rooms of society—and look in the villages—leave the villages and search in the schools—and you can hardly find a girl whose heart has not been *had*—is not an old thing half worn out by some He or another. If men only knew the staleness of the freshest of us! that nine times out of ten the 'first love' they think they are winning from a woman is but the hulk of an old wrecked affection, fitted with new sails and re-used. O, Cytherea, can it be that you, too, are like the rest?"

"No, no, no," urged Cytherea, awed by the storm she had raised in the impetuous woman's mind. "He only kissed me once—twice, I mean."

"He might have a thousand times if he had cared to, there's no doubt about that, whoever his lordship is. You are as bad as I—we are all alike; and I—an old fool—have been sipping at your mouth as if it were honey, because I fancied no wasting lover knew the spot. But a minute ago, and you seemed to me like a fresh spring meadow—now you seem a dusty highway."

"O no, no!" Cytherea was not weak enough to shed tears except on extraordinary occasions, but she was fain to begin sobbing now. She wished Miss Aldclyffe would go to her own room, and leave her and her treasured dreams alone. This vehement imperious affection was in one sense soothing, but yet it was not of the kind that Cytherea's instincts desired. Though it was generous, it seemed somewhat too rank, sensuous, and capricious for endurance.

"Well," said the lady in continuation, "who is he?"

Her companion was desperately determined not to tell his name: she too much feared a taunt when Miss Aldclyffe's fiery mood again ruled her tongue.

"Won't you tell me? not tell me after all the affection I have shown?"

"I will perhaps, another day."

"Did you wear a hat and white feather in Creston for the week or two previous to your coming here?"

"Yes."

"Then I have seen you and your sweetheart at a distance! He rowed you round the bay with your brother."

"Yes."

"And without your brother—fie! There, there, don't let that little heart beat itself to death: throb, throb: it shakes the bed, you silly thing. I didn't mean that there was any harm in going alone with him. I only saw you from the esplanade, in common with the rest of the people. I often run down to Creston. He was a very good figure: now who was he?"

"I—I won't tell, madam—I cannot indeed!"

"Won't tell—very well, don't. You are very foolish to treasure up

his name and image as you do. Why he has had Loves before you,
trust him for that, whoever he is, and you are but a temporary link in
a long chain of others like you; who only have your little day as they
have had theirs."

" 'Tisn't true! 'tisn't true, 'tisn't true!" cried Cytherea in an agony
of torture. "He has never loved anybody else, I know—I am sure he
hasn't!"

Miss Aldclyffe was as jealous as any man could have been. She
continued—

"He sees a beautiful face and thinks he will never forget it, but in a
few weeks the feeling passes off and he wonders how he could have
cared for anybody so absurdly much."

"No, no, he doesn't—What does he do when he has thought
that—come, tell me—tell me!"

"You are as hot as fire, and the throbbing of your heart makes me
nervous. I can't tell you if you get in that flustered state."

"Do, do tell—O, it makes me so miserable! but tell—come tell
me!"

"Ah—the tables are turned now, dear!" she continued, in a tone
which mingled pity with derision:—

> "Love's passions shall rock thee
> As the storms rock the ravens on high,
> Bright reason will mock thee
> Like the sun from a wintry sky."*

"What does he do next?—Why this is what he does next: rumin-
ate on what he has heard of women's romantic impulses, and how
easily men torture them when they have given way to those feelings,
and have resigned everything for their hero. It may be that though he
loves you heartily now—that is, as heartily as a man can—and you
love him in return, your loves may be impracticable and hopeless and
you may be separated for ever. You, as the weary weary years pass by
will fade and fade—bright eyes will fade—and you will perhaps then
die early—true to him to your latest breath and believing him to be
true to the latest breath also; whilst he, in some gay and busy spot far
away from your last quiet nook, will have married some dashing lady,
and not purely oblivious of you, will long have ceased to regret
you—will chat about you, as you were in long past years—will say,
'Ah, little Cytherea used to tie her hair like that—poor innocent

trusting thing! it was a pleasant useless idle dream—that dream of mine for the maid with the bright eyes and simple, silly, heart; but I was a foolish lad at that time.' Then he will tell the tale of all your little Wills and Won'ts, and particular ways, and as he speaks, turn to his wife with a placid smile."

"It is not true! He can't, he c—can't be s—so cruel—and you are cruel to me—you are, you are!" She was at last driven to desperation: her natural common sense and shrewdness had seen all through the piece how imaginary her emotions were—she felt herself to be weak and foolish in permitting them to rise; but even then she could not control them: be agonised she must. She was only eighteen, and the long day's labour, her weariness, her excitement, had completely unnerved her, and worn her out; she was bent hither and thither by this tyrannical working upon her imagination, as a young rush in the wind. She wept bitterly.

"And now think how much I like you," resumed Miss Aldclyffe, when Cytherea grew calmer. "*I* shall never forget you for anybody else, as men do—never. I will be exactly as a mother to you. Now will you promise to live with me always, and always be taken care of, and never deserted?"

"I cannot. I will not be anybody's maid for another day on any consideration."

"No, no, no. You shan't be a lady's maid, You shall be my companion. I will get another maid."

Companion—that was a new idea. Cytherea could not resist the evidently heartfelt desire of the strange-tempered woman for her presence. But she could not trust to the moment's impulse.

"I will stay, I think. But do not ask for a final answer to night."

"Never mind now, then. Put your hair round your mamma's neck and give me one good long kiss and I won't talk any more in that way about your lover. After all, some young men are not so fickle as others; but even if he's the ficklest, there is consolation. The love of an inconstant man is ten times more ardent than that of a faithful man—that is, while it lasts."

Cytherea did as she was told, to escape the punishment of further talk; flung the twining tresses of her long, rich hair over Miss Aldclyffe's shoulders as directed, and the two ceased conversing, making themselves up for sleep. Miss Aldclyffe seemed to give herself over to a luxurious sense of content and quiet, as if the maiden at her side afforded her a protection against dangers which had menaced her for years; she was soon sleeping calmly.

§ 2. *Two to five, a.m.*

With Cytherea it was otherwise. Unused to the place and circumstances, she continued wakeful, ill at ease, and mentally distressed. She withdrew herself from her companion's embrace, turned to the other side, and endeavoured to relieve her busy brain by looking at the window-blind, and noticing the light of the rising moon—now in her last quarter—creep round upon it: it was the light of an old waning moon which had but a few days longer to live.

The sight led her to think again of what had happened under the rays of the same month's moon, a little before its full, the delicious* evening scene with Edward; the kiss, and the shortness of those happy moments—maiden imagination bringing about the apotheosis of a *status quo* which had had several unpleasantnesses in its earthly reality.

But sounds were in the ascendant that night. Her ears became aware of a strange and gloomy murmur.

She recognised it: it was the gushing of the waterfall, faint and low, brought from its source to the unwonted distance of the House by a faint breeze which made it distinct and recognisable by reason of the utter absence of all disturbing sounds. The groom's melancholy representation lent to the sound a more dismal effect than it would have had of its own nature. She began to fancy what the waterfall must be like at that hour, under the trees in the ghostly moonlight. Black at the head, and over the surface of the deep cold hole into which it fell; white and frothy at the fall; black and white, like a pall and its border; sad everywhere.

She was in the mood for sounds of every kind now, and strained her ears to catch the faintest, in wayward enmity to her quiet of mind. Another soon came.

The second was quite different from the first—a kind of intermittent whistle it seemed primarily: no, a creak, a metallic creak, ever and anon, like a plough, or a rusty wheelbarrow, or at least a wheel of some kind. Yes, it was a wheel—the water-wheel in the shrubbery by the old manor-house, which the coachman had said would drive him mad.

She determined not to think any more of these gloomy things; but now that she had once noticed the sound there was no sealing her ears to it. She could not help timing its creaks, and putting on a dread expectancy just before the end of each half minute that brought them. To imagine the inside of the engine-house, whence these noises proceeded, was now a necessity. No window, but crevices in the door, through which, probably, the moon-beams streamed in the most attenuated and skeleton-like rays, striking sharply upon portions of wet rusty cranks and chains; a glistening wheel, turning incessantly, labouring in the dark like a captive starving in a dungeon; and instead of a floor below, gurgling water, which on account of the darkness could only be heard; water which laboured up dark pipes almost to where she lay.

She shivered. Now she was determined to go to sleep; there could be nothing else left to be heard or to imagine—it was horrid that her imagination should be so restless. Yet just for an instant before going to sleep she would think this—suppose another sound *should* come—just suppose it should! Before the thought had well passed through her brain, a third sound came.

The third was a very soft gurgle or rattle—of a strange and abnormal kind—yet a sound she had heard before at some past period of her life—when, she could not recollect. To make it the more disturbing, it seemed to be almost close to her—either close outside the window, close under the floor, or close above the ceiling. The accidental fact of its coming so immediately upon the heels of her supposition, told so powerfully upon her excited nerves, that she jumped up in the bed. The same instant, a little dog in some room near, having probably heard the same noise, set up a low whine. The watchdog in the yard, hearing the moan of his associate, began to howl loudly and distinctly. His melancholy notes were taken up directly afterwards by the dogs in the kennel a long way off, in every variety of wail.

One logical thought alone was able to enter her flurried brain. The little dog that began the whining must have heard the other two sounds even better than herself. He had taken no notice of them, but he had taken notice of the third. The third, then, was an unusual sound.

It was not like water, it was not like wind, it was not the night-jar, it was not a clock, nor a rat, nor a person snoring.

She crept under the clothes, and flung her arms tightly round Miss Aldclyffe, as if for protection. Cytherea perceived that the lady's late peaceful warmth had given place to a sweat. At the maiden's touch, Miss Aldclyffe awoke with a low scream.

She remembered her position instantly. "Oh such a terrible dream!" she cried, in a hurried whisper, holding to Cytherea in her turn; "and your touch was the end of it. It was dreadful. Time, with his wings, hour-glass, and scythe, coming nearer and nearer to me— grinning and mocking: then he seized me, took a piece of me only. . . . But I can't tell you. I can't bear to think of it. How those dogs howl! People say it means death."*

The return of Miss Aldclyffe to consciousness was sufficient to dispel the wild fancies which the loneliness of the night had woven in Cytherea's mind. She dismissed the third noise as something which in all likelihood could easily be explained, if trouble were taken to inquire into it: large houses had all kinds of strange sounds floating about them. She was ashamed to tell Miss Aldclyffe her terrors.

A silence of five minutes.

"Are you asleep?" said Miss Aldclyffe.

"No," said Cytherea, in a long-drawn whisper.

"How those dogs howl, don't they?"

"Yes. A little dog in the house began it."

"Ah, yes: that was Totsy. He sleeps on the mat outside my father's bedroom door. A nervous creature."

There was a silent interval of nearly half-an-hour. A clock on the landing struck three.

"Are you asleep, Miss Aldclyffe?" whispered Cytherea.

"No," said Miss Aldclyffe. "How wretched it is not to be able to sleep, isn't it?"

"Yes," replied Cytherea, like a docile child.

Another hour passed, and the clock struck four. Miss Aldclyffe was still awake.

"Cytherea," she said, very softly.

Cytherea made no answer. She was sleeping soundly.

The first glimmer of dawn was now visible. Miss Aldclyffe arose, put on her dressing-robe, and went softly downstairs to her own room.

"I have not told her who I am after all, or found out the particulars of Ambrose's history," she murmured. "But her being in love alters everything."

§ 3. *Half-past seven to ten o'clock, a.m.*

Cytherea awoke, quiet in mind and refreshed. A conclusion to remain at Knapwater was already in possession of her.

Finding Miss Aldclyffe gone, she dressed herself and sat down at the window to write an answer to Edward's letter, and an account of her arrival at Knapwater to Owen. The dismal and heart-breaking pictures that Miss Aldclyffe had placed before her the preceding evening, the later terrors of the night, were now but as shadows of shadows, and she smiled in derision at her own excitability.

But writing Edward's letter was the great consoler, the effect of each word upon him being enacted in her own face as she wrote it. She felt how much she would like to share his trouble—how well she could endure poverty with him—and wondered what his trouble was. But all would be explained at last, she knew.

At the appointed time she went to Miss Aldclyffe's room, intending, with the contradictoriness common in people, to perform with pleasure, as a work of supererogation, what as a duty was simply intolerable.

Miss Aldclyffe was already out of bed. The bright penetrating light of morning made a vast difference in the elder lady's behaviour to her dependent; the day, which had restored Cytherea's judgment, had effected the same for Miss Aldclyffe. Though practical reasons forbade her regretting that she had secured such a companionable creature to read, talk, or play to her whenever her whim required, she was inwardly vexed at the extent to which she had indulged in the womanly luxury of making confidences and giving way to emotions. Few would have supposed that the calm lady sitting aristocratically at the toilet table, seeming scarcely conscious of Cytherea's presence in the room, even when greeting her, was the passionate creature who had asked for kisses a few hours before.

It is both painful and satisfactory to think how often these antitheses are to be observed in the individual most open to our observation—ourselves. We pass the evening with faces lit up by some flaring illumination or other: we get up the next morning—the fiery jets have all gone out, and nothing confronts us but a few crinkled pipes and sooty wirework, hardly even recalling the outline of the blazing picture that arrested our eyes before bedtime.

Emotions would be half starved if there were no candlelight. Probably nine-tenths of the gushing letters of indiscreet confidences are written after nine or ten o'clock in the evening, and sent off before day returns to leer invidiously upon them.* Few that remain open to catch our glance as we rise in the morning, survive the frigid criticism of dressing time.

The subjects uppermost in the minds of the two women who had thus cooled from their fires, were not the visionary ones of the later hours, but the hard facts of their earlier conversation. After a remark that Cytherea need not assist her in dressing unless she wished to, Miss Aldclyffe said, abruptly,—

"I can tell that young man's name." She looked keenly at Cytherea. "It is Edward Springrove, my tenant's son."

The inundation of colour upon the younger lady at hearing a name, which to her was a world, handled as if it were only an atom, told Miss Aldclyffe that she had divined the truth at last.

"Ah—it is he, is it?" she continued. "Well, I wanted to know for practical reasons. His example shows that I was not so far wrong in my estimate of men after all, though I only generalised, and had no thought of him." This was perfectly true.

"What do you mean?" said Cytherea, visibly alarmed.

"Mean? Why that all the world knows him to be engaged to be married, and that the wedding is soon to take place." She made the remark bluntly and superciliously, as if to obtain absolution at the hands of her family pride for the weak confidences of the night.

But even the frigidity of Miss Aldclyffe's morning mood was overcome by the look of sick and blank despair which the carelessly uttered words had produced upon Cytherea's face. She sank back into a chair, and buried her face in her hands.

"Don't be so foolish," said Miss Aldclyffe. "Come, make the best of it. I cannot upset the fact I have told you of, unfortunately. But I believe the match can be broken off."

"O no, no."

"Nonsense. I liked him much as a youth, and I like him now. I'll help you to captivate and chain him down. I have got over my absurd feeling of last night in not wanting you ever to go away from me—of course I could not expect such a thing as that. There, now I have said

I'll help you, and that's enough. He's tired of his first sweetheart now that he's been away from home for a while. The love which no outer attack can frighten away quails before its idol's own homely ways; 'tis always so . . . . . Come, finish what you are doing if you are going to, and don't be a little goose about such a trumpery affair as that."

"Who—is he engaged to?" Cytherea enquired by a movement of her lips but no sound of her voice. But Miss Aldclyffe did not answer. It mattered not, Cytherea thought. Another woman—that was enough for her: curiosity was stunned.

She applied herself to the work of dressing, scarcely knowing how. Miss Aldclyffe went on:—

"You were too easily won. I'd have made him or anybody else speak out before he should have kissed my face for his pleasure. But you are one of those precipitantly fond things who are yearning to throw away their hearts upon the first worthless fellow who says Good morning. In the first place, you shouldn't have loved him so quickly: in the next, if you must have loved him off-hand, you should have concealed it. It tickled his vanity: 'By Jove, that girl's in love with me already!' he thought."

To hasten away at the end of the toilet, to tell Mrs. Morris—who stood waiting in a little room prepared for her, with tea poured out, bread-and-butter cut into diaphanous slices, and eggs arranged—that she wanted no breakfast: then to shut herself alone in her bedroom, was her only thought. She was followed thither by the well-intentioned matron with a cup of tea and one piece of bread-and-butter on a tray, cheerfully insisting that she should eat it.

To those who grieve, innocent cheerfulness seems heartless levity. "No, thank you, Mrs. Morris," she said, keeping the door closed. Despite the incivility of the action, Cytherea could not bear to let a pleasant person see her face then.

Immediate revocation—even if revocation would be more effective by postponement—is the impulse of young wounded natures. Cytherea went to her blotting-book,* took out the long letter so carefully written, so full of gushing remarks and tender hints, and sealed up so neatly with a little seal bearing "Good Faith" as its motto, tore the missive into fifty pieces, and threw them into the grate. It was then the bitterest of anguishes to look upon some of the words she had so lovingly written, and see them existing only in mutilated forms without meaning—to feel that his eye would never read them, nobody ever know how ardently she had penned them.

Pity for one's self for being wasted is mostly present in these moods of abnegation.

The meaning of all his allusions, his abruptness in telling her of his love; his constraint at first, then his desperate manner of speaking, was clear. They must have been the last flickering of a conscience not quite dead to all sense of perfidiousness and fickleness. Now he had gone to London: she would be dismissed from his memory, in the same way as Miss Aldclyffe had said. And here she was in Edward's own parish, reminded continually of him by what she saw and heard. The landscape, yesterday so much and so bright to her, was now but as the banquet-hall deserted*—all gone but herself.

Miss Aldclyffe had wormed her secret out of her, and would now be continually mocking her for her trusting simplicity in believing him. It was altogether unbearable: she would not stay there.

She went downstairs and found that Miss Aldclyffe had gone into the breakfast-room, but that Captain Aldclyffe, who rose later with increasing infirmities, had not yet made his appearance. Cytherea entered. Miss Aldclyffe was looking out of the window, watching a trail of white smoke along the distant landscape—signifying a passing train. At Cytherea's entry she turned and looked enquiry.

"I must tell you now," began Cytherea, in a tremulous voice.

"Well, what?" Miss Aldclyffe said.

"I am not going to stay with you. I must go away—a very long way. I am very sorry, but indeed I can't remain!"

"Pooh—what shall we hear next?" Miss Aldclyffe surveyed Cytherea's face with leisurely criticism. "You are breaking your heart again about that worthless young Springrove. I knew how it would be. It is as Hallam says of Juliet—what little reason you may have possessed originally has all been whirled away by this love.* I shan't take this notice, mind."

"Do let me go?"

Miss Aldclyffe took her new pet's hand, and said with severity, "As to hindering you, if you are determined to go, of course that's absurd. But you are not now in a state of mind fit for deciding upon any such proceeding, and I shall not listen to what you have to say. Now, Cythie, come with me; we'll let this volcano burst and spend

itself, and after that we'll see what had better be done." She took
Cytherea into her workroom, opened a drawer, and drew forth a roll
of linen.

"This is some embroidery I began one day, and now I should like
it finished."

She then preceded the maiden upstairs to Cytherea's own room.
"There," she said, "now sit down here, go on with this work, and
remember one thing—that you are not to leave the room on any
pretext whatever for two hours unless I send for you—I insist kindly,
dear. Whilst you stitch—you are to stitch, recollect, and not go
mooning out of the window—think over the whole matter, and get
cooled; don't let the foolish love-affair prevent your thinking as a
woman of the world. If at the end of that time you still say you must
leave me, you may. I will have no more to say in the matter. Come, sit
down, and promise to sit here the time I name."

To hearts in a despairing mood, compulsion seems a relief; and
docility was at all times natural to Cytherea. She promised, and sat
down. Miss Aldclyffe shut the door upon her and retreated.

She sewed, stopped to think, shed a tear or two, recollected the
articles of the treaty, and sewed again; and at length fell into a reverie
which took no account whatever of the lapse of time.

§ 4. *Ten to twelve o'clock, a.m.*

A quarter of an hour might have passed when her thoughts became
attracted from the past to the present by unwonted movements
downstairs. She opened the door and listened.

There was hurrying along passages, opening and shutting of
doors, trampling in the stable-yard. She went across into another
bed-room from which a view of the stable-yard could be obtained,
and arrived there just in time to see the figure of the man who had
driven her from the station vanishing down the coach-road on a
black horse—galloping at the top of the animal's speed.

Another man went off in the direction of the village.

Whatever had occurred, it did not seem to be her duty to inquire
or meddle with it, stranger and dependent as she was, unless she
were requested to, especially after Miss Aldclyffe's strict charge to
her. She sat down again, determined to let no idle curiosity influence
her movements.

Her window commanded the front of the house; and the next thing she saw was a clergyman walk up and enter the door.

All was silent again till, a long time after the first man had left, he returned again on the same horse, now matted with sweat and trotting behind a carriage in which sat an elderly gentleman driven by a lad in livery. These came to the house, entered, and all was again the same as before.

The whole household—master, mistress, and servants—appeared to have forgotten the very existence of such a being as Cytherea. She almost wished she had not vowed to have no idle curiosity.

Half an hour later, the carriage drove off with the elderly gentleman, and two or three messengers left the house, speeding in various directions. Rustics in smock-frocks* began to hang about the road opposite the house, or lean against trees, looking idly at the windows and chimneys.

A tap came to Cytherea's door. She opened it to a young maid-servant.

"Miss Aldclyffe wishes to see you, ma'am." Cytherea hastened down.

Miss Aldclyffe was standing on the hearth-rug, her elbow on the mantel, her hand to her temples, her eyes on the ground; perfectly calm, but very pale.

"Cytherea," she said, in a whisper, "come here."

Cytherea went close.

"Something very serious has taken place," she said again, and then paused, with a tremulous movement of her mouth.

"Yes," said Cytherea.

"My father. He was found dead in his bed this morning."

"Dead!" echoed the younger woman. It seemed impossible that the announcement could be true: that knowledge of so great a fact could be contained in a statement so small.

"Yes, dead," murmured Miss Aldclyffe, solemnly. "He died alone, though within a few feet of me. The room we slept in is exactly over his own."

Cytherea said, hurriedly, "Do they know at what hour?"

"The doctor says it must have been between two and three o'clock this morning."

"Then I heard him!"

"Heard him?"

"Heard him die!"

"You heard him die? What did you hear?"

"A sound I had heard once before in my life—at the death-bed of my mother. I could not identify it—though I recognised it. Then the dog howled: you remarked it. I did not think it worth while to tell you what I had heard a little earlier." She looked agonised.

"It would have been useless," said Miss Aldclyffe. "All was over by that time." She addressed herself as much as Cytherea when she continued, "Is it a Providence who sent you here at this juncture that I might not be left entirely alone?"

Till this instant Miss Aldclyffe had forgotten the reason of Cytherea's seclusion in her own room. So had Cytherea herself. The fact now recurred to both in one moment.

"Do you still wish to go?" said Miss Aldclyffe, anxiously.

"I don't want to go now," Cytherea had remarked simultaneously with the other's question. She was pondering on the strange likeness which Miss Aldclyffe's bereavement bore to her own: it had the appearance of being still another call to her not to forsake this woman so linked to her life, for the sake of any trivial vexation.

Miss Aldclyffe held her almost as a lover would have held her, and said musingly,—

"We get more and more into one groove. I now am left fatherless and motherless as you were." Other ties lay behind in her thoughts, but she did not mention them.

"You loved your father, Cytherea, and wept for him?"

"Yes: I did. Poor papa!"

"I was always at variance with mine, and can't weep for him now! But you must stay here always and make a better woman of me."

The compact was thus sealed, and Cytherea, in spite of the failure of her advertisements was installed as a veritable Companion. And, once more in the history of human endeavour, a position which it was impossible to reach by any direct attempt, was come to by the seeker's swerving from the path, and regarding the original object as one of secondary importance.

CHAPTER VII

THE EVENTS OF EIGHTEEN DAYS

§ 1. *August the seventeenth*

The time of day was four o'clock in the afternoon. The place was the lady's study or boudoir, Knapwater House. The person was Miss Aldclyffe sitting there alone, clothed in deep mourning.

The funeral of the old Captain had taken place, and his will had been read. It was very concise, and had been executed about five years previous to his death. It was attested by his solicitors, Messrs. Nyttleton and Tayling, of Lincoln's-Inn-Fields. The whole of his estate real and personal, was bequeathed to his daughter Cytherea, for her sole and absolute use, subject only to the payment of a legacy to the rector, their relative, and a few small amounts to the servants.

Miss Aldclyffe had not chosen the easiest chair of her boudoir to sit in, or even a chair of ordinary comfort; but an uncomfortable, high, narrow-backed, oak-framed and seated chair, which was allowed to remain in the room only on the ground of being a companion in artistic quaintness to an old coffer beside it, and was never used except to stand in to reach for a book from the highest row of shelves. But she had sat erect in this chair for more than an hour, for the reason that she was utterly unconscious of what her actions and bodily feelings were. The chair had stood nearest her path on entering the room, and she had gone to it in a dream.

She sat in the attitude which denotes unflagging, intense, concentrated thought—as if she were cast in bronze. Her feet were together, her body bent a little forward, and quite unsupported by the back of the chair; her hands on her knees, her eyes fixed intently on the corner of a footstool.

At last she moved and tapped her fingers upon the table at her side. Her pent-up ideas had finally found some channel to advance in. Motions became more and more frequent as she laboured to carry farther and farther the problem which occupied her brain. She sat back and drew a long breath: she sat sideways and leant her forehead upon her hand. Later still she arose, walked up and down the room—at first abstractedly, with her features as firmly set as ever;

but by degrees her brow relaxed, her footsteps became lighter and more leisurely; her head rose gracefully and was no longer bowed. She plumed herself like a swan after exertion.

"Yes," she said aloud. "To get *him* here without letting him know that I have any other object than that of getting a useful man—that's the difficulty—and that I think I can master."

She rang for the new maid, a placid woman of forty, with a few grey hairs.

"Ask Miss Graye if she can come to me."

Cytherea was not far off, and came in.

"Do you know anything about architects and surveyors?" said Miss Aldclyffe, abruptly.

"Know anything?" replied Cytherea poising herself on her toe to consider the compass of the question.

"Yes—know anything," said Miss Aldclyffe.

"Owen is an architect and surveyor's clerk," the maiden said, and thought of somebody else who was likewise.

"Yes: that's why I asked you. What are the different kinds of work comprised in an architect's practice? They lay out estates, and superintend the various works done upon them, I should think, among other things?"

"Those are, more properly, a land or building steward's duties—at least I have always imagined so. Country architects include those things in their practice: city architects don't."

"I know that. But a steward's is an indefinite fast-and-loose profession, it seems to me. Shouldn't you think that a man who had been brought up as an architect would do for a steward?"

Cytherea had doubts whether an architect pure would do.

The chief pleasure connected with asking an opinion lies in not adopting it. Miss Aldclyffe replied decisively:

"Nonsense; of course he would. Your brother Owen makes plans for country buildings—such as cottages, stables, homesteads, and so on?"

"Yes; he does."

"And superintends the building of them?"

"Yes; he will soon."

"And he surveys land?"

"O yes."

"And he knows about hedges and ditches—how wide they ought to be, boundaries, levelling, planting trees to keep away the winds, measuring timber, houses for ninety-nine years, and such things?"

"I have never heard him say that; but I think Mr. Gradfield does those things. Owen, I am afraid, is inexperienced as yet."

"Yes; your brother is not old enough for such a post yet, of course. And then there are rent days, the audit and winding-up of tradesmen's accounts. I am afraid, Cytherea, you don't know much more about the matter than I do myself. . . . . I am going out just now," she continued. "I shall not want you to walk with me to-day. Run away till dinner-time."

Miss Aldclyffe went out of doors, and down the steps to the lawn; then turning to the right, through a shrubbery, she opened a wicket and passed into a neglected and leafy carriage-drive, leading down the hill. This she followed till she reached the point of its greatest depression, which was also the lowest ground in the whole grove.

The trees here were so interlaced, and hung their branches so near the ground, that a whole summer's day was scarcely long enough to change the air pervading the spot from its normal state of coolness to even a temporary warmth. The unvarying freshness was helped by the nearness of the ground to the level of the springs, and by the presence of a deep, sluggish stream close by, equally well shaded by bushes and a high wall. Following the road, which now ran along at the margin of the stream, she came to an opening in the wall, on the other side of the water, revealing a large rectangular nook from which the stream proceeded, covered with froth, and accompanied by a dull roar. Two more steps, and she was opposite the nook, in full view of the cascade forming its further boundary. Over the top could be seen the bright outer sky in the form of a crescent, caused by the curve of a bridge across the rapids, and the trees above.

Beautiful as was the scene she did not look in that direction. The same standing ground afforded another prospect, straight in the front, less sombre than the water on the right or the trees on the left. The avenue and grove which flanked it abruptly terminated a few yards ahead, where the ground began to rise, and on the remote edge of the greensward thus laid open, stood all that remained of the original manor-house, to which the dark marginal line of the trees in the avenue formed an adequate and well-fitting frame. It was the picture thus presented that was now interesting Miss Aldclyffe—not artistically or historically, but practically—as regarded its fitness for adaptation to modern requirements.

In front, detached from everything else, rose the most ancient portion of the structure—an old arched gateway, flanked by the bases of two small towers, and nearly covered with creepers, which had clambered over the eaves of the sinking roof, and up the gable to the crest of the Aldclyffe family perched on the apex. Behind this, at a distance of ten or twenty yards, came the only portion of the main building that still existed—an Elizabethan fragment, consisting of as much as could be contained under three gables and a cross roof* behind. Against the wall could be seen ragged lines indicating the form of other destroyed gables which had once joined it there. The mullioned and transomed windows, containing five or six lights,* were mostly bricked up to the extent of two or three, and the remaining portion fitted with cottage window frames carelessly inserted, to suit the purpose to which the old place was now applied, it being partitioned out into small rooms down-stairs to form cottages for two labourers and their families; the upper portion was arranged as a storehouse for divers kinds of roots and fruit.

The owner of the picturesque spot, after her survey from this point, went up to the walls and walked into the old court, where the paving stones were pushed sideways and upwards by the thrust of the grasses between them. Two or three little children, with their fingers in their mouths, came out to look at her, and then ran in to tell their mothers in loud tones of secrecy that Miss Aldclyffe was coming. Miss Aldclyffe, however, did not come in. She concluded her survey of the exterior by making a complete circuit of the building; then turned into a nook a short distance off, where round and square timber, a saw-pit,* planks, grindstones, heaps of building stone and brick, explained that this spot was the centre of operations for the building work done on the estate.

She paused, and looked around. A man who had seen her from the window of the workshops behind, came out and respectfully lifted his hat to her. It was the first time she had been seen walking outside the house since her father's death.

"Burden, could the Old House be made a decent residence of, without much trouble?" she inquired.

The tradesman considered, and spoke as each consideration completed itself.

"You don't forget, madam, that two-thirds of the place is already pulled down, or gone to ruin?"

"Yes; I know."

"And that what's left may almost as well be, madam."

"Why may it?"

" 'Twas so cut up inside when they made it into cottages, that the whole carcase is full of cracks."

"Still by pulling down the inserted partitions, and adding a little outside, it could be made to answer the purpose of an ordinary six or eight-roomed house?"

"Yes, madam."

"About what would it cost?" was the question which had invariably come next in every communication of this kind, to which the clerk of works had been a party during his whole experience. To his surprise, Miss Aldclyffe did not put it. The man thought her object in altering an old house must have been an unusually absorbing one not to prompt what was so instinctive in owners as hardly to require any prompting at all.

"Thank you: that's sufficient, Burden," she said. "You will understand that it is not unlikely some alteration may be made here in a short time, with reference to the management of affairs."

Burden said "Yes," in a complex voice, and looked uneasy.

"During the life of Captain Aldclyffe, with you as the foreman of works, and he himself as his own steward, everything worked well. But now it may be necessary to have a steward, whose management will encroach further upon things which have hitherto been left in your hands than did your late master's. What I mean is, that he will directly and in detail superintend all."

"Then—I shall not be wanted, madam?" he faltered.

"O yes; if you like to stay on as foreman in the yard and workshops only. I should be sorry to lose you. However, you had better consider. I will send for you in a few days."

Leaving him to suspense, and all the ills that came in its train, distracted application to his duties, and an undefined number of sleepless nights, and untasted dinners, Miss Aldclyffe looked at her watch and returned to the House. She was about to keep an appointment with her solicitor, Mr. Nyttleton, who had been to Creston, and was coming to Knapwater on his way back to London.

§ 2. *August the twentieth*

On the Saturday subsequent to Mr. Nyttleton's visit to Knapwater House, the subjoined advertisement appeared in the *Field* and the *Builder** newspapers:—

"LAND STEWARD.

"A gentleman of integrity and professional skill is required immediately for the MANAGEMENT of an ESTATE, containing about 800 acres, upon which agricultural improvements and the erection of buildings are contemplated. He must be a man of superior education, unmarried, and not more than thirty years of age. Considerable preference will be shown for one who possesses an artistic as well as a practical knowledge of planning and laying out. The remuneration will consist of a salary of £220, with the old manor-house as a residence. Address Messrs. Nyttleton and Tayling, solicitors, Lincoln's-Inn-Fields."

A copy of each paper was sent to Miss Aldclyffe on the day of publication. The same evening she told Cytherea that she was advertising for a steward, who would live at the old manor-house, showing her the papers containing the announcement.

What was the drift of that remark? thought the maiden; or was it merely made to her in confidential intercourse, as other arrangements were told her daily. Yet it seemed to have more meaning than common. She remembered the conversation about architects and surveyors, and her brother Owen. Miss Aldclyffe knew that his situation was precarious, that he was well educated and practical, and was applying himself heart and soul to the details of the profession and all connected with it. Miss Aldclyffe might be ready to take him if he could compete successfully with others who would reply. She hazarded a question:—

"Would it be desirable for Owen to answer it?"

"Not at all," said Miss Aldclyffe, peremptorily.

A flat answer of this kind had ceased to alarm Cytherea. Miss Aldclyffe's blunt mood was not her worst. Cytherea thought of another man, whose name, in spite of resolves, tears, renunciations and injured pride, lingered in her ears like an old familiar strain. That man was qualified for a stewardship under a king.

"Would it be of any use if Edward Springrove were to answer it?" she said, resolutely enunciating the name.

"None whatever," replied Miss Aldclyffe, again in the same decided tone.

"You are very unkind to speak in that way."

"Now don't pout like a goosie, as you are. I don't want men like either of them, for, of course, I must look to the good of the estate rather than to that of any individual. The man I want must have been more specially educated. I have told you that we are going to London next week; it is mostly on this account."

Cytherea thus found that she had mistaken the drift of Miss Aldclyffe's peculiar explicitness on the subject of advertising, and wrote to tell her brother that if he saw the notice it would be useless to reply.

§ 3. *August the twenty-fifth*

Five days after the above-mentioned dialogue took place they went to London, and, with scarcely a minute's pause, to the solicitor's offices in Lincoln's-Inn-Fields.*

They alighted opposite one of the characteristic entrances about the place—a gate which was never, and could never be, closed, flanked by lamp-standards carrying no lamp. Rust was the only active agent to be seen there at this time of the day and year. The palings along the front were rusted away at their base to the thinness of wires, and the successive coats of paint, with which they were overlaid in bygone days, had been completely undermined by the same insidious canker, which lifted off the paint in flakes, leaving the raw surface of the iron on palings, standards, and gate hinges, of a staring blood red.

But once inside the railings the picture changed. The court and offices were a complete contrast to the grand ruin of the outwork which enclosed them. Well-painted respectability extended over, within, and around the doorstep; and in the carefully swept yard not a particle of dust was visible.

Mr. Nyttleton, who had just come up from Margate, where he was staying with his family, was standing at the top of his own staircase as the pair ascended. He politely took them inside.

"Is there a comfortable room in which this young lady can sit during our interview?" said Miss Aldclyffe.

It was rather a favourite habit of hers to make much of Cytherea when they were out, and snub her for it afterwards when they got home.

"Certainly—Mr. Tayling's." Cytherea was shown into an inner room.

Social definitions are all made relatively: an absolute datum is only imagined. The small gentry about Knapwater seemed unpractised to Miss Aldclyffe, Miss Aldclyffe herself seemed unpractised to Mr. Nyttleton's experienced old eyes.

"Now then," the lady said, when she was alone with the lawyer; "what is the result of our advertisement?"

It was late summer: the estate-agency, building, engineering, and surveying worlds were dull. There were forty-five replies to the advertisement.

Mr. Nyttleton spread them one by one before Miss Aldclyffe. "You will probably like to read some of them yourself, madam?" he said.

"Yes, certainly," said she.

"I will not trouble you with those which are from persons manifestly unfit at first sight," he continued; and began selecting from the heap twos and threes which he had marked, collecting others into his hand. "The man we want lies among these, if my judgment doesn't deceive me, and from them it would be advisable to select a certain number to be communicated with."

"I should like to see every one—only just to glance them over—exactly as they came," she said, suasively.

He looked as if he thought this a waste of his time, but dismissing his sentiment unfolded each singly and laid it before her. As he laid them out, it struck him that she studied them quite as rapidly as he could spread them. He slyly glanced up from the outer corner of his eye to hers, and noticed that all she did was look at the name at the bottom of the letter, and then put the enclosure aside without further ceremony. He thought this an odd way of enquiring into the merits of forty-five men who at considerable trouble gave in detail reasons why they believed themselves well qualified for a certain post. She came to the final one, and put it down with the rest.

Then the lady said that in her opinion it would be best to get as many replies as they possibly could before selecting—"to give us a wider choice. What do you think, Mr. Nyttleton?"

It seemed to him, he said, that a greater number than those they already had would scarcely be necessary, and if they waited for more, there would be this disadvantage attending it, that some of those they now could command would possibly not be available.

"Never mind, we will run that risk," said Miss Aldclyffe. "Let the advertisement be inserted once more, and then we will certainly settle the matter."

Mr. Nyttleton bowed, and seemed to think Miss Aldclyffe, for a single woman, and one who till so very recently had never concerned herself with business of any kind, a very meddlesome client. But she was rich, and handsome still. "She's a new broom in estate-management as yet," he thought. "She will soon get tired of this," and he parted from her without a sentiment which could mar his habitual blandness.

The two ladies then proceeded westward. Dismissing the cab in Waterloo Place, they went along Pall Mall on foot, where in place of the usual well-dressed clubbists*—rubicund with alcohol—were to be seen in linen pinafores, flocks of house-painters pallid from white lead. When they had reached the Green Park, Cytherea proposed that they should sit down awhile under the young elms at the brow of the hill. This they did—the growl of Piccadilly on their left hand—the monastic seclusion of the Palace on their right: before them, the clock tower of the Houses of Parliament, standing forth with a metallic lustre against a livid Lambeth sky.

Miss Aldclyffe still carried in her hand a copy of the newspaper, and while Cytherea had been interesting herself in the picture around, glanced again at the advertisement.

She heaved a slight sigh, and began to fold it up again. In the action her eye caught sight of two consecutive advertisements on the cover, one relating to some lecture on Art, and addressed to members of the Society of Architects.* The other emanated from the same source, but was addressed to the public, and stated that the exhibition of drawings at the Society's rooms would close at the end of that week.

Her eye lighted up. She sent Cytherea back to the hotel in a cab, then turned round by Piccadilly into Bond Street, and proceeded to the rooms of the Society. The secretary was sitting in the lobby. After making her payment, and looking at a few of the drawings on the walls, in the company of three gentlemen, the only other visitors to the exhibition, she turned back and asked if she might be allowed to see a list of the members. She was a little connected with the architectural world, she said, with a smile, and was interested in some of the names.

"Here it is, madam," he replied, politely handing her a pamphlet containing the names.

Miss Aldclyffe turned the leaves till she came to the letter M. The name she hoped to find there was there, with the address appended, as was the case with all the rest.

The address was at some chambers in a street not far from Charing Cross. "Chambers" as a residence, had always been assumed by the lady to imply the condition of a bachelor. She murmured two words, "There still."

Another request had yet to be made, but it was of a more noticeable kind than the first, and might compromise the secrecy with which she wished to act throughout this episode. Her object was to get one of the envelopes lying on the secretary's table, stamped with the die of the Society; and in order to get it she was about to ask if she might write a note.

But the secretary's back chanced to be turned, and he now went towards one of the men at the other end of the room, who had called him to ask some question relating to an etching on the wall. Quick as thought, Miss Aldclyffe stood before the table, slipped her hand behind her, took one of the envelopes and put it in her pocket.

She sauntered round the rooms for two or three minutes longer, then withdrew and returned to her hotel.

Here she cut the Knapwater advertisement from the paper, put it into the envelope she had stolen, embossed with the society's stamp, and directed it in a round clerkly hand to the address she had seen in the list of members' names submitted to her:—

> ÆNEAS MANSTON, ESQ.,*
> WYKEHAM CHAMBERS,
> SPRING GARDENS.

This ended her first day's work in London.

§4. *From August the twenty-sixth to September the first*

The two Cythereas continued at the Westminster Hotel, Miss Aldclyffe informing her companion that business would detain them in

London another week. The days passed as slowly and drearily as days can pass in a city at that time of the year, the shuttered windows about the squares and terraces confronting their eyes like the white and sightless orbs of a blind man. On Thursday Mr. Nyttleton called, bringing the whole number of replies to the advertisement. Cytherea was present at the interview, by Miss Aldclyffe's request—either from whim or design.

Ten additional letters were the result of the second week's insertion, making fifty-five in all. Miss Aldclyffe looked them over as before. One was signed—

ÆNEAS MANSTON,
133, Durngate Street,
Liverpool.

"Now then, Mr. Nyttleton, will you make a selection, and I will add one or two," Miss Aldclyffe said.

Mr. Nyttleton scanned the whole heap of letters, testimonials, and references, sorting them into two heaps. Manston's missive, after a mere glance, was thrown amongst the summarily rejected ones.

Miss Aldclyffe read, or pretended to read after the lawyer. When he had finished, five lay in the group he had selected. "Would you like to add to the number?" he said, turning to the lady.

"No," she said, carelessly. "Well, two or three additional ones rather took my fancy," she added, searching for some in the larger collection.

She drew out three. One was Manston's.

"These eight, then, shall be communicated with," said the lawyer, taking up the eight letters and placing them by themselves.

They stood up. "If I myself, madam, were only concerned personally," he said, in an off-hand way, and holding up a letter singly; "I should choose this man unhesitatingly. He writes honestly, is not afraid to name what he does not consider himself well acquainted with—a rare thing to find in answers to advertisements; he is well recommended, and possesses some qualities rarely found in combination. Oddly enough, he is not really a steward. He was bred a farmer, studied building affairs, served on an estate for some time, then went with an architect, and is now well qualified as architect, estate agent, and surveyor. That man is sure to have a fine head for a manor like yours." He tapped the letter as he spoke. "Yes, I should choose him without hesitation—speaking personally."

"And I think," she said, artificially, "I should choose this one as a matter of mere personal whim, which, of course, can't be given way to when practical questions have to be considered."

Cytherea, after looking out of the window, and then at the newspapers, had become interested in the proceedings between the clever Miss Aldclyffe and the keen old lawyer, which reminded her of a game at cards. She looked inquiringly at the two letters—one in Miss Aldclyffe's hand, the other in Mr. Nyttleton's.

"What is the name of your man?" said Miss Aldclyffe.

"His name—" said the lawyer, looking down the page; "What is his name—it is Edward Springrove."

Miss Aldclyffe glanced towards Cytherea, who was getting red and pale by turns. She looked imploringly at Miss Aldclyffe.

"The name of my man," said Miss Aldclyffe, looking at her letter in turn; "is, I think—yes—Æneas Manston."

§ 5. *September the third*

The next morning but one was appointed for the interviews, which were to be at the lawyer's offices. Mr. Nyttleton and Mr. Tayling were both in town for the day, and the candidates were admitted one by one into a private room. In the window recess was seated Miss Aldclyffe, wearing her veil down.

The lawyer had, in his letters to the selected number, timed each candidate at an interval of ten or fifteen minutes from those preceding and following. They were shown in as they arrived, and had short conversations with Mr. Nyttleton—terse, and to the point. Miss Aldclyffe neither moved nor spoke during this proceeding; it might have been supposed that she was quite unmindful of it, had it not been for what was revealed by a keen penetration of the veil covering her countenance—the rays from two bright black eyes, directed towards the lawyer and his interlocutor.

Springrove came fifth; Manston seventh. When the examination of all was ended, and the last man had retired, Nyttleton, again as at the former time, blandly asked his client which of the eight she personally preferred. "I still think the fifth we spoke to, Springrove, the man whose letter I pounced upon at first, to be by far the best qualified, in short, most suitable generally."

"I am sorry to say that I differ from you; I lean to my first notion still—that Mr.—Mr. Manston is most desirable in tone and bearing, and even specifically, I think he would suit me best in the long run."

Mr. Nyttleton looked out of the window at the whitened wall of the court.

"Of course, madam, your opinion may be perfectly sound and reliable; a sort of instinct, I know, often leads ladies by a short cut to conclusions truer than those come to by men after laborious round-about calculations, based on long experience. I must say I shouldn't recommend him."

"Why, pray?"

"Well, let us look first at his letter of answer to the advertisement. He didn't reply till the last insertion; that's one thing. His letter is bold and frank in tone, so bold and frank that the second thought after reading it is that not honesty, but unscrupulousness of con-science dictated it. It is written in an indifferent mood, as if he felt that he was humbugging us in his statement that he was the right man for such an office, that he tried hard to get it only as a matter of form which required that he should neglect no opportunity that came in his way."

"You may be right, Mr. Nyttleton, but I don't quite see the grounds of your reasoning."

"He has been, as you perceive, almost entirely used to the office duties of a city architect, the experience we don't want. You want a man whose acquaintance with rural landed properties is more prac-tical and closer—somebody who, if he has not filled exactly such an office before, has lived a country life, knows the ins and outs of country tenancies, building, farming, and so on."

"He's by far the most intellectual looking of them all."

"Yes; he may be—your opinion, madam, is worth more than mine in that matter. And more than you say, he is a man of parts—his brain-power would soon enable him to master details and fit him for the post, I don't much doubt that. But to speak clearly" (here his words started off at a jog-trot) "I wouldn't run the risk of placing the management of an estate of mine in his hands on any account what-ever. There, that's flat and plain, madam."

"But, definitely," she said, with a show of impatience; "what is your reason?"

"He is a voluptuary with activity;* which is a very bad form of man—as bad as it is rare."

"Oh. Thank you for your explicit statement, Mr. Nyttleton," said Miss Aldclyffe, starting a little and flushing with displeasure.

Mr. Nyttleton nodded slightly, as a sort of neutral motion, simply signifying a receipt of the information, good or bad.

"And I really think it is hardly worth while to trouble you further in this," continued the lady. "He's quite good enough for a little insignificant place like mine at Knapwater; and I know that I could not get on with one of the others for a single month. We'll try him."

"Certainly, madam," said the lawyer. And Mr. Manston was written to, to the effect that he was the successful competitor.

"Did you see how unmistakeably her temper was getting the better of her, that minute you were in the room?" said Nyttleton to Tayling, when their client had left the house. Nyttleton was a man who surveyed everybody's character in a sunless and shadowless northern light. A culpable slyness, which marked him as a boy, had been moulded by Time, the Improver, into honourable circumspection.

We frequently find that the quality which, conjoined with the simplicity of the child, is vice, is virtue when it pervades the knowledge of the man.

"She was as near as damn-it to boiling over when I added up her man," continued Nyttleton. "His handsome face is his qualification in her eyes. They have met before; I saw that."

"He didn't seem conscious of it," said the junior.

"He didn't. That was rather puzzling to me. But still, if ever a woman's face spoke out plainly that she was in love with a man, hers did that she was with him. Poor old maid, she's almost old enough to be his mother. If that Manston's a schemer he'll marry her, as sure as I am Nyttleton. Let's hope he's honest, however."

"I don't think she's in love with him," said Tayling. He had seen but little of the pair, and yet he could not reconcile what he had noticed in Miss Aldclyffe's behaviour with the idea that it was the bearing of a woman towards her lover.

"Well, your experience of the fiery phenomenon is more recent than mine," rejoined Nyttleton carelessly. "And you may remember the nature of it best."

CHAPTER VIII

THE EVENTS OF EIGHTEEN DAYS

§ 1. *From the third to the nineteenth of September*

Miss Aldclyffe's tenderness towards Cytherea, between the hours of her irascibility, increased till it became no less than doting fondness. Like Nature in the tropics, with her hurricanes and the subsequent luxuriant vegetation effacing their ravages, Miss Aldclyffe compensated for her outbursts by excess of generosity afterwards. She seemed to be completely won out of herself by close contact with a young woman whose modesty was absolutely unimpaired, and whose artlessness was as perfect as was compatible with the complexity necessary to produce the due charm of womanhood. Cytherea, on her part, perceived with honest satisfaction that her influence for good over Miss Aldclyffe was considerable. Ideas and habits peculiar to the younger, which the elder lady had originally imitated in a mere whim, she grew in course of time to take a positive delight in. Among others were evening and morning prayers, dreaming over out-door scenes, learning a verse from some poem whilst dressing.

Yet try to force her sympathies as much as she would, Cytherea could feel no more than thankful for this, even if she always felt as much as that. The mysterious cloud hanging over the past life of her companion, of which the uncertain light already thrown upon it only seemed to render still darker the unpenetrated remainder, nourished in her a feeling which was scarcely too slight to be called dread. She would have infinitely preferred to be treated distantly, as the mere dependent, by such a changeable nature—like a fountain, always herself, yet always another. That a crime of any deep dye had ever been perpetrated or participated in by her namesake, she would not believe; but the reckless adventuring of the lady's youth seemed connected with deeds of darkness rather than light.

Sometimes Miss Aldclyffe appeared to be on the point of making some absorbing confidence, but reflection invariably restrained her. Cytherea hoped that such a confidence would come with time, and that she might thus be a means of soothing a mind which had obviously known extreme suffering.

But Miss Aldclyffe's reticence concerning her past was not imitated by Cytherea. Though she never disclosed the one fact of her knowledge that the love-suit between Miss Aldclyffe and her father terminated abnormally, the maiden's natural ingenuousness on subjects not set down for special guard had enabled Miss Aldclyffe to worm from her, fragment by fragment, every detail of her father's history. Cytherea saw how deeply Miss Aldclyffe sympathised—and it compensated her, to some extent, for the hasty resentments of other times.

Thus uncertainly she lived on. It was perceived by the servants of the House, that some secret bond of connexion existed between Miss Aldclyffe and her companion. But they were woman and woman, not woman and man,* the facts were ethereal and refined, and so they could not be worked up into a taking story. Whether, as critics dispute, a supernatural machinery be necessary to an epic or no, a carnal plot* is decidedly necessary to a scandal.

Another letter had come to her from Edward—very short, but full of entreaty, asking why she would not write just one line—just one line of cold friendship at least? She then allowed herself to think, little by little, whether she had not perhaps been too harsh with him; and at last wondered if he were really much to blame for being engaged to another woman. "Ah, Brain, there is one in me stronger than you!" she said. The young maid now continually pulled out his letter, read it and re-read it, almost crying with pity the while, to think what wretched suspense he must be enduring at her silence, till her heart chid her for her cruelty. She felt that she must send him a line—one little line—just a wee line to keep him alive, poor thing; sighing like Donna Clara:—

> "Ah, were he now before me,
> In spite of injured pride,
> I fear my eyes would pardon
> Before my tongue could chide."*

§2. *September the twentieth. Three to four, p.m.*

It was the third week in September, about five weeks after Cytherea's arrival, when Miss Aldclyffe requested her one day to go through the village of Carriford and assist herself in collecting the subscriptions made by some of the inhabitants of the parish to a religious society she patronised. Miss Aldclyffe formed one of what was called a Ladies' Association, each member of which collected tributary streams of shillings from her inferiors, to add to her own pound at the end.

Miss Aldclyffe took particular interest in Cytherea's appearance that afternoon, and the object of her attention was, indeed, gratifying to look at. The sight of the lithe girl, set off by an airy dress, coquettish jacket, flexible hat, a ray of starlight in each eye and a war of lilies and roses* in each cheek, was a palpable pleasure to the mistress of the mansion, yet a pleasure which appeared to partake less of the nature of affectionate satisfaction than of mental gratification.

Eight names were printed in the report as belonging to Miss Aldclyffe's list, with the amount of subscription-money attached to each.

"I will collect the first four, whilst you do the same with the last four," said Miss Aldclyffe.

The names of two tradespeople stood first in Cytherea's share: then came a Miss Hinton: last of all in the printed list was Mr. Springrove the elder. Underneath his name was pencilled, in Miss Aldclyffe's handwriting, "Mr. Manston."

Manston had arrived on the estate, in the capacity of steward, three or four days previously, and occupied the old manor-house, which had been altered and repaired for his reception.

"Call on Mr. Manston," said the lady, impressively, looking at the name written under Cytherea's portion of the list.

"But he does not subscribe yet?"

"I know it; but call and leave him a report. Don't forget it."

"Say you would be pleased if he would subscribe?"

"Yes—say I should be pleased if he would," repeated Miss Aldclyffe, smiling. "Good-bye. Don't hurry in your walk. If you can't get easily through your task to-day put off some of it till to-morrow."

Each then started on her rounds: Cytherea going in the first place to the old manor-house. Mr. Manston was not indoors, which was a relief to her. She called then on the two gentleman-farmers' wives, who soon transacted their business with her, frigidly indifferent to her personality. A person who socially is nothing is thought less of by people who are not much than by those who are a great deal.*

She then turned towards Peakhill Cottage, the residence of Miss

Hinton, who lived there happily enough, with an elderly servant and a house-dog as companions. Her father, and last remaining parent, had retired thither four years before this time, after having filled the post of editor to the *Froominster Chronicle* for eighteen or twenty years. There he died soon after, and though comparatively a poor man, he left his daughter sufficiently well provided for as a modest fundholder and claimant of sundry small sums in dividends to maintain herself as mistress at Peakhill.

At Cytherea's knock an inner door was heard to open and close, and footsteps crossed the passage hesitatingly. The next minute Cytherea stood face to face with the lady herself.

Adelaide Hinton was about nine-and-twenty years of age. Her hair was plentiful, like Cytherea's own; her teeth equalled Cytherea's in regularity and whiteness. But she was much paler, and had features too transparent to be in place among household surroundings. Her mouth expressed love less forcibly than Cytherea's, and, as a natural result of her greater maturity, her tread was less elastic, and she was more self-possessed.

She had been a girl of that kind which mothers praise as not forward, by way of contrast, when disparaging those nobler ones with whom loving is an end and not a means. Men of forty, too, said of her, "a good sensible wife for any man, if she cares to marry," the caring to marry being thrown in as the vaguest hypothesis, because she was so practical. Yet it would be singular if, in such cases, the important subject of marriage should be excluded from manipulation by hands that are ready for practical performance in every domestic concern besides.

Cytherea was an acquisition, and the greeting was hearty.

"Good afternoon! O yes—Miss Graye, from Miss Aldclyffe's. I have seen you at church, and I am so glad you have called! Come in. I wonder if I have change enough to pay my subscription." She spoke girlishly.

Adelaide, when in the company of a younger woman, always levelled herself down to that younger woman's age from a sense of justice to herself—as if, though not her own age at common law, it was in equity.

"It doesn't matter. I'll come again."

"Yes, do at any time; not only on this errand. But you must step in for a minute. Do."

"I have been wanting to, for several weeks."

"That's right. Now you must see my house—lonely, isn't it, for a single lady? People said it was odd for a young woman like me to keep on a house; but what did I care? If you knew the pleasure of locking up your own door, with the sensation that you reigned supreme inside it, you would say it was worth the risk of being called odd. Mr. Springrove attends to my gardening, the dog attends to robbers, and whenever there is a snake or toad to kill, Jane does it."

"How nice. It is better than living in a town."

"Far better. A town makes a cynic of me."

The remark recalled, somewhat startlingly, to Cytherea's mind, that Edward had used those very words to herself one evening at Creston.

Miss Hinton opened an interior door and led her visitor into a small drawing-room commanding a view of the country for miles.

The missionary business was soon settled; but the chat continued.

"How lonely it must be here at night," said Cytherea. "Aren't you afraid?"

"At first, I was slightly. But I got used to the solitude. And you know a sort of common-sense will creep even into timidity. I say to myself sometimes at night, 'If I were anybody but a harmless woman, not worth the trouble of a worm's ghost to appear to me, I should think that every sound I hear was a spirit.' But you must see all over my house."

Cytherea was very interested in seeing.

"I say you *must* do this, and you *must* do that, as if you were a child," remarked Adelaide. "A privileged friend of mine tells me this use of the imperative comes of being so constantly in nobody's society but my own."

"Ah, yes. I suppose she is right."

Cytherea called the friend "she" by a rule of lady-like practice; for a woman's "friend" is delicately assumed by another friend to be of their own sex in the absence of knowledge to the contrary; just as cats are called shes until they prove themselves hes.

Miss Hinton laughed mysteriously.

"I get a humorous reproof for it now and then, I assure you," she continued.

" 'Humorous reproof:' that's not from a woman: who can reprove humorously but a man?" was the groove of Cytherea's thought at the remark. "Your brother reproves you, I expect," said that innocent young lady.

"No," said Miss Hinton, with a candid air. " 'Tis only a gentleman I am acquainted with." She looked out of the window.

Women are persistently imitative. No sooner did a thought flash through Cytherea's mind that the gentleman was a lover than she became a Miss Aldclyffe in a mild form.

"I imagine he's a sweetheart," she said.

Miss Hinton smiled a smile of experience in that line.

Few women, if taxed with having an admirer, are so free from vanity as to deny the impeachment, even if it is utterly untrue. When it does happen to be true, they look pityingly away from the person who is so benighted as to have got no farther than suspecting it.

"There now—Miss Hinton; you are engaged to be married!" said Cytherea, accusingly.

Adelaide nodded her head practically. "Well yes, I am," she said.

The word "engaged" had no sooner passed Cytherea's lips than the sound of it—the mere sound by her own lips—carried her mind to the time and circumstances under which Miss Aldclyffe had used it towards herself. A sickening thought followed—based but on a mere surmise; yet its presence took every other idea away from Cytherea's mind. Miss Hinton had used Edward's words about towns; she mentioned Mr. Springrove as attending to her garden. It could not be that Edward was the man! that Miss Aldclyffe had planned to reveal her rival thus!

"Are you going to be married soon?" she inquired, with a steadiness the result of a sort of fascination, but apparently of indifference.

"Not very soon—still, soon."

"Ah—ha. In less than three months?" said Cytherea.

"Two."

Now that the subject was well in hand, Adelaide wanted no more prompting. "You won't tell anybody if I show you something?" she said with eager mystery.

"O no, nobody. But does he live in this parish?"

"No."

Nothing proved yet.

"What's his name?" said Cytherea, flatly. Her breath and heart had begun their old tricks, and came and went hotly. Miss Hinton could not see her face.

"What do you think?" said Miss Hinton.

"George?" said Cytherea, with deceitful agony.

"No," said Adelaide. "But now, you shall see him first; come here;" and she led the way upstairs into her bed-room. There, standing on the dressing-table in a little frame, was the unconscious portrait of Edward Springrove.

"There he is," Miss Hinton said, and a silence ensued.

"Are you very fond of him?" continued the miserable Cytherea at length.

"Yes, of course I am," her companion replied, but in the tone of one who lived in Abraham's bosom all the year,* and was therefore untouched by solemn thought at the fact. "He's my cousin—a native of this village. We were engaged before my father's death left me so lonely. I was only twenty, and a much greater belle than I am now. We know each other thoroughly as you may imagine. I give him a little sermonising now and then."

"Why?"

"O it's only in fun. He's very naughty sometimes—not really you know—but he will look at any pretty face when he sees it."

Storing up this statement of his susceptibility as another item to be miserable upon when she had time, "How do you know that?" Cytherea asked, with a swelling heart.

"Well, you know how things do come to women's ears. He used to live at Creston as an assistant-architect, and I found out that a young giddy thing of a girl, who lives there somewhere, took his fancy for a day or two. But I don't feel jealous at all—our engagement is so matter-of-fact that neither of us can be jealous. And it was a mere flirtation—she was too silly for him. He's fond of rowing, and kindly gave her an airing for an evening or two. I'll warrant they talked the most unmitigated rubbish under the sun—all shallowness and pastime, just as everything is at watering-places—neither of them caring a bit for the other—she giggling like a goose all the time——"

Concentrated essence of woman pervaded the room rather than air. "She didn't! and 'twasn't shallowness!" Cytherea burst out with brimming eyes. " 'Twas deep deceit on one side, and entire confidence on the other—yes, it was!" The pent-up emotion had swollen and swollen inside the young thing till the dam could no longer embay it. The instant the words were out she would have given worlds to have been able to recall them.

"Do you know her—or him?" said Miss Hinton, starting with suspicion at the warmth shown.

The two women had now lost their personality quite. There was the same keen brightness of eye, the same movement of the mouth, the same mind in both, as they looked doubtingly and excitedly at each other. As is invariably the case with women where a man they care for is the subject of an excitement among them, the situation abstracted the differences which distinguished them as individuals, and left only the properties common to them as atoms of a sex.

Cytherea caught at the chance afforded her of not betraying herself. "Yes, I know her," she said.

"Well," said Miss Hinton, "I am really vexed if my speaking so lightly of any friend of yours has hurt your feelings, but——"

"O never mind," Cytherea returned; "It doesn't matter, Miss Hinton. I think I must leave you now. I have to call at other places. Yes—I must go."

Miss Hinton, in a perplexed state of mind, showed her visitor politely down stairs to the door. Here Cytherea bade her a hurried adieu, and flitted down the garden into the lane.

She persevered in her duties with a wayward pleasure in giving herself misery, as was her wont. Mr. Springrove's name was next on the list, and she turned towards his dwelling, the Three Tranters Inn.

§ 3. *Four to five, p.m.*

The cottages along Carriford village street were not so close but that on one side or other of the road was always a hedge of hawthorn or privet, over or through which could be seen gardens or orchards rich with produce. It was about the middle of the early apple-harvest, and the laden trees were shaken at intervals by the gatherers; the soft pattering of the falling crop upon the grassy ground being diversified by the loud rattle of vagrant ones upon a rail, hencoop, basket, or lean-to roof, or upon the rounded and stooping backs of the collectors—mostly children, who would have cried bitterly at receiving such a smart blow from any other quarter, but smilingly assumed it to be but fun in apples.

The Three Tranters Inn, a many-gabled, mediæval building, constructed almost entirely of timber, plaster, and thatch, stood close to the line of the roadside, almost opposite the churchyard, and was connected with a row of cottages on the left by thatched outbuildings. It was an uncommonly characteristic and handsome specimen of the genuine roadside inn of bygone times; and standing on the great highway to the South-west of England, (which ran through Carriford), had in its time been the scene of as much of what is now looked upon as the romantic and genial experience of stage-coach travelling as any halting-place in the country. The railway had absorbed the whole stream of traffic which formerly flowed through the village* and along by the ancient door of the inn, reducing the empty-handed landlord, who used only to farm a few fields at the back of the house, to the necessity of eking out his attenuated income by increasing the extent of his agricultural business if he would still maintain his social standing. Next to the general stillness pervading the spot, the long line of outbuildings adjoining the house was the most striking and saddening witness to the passed-away fortunes of the Three Tranters Inn. It was the bulk of the original stabling, and where once the hoofs of two-score horses had daily rattled over the stony yard, to and from the stalls within, thick grass now grew, whilst the line of roofs—once so straight—over the decayed stalls, had sunk into vast hollows till they seemed like the cheeks of toothless age.

On a green plot at the other end of the building grew two or three large, wide spreading elm trees, from which the sign was suspended—representing the three men called tranters (irregular carriers), standing side by side, and exactly alike to a hair's breadth, the grain of the wood and joints of the boards being visible through the thin paint depicting their forms, which were still further disfigured by red stains running downwards from the rusty nails above.

Under the trees now stood a cider-mill and press, and upon the spot sheltered by the boughs were gathered Mr. Springrove himself, his men, the parish clerk, two or three other men, grinders and supernumeraries, a woman with an infant in her arms, a flock of pigeons, and some little boys with straws in their mouths, endeavouring, whenever the men's backs were turned, to get a sip of the sweet juice issuing from the vat.

Edward Springrove the elder, the landlord, now more particularly a farmer, and for two months in the year a cider-maker, was an employer of labour of the old school, who worked himself among his men. He was now engaged in packing the pomace* into horsehair bags with a rammer,* and Gad Weedy, his man, was occupied in shovelling up more from a tub at his side. The shovel shone like silver from the action of the juice, and ever and anon, in its motion to and fro, caught the rays of the declining sun and reflected them in bristling stars of light.

Mr. Springrove had been too young a man when the pristine days of the Three Tranters had departed for ever to have much of the host left in him now. He was a poet with a rough skin: one whose sturdiness was more the result of external circumstances than of intrinsic nature. Too kindly constitutioned to be very provident, he was yet not imprudent. He had a quiet humorousness of disposition, not out of keeping with a frequent melancholy, the general expression of his countenance being one of abstraction. Like Walt Whitman he felt as his years increased,

> "I foresee too much; it means more than I thought."*

On the present occasion he wore gaiters and a leathern apron, and worked with his shirt sleeves rolled up beyond his elbows, disclosing solid and fleshy rather than muscular arms. They were stained by the cider, and two or three brown apple-pips from the pomace he was handling were to be seen sticking on them here and there among the hairs.

The other prominent figure was that of Richard Crickett, the parish clerk, a kind of Bowdlerized rake,* who ate only the quantity of a woman, and had the rheumatism in his left hand. The remainder of the group, brown-faced peasants, wore smock-frocks embroidered on the shoulders with hearts and diamonds, and were girt round their middle with a strap, another being worn round the right wrist.

"And have you seen the steward, Mr. Springrove?" said the clerk.

"Just a glimpse of him; but 'twas just enough to show me that he's not here for long."

"Why m't that be?"

"He'll never stand the vagaries of the female figure holden the reins—not he."

"She d' pay en well," said a grinder;* "and money's money."

"Ah—'tis: very much so," the clerk replied.

"Yes, yes, naibour Crickett," said Springrove, "but she'll flee in a passion—all the fat will be in the fire—and there's an end. . . . . Yes, she is a one," continued the farmer, resting, raising his eyes, and reading the features of a distant apple.

"She is," said Gad, resting too (it is wonderful how prompt a journeyman is in following his master's initiative to rest) and reflectively regarding the ground in front of him.

"True: a one is she," the clerk chimed in, shaking his head ominously.

"She has such a temper," said the farmer, "and is so wilful too. You may as well try to stop a footpath* as stop her when she has taken anything into her head. I'd as soon grind little green crabs* all day as live wi' her."

" 'Tis a temper she hev, 'tis," the clerk replied, "though I be a servant of the church that say it. But she isn't goen to flee in a passion this time."

The company waited for the continuation of the speech, as if they knew from experience the exact distance off it lay in the future.

The clerk swallowed nothing as if it were a great deal, and then went on, "There's some'at between them: mark my words, naibours—there's some'at between 'em."

"D'ye mean it?"

"I d' know it. He came last Saturday, didn't he."

" 'A did, truly," said Gad Weedy, at the same time taking an apple from the hopper* of the mill, eating a piece, and flinging back the remainder to be ground up for cider.

"He went to church a-Sunday," said the clerk again.

" 'A did."

"And she kept her eye upon en all the service, her face flickeren between red and white, but never stoppen at either."

Mr. Springrove nodded, and went to the press.

"Well," said the clerk, "you don't call her the kind o' woman to make mistakes in just trotten through the weekly service o' God? Why, as a rule she's as right as I be myself."

Mr. Springrove nodded again, and gave a twist to the screw of the press, followed in the movement by Gad at the other side; the two grinders expressing by looks of the greatest concern that, if Miss Aldclyffe were as right at church as the clerk, she must be right indeed.

"Yes, as right in the service o' God as I be myself," repeated the clerk, adding length to such a solemn sound, like St. Cecilia.* "But last Sunday, when we were in the tenth commandment, says she, 'Incline our hearts to keep this law,' says she, when 'twas 'Laws in our hearts we beseech thee,'* all the church through. Her eye was upon *him*—she was quite lost—'Hearts to keep this law,' says she; she was no more than a mere shadder at that tenth time—a mere shadder. You mi't ha' mouthed across to her 'Laws in our hearts we beseech thee,' fifty times over—she'd never ha' noticed ye. She's in love wi' the man, that's what she is."

"Then she's a bigger stunpoll* than I took her for," said Mr. Springrove. "Why she's old enough to be his mother."

"The row 'ill be between her and that young Curly-wig, you'll see. She won't run the risk of that pretty face beën near."

"Clerk Crickett, I d' fancy you d' know everything about everybody," said Gad.

"Well so's," said the clerk modestly. "I do know a little. It comes to me."

"And I d' know where from."

"Ah."

"That wife o' thine. She's an entertainen woman, not to speak disrespectfully."

"She is: and a winnen one. Look at the husbands she've had— God bless her!"

"I wonder you could stand third in that list, Clerk Crickett," said Mr. Springrove.

"Well, 't has been a power o' marvel to myself oftentimes. Yes, matrimony d' begin 'Dearly beloved,' and ends wi' 'Amazement,'* as the prayer book says. But what could I do, naibour Springrove? 'Twas ordained to be. Well do I remember what your poor lady said to me when I had just married. 'Ah, Mr. Crickett,' says she, 'your wife will soon settle you as she did her other two: here's a glass o' rum, for I shan't see your poor face this time next year.' I swallered the rum, called again next year, and said, 'Mrs. Springrove, you gave me a glass o' rum last year because I was going to die—here I be alive still, you see.' 'Well said, Clerk! Here's two glasses for you now then,' says she. 'Thank you mem,' I said, and swallered the rum. Well, dang my old sides, next year I thought I'd call again and get three. And call I did. But she wouldn't give me a drop o' the commonest. 'No, clerk,' says she, 'you are too tough for a woman's pity.' .... Ah, poor soul, 'twas true enough. Here be I that was expected to die alive and hard as a nail, you see, and there's she moulderen in her grave."

"I used to think 'twas your wife's fate not to have a liven husband when I sid 'em die off so," said Gad.

"Fate? Bless thy simplicity, so 'twas her fate; but she struggled to have one, and would, and did. Fate's nothen beside a woman's schemen!"

"I suppose, then, that Fate is a He, like us, and the Lord, and the rest o' em up above there," said Gad, lifting his eyes to the sky.

"Hullo! Here's the young woman comen that we were a-talken about by-now," said a grinder, suddenly interrupting. "She's comen up here, as I be alive!"

The two grinders stood and regarded Cytherea as if she had been a ship tacking into a harbour, nearly stopping the mill in their new interest.

"Stylish accoutrements about the head and shoulders, to my thinken," said the clerk. "Sheenen curls, and plenty o' em."

"If there's one kind of pride more excusable than another in a young woman, 'tis beën proud of her hair," said Mr. Springrove.

"Dear man!—the pride there is only a small piece o' the whole. I warrant now, though she can show such a figure, she ha'n't a stick o' furniture to call her own."

"Come, clerk Crickett, let the maid be a maid while she is a maid,"* said Farmer Springrove, chivalrously.

"O," replied the servant of the church; "I've nothen to say against it—O, no:—

> " 'The chimney-sweeper's daughter Sue,
> As I have heard declare, O,
> Although she's neither sock nor shoe
> Will curl and deck her hair, O.' "*

Cytherea was rather disconcerted at finding that the gradual cessation of the chopping of the mill was on her account, and still more when she saw all the cidermakers' eyes fixed upon her except Mr. Springrove's, whose natural delicacy restrained him. She neared the plot of grass, but instead of advancing farther, hesitated on its border.

Mr. Springrove perceived her embarrassment, which was relieved when she saw his old-established figure coming across to her, wiping his hands in his apron.

"I know your errand, Missie," he said, "and am glad to see you and attend to it. I'll step indoors."

"If you are busy I am in no hurry for a minute or two," said Cytherea.

"Then if so be you really wouldn't mind, we'll wring down this last filling to let it drain all night?"

"Not at all. I like to see you."

"We are only just grinden down the early pickthongs and griffins,"* continued the farmer, in a half-apologetic tone for being caught cider-making by any well-dressed lady. "They rot as black as a chimney-crook* if we keep 'em till the regulars turn in." As he spoke he went back to the press, Cytherea keeping at his elbow. "I'm later than I should have been by rights," he continued, taking up a lever for propelling the screw, and beckoning to the men to come forward. "The truth is, my son Edward had promised to come to-day, and I made preparations; but instead of him comes a letter: 'London, September the eighteenth, Dear Father,' says he, and went on to tell me he couldn't. It threw me out a bit."

"Of course," said Cytherea.

"He's got a place a b'lieve?" said the clerk, drawing near.

"No, poor mortal fellow, no. He tried for this one here, you know, but couldn't manage to get it. I don't know the rights o' the matter, but willy-nilly they wouldn't have him for steward. Now mates, form in line."

Springrove, the clerk, the grinders, and Gad, all ranged themselves behind the lever of the screw, and walked round like soldiers wheeling.

"The man that the old quean* hev got is a man you can hardly get upon your tongue to gainsay, by the look o' en," rejoined Clerk Crickett.

"One o' them people that can continue to be thought no worse o' for stealen a horse than another man for looken over hedge at en," said a grinder.

"Well, he's all there as steward, and is quite the gentleman—no doubt about that."

"So would my Ted ha' been, for the matter o' that," the farmer said.

"That's true: 'a would, sir."

"I said, I'll give Ted a good education if it do cost me my eyes, and I would have."

"Ay, that you would so," said the chorus of assistants, solemnly.

"But he took to books naturally, and cost very little; and as a wind-up the women-folk hatched up a match between en and his cousin."

"When's the wedden to be, Mr. Springrove?"

"Uncertain—but soon I suppose. Edward, you see, can do any-thing pretty nearly, and yet can't get a straightforward liven. I wish sometimes I had kept en here, and let professions go. But he was such a one for the prent."

He dropped the lever in the hedge, and turned to his visitor.

"Now then, Missie, if you'll come indoors, please."

Gad Weedy looked with a placid criticism at Cytherea as she withdrew with the farmer.

"I could tell by the tongue o' her that she didn't take her degrees in our country," he said, in an undertone.

"The railways have left you lonely here," she observed, when they were indoors.

Save the withered old flies, which were quite tame from the soli-tude, not a being was in the house. Nobody seemed to have entered it since the last passenger had been called out to mount the last stage coach that had run by.

"Yes, the Inn and I seem almost a pair of fossils," the farmer replied, looking at the room and then at himself.

"O Mr. Springrove," said Cytherea, suddenly recollecting herself; "I am much obliged to you for recommending me to Miss Ald-clyffe." She began to warm towards the old man; there was in him a gentleness of disposition which reminded her of her own father.

"Recommending? Not at all, Miss. Ted—that's my son,—Ted said a fellow clerk of his had a sister who wanted to be doing some-thing in the world, and I mentioned it to the housekeeper, that's all. Ay, I miss my son very much."

She kept her back to the window that he might not see her rising colour.

"Yes," he continued, "sometimes I can't help feelen uneasy about en. You know, he seems not made for a town life exactly: he gets very queer over it sometimes, I think. Perhaps he'll be better when he's married to Adelaide."

A half-impatient feeling arose in her, like that which possesses a sick person when he hears a recently-struck hour struck again by a slow clock. She had lived further on.

"Everything depends upon whether he loves her," she said, tremulously.

"He used to—he doesn't show it so much now: but that's because he's older. You see, it was several years ago they first walked together as young man and young woman. She's altered too from what she was when he first coorted her."

"How, sir?"

"O, she's more sensible by half. When he used to write to her she'd creep up the lane, and look back over her shoulder, and slide out the letter, and kiss it, and look over one shoulder and t'other again, and read a word and stand in thought looken at the hills and seën none. Then the cuckoo would cry*—away the letter would slip, and she'd start a span wi' fright at the mere bird, and have a red skin before the quickest man among you could say, 'Blood, rush up.' "

He came forward with the money and dropped it into her hand. His thoughts were still with Edward, and he absently took her little fingers in his as he said, earnestly and ingenuously,—

" 'Tis so seldom I get a gentlewoman to speak to that I can't help speaken to you, Miss Graye, on my fears for Edward; I sometimes am afraid that he'll never get on—that he'll die poor and despised under the worst mental conditions, a keen sense of haven been passed in the race by men whose brains are nothen to his own, all through his seën too far into things—beën discontented with make-shifts—thinken o' perfection in things, and then sickened that there's no such thing as perfection. I shan't be sorry to see him marry, since it may settle him down and do him good . . . Ay, we'll hope for the best."

He let go her hand and accompanied her to the door, saying, "If you should care to walk this way and talk to an old man once now and then, it will be a great delight to him, Miss Graye. Good-evenen to ye . . . Ah look! a thunderstorm is brewing—be quick home. Or shall I step up with you?"

"No, thank you, Mr. Springrove. Good evening," she said in a low voice and hurried away. One thought still possessed her: Edward had trifled with her love.

§ 4. *Five to six, p.m.*

She followed the road into a bower of trees, overhanging it so densely that the pass appeared like a rabbit's burrow, and presently reached a side entrance to the park. The clouds rose more rapidly than the farmer had anticipated: the sheep moved in a trail, and complained incoherently. Livid grey shades, like those of the modern French artists,* made a mystery of the remote and dark parts of the vista, and seemed to insist upon a suspension of breath. Before she was half-way across the park the thunder rumbled distinctly.

The direction in which she had to go would take her close by the old manor-house. The air was perfectly still, and between each low rumble of the thunder behind she could hear the roar of the waterfall before her, and the creak of the engine among the bushes hard by it. Hurrying on, with a growing dread of the gloom and of the approaching storm, she drew near the Old House, now rising before her against the dark foliage and sky in tones of strange whiteness.

On the flight of steps, which descended from a terrace in front to the level of the park, stood a man. He appeared, partly from the relief the position gave to his figure, and partly from fact, to be of towering height. He was dark in outline, and was looking at the sky, with his hands behind him.

It was necessary for Cytherea to pass directly across the line of his front. She felt so reluctant to do this, that she was about to turn under the trees out of the path and enter it again at a point beyond the Old House; but he had seen her, and she came on mechanically, unconsciously averting her face a little, and dropping her glance to the ground.

Her eyes unswervingly lingered along the path until they fell upon another path branching in a right line from the path she was pursuing. It came from the steps of the Old House. "I am exactly opposite him now," she thought, "and his eyes are going through me."

A clear, masculine voice said, at the same instant,

"Are you afraid?"

She, interpreting his question by her feelings at the moment, assumed himself to be the object of fear, if any. "I don't think I am," she stammered.

He seemed to know that she thought in that sense.

"Of the thunder, I mean," he said; "not of myself."

She must turn to him now. "I think it is going to rain," she remarked for the sake of saying something.

He could not conceal his surprise and admiration of her face and bearing. He said courteously. "It may possibly not rain before you reach the House, if you are going there?"

"Yes I am."

"May I walk up with you? It is lonely under the trees."

"No." Fearing his courtesy arose from a belief that he was addressing a woman of higher station than was hers, she added, "I am Miss Aldclyffe's companion. I don't mind the loneliness."

"Oh, Miss Aldclyffe's companion. Then will you be kind enough to take a subscription to her? She sent to me this afternoon to ask me to become a subscriber to her Society, and I was out. Of course I'll subscribe if she wishes it. I take a great interest in the Society."

"Miss Aldclyffe will be glad to hear that, I know."

"Yes: let me see—what Society did she say it was? I am afraid I haven't enough money in my pocket, and yet it would be a satisfaction to her to have practical proof of my willingness. I'll get it, and be out in one minute."

He entered the house and was at her side again within the time he had named. "This is it," he said pleasantly.

She held up her hand. The soft tips of his fingers brushed the palm of her glove as he placed the money within it. She wondered why his fingers should have touched her.

"I think after all," he continued, "that the rain is upon us, and will drench you before you reach the House. Yes: see there."

He pointed to a round wet spot as large as a nasturtium leaf, which had suddenly appeared upon the white surface of the step.

"You had better come into the porch. It is not nearly night yet. The clouds make it seem later than it really is."

Heavy drops of rain, followed immediately by a forked flash of lightning and sharp rattling thunder, compelled her, willingly or no, to accept his invitation. She ascended the steps, stood beside him just within the porch, and for the first time obtained a series of short views of his person, as they waited there in silence.

He was an extremely handsome man, well-formed, and well-dressed, of an age which seemed to be two or three years less than thirty.

The most striking point in his appearance was the wonderful, almost preternatural, clearness of his complexion. There was not a blemish or speck of any kind to mar the smoothness of its surface or the beauty of its hue. Next, his forehead was square and broad, his brows straight and firm, his eyes penetrating and clear. By collecting the round of expressions they gave forth, a person who theorised on such matters would have imbibed the notion that their owner was of a nature to kick against the pricks; the last man in the world to put up with a position because it seemed to be his destiny to do so; one who took upon himself to resist fate with the vindictive determination of a Theomachist.* Eyes and forehead both would have expressed keenness of intellect too severely to be pleasing, had their force not been counteracted by the lines and tone of the lips. These were full and luscious to a surprising degree, possessing a woman-like softness of curve, and a ruby redness so intense, as to testify strongly to much susceptibility of heart where feminine beauty was concerned—a susceptibility that might require all the ballast of brain with which he had previously been credited to confine within reasonable channels.

His manner was elegant: his speech well-finished and unconstrained.

The break in their discourse, which had been caused by the peal of thunder, was unbroken by either for a minute, or two, during which the ears of both seemed to be absently following the low roar of the waterfall as it became gradually rivalled by the increasing rush of rain upon the trees and herbage of the grove. After her short looks at him, Cytherea had turned her head towards the avenue for a while, and now, glancing back again for an instant, she discovered that his eyes were engaged in a steady, though delicate, regard of her face and form.

At this moment, by reason of the narrowness of the porch, their dresses touched, and remained in contact.

His clothes are something exterior to every man; but to a woman her dress is part of her body.* Its motions are all present to her intelligence if not to her eyes; no man knows how his coat-tails swing. By the slightest hyperbole it may be said that her dress has sensation. Crease but the very Ultima Thule* of fringe or flounce, and it hurts her as much as pinching her. Delicate antennæ, or feelers, bristle on every outlying frill. Go to the uppermost: she is there; tread on the lowest: the fair creature is there almost before you.

Thus the touch of clothes, which was nothing to Manston, sent a thrill through Cytherea, seeing, moreover, that he was of the nature of a mysterious stranger. She looked out again at the storm, but still felt him. At last to escape the sensation she moved away, though by so doing it was necessary to advance a little into the rain.

"Look, the rain is coming into the porch upon you," he said. "Step inside the door."

Cytherea hesitated.

"Perfectly safe, I assure you," he added laughing, and holding the door open. "You shall see what a state of disorganisation I am in— boxes on boxes, furniture, straw, crockery, in every form of transposition. An old woman is in the back quarters somewhere, beginning to put things to rights . . . You know the inside of the house, I dare say?"

"I have never been in."

"Oh well, come along. Here, you see, they have made a door through; here they have put a partition dividing the old hall into two, one part is now my parlour; there they have put a plaster ceiling, hiding the old chestnut carved roof because it was too high and would have been chilly for me; you see, being the original hall, it was open right up to the top, and here the lord of the manor and his retainers used to meet and be merry by the light from the monstrous fire which shone out from that monstrous fire-place, now narrowed to a mere nothing for my grate, though you can see the old outline still.* I almost wish I could have had it in its original state."

"With more romance and less comfort."

"Yes, exactly. Well, perhaps the wish is not deep-seated. You will see how the things are tumbled in anyhow, packing-cases and all. The only piece of ornamental furniture yet unpacked is this one."

"An organ?"

"Yes, an organ. I made it myself, except the pipes. I opened the case this afternoon to commence soothing myself at once. It is not a very large one, but quite big enough for a private house. You play, I dare say?"

"The piano. I am not at all used to an organ."

"You would soon acquire the touch for an organ, though it would spoil your touch for the piano. Not that that matters a great deal. A piano isn't much as an instrument."

"It is the fashion to say so now. I think it is quite good enough."

"That isn't altogether a right sentiment about things being good enough."

"No—no. What I mean is, that the men who despise pianos do it as a rule from their teeth,* merely for fashion's sake, because cleverer men have said it before them—not from the experience of their ears."

Now Cytherea all at once broke into a blush at the consciousness of a great snub she had been guilty of in her eagerness to explain herself. He charitably expressed by a look that he did not in the least mind her blunder, if it were one; and this attitude forced him into a position of mental superiority which vexed her.

"I play for my private amusement only," he said. "I have never learnt scientifically. All I know is what I taught myself."

The thunder, lightning, and rain had now increased to a terrific force. The clouds, from which darts, forks, zigzags, and balls of fire continually sprang, did not appear to be more than a hundred yards above their heads, and every now and then a flash and a peal made gaps in the steward's descriptions. He went towards the organ, in the midst of a volley which seemed to shake the aged house from foundations to chimney.

"You are not going to play now, are you?" said Cytherea, uneasily.

"O yes. Why not now?" he said. "You can't go home, and therefore we may as well be amused, if you don't mind sitting on this box. The few chairs I have unpacked are in the other room."

Without waiting to see whether she sat down or not, he turned to the organ and began extemporising a harmony which meandered through every variety of expression of which the instrument was capable. Presently he ceased, and began searching for some music-book.

"What a splendid flash!" he said, as the lightning again shone in through the mullioned window, which, of a proportion to suit the whole extent of the original hall, was much too large for the present room. The thunder pealed again. Cytherea, in spite of herself, was frightened, not only at the weather, but at the general unearthly weirdness which seemed to surround her there.

"I wish I—the lightning wasn't so bright. Do you think it will last long?" she said, timidly.

"It can't last much longer," he murmured, without turning, running his fingers again over the keys. "But this is nothing," he continued, suddenly stopping and regarding her. "It seems brighter because of the deep shadow under those trees yonder. Don't mind it; now look at me—look in my face—now."

He had faced the window, looking fixedly at the sky with his dark strong eyes. She seemed compelled to do as she was bidden, and looked in the too-delicately beautiful face.

The flash came; but he did not turn or blink, keeping his eyes fixed as firmly as before. "There," he said, turning to her, "that's the way to look at lightning."

"O, it might have blinded you!" she exclaimed.

"Nonsense—not lightning of this sort—I shouldn't have stared at it if there had been danger. It is only sheet-lightning now. Now, will you have another piece? Something from an oratorio this time?"

"No, thank you—I don't want to hear it whilst it thunders so." But he had commenced without heeding her answer, and she stood motionless again, marvelling at the wonderful indifference to all external circumstance which was now evinced by his complete absorption in the music before him.

"Why do you play such saddening chords?" she said, when he next paused.

"H'm—because I like them, I suppose," he said lightly. "Don't you like sad impressions sometimes?"

"Yes, sometimes, perhaps."

"When you are full of trouble."

"Yes."

"Well, why shouldn't I when I am full of trouble?"

"Are you troubled?"

"I am troubled." He said this thoughtfully and abruptly—so abruptly that she did not push the dialogue further.

He now played more powerfully. Cytherea had never heard music in the completeness of full orchestral power, and the tones of the organ, which reverberated with considerable effect in the comparatively small space of the room, heightened by the elemental strife of light and sound outside, moved her to a degree out of proportion to the actual power of the mere notes, practised as was the hand that produced them. The varying strains—now loud, now soft; simple, complicated, weird, touching, grand, boisterous, subdued; each phase distinct, yet modulating into the next with a graceful and easy flow—shook and bent her to themselves, as a gushing brook shakes and bends a shadow cast across its surface.* The power of the music did not show itself so much by attracting her attention to the subject of the piece, as by taking up and developing as its libretto the poem of her own life and soul, shifting her deeds and intentions from the hands of her judgment, and holding them in its own.

She was swayed into emotional opinions concerning the strange man before her; new impulses of thought came with new harmonies, and entered into her with a gnawing thrill. A dreadful flash of lightning then, and the thunder close upon it. She found herself involuntarily shrinking up beside him, and looking with parted lips at his face.

He turned his eyes and saw her emotion, which greatly increased the ideal element in her expressive face. She was in the state in which woman's instinct to conceal has lost its power over her impulse to tell; and he saw it. Bending his handsome face over her till his lips almost touched her ear, he murmured without breaking the harmonies:—

"Do you very much like this piece?"

"Very much indeed," she said.

"I could see you were affected by it. I will copy it for you."

"Thank you much."

"I will bring it to the House to you to-morrow. Who shall I ask for?"

"O, not for me. Don't bring it," she said, hastily. "I shouldn't like you to."

"Let me see—to-morrow evening at seven or a few minutes past I shall be passing the waterfall on my way home. I could conveniently give it you there, and I should like you to have it."

He modulated into the Pastoral Symphony,* still looking in her eyes.

"Very well," she said, to get rid of the look.

The storm had by this time considerably decreased in violence, and in seven or ten minutes the sky partially cleared, the clouds around the western horizon becoming lighted up with the rays of the sinking sun.

Cytherea drew a long breath of relief and prepared to go away. She was full of a distressing sense that her detention in the old manor-house, and the acquaintanceship it had set on foot, was not a thing she wished. It was such a foolish thing to have been excited and dragged into frankness by the wiles of a stranger.

"Allow me to come with you," he said, accompanying her to the door, and again showing by his behaviour how powerfully he was impressed with her. His influence over her had vanished with the musical chords, and she turned her back upon him. "May I come?" he repeated.

"No, no. The distance is not three hundred yards—it is really not necessary, thank you," she said, quietly. And wishing him good evening, without meeting his eyes, she went down the steps, leaving him standing at the door.

"O, how is it that man has so fascinated me!" was all she could think. Her own self, as she had sat spell-bound before him, was all she could see. Her gait was constrained, from the knowledge that his eyes were upon her until she had passed the hollow by the waterfall, and by ascending the rise had become hidden from his view by the boughs of the overhanging trees.

§ 5. *Six to seven, p.m.*

The wet shining road threw the western glare into her eyes with an invidious lustre which rendered the restlessness of her mood more wearying. Her thoughts flew from idea to idea without asking for the slightest link of connection between one and another. One moment she was full of the wild music and stirring scene with Manston—the next, Edward's image rose before her like a shadowy ghost. Then Manston's black eyes seemed piercing her again, and the reckless voluptuous mouth appeared bending to the curves of his special words. What could be those troubles to which he had alluded? Perhaps Miss Aldclyffe was at the bottom of them. Sad at heart she paced on: her life was bewildering her.

On coming into Miss Aldclyffe's presence, Cytherea told her of the incident, not without a fear that she would burst into one of her ungovernable fits of temper at learning Cytherea's slight departure from the programme. But, strangely to Cytherea, Miss Aldclyffe looked delighted. The usual cross-examination followed.

"And so you were with him all that time?" said the lady, with assumed severity.

"Yes, I was."

"I did not tell you to call at the Old House twice."

"I didn't call, as I have said. He made me come into the porch."

"What remarks did he make, do you say?"

"That the lightning was not so bad as I thought."

"A very important remark, that. Did he—" she turned her glance full upon the girl, and eyeing her searchingly, said,—

"Did he say anything about *me?*"

"Nothing," said Cytherea, returning her gaze calmly, "except that I was to give you the subscription."

"You are quite sure?"

"Quite."

"I believe you. Did he say anything striking or strange about himself?"

"Only one thing—that he was troubled."

"Troubled!"

After saying the word, Miss Aldclyffe relapsed into silence. Such behaviour as this had ended, on most previous occasions, by her making a confession, and Cytherea expected one now. But for once she was mistaken, nothing more was said.

When she had returned to her room she sat down and penned a farewell letter to Edward Springrove, as little able as any other excitable and brimming young woman of nineteen, to feel that the wisest and only dignified course at that juncture was to do nothing at all. She told him that, to her painful surprise, she had learnt that his engagement to another woman was a matter of notoriety. She insisted that all honour bade him marry his early love—a woman far better than her unworthy self, who only deserved to be forgotten, and begged him to remember that he was not to see her face again. She upbraided him for levity and cruelty in meeting her so frequently at Creston, and above all in stealing the kiss from her lips on the last evening of the water excursions. "I never, never can forget it!" she said, and then felt a sensation of having done her duty, ostensibly persuading herself that her reproaches and commands were of such a force that no man to whom they were uttered could ever approach her more.

Yet it was all unconsciously said in words which betrayed a lingering tenderness of love at every unguarded turn. Like Beatrice accusing Dante from the chariot,* try as she might to play the superior being who contemned such mere eye-sensuousness, she betrayed at every point a pretty woman's jealousy of a rival, and covertly gave her old lover hints for excusing himself at each fresh indictment.

This done, Cytherea, still in a practical mood, upbraided herself with weakness in allowing a stranger like Mr. Manston to influence her as he had that evening. What right on earth had he to suggest so suddenly that she might meet him at the waterfall to receive his music? She would have given much to be able to annihilate the ascendency he had obtained over her during that extraordinary interval of melodious sound. Not being able to endure the notion of his living a minute longer in the belief he was then holding, she took her pen and wrote to him also:—

> "Knapwater House,
> "*September 20th.*
>
> "I find I cannot meet you at seven o'clock by the waterfall as I promised. The emotion I felt made me forgetful of realities.*
> "C. Graye."

A great statesman thinks several times, and acts; a young lady acts, and thinks several times. When, a few minutes later, she saw the postman carry off the bag containing one of the letters, and a messenger with the other, she, for the first time, asked herself the question whether she had acted very wisely in writing to either of the two men who had so influenced her.

END OF VOL. I

VOLUME II

VOLUME II

CHAPTER I

THE EVENTS OF TEN WEEKS

§ 1. *From September the twenty-first to the middle of November*

The foremost figure within Cytherea's horizon, exclusive of the inmates of Knapwater House, was now the steward, Mr. Manston. It was impossible that they should live within a quarter of a mile of each other, be engaged in the same service, and attend the same Church, without meeting at some spot or another, twice or thrice a week. On Sundays, in her pew, when by chance she turned her head, Cytherea found his eyes waiting desirously for a glimpse of hers, and, at first more strangely, the eyes of Miss Aldclyffe furtively resting on him. On coming out of Church he frequently walked beside Cytherea till she reached the gate at which residents in the House turned into the shrubbery. By degrees a conjecture grew to a certainty. She knew that he loved her.

But this strange fact was connected with the development of his love.

He was palpably making the strongest efforts to subdue, or at least to hide, the weakness, and as it sometimes seemed, rather from his own conscience than from surrounding eyes. Hence she found that not one of his encounters with her was anything more than the result of pure accident. He made no advances whatever: without avoiding her, he never sought her: the words he had whispered at their first interview now proved themselves to be quite as much the result of unguarded impulse as was her answer. Something held him back, bound his impulse down, but she saw that it was neither pride of his person, nor fear that she would refuse him,—a course she unhesitatingly resolved to take should he think fit to declare himself. She was interested in him and his marvellous beauty, as she might have been in some fascinating panther or leopard,—for some undefinable reason she shrank from him, even whilst she admired. The key-note of her nature, a warm "precipitance of soul",* as Coleridge happily writes it, which Manston had so directly pounced upon at their very first interview, gave her now a tremulous sense of being in some way in his power.

The state of mind was on the whole a dangerous one for a young and inexperienced woman; and perhaps the circumstance which, more than any other, led her to cherish Edward's image now, was that he had taken no notice of the receipt of her letter, stating that she discarded him. It was plain then, she said, that he did not care deeply for her, and she thereupon could not quite leave off caring deeply for him:—

> "——Ingenium mulierum,
> Nolunt ubi velis, ubi nolis cupiunt ultro."*

The month of October passed, and November began its course. The inhabitants of the village of Carriford grew weary of supposing that Miss Aldclyffe was going to marry her steward. New whispers arose and became very distinct (though they did not reach Miss Aldclyffe's ears) to the effect that, the steward was deeply in love with Cytherea Graye. Indeed the fact became so obvious that there was nothing left to say about it except that their marriage would be an excellent one for both;—for her in point of money—and for him in point of love.

As circles in a pond grow wider and wider, the next fact, which at first had been patent only to Cytherea herself, in due time spread to her neighbours, and they too wondered that he made no overt advances. By the middle of November, a theory made up of a combination of the other two was received with general favour: its substance being, that a guilty intrigue had been commenced between Manston and Miss Aldclyffe, some years before, when he was a very young man, and she still in the enjoyment of some womanly beauty, but now that her seniority began to grow emphatic she was becoming distasteful to him. His fear of the effect of the lady's jealousy, would, they said, thus lead him to conceal from her his new attachment to Cytherea. Almost the only woman who did not believe this was Cytherea herself, on unmistakable grounds, which were hidden from all besides. It was not only in public, but even more markedly in secluded places, on occasions when gallantry would have been safe from all discovery, that this guarded course of action was pursued, all the strength of a consuming passion burning in his eyes the while.

§ 2. *November the eighteenth*

It was on a Friday in this month of November that Owen Graye paid a visit to his sister.

His zealous integrity still retained for him the situation at Creston, and in order that there should be as little interruption as possible to his duties there, he had decided not to come to Knapwater till late in the afternoon, and to return to Creston by the first train the next morning, Miss Aldclyffe having made a point of frequently offering him lodging for an unlimited period, to the great pleasure of Cytherea.

He reached the house about four o'clock, and ringing the bell of the side entrance, asked of the page who answered it for Miss Graye.

When Graye spoke the name of his sister, Manston, who was just coming out from an interview with Miss Aldclyffe, passed him in the vestibule and heard the question. The steward's face grew hot, and he secretly clenched his hands. He half crossed the Court, then turned his head and saw that the lad still stood at the door, though Owen had been shown into the house. Manston went back to him.

"Who was that man?" he said.

"I don't know, sir."

"Has he ever been here before?"

"Yes, sir."

"How many times?"

"Three."

"You are sure you don't know him?"

"I think he is Miss Graye's brother, sir."

"Then, why the devil didn't you say so before!" Manston exclaimed, and again went on his way.

"Of course, that was not the man of my dreams—of course, it couldn't be!" he said to himself. "That I should be such a fool—such an utter fool. Good God! to allow a girl to influence me like this, day after day, till I am jealous of her very brother. A lady's dependent, a waif, a helpless thing entirely at the mercy of the world; yes, curse it; that is just why it is; that fact of her being so helpless against the blows of circumstances which renders her so deliciously sweet!"

He paused opposite his house. Should he get his horse saddled? No.

He went down the drive and out of the park, having started to proceed to an outlying spot on the estate concerning some draining, and to call at the potter's yard to make an arrangement for the supply of pipes. But a remark which Miss Aldclyffe had dropped in relation to Cytherea, was what still occupied his mind, and had been the immediate cause of his excitement at the sight of her brother. Miss Aldclyffe had meaningly remarked during their intercourse, that Cytherea was wildly in love with Edward Springrove, in spite of his engagement to his cousin Adelaide.

"How I am harassed!" he said aloud, after deep thought for half an hour, while still continuing his walk with the greatest vehemence. "How I am harassed by these emotions of mine!" He calmed himself by an effort. "Well, duty after all it shall be, as nearly as I can effect it. 'Honesty is the best policy,' " with which vigorously uttered resolve, he once more attempted to turn his attention to the prosy object of his journey.

The evening had closed in to a dark and dreary night when the steward came from the potter's door to proceed homewards again. The gloom did not tend to raise his spirits, and in the total lack of objects to attract his eye, he soon fell to introspection as before. It was along the margin of turnip fields that his path lay, and the large leaves of the crop struck flatly against his feet at every step, pouring upon them the rolling drops of moisture gathered upon their broad surfaces; but the annoyance was unheeded. Next reaching a fir-plantation, he mounted the stile and followed the path into the midst of the darkness produced by the overhanging trees.

After walking under the dense shade of the inky boughs for a few minutes, he fancied he had mistaken the path, which as yet was scarcely familiar to him. This was proved directly afterwards by his coming at right angles upon some obstruction, which careful feeling with outstretched hands soon told him to be a rail fence. However, as the wood was not large, he experienced no alarm about finding the path again, and with some sense of pleasure halted awhile against the rails, to listen to the intensely melancholy yet musical wail of the fir-tops, and as the wind passed on, the prompt moan of an adjacent plantation in reply. He could just dimly discern the airy summits of the two or three trees nearest him waving restlessly backwards and forwards, and stretching out their boughs like hairy arms into the dull sky. The scene, from its striking and emphatic loneliness, began to grow congenial to his mood; all of human kind seemed at the antipodes.

A sudden rattle on his right hand caused him to start from his reverie, and turn in that direction.

There, before him, he saw rise up from among the trees a fountain of sparks and smoke, then a red glare of light coming forward towards him; then a flashing panorama of illuminated oblong pictures; then the old darkness, more impressive than ever.

The surprise, which had owed its origin to his imperfect acquaintance with the topographical features of that end of the estate, had been but momentary.

The disturbance, a well-known one to dwellers by a railway, was caused by the 6.50 down-train passing along a shallow cutting in the midst of the wood immediately below where he stood, the driver having the fire door of the engine open at the minute of going by. The train had, when passing him, already considerably slackened speed, and now a whistle was heard, announcing that Carriford-Road Station was not far in its van.

But contrary to the natural order of things, the discovery that it was only a common-place train had not caused Manston to stir from his position of facing the railway.

If the 6.50 down-train had been a flash of forked lightning transfixing him to the earth, he could scarcely have remained in a more trance-like state. He still leant against the railings, his right hand still continued pressing on his walking-stick, his weight on one foot, his other heel raised, his eyes wide open towards the blackness of the cutting. The only movement in him was a slight dropping of the lower jaw, separating his previously closed lips a little way, as when a strange conviction rushes home suddenly upon a man.

A new surprise, not nearly so trivial as the first, had taken possession of him.

It was on this account. At one of the illuminated windows of a second-class carriage in the series gone by, he had seen a pale face, reclining upon one hand, the light from the lamp falling full upon it. The face was a woman's.

At last he moved; gave a whispering kind of whistle, adjusted his hat, and walked on again.

He was cross-questioning himself in every direction as to how a piece of knowledge he had carefully concealed had found its way to another person's intelligence. "How can my address have become known," he said at length, audibly. "Well, it is a blessing I have been circumspect and honourable, in relation to that—yes, I will say it, for once, even if the words choke me, that darling of mine, Cytherea, never to be my own, never. I suppose all will come out now. All!" The great sadness of his utterance proved that no mean force had been exercised upon himself to sustain the circumspection he had just claimed.

He wheeled to the left, pursued the ditch beside the railway fence, and presently emerged from the wood, stepping into a road which crossed the railway by a bridge.

As he neared home, the anxiety lately written in his face, merged by degrees into a grimly humorous smile, which hung long upon his lips, and he quoted aloud a line from the Book of Jeremiah:—

"A woman shall compass a man."*

§ 3. *November the nineteenth. Daybreak*

Before it was light the next morning, two little naked feet pattered along the passage in Knapwater House, from which Owen Graye's bedroom opened, and a tap was given upon his door.

"Owen, Owen, are you awake?" said Cytherea in a whisper through the keyhole. "You must get up directly, or you'll miss the train."

When he descended to his sister's little room, he found her there already waiting with a cup of cocoa and a grilled rasher on the table for him. A hasty meal was despatched in the intervals of putting on his overcoat and finding his hat, and they then went softly through the long deserted passages, the kitchen-maid who had prepared their breakfast walking before them with a lamp held high above her head, which cast long wheeling shadows down corridors intersecting the one they followed, their remoter ends being lost in darkness. The door was unbolted and they stepped out.

Owen had preferred walking to the station to accepting the pony-carriage which Miss Aldclyffe had placed at his disposal, having a morbid horror of giving trouble to people above him in rank, and especially to their men-servants, who looked down upon him as a hybrid monster from regions far below the touch-my-hat stage of supremacy.* Cytherea proposed to walk a little way with him.

"I want to talk to you as long as I can," she said, tenderly.

Brother and sister then emerged by the heavy door into the drive. The feeling and aspect of the hour were precisely similar to those under which the steward had left the house the evening previous, excepting that apparently unearthly reversal of natural sequence, which is caused by the world getting lighter instead of darker. "The tearful glimmer of the languid dawn"* was just sufficient to reveal to them the melancholy red leaves, lying thickly in the channels by the roadside, ever and anon loudly tapped on by heavy drops of water, which the boughs above had collected from the foggy air.

They passed the Old House engaged in a deep conversation, and had proceeded about twenty yards by a cross route, in the direction of the turnpike road, when the form of a woman emerged from the porch of the building.

She was wrapped in a grey waterproof cloak, the hood of which was drawn over her head and closely round her face—so closely that her eyes were the sole features uncovered.

With this one exception of her appearance there, the most perfect stillness and silence pervaded the steward's residence from basement to chimney. Not a shutter was open; not a twine of smoke came forth.

Underneath the ivy-covered gateway she stood still and listened for two, or possibly three minutes, till she became conscious of others in the park.

Seeing the pair she stepped back, with the apparent intention of letting them pass out of sight, and evidently wishing to avoid observation. But looking at her watch, and returning it rapidly to her pocket, as if surprised at the lateness of the hour, she hurried out again, and across the park by a still more oblique line than that traced by Owen and his sister.

These in the meantime had got into the road, and were walking along it as the woman came up on the other side of the boundary hedge, looking for a gate or stile, by which she too might get off the grass upon hard ground.

Their conversation, of which every word was clear and distinct, in the still air of the dawn, to the distance of a quarter of a mile, reached her ears, and withdrew her attention from all other matters and sights whatsoever. Thus arrested she stood for an instant as precisely in the attitude of Imogen by the cave of Belarius,* as if she had studied the position from the play.

When they had advanced a few steps, she followed them in some doubt, still screened by the hedge.

"Do you believe in such odd coincidences?" said Cytherea.

"How do you mean, believe in them? They occur sometimes."

"Yes, one will occur often enough—that is, two disconnected events will fall strangely together by chance, and people scarcely notice the fact beyond saying, 'Oddly enough it happened that so and so were the same,' and so on. But when three such events coincide without any apparent reason for the coincidence, it seems as if there must be invisible means at work. You see, three things falling together in that manner are ten times as singular as two cases of coincidence which are distinct."*

"Well of course: what a mathematical head you have, Cytherea. But I don't see so much to marvel at in our case. That the man who kept the public-house in which Miss Aldclyffe fainted, and who found out her name and position, lives in this neighbourhood, is accounted for by the fact that she got him the berth to stop his tongue. That you came here was simply owing to Springrove."

"Ah, but look at this. Miss Aldclyffe is the woman our father first loved, and I have come to Miss Aldclyffe's; you can't get over that."

From these premises, she proceeded to argue like an elderly divine on the designs of Providence which were apparent in such conjunctures, and went into a variety of details connected with Miss Aldclyffe's history.

"Had I better tell Miss Aldclyffe that I know all this?" she inquired at last.

"What's the use?" he said. "Your possessing the knowledge does no harm; you are at any rate comfortable here, and a confession to Miss Aldclyffe might only irritate her. No, hold your tongue, Cytherea."

"I fancy I should have been tempted to tell her too," Cytherea went on, "had I not found out that there exists a very odd, almost imperceptible, and yet real connection of some kind between her and Mr. Manston, which is more than that of a mutual interest in the estate."

"She is in love with him!" exclaimed Owen, "fancy that!"

"Ah—that's what every body says who has been keen enough to

notice anything. I said so at first. And yet now I cannot persuade myself that she is in love with him at all."

"Why can't you?"

"She doesn't act as if she were. She isn't—you will know I don't say it from any vanity, Owen,—she isn't the least jealous of me."

"Perhaps she is in some way in his power."

"No—she is not. He was openly advertised for, and chosen from forty or fifty who answered the advertisement, without knowing whose it was. And since he has been here, she has certainly done nothing to compromise herself in any way. Besides, why should she have brought an enemy here at all?"

"Then she must have fallen in love with him. You know as well as I do, Cyth, that with women there's nothing between the two poles of emotion towards an interesting male acquaintance. 'Tis either love or hate."

They walked for a few minutes in silence, when Cytherea's eyes accidentally fell upon her brother's feet.

"Owen," she said, "do you know that there is something unusual in your manner of walking?"

"What is it like?" be asked.

"I can't quite say, except that you don't walk so regularly as you used to."

The woman behind the hedge, who had still continued to dog their footsteps, made an impatient movement at this change in their conversation, and looked at her watch again.

Yet she seemed reluctant to give over listening.

"Yes," Owen returned with assumed carelessness, "I do know it. I think the cause of it, is that mysterious pain which comes just above my ankle sometimes. You remember the first time I had it? That day we went by steam-packet to Lewborne Bay, when it hindered me from coming back to you, and compelled me to sleep with the gateman we have been talking about."

"But is it anything serious, dear Owen?" Cytherea exclaimed with some alarm.

"O nothing at all. It is sure to go off again. I never find a sign of it when I sit in the office."

Again their unperceived companion made a gesture of vexation, and looked at her watch.

But the dialogue still flowed on upon this new subject, and showed no sign of returning to its old channel.

Gathering up her skirt decisively she renounced all further hope, and hurried along the ditch till she had dropped into a valley, and came to a gate which was beyond the view of those coming behind. This she softly opened, and came out upon the road, following it in the direction of the railway station.

Presently she heard Owen Graye's footsteps in her rear, his quickened pace implying that he had parted from his sister. The woman thereupon increased her rapid walk to a run, and in a few minutes safely distanced* her fellow traveller.

The railway at Carriford-Road consisted only of a single line of rails; and the short local down-train by which Owen was going to Creston was shunted on to a siding, whilst the first up-train passed. Graye entered the waiting room, and the door being open he listlessly observed the movements of a woman wearing a long grey cloak, and closely hooded, who had asked for a ticket for London.

He followed her with his eyes on to the platform, saw her waiting there and afterwards stepping into the train: his recollection of her ceasing with the perception.

§ 4.   *Eight to ten o'clock, a.m.*

Mrs. Crickett, twice a widow, and now the parish clerk's wife, a fine-framed, scandal-loving woman, with a peculiar corner to her eye by which, without turning her head, she could see what people were doing almost behind her,* lived in a cottage standing nearer to the old manor-house than any other in the village of Carriford, and she had on that account been temporarily engaged by the steward, as a respectable kind of charwoman and general servant, until a settled arrangement could be made with some person as permanent domestic.

Every morning, therefore, Mrs. Crickett, immediately she had lighted the fire in her own cottage, and prepared the breakfast for herself and husband, wended her way to the Old House to do the same for Mr. Manston. Then she went home to breakfast, and when the steward had partaken of his, and had gone out on his rounds, she returned again to clear away, make his bed, and put the house in order for the day.

On the morning of Owen Graye's departure, she went through the operations of her first visit as usual—proceeded home to breakfast, and went back again, to perform those of the second.

Entering Manston's empty bedroom, with her hands on her hips, she indifferently cast her eyes upon the bed, previously to dismantling it.

Whilst she looked, she thought in an inattentive manner, "What a remarkably quiet sleeper Mr. Manston must be!" The upper bedclothes were flung back, certainly, but the bed was scarcely disarranged. "Anybody would almost fancy," she thought, "that he had made it himself after rising."

But these evanescent thoughts vanished as they had come, and Mrs. Crickett set to work; she dragged off the counterpane, blankets and sheets, and stooped to lift the pillows. Thus stooping, something arrested her attention; she looked closely—more closely—very closely. "Well, to be sure!" was all she could say. The clerk's wife stood as if the air had suddenly set to amber, and held her fixed like a fly in it.

The object of her wonder was a trailing brown hair, very little less than a yard long, which proved it clearly to be a hair from some woman's head. She drew it off the pillow, and took it to the window; there holding it out she looked fixedly at it, and became utterly lost in meditation: her gaze, which had at first actively settled on the hair, involuntarily dropped past its object by degrees and was lost on the floor, as the inner vision obscured the outer one.

She at length moistened her lips, returned her eyes to the hair, wound it round her fingers, put it in some paper, and secreted the whole in her pocket. Mrs. Crickett's thoughts were with her work no more that morning.

She searched the house from roof-tree to cellar, for some other trace of feminine existence or appurtenance; but none was to be found.

She went out into the yard, coal-hole, stable, hay-loft, greenhouse, fowl-house, and piggery, and still there was no sign. Coming in again, she saw a bonnet, eagerly pounced upon it, and found it to be her own.

Hastily completing her arrangements in the other rooms, she entered the village again, and called at once on the post-mistress, Mrs. Leat, an intimate friend of hers, and a female who sported several unique diseases and afflictions.

Mrs. Crickett unfolded the paper, took out the hair, and waved it on high before the perplexed eyes of Mrs. Leat, which immediately mooned and wandered after it like a cat's.

"What is it?" said Mrs. Leat, contracting her eyelids, and stretching out towards the invisible object a narrow bony hand that would have been an unmitigated delight to the pencil of Carlo Crivelli.*

"You shall hear," said Mrs. Crickett, complacently gathering up the treasure into her own fat hand; and the secret was then solemnly imparted, together with the accident of its discovery.

A shaving-glass was taken down from a nail, laid on its back in the middle of a table by the window, and the hair spread carefully out upon it. The pair then bent over the table from opposite sides, their elbows on the edge, their hands supporting their heads, their foreheads nearly touching, and their eyes upon the hair.

"He ha' been mad a'ter my lady Cytherea," said Mrs. Crickett, "and 'tis my very belief the hair is——"

"No 'tidn'. Hers id'n so dark as that," said Mrs. Leat.

"Mrs. Leat, you know me, and have known me for many years," said the clerk's wife parenthetically.

"True, I have, Mrs. Crickett."

"And you know that as the faithful wife of a servant of the Church, I should be glad to think as you do about the hair. Mind I don't wish to say anything against Miss Graye, but this I do say, that I believe her to be a nameless thing,* and she's no right to stick a moral clock in her face,* and deceive the country in such a way. If she wasn't of a bad stock at the outset, she was bad in the planten, and if she wasn't bad in the planten, she was bad in the growen, and if not in the growen, she's made bad by what she's gone through since."

"But I have another reason for knowing it idn' hers," said Mrs. Leat.

"Ah! I know whose it is then—Miss Aldclyffe's, upon my song!"

" 'Tis the colour of hers, but I don't believe it to be hers either."

"Don't you believe what they d' say about her and him?"

"I say nothen about that; but you don't know what I know about his letters."

"What about 'em?"

"He d' post all his letters here except them for one person, and they he d' take to Creston. My son is in Creston Post Office, as you know, and as he d' sit at desk he can see over the blind of the window all the people who d' post letters. Mr. Manston d' unvariably go there wi' letters for that person; my boy d' know 'em by sight well enough now."

"Is it a she?"

" 'Tis a she."

"What's her name?"

"The litttle stunpoll of a fellow couldn't call to mind more than that 'tis Miss Somebody of London. However, that's the woman who ha' been here, depend upon't—a wicked one—some poor street-wench escaped from Sodom, I warrant ye."

"Only to find herself in Gomorrah,* seemingly."

"That may be."

"No, no, Mrs. Leat, this is clear to me. 'Tis no Miss who came here to see our steward last night—whenever she came, or wherever she vanished. Do you think he would ha' let a Miss, get here how she could, go away how she would, without breakfast or help of any kind?"

Mrs Leat shook her head—Mrs. Crickett looked at her solemnly.

"Mrs. Leat, I ask you, have you, or ha'n't you known me many years?"

"True, I have."

"And I say I d' know she had no help of any kind, I know it was so, for the grate was quite cold when I touched it this morning with these fingers, and he was still in bed. No, he wouldn't take the trouble to write letters to a girl and then treat her so off-hand as that. There's a tie between 'em stronger than feelen. She's his wife."

"He married! The Lord so 's, what shall we hear next. Do he look married now? His are not the abashed eyes and lips of a married man."

"Perhaps she's a tame one—but she's his wife still."

"No, no: he's not a married man."

"Yes, yes he is. I've had three, and I ought to know."

"Well, well," said Mrs Leat, giving way, "Whatever may be the truth on't I trust Providence will settle it all for the best, as he always do."

"Ay, ay, Elizabeth," rejoined Mrs. Crickett with a satirical sigh, as she turned on her foot to go home, "good people like you may say so, but I have always found Providence a different sort of feller."

§ 5. *November the twentieth*

It was Miss Aldclyffe's custom, a custom originated by her father, and nourished by her own exclusiveness, to unlock the post-bag herself every morning, instead of allowing the duty to devolve on the butler, as was the case in most of the neighbouring county families. The bag was brought up-stairs each morning to her dressing-room, where she took out the contents, mostly in the presence of her maid and Cytherea, who had the entrée of the chamber at all hours, and attended there in the morning at a kind of reception on a small scale, which was held by Miss Aldclyffe of her namesake only.

Here she read her letters before the glass, whilst undergoing the operation of being brushed and dressed.

"What woman can this be, I wonder?" she said on the morning succeeding that of the last section, " 'London, N!' It is the first time in my life I ever had a letter from that outlandish place the North side of London."

Cytherea had just come into her presence to learn if there was anything for herself; and on being thus addressed, walked up to Miss Aldclyffe's corner of the room to look at the curiosity which had raised such an exclamation. But the lady, having opened the envelope and read a few lines, put it quickly in her pocket, before Cytherea could reach her side.

"Oh, 'tis nothing," she said. She proceeded to make general remarks in a noticeably forced tone of sang-froid, from which she soon lapsed into silence. Not another word was said about the letter: she seemed very anxious to get her dressing done, and the room cleared. Thereupon Cytherea went away to the other window, and a few minutes later left the room to follow her own pursuits.

It was late when Miss Aldclyffe descended to the breakfast-table, and then she seemed there to no purpose; tea, coffee, eggs, cutlets, and all their accessories, were left absolutely untasted. The next that was seen of her was when walking up and down the south terrace, and round the flower beds; her face was pale, and her tread was fitful, and she crumpled a letter in her hand.

Dinner-time came round as usual; she did not speak ten words, or indeed seem conscious of the meal; for all that Miss Aldclyffe did in the way of eating, dinner might have been taken out as perfect as it was taken in.

In her own private apartment Miss Aldclyffe again pulled out the letter of the morning. One passage in it ran thus:—

"Of course, being his wife, I could publish the fact, and compel him to acknowledge me at any moment, notwithstanding his threats, and reasonings that it will be better to wait. I have waited, and waited again, and the time for such acknowledgment seems no nearer than at first. To show you how patiently I have waited, I can tell you that not till a fortnight ago, when by stress of circumstances I had been driven to new lodgings, have I ever assumed my married name, solely on account of its having been his request all along that I should not. This writing to you, madam, is my first disobedience, and I am justified in it. A woman who is driven to visit her husband like a thief in the night and then sent away like a street dog;* left to get up, unbolt, unbar, and find her way out of the house as she best may, is justified in doing anything.

"But should I demand of him a restitution of rights,* there would be involved a publicity which I could not endure, and a noisy scandal flinging my name the length and breadth of the country.

"What I still prefer to any such violent means is that you reason with him privately, and compel him to bring me home to your parish in a decent and careful manner, in the way that would be adopted by any respectable man, whose wife had been living away from him for some time, by reason, say, of peculiar family circumstances which had caused disunion, but not enmity, and who at length was enabled to reinstate her in his house.

"You will, I know, oblige me in this, especially as knowledge of a peculiar transaction of your own, which took place some years ago, has lately come to me in a singular way. I will not at present trouble you by describing how. It is enough, that I alone, of all people living, know *all the sides of the story*, those from whom I collected it having each only a partial knowledge which confuses them and points to nothing. One person knows of your early engagement and its sudden termination; another, of the reason of those strange meetings at inns and coffee-houses; another, of what was sufficient to cause all this, and so on. I know what fits one and all the circumstances like a key, and shows them to be the natural outcrop of a rational (though rather rash) line of conduct for a young lady. You will at once perceive how it was that some at least of these things were revealed to me.

"This knowledge then, common to, and secretly treasured by us both, is the ground upon which I beg for your friendship and help, with a feeling that you will be too generous to refuse it to me.

"I may add that, as yet, my husband knows nothing of this, neither need he if you remember my request."

*   *   *   *   *   *   *   *   *   *

"A threat—a flat, stinging threat! as delicately wrapped up in words as the woman could do it; a threat from a miserable unknown wench to an Aldclyffe, and not the least proud member of the family either! A threat on his account—O, O, shall it be?"

Presently this humour of defiance vanished, and the members of her body became supple again, her proceedings proving that it was absolutely necessary to give way, Aldclyffe as she was. She wrote a short answer to Mrs. Manston, saying civilly that Mr. Manston's possession of such a near relation was a fact quite new to herself, and that she would see what could be done in such an unfortunate affair.

§ 6. *November the twenty-first*

Manston received a message the next day requesting his attendance at the house punctually at eight o'clock the ensuing evening. Miss Aldclyffe was brave and imperious, but with the purpose she had in view she could not look him in the face whilst daylight shone upon her.

The steward was shown into the library. On entering it, he was immediately struck with the unusual gloom which pervaded the apartment. The fire was dead and dull, one lamp, and that a comparatively small one, was burning at the extreme end, leaving the main proportion of the lofty and sombre room in an artificial twilight, scarcely powerful enough to render visible the titles of the folio and quarto volumes which were jammed into the lower tiers of the book-shelves.

After keeping him waiting for more than twenty minutes (Miss Aldclyffe knew that excellent recipe for taking the stiffness out of human flesh, and for extracting all pre-arrangement from human speech) she entered the room.

Manston sought her eye directly. The hue of her features was not discernible, but the calm glance she flung at him, from which all attempt at returning his scrutiny was absent, awoke him to the perception that probably his secret was by some means or other known to her; how it had become known he could not tell.

She drew forth the letter, unfolded it, and held it up to him, letting it hang by one corner from between her finger and thumb, so that the light from the lamp, though remote, fell directly upon its surface.

"You know whose writing this is?" she said.

He saw the strokes plainly, instantly resolving to burn his ships and hazard all on an advance.

"My wife's," he said calmly.

His quiet answer threw her off her balance. She had no more expected an answer than does a preacher when he exclaims from the pulpit, "Do you feel your sin?" She had clearly expected a sudden alarm.

"And why all this concealment?" she said again, her voice rising, as she vainly endeavoured to control her feelings, whatever they were.

"It doesn't follow that, because a man is married, he must tell every stranger of it, madam," he answered, just as calmly as before.

"Stranger! well, perhaps not; but Mr. Manston, why did you choose to conceal it, I ask again? I have a perfect right to ask this question, as you will perceive, if you consider the terms of my advertisement."

"I will tell you. There were two simple reasons. The first was this practical one; you advertised for an unmarried man, if you remember?"

"Of course I remember."

"Well, an incident suggested to me that I should try for the situation. I was married; but, knowing that in getting an office where there is a restriction of this kind, leaving one's wife behind is always accepted as a fulfilment of the article, I left her behind for a while. The other reason is, that these terms of yours afforded me a plausible excuse for escaping (for a short time) the company of a woman I had been mistaken in marrying."

"Mistaken! what was she?" the lady inquired.

"A third-rate actress, whom I met with during my stay in Liverpool last summer, where I had gone to fulfil a short engagement with an architect."

"Where did she come from?"

"She is an American* by birth, and I grew to dislike her when we had been married a week."

"She was ugly, I imagine?"

"She is not an ugly woman by any means."

"Up to the ordinary standard?"

"Quite up to the ordinary standard, indeed handsome. After a while we quarrelled and separated."

"You did not ill-use her, of course," said Miss Aldclyffe, with a little sarcasm.

"I did not."

"But at any rate, you got thoroughly tired of her."

Manston looked as if he began to think her questions out of place; however, he said quietly, "I did get tired of her. I never told her so, but we separated; I to come here, bringing her with me as far as London and leaving her there in perfectly comfortable quarters; and though your advertisement expressed a single man, I have always intended to tell you the whole truth; and this was when I was going to tell it, when your satisfaction with my careful management of your affairs should have proved the risk to be a safe one to run."

She bowed.

"Then I saw that you were good enough to be interested in my welfare to a greater extent than I could have anticipated or hoped, judging you by the frigidity of other employers, and this caused me to hesitate. I was vexed at the complication of affairs. So matters stood till three nights ago; I was then walking home from the pottery, and came up to the railway. The down-train came along close to me, and there, sitting at a carriage window, I saw my wife: she had found out my address, and had thereupon determined to follow me here. I had not been home many minutes before she came in, next morning early she left again—"

"Because you treated her so cavalierly?"

"—And as I suppose, wrote to you directly. That's the whole story of her, madam." Whatever were Manston's real feelings towards the lady who had received his explanation in these supercilious tones they remained locked within him as within a casket of steel.

"Did your friends know of your marriage, Mr. Manston?" she continued.

"Nobody at all; we kept it a secret for various reasons."

"It is true then that as your wife tells me in this letter, she has not passed as Mrs. Manston till within these last few days?"

"It is quite true; I was in receipt of a very small and uncertain income when we married; and so she continued playing at the theatre as before our marriage, and in her maiden name."

"Has she any friends?"

"I have never heard that she has any in England. She came over here on some theatrical speculation, as one of a company who were going to do much, but who never did anything; and here she has remained."

A pause ensued, which was terminated by Miss Aldclyffe.

"I understand," she said. "Now, though I have no direct right to concern myself with your private affairs, (beyond those which arise from your misleading me and getting the office you hold)—"

"As to that, madam," he interrupted, rather hotly, "as to coming here, I am vexed as much as you. Somebody, a member of the Society of Architects,—who, I could never tell—sent to my old address in London your advertisement cut from the paper; it was forwarded to me; I wanted to get away from Liverpool, and it seemed as if this was put in my way on purpose, by some old friend or other. I answered the advertisement certainly, but I was not particularly anxious to come here, nor am I anxious to stay."

Miss Aldclyffe descended from haughty superiority to womanly persuasion with a haste which was almost ludicrous. Indeed the *Quos ego* of the whole lecture had been less the genuine menace of the imperious ruler of Knapwater than an artificial utterance to hide a failing heart.*

"Now, now, Mr. Manston, you wrong me; don't suppose I wish to be overbearing, or anything of the kind; and you will allow me to say this much at any rate, that I have become interested in your wife, as well as in yourself."

"Certainly, madam," he said, slowly, like a man feeling his way in the dark. Manston was utterly at fault now. His previous experience of the effect of his form and features upon womankind *en masse*, had taught him to flatter himself that he could account by the same law of natural selection* for the extraordinary interest Miss Aldclyffe had hitherto taken in him, as an unmarried man; an interest he did not at all object to, seeing that it kept him near Cytherea, and enabled him, a man of no wealth, to rule on the estate as if he were its lawful owner. Like Curius at his Sabine farm, he had counted it his glory not to possess gold himself, but to have power over her who did.* But at this hint of the lady's wish to take his wife under her wing also, he was perplexed: could she have any sinister motive in doing so? But he did not allow himself to be troubled with these doubts, which only concerned his wife's happiness.

"She tells me," continued Miss Aldclyffe, "how utterly alone in the world she stands, and that is an additional reason why I should sympathise with her. Instead, then, of requesting the favour of your retirement from the post, and dismissing your interests altogether, I will retain you as my steward still, on condition that you bring home your wife, and live with her respectably, in short, as if you loved her; you understand. I *wish* you to stay here if you grant that everything shall flow smoothly between yourself and her."

The breast and shoulders of the steward rose, as if an expression of defiance was about to be poured forth; before it took form, he controlled himself and said, in his natural voice,—

"My part of the performance shall be carried out, madam."

"And her anxiety to obtain a standing in the world ensures that her's will," replied Miss Aldclyffe. "That will be satisfactory, then."

After a few additional remarks, she gently signified that she wished to put an end to the interview. The steward took the hint and retired.

He felt vexed and mortified; yet in walking homeward, he was convinced that telling the whole truth as he had done, with the single exception of his love for Cytherea (which he tried to hide even from himself,) had never served him in better stead than it had that night.

Manston went to his desk and thought of Cytherea's beauty with the bitterest, wildest regret. After the lapse of a few minutes he calmed himself by a stoical effort, and wrote the subjoined letter to his wife.

"KNAPWATER, *Nov. 21st*, 1864.

"DEAR EUNICE,

"I hope you reached London safely after your flighty visit to me.

"As I promised, I have thought over our conversation that night, and your wish that your coming here should be no longer delayed. After all, it was perfectly natural that you should have spoken unkindly as you did, ignorant as you were of the circumstances which bound me.

"So I have made arrangements to fetch you home at once. It is hardly worth while for you to attempt to bring with you any luggage you may have gathered about you (beyond mere clothing). Dispose of superfluous things at a broker's;* your bringing them would only make a talk in this parish, and lead people to believe we had long been keeping house separately.

"Will next Monday suit you for coming? You have nothing to do that can occupy you for more than a day or two, as far as I can see, and the remainder of this week will afford ample time. I can be in London the night before, and we will come down together by the mid-day train.

"Your very affectionate husband,

"ÆNEAS MANSTON.

"Now, of course, I shall no longer write to you as Mrs. Rondley."

The address on the envelope was,—

"MRS. MANSTON,
"41, CHARLES SQUARE,
"HOXTON,
"LONDON, N."

He took the letter to the house, and it being too late for the country post, sent one of the stable-men with it to Froominster, instead of troubling to go to Creston with it himself as heretofore. He had no longer any necessity to keep his condition a secret.

§ 7. *From the twenty-second to the twenty-seventh of November*

But the next morning Manston found he had been forgetful of another matter, in naming the following Monday to his wife for the journey.

The fact was this. A letter had just come, reminding him that he had left the whole of the succeeding week open for an important business engagement with a neighbouring land-agent, at that gentleman's residence thirteen miles off.

The particular day he had suggested to his wife, had, in the interim, been appropriated by his correspondent. The meeting could not now be put off.

So he wrote again to his wife, stating that business, which could not be postponed, called him away from home on Monday, and would entirely prevent him coming all the way to fetch her on Sunday night as he had intended, but that he would meet her at the Carriford-Road Station with a conveyance when she arrived there in the evening.

The next day came his wife's answer to his first letter, in which she said that she would be ready to be fetched at the time named.

Having already written his second letter, which was by that time in her hands, he made no further reply.

The week passed away. The steward had, in the meantime, let it become generally known in the village that he was a married man, and by a little judicious management, sound family reasons for his past secrecy upon the subject, which were floated as adjuncts to the story, were placidly received; they seemed so natural and justifiable to the unsophisticated minds of nine-tenths of his neighbours, that curiosity in the matter, beyond a strong curiosity to see the lady's face, was well-nigh extinguished.

CHAPTER II

THE EVENTS OF A DAY AND NIGHT

§ 1. *November the twenty-eighth. Until ten, p.m.*

Monday came, the day named for Mrs. Manston's journey from London to her husband's house; a day of singular and great events, influencing the present and future of nearly all the personages whose actions in a complex drama form the subject of this record.

The proceedings of the steward demand the first notice. Whilst taking his breakfast on this particular morning, the clock pointing to eight, the horse and gig* that was to take him to Chettlewood waiting ready at the door, Manston hurriedly cast his eyes down the column of *Bradshaw** which showed the details and duration of the selected train's journey.

The inspection was carelessly made, the leaf being kept open by the aid of one hand, whilst the other still held his cup of coffee; much more carelessly than would have been the case had the expected new-comer been Cytherea Graye, instead of his lawful wife.

He did not perceive, branching from the column down which his finger ran, a small twist, called a shunting-line, inserted at a particular place, to imply that at that point the train was divided into two. By this oversight he understood that the arrival of his wife at Carriford-Road Station would not be till late in the evening: by the second half of the train, containing the third-class passengers, and passing two hours and three-quarters later than the previous one, by which the lady, as a second-class passenger, would really be brought.

He then considered that there would be plenty of time for him to return from his day's engagement to meet this train. He finished his breakfast, gave proper and precise directions to his servant on the preparations that were to be made for the lady's reception, jumped into his gig, and drove off to Lord Claydonfield's at Chettlewood.

He went along by the front of Knapwater House. He could not help turning to look at what he knew to be the window of Cytherea's room. Whilst he looked, a hopeless expression of passionate love and sensuous anguish came upon his face and lingered there for a few seconds; then, as on previous occasions, it was resolutely repressed, and he trotted along the smooth white road, again endeavouring to banish all thought of the young girl whose beauty and grace had so enslaved him.

Thus it was that when, in the evening of the same day, Mrs. Manston reached Carriford-Road Station, her husband was still at Chettlewood ignorant of her arrival, and on looking up and down the platform, dreary with autumn gloom and wind, she could see no sign that any preparation whatever had been made for her reception and conduct home.

The train went on. She waited, fidgeted with the handle of her umbrella, walked about, strained her eyes into the gloom of the chilly night, listened for wheels, tapped with her foot, and showed all the usual signs of annoyance and irritation: she was the more irritated in that this seemed a second and culminating instance of her husband's neglect—the first having been shown in his not fetching her.

Reflecting awhile upon the course it would be best to take, in order to secure a passage to Knapwater, she decided to leave all her luggage, except a carpet-bag,* in the cloak-room, and walk to her husband's house, as she had done on her first visit. She asked one of the porters if he could find a lad to go with her and carry her bag: he offered to do it himself.

The porter was a good-tempered, shallow-minded, ignorant man. Mrs. Manston, being apparently in very gloomy spirits, would probably have preferred walking beside him without saying a word: but her companion would not allow silence to continue between them for a longer period than two or three minutes together.

He had volunteered several remarks upon her arrival, chiefly to the effect that it was very unfortunate Mr. Manston had not come to the station for her, when she suddenly asked him concerning the inhabitants of the parish.

He told her categorically the names of the chief—first the chief possessors of property; then of brains; then of good looks. As first among the latter he mentioned Miss Cytherea Graye.

After getting him to describe her appearance as completely as lay in his power, she wormed out of him the statement that everybody had been saying—before Mrs. Manston's existence was heard of—how well the handsome Mr. Manston and the beautiful Miss Graye were suited for each other as man and wife, and that Miss Aldclyffe was the only one in the parish who took no interest in bringing about the match.

"He rather liked her you think?"

The porter began to think he had been too explicit, and hastened to correct the error.

"O no, he doesn't care a bit about her, madam," he said, solemnly.

"Any more than he does about me?"

"Not a bit."

"Then that must be little indeed," Mrs. Manston murmured. She stood still, as if reflecting upon the painful neglect her words had recalled to her mind; then with a sudden impulse, turned round, and walked petulantly a few steps back again in the direction of the station.

The porter stood still and looked surprised.

"I'll go back again, yes, indeed, I'll go back again!" she said plaintively. Then she paused and looked anxiously up and down the deserted road.

"No, I mustn't go back now," she continued, in a tone of resignation. Seeing that the porter was watching her, she turned about and came on as before, giving vent to a slight laugh.

It was a laugh full of character; the low forced laugh which seeks to hide the painful perception of a humiliating position under the mask of indifference.

Altogether her conduct had shown her to be what in fact she was, a weak, though a calculating woman, one clever to conceive, weak to execute: one whose best-laid schemes were for ever liable to be frustrated by the ineradicable blight of vacillation at the critical hour of action.

"O if I had only known that all this was going to happen!" she murmured again, as they paced along upon the rustling leaves.

"What did you say, madam?" said the porter.

"O nothing particular; we are getting near the old manor-house by this time, I imagine?"

"Very near now, madam."

They soon reached Manston's residence, round which the wind blew mournfully and chill.

Passing under the detached gateway, they entered the porch. The porter stepped forward, knocked heavily, and waited.

Nobody came.

Mrs. Manston then advanced to the door and gave a different series of rappings—less forcible, but more sustained.

There was not a movement of any kind inside, not a ray of light visible; nothing but the echo of her own knocks through the passages, and the dry scratching of the withered leaves blown about her feet upon the floor of the porch.

The steward, of course, was not at home. Mrs. Crickett, not expecting that anybody would arrive till the time of the later train, had set the place in order, laid the supper-table, and then locked the door, to go into the village and converse with her friends.

"Is there an inn in the village?" said Mrs. Manston, after the fourth and loudest rapping upon the iron-studded old door had resulted only in the fourth and loudest echo from the passages inside.

"Yes, madam."

"Who keeps it?"

"Farmer Springrove."

"I will go there to-night," she said, decisively. "It is too cold, and altogether too bad, for a woman to wait in the open road on anybody's account, gentle or simple."*

They went down the park and through the gate, into the village of Carriford. By the time they reached the Three Tranters, it was verging upon ten o'clock. There, on the spot where two months earlier in the season the sunny and lively group of villagers making cider under the trees had greeted Cytherea's eyes, was nothing now intelligible but a vast cloak of darkness, from which came the low sough of the elms, and the occasional creak of the swinging sign.

They went to the door, Mrs. Manston shivering; but less from the cold, than from the dreariness of her emotions. Neglect is the coldest of winter winds.

It so happened that Edward Springrove was expected to arrive from London either on that evening or the next, and at the sound of voices, his father came to the door fully expecting to see him. A picture of disappointment seldom witnessed in a man's face was visible in old Mr. Springrove's, when he saw that the comer was a stranger.

Mrs. Manston asked for a room, and one that had been prepared for Edward was immediately named as being ready for her, another being adaptable for Edward, should he come in.

Without partaking of any refreshment, or entering any room downstairs, or even lifting her veil, she walked straight along the passage and up to her apartment, the chambermaid preceding her.

"If Mr. Manston comes to-night," she said, sitting on the bed as she had come in, and addressing the woman, "tell him I cannot see him."

"Yes, madam."

The woman left the room, and Mrs. Manston locked the door. Before the servant had gone down more than two or three stairs, Mrs. Manston unfastened the door again, and held it ajar.

"Bring me some brandy," she said.

The chambermaid went down to the bar and brought up the spirit in a tumbler. When she came into the room, Mrs. Manston had not removed a single article of apparel, and was walking up and down, as if still quite undecided upon the course it was best to adopt.

Outside the door, when it was closed upon her, the maid paused to listen for an instant. She heard Mrs. Manston talking to herself.

"This is welcome home!" she said.

§ 2. *From ten to half-past eleven, p.m.*

A strange concurrence of phenomena* now confronts us.

During the autumn in which the past scenes were enacted, Mr. Springrove had ploughed, harrowed, and cleaned a narrow and shaded piece of ground, lying at the back of his house, which for many years had been looked upon as irreclaimable waste.

The couch-grass extracted from the soil had been left to wither in the sun; afterwards it was raked together, lighted in the customary way, and now lay smouldering in a large heap in the middle of the plot.

It had been kindled three days previous to Mrs. Manston's arrival, and one or two villagers, of a more cautious and less sanguine temperament than Springrove, had suggested that the fire was almost too near the back of the house for its continuance to be unattended with risk; for though no danger could be apprehended whilst the air remained moderately still, a brisk breeze blowing towards the house might possibly carry a spark across.

"Ay, that's true enough," said Springrove. "I must look round before going to bed and see that everything's safe; but to tell the truth I am anxious to get the rubbish burnt up before the rain comes to wash it into ground again. As to carrying the couch into the back field to burn, and bringing it back again, why 'tis more than the ashes would be worth."

"Well, that's very true," said the neighbours, and passed on.

Two or three times during the first evening after the heap was lit, he went to the back door to take a survey. Before bolting and barring up for the night, he made a final and more careful examination. The slowly-smoking pile showed not the slightest signs of activity.

Springrove's perfectly sound conclusion was, that as long as the heap was not stirred, and the wind continued in the quarter it blew from then, the couch would not flame, and that there could be no shadow of danger to anything, even a combustible substance, and if it were no more than a yard off.

The next morning the burning couch was discovered in precisely the same state as when he had gone to bed the preceding night. The heap smoked in the same manner the whole of that day: at bed-time the farmer looked towards it, but less carefully than on the first night.

The morning and the whole of the third day still saw the heap in its old smouldering condition; indeed, the smoke was less, and there seemed a probability that it might have to be re-kindled on the morrow.

After admitting Mrs. Manston to his house in the evening, and hearing her retire, Mr. Springrove returned to the front door to listen for a sound of his son, and inquired concerning him of the railway-porter, who sat for a while in the kitchen.

The porter had not noticed young Mr. Springrove get out of the train, at which intelligence the old man concluded that he would probably not see his son till the next day, as Edward had hitherto made a point of coming by the train which brought Mrs. Manston.

Half an hour later the porter left the inn, Springrove at the same time going to the door to listen again for an instant, then he walked round and in at the back of the house.

The farmer glanced at the heap casually and indifferently in passing; two nights of safety seemed to ensure the third; and he was about to bolt and bar as usual, when the idea struck him that there was just a possibility of his son's return by the latest train, unlikely as it was that he would be so delayed.

The old man thereupon left the door unfastened, looked to his usual matters indoors, and then went to bed. This was at half-past ten o'clock.

Farmers and horticulturists well know that it is the nature of a heap of couch-grass, when kindled in calm weather, to smoulder for many days, and even weeks, until the whole mass is reduced to a powdery charcoal ash, displaying the while scarcely a sign of combustion beyond the volcano-like smoke from its summit; but the continuance of this quiet process is throughout its length at the mercy of one particular freak of Nature: that is, a sudden breeze, by which the heap is liable to be fanned into a flame so brisk as to consume the whole in an hour or two.

Had the farmer narrowly watched the pile when he went to close the door, he would have seen, besides the familiar twine of smoke from its summit, a quivering of the air around the mass, showing that a considerable heat had arisen inside.

As the railway-porter turned the corner of the row of houses adjoining the Three Tranters, a brisk new wind greeted his face, and spread past him into the village. He walked along the high-road till he came to a gate, about three hundred yards from the inn. Over the gate could be discerned the situation of the building he had just quitted.

He carelessly turned his head in passing, and saw behind him a clear red glow indicating the position of the couch-heap: a glow without a flame, increasing and diminishing in brightness as the breeze quickened or fell, like the coal of a newly-lighted cigar. If those cottages had been his, he thought, he should not care to have a fire so near to them as that—and the wind rising. But the cottages not being his, he went on his way to the station, where he was about to resume duty for the night.

The road was now quite deserted: till four o'clock the next morning, when the carters would go by to the stables, there was little probability of any human being passing the Three Tranters Inn.

By eleven, everybody in the house was asleep. It truly seemed as if the treacherous element knew there had arisen a grand opportunity for devastation.

At a quarter-past eleven a slight stealthy crackle made itself heard amid the increasing moans of the night wind; the heap glowed brighter still, and burst into a flame; the flame sank, another breeze entered it, sustained it, and it grew to be first continuous and weak, then continuous and strong.

At twenty minutes past eleven a blast of wind carried an airy bit of ignited fern several yards forward, in a direction parallel to the houses and inn, and there deposited it on the ground.

Five minutes later another puff of wind carried a similar piece to a distance of five-and-twenty yards, where it also was dropped softly on the ground.

Still the wind did not blow in the direction of the houses, and even now to a casual observer they would have appeared safe.

But Nature does few things directly. A minute later still, an ignited fragment fell upon the straw covering of a long thatched heap or "grave"* of mangel-wurzel,* lying in a direction at right angles to the house, and down toward the hedge. There the fragment faded to darkness.

A short time subsequent to this, after many intermediate deposits and seemingly baffled attempts, another fragment fell on the mangel-wurzel grave, and continued to glow; the glow was increased by the wind; the straw caught fire and burst into flame. It was inevitable that the flame should run along the ridge of the thatch towards a piggery at the end. Yet had the piggery been tiled, the time-honoured hostel would even now at this last moment have been safe; but it was constructed as piggeries are mostly constructed, of wood and thatch. The hurdles and straw roof of the frail erection became ignited in their turn, and abutting as the shed did on the back of the inn, flamed up to the eaves of the main roof in less than thirty seconds.

§ 3. *Half-past eleven to twelve, p.m.*

A hazardous length of time elapsed before the inmates of the Three Tranters knew of their danger. When at length the discovery was made, the rush was a rush for bare life.

A man's voice calling, then screams, then loud stamping and shouts were heard.

Mr. Springrove ran out first. Two minutes later appeared the ostler* and chambermaid, who were man and wife. The inn, as has been stated, was a quaint old building, and as inflammable as a bee-hive; it overhung the base at the level of the first floor, and again overhung at the eaves, which were finished with heavy oak barge-boards;* every atom in its substance, every feature in its construction, favoured the fire.

The forked flames, lurid and smoky, became nearly lost to view, bursting forth again with a bound and loud crackle, increased tenfold in power and brightness. The crackling grew sharper. Long quiver-ing shadows began to be flung from the stately trees at the end of the house; the square outline of the church tower, on the other side of the way, which had hitherto been a dark mass against a sky compara-tively light, now began to appear as a light object against a sky of darkness; and even the narrow surface of the flag-staff at the top could be seen in its dark surrounding, brought out from its obscurity by the rays from the dancing light.

Shouts and other noises increased in loudness and frequency. The lapse of ten minutes brought most of the inhabitants of that end of the village into the street, followed in a short time by the rector.

Casting a hasty glance up and down, he beckoned to one or two of the men, and vanished again. In a short time wheels were heard, and Mr. Raunham and the men reappeared with the garden engine,* the only one in the village, except that at Knapwater House. After some little trouble the hose was connected with a tank in the old stable-yard, and the puny instrument began to play.

Several seemed paralysed at first, and stood transfixed, their rigid faces looking like red-hot iron in the glaring light. In the confusion a woman cried, "Ring the bells backwards!"* and three or four of the old and superstitious entered the belfry and jangled them indescrib-ably. Some were only half-dressed, and, to add to the horror, among them was Clerk Crickett, running up and down with a face stream-ing with blood, ghastly and pitiful to see, his excitement being so great that he had not the slightest conception of how, when, or where, he came by the wound.

The crowd was now busy at work, and tried to save a little of the furniture of the inn. The only room they could enter was the par-lour, from which they managed to bring out the bureau, a few chairs, some old silver candlesticks, and half-a-dozen light articles; but these were all.

Fiery mats of thatch slid off the roof and fell into the road with a

deadened thud, whilst white flakes of straw and wood-ash were flying in the wind like feathers. At the same time two of the cottages
adjoining, upon which a little water had been brought to play from
the rector's engine, were seen to be on fire. The attenuated spurt of
water was as nothing upon the heated and dry surface of the
thatched roof; the fire prevailed without a minute's hindrance, and
dived through to the rafters.

Suddenly arose a cry, "Where's Mr. Springrove?"

He had vanished from the spot by the churchyard wall, on which
he had been standing a few minutes earlier.

"I fancy he's gone inside," said a voice.

"Madness and folly, what can he save!" said another; "Good God,
find him! Help here!"

A wild rush was made at the door, which had fallen to, and in
defiance of the scorching flame that burst forth, three men forced
themselves through it. Immediately inside the threshold they found
the object of their search, lying senseless on the floor of the passage.

To bring him out and lay him on a bank was the work of an
instant; a basin of cold water was dashed in his face, and he began to
recover consciousness, but very slowly. He had been saved by a mir-
acle. No sooner were his preservers out of the building than the win-
dow-frames lit up as if by magic with deep and waving fringes of
flames. Simultaneously, the joints of the boards forming the front
door started into view as glowing bars of fire; a star of red light
penetrated the centre, gradually increasing in size till the flames
rushed forth.

Then the staircase fell.

"Everybody is out safe," said a voice.

"Yes, thank God!" said three or four others.

"Oh, we forgot that a stranger came! I think she is safe."

"I hope she is," said the weak voice of some one coming up from
behind. It was the chambermaid's.

Springrove at that moment aroused himself; he staggered to his
feet, and threw his hand up wildly.

"Everybody, no! no! The lady who came by train, Mrs. Manston! I
tried to fetch her out, but I fell."

An exclamation of horror burst from the crowd; it was caused
partly by this disclosure of Springrove, more by the added
perception which followed his words.

An average interval of about three minutes had elapsed between one intensely fierce gust of wind and the next, and now another poured over them; the roof swayed, and a moment afterwards fell in with a crash, pulling the gable after it, and thrusting outwards the front wall of wood-work, which fell into the road with a rumbling echo; a cloud of black dust, myriads of sparks, and a great outburst of flame followed the uproar of the fall.

"Who is she,—what is she!" burst from every lip again and again, incoherently, and without leaving a sufficient pause for a reply, had a reply been volunteered.

The autumn wind, tameless, and swift, and proud,* still blew upon the dying old house, which was constructed so entirely of combustible materials that it burnt almost as fiercely as a corn-rick. The heat in the road increased, and now for an instant at the height of the conflagration all stood still, and gazed silently, awe-struck and helpless, in the presence of so irresistible an enemy. Then, with minds full of the tragedy unfolded to them, they rushed forward again with the obtuse directness of waves, to their labour of saving goods from the houses adjoining, which it was evident were all doomed to destruction.

The minutes passed by. The Three Tranters Inn sank into a mere heap of red-hot charcoal: the fire pushed its way down the row as the church clock opposite slowly struck the hour of midnight, and the bewildered chimes, scarcely heard amid the crackling of the flames, wandered through the wayward air of the Old Hundred-and-Thirteenth Psalm.*

§ 4. *Nine to eleven, p.m.*

Manston mounted his gig and set out from Chettlewood that evening in no very enviable frame of mind. The thought of domestic life in Knapwater Old House, with the now eclipsed wife of the past, was more than disagreeable, was positively distasteful to him.

Yet he knew that the influential position which, from whatever fortunate cause, he held on Miss Aldclyffe's manor, would never again fall to his lot on any other; and he tacitly assented to this dilemma, hoping that some consolation or other would soon suggest itself to him; married as he was, he was near Cytherea.

He occasionally looked at his watch as he drove along the lanes,

timing the pace of his horse by the hour, that he might reach Carriford-Road Station just soon enough to meet the last London train.

He soon began to notice in the sky a slight yellow halo, near the
horizon. It rapidly increased; it changed colour, and grew redder;
then the glare visibly brightened and dimmed at intervals, showing
that its origin was affected by the strong wind prevailing.

Manston reined in his horse at the summit of a hill, and
considered.

"It is a rick-yard on fire," he thought; "no house could produce
such a raging flame so suddenly."

He trotted on again, attempting to particularise the local features
in the neighbourhood of the fire; but this it was too dark to do, and
the excessive winding of the roads misled him as to its direction, not
being an inhabitant of the district, or a countryman used to forming
such judgments; whilst the brilliancy of the light shortened its real
remoteness to an apparent distance of not more than half: it seemed
so near that he again stopped his horse, this time to listen; but he
could hear no sound.

Entering now a narrow valley, the sides of which obscured the sky
to an angle of perhaps thirty or forty degrees above the mathematical
horizon,* he was obliged to suspend his judgment till he was in possession of further knowledge, having however assumed in the
interim, that the fire was somewhere between Carriford-Road Station and the village.

The self-same glare had just arrested the eyes of another man. He
was at that minute gliding along several miles to the east of the
steward's position, but nearing the same point as that to which Manston tended. The younger Edward Springrove was returning from
London to his father's house by the identical train which the steward
was expecting to bring his wife, the truth being that Edward's lateness was owing to the simplest of all causes, his temporary want of
money, which led him to make a slow journey for the sake of travelling at third-class fare.

Springrove had received Cytherea's bitter and admonitory letter,
and he was clearly awakened to a perception of the false position in
which he had placed himself, by keeping silence at Creston on his
long engagement. An increasing reluctance to put an end to those
few days of ecstasy with Cytherea had over-ruled his conscience, and
tied his tongue till speaking was too late.

"Why did I do it, how could I dream of loving her," he asked himself as he walked by day, as he tossed on his bed by night; "miserable folly!"

An impressible heart had for years—perhaps as many as six or seven years—been distracting him, by unconsciously setting itself to yearn for somebody wanting,* he scarcely knew whom. Echoes of himself, though rarely, he now and then found. Sometimes they were men, sometimes women, his cousin Adelaide being one of these; for in spite of a fashion which pervades the whole community at the present day—the habit of exclaiming that woman is not undeveloped man, but diverse, the fact remains that, after all, women are Mankind, and that in many of the sentiments of life the difference of sex is but a difference of degree.*

But the indefinable helpmate to the remoter sides of himself still continued invisible. He grew older, and concluded that the ideas, or rather emotions, which possessed him on the subject, were probably too unreal ever to be found embodied in the flesh of a woman.* Thereupon, he developed a plan of satisfying his dreams by wandering away to the heroines of poetical imagination, and took no further thought on the earthly realization of his formless desire, in more homely matters satisfying himself with his cousin.

Cytherea appeared in the sky: his heart started up and spoke:—

> "'Tis she, and here.
> Lo! I unclothe and clear
> My wishes' cloudy character."*

Some women kindle emotion so rapidly in a man's heart, that the judgment cannot keep pace with its rise, and finds, on comprehending the situation, that faithfulness to the old love is already treachery to the new. Such women are not necessarily the greatest of their sex, but there are very few of them. Cytherea was one.

On receiving the letter from her he had taken to thinking over these things, and had not answered it at all. But "hungry generations" soon tread down the muser in a city.* At length he thought of the strong necessity of living. After a dreary search, the negligence of which was ultimately overcome by mere conscientiousness, he obtained a situation as assistant to an architect in the neighbourhood of Charing Cross: the duties would not commence till after the lapse of a month.

He could not at first decide whither he should go to spend the intervening time; but in the midst of his reasonings he found himself on the road homeward, impelled by a secret and unowned hope of getting a last glimpse of Cytherea there.

§ 5. *Midnight*

It was a quarter to twelve when Manston drove into the station yard. The train was punctual, and the bell, announcing its arrival, rang as he crossed the booking-office to go out upon the platform.

The porter who had accompanied Mrs. Manston to Carriford, and had returned to the station on his night duty, recognised the steward as he entered, and immediately came towards him.

"Mrs. Manston came by the nine o'clock train, sir," he said.

The steward gave vent to an expression of vexation.

"Her luggage is here, sir," the porter said.

"Put it up behind me in the gig if it is not too much," said Manston.

"Directly this train is in and gone, sir."

The man vanished and crossed the line to meet the entering train.

"Where is that fire?" Manston said to the booking-clerk.

Before the clerk could speak, another man ran in and answered the question without having heard it.

"Half Carriford is burnt down, or will be!" he exclaimed. "You can't see the flames from this station on account of the trees, but step on the bridge—'tis tremendous!"

He also crossed the line to assist at the entry of the train, which came in the next minute.

The steward stood in the office. One passenger alighted, gave up his ticket, and crossed the room in front of Manston: a young man with a black bag and umbrella in his hand. He passed out of the door, down the steps, and struck out into the darkness.

"Who was that young man?" said Manston, when the porter had returned. The young man, by a kind of magnetism, had drawn the steward's thoughts after him.

"He's an architect's clerk."

"My own old profession. I could have sworn it by the cut of him," Manston murmured. "What's his name?" he said again.

"Springrove—Farmer Springrove's son, Edward."

"Farmer Springrove's son, Edward," the steward repeated to himself, and considered a matter to which the words had painfully recalled his mind.

The matter was Miss Aldclyffe's mention of the young man as Cytherea's lover, which, indeed, had scarcely ever been absent from his thoughts.

"But for the existence of my wife that man might have been my rival," he pondered, following the porter, who had now come back to him, into the luggage-room. And whilst the man was carrying out and putting in one box, which was sufficiently portable for the gig, Manston still thought, as his eyes watched the process,—

"But for my wife, Springrove might have been my rival."

He examined the lamps of his gig, carefully laid out the reins, mounted the seat and drove along the turnpike-road towards Knapwater Park.

The exact locality of the fire was plain to him as he neared home. He soon could hear the shout of men, the flapping of the flames, the crackling of burning wood, and could smell the smoke from the conflagration.

Of a sudden, a few yards a-head, within the compass of the rays from the right-hand lamp, burst forward the figure of a man. Having been walking in darkness the new-comer raised his hands to his eyes, on approaching nearer, to screen them from the glare of the reflector.

Manston saw that he was one of the villagers: a small farmer originally, who had drunk himself down to a day-labourer and reputed poacher.

"Hoy!" cried Manston, aloud, that the man might step aside out of the way.

"Is that Mr. Manston?" said the man.

"Yes."

"Somebody ha' come to Carriford: and the rest of it may concern you, sir."

"Well, well."

"Did you expect Mrs. Manston to-night, sir?"

"Yes, unfortunately she's come, I know, and asleep long before this time, I suppose?"

The labourer leant his elbow upon the shaft of the gig and turned his face, pale and sweating from his late work at the fire, up to Manston's.

"Yes, she did come," he said. . . . "I beg pardon, sir, but I should be glad of—of——"

"What?"

"Glad of a trifle for bringen ye the news."

"Not a farthing! I didn't want your news, I knew she was come."

"Won't you give me a shillen, sir?"

"Certainly not."

"Then will you lend me a shillen, sir? I be tired out and don't know what to do. If I don't pay you back some day I'll be d——d."

"The devil is so cheated that perdition isn't worth a penny as a security."

"Oh!"

"Let me go on," said Manston.

"Thy wife is *dead*; that's the rest o' the news," said the labourer, slowly. He waited for a reply; none came.

"She went to the Three Tranters, because she couldn't get into thy house, the burnen roof fell in upon her before she could be called up, and she's a cinder, as thou'lt be some day."

"That will do, let me drive on," said the steward, calmly.

Expectation of a concussion* may be so intense that its failure strikes the brain with more force than its fulfilment. The labourer sank back into the ditch. Such a Cushi could not realize the possibility of such an unmoved king.*

Manston drove hastily to the turning of the road, tied his horse, and ran on foot to the site of the fire.

The stagnation caused by the awful accident had been passed through, and all hands were helping to remove from the remaining cottages what furniture they could lay hold of; the thatch of the roofs being already on fire. The Knapwater fire-engine had arrived on the spot, but it was small, and ineffectual. A group was collected round the rector, who in a coat which had become bespattered, scorched, and torn in his exertions, was directing on one hand the proceedings relative to the removal of goods into the church, and with the other was pointing out the spot on which it was most desirable that the puny engines at their disposal should be made to play. Every tongue was instantly silent at the sight of Manston's pale and clear countenance, which contrasted strangely with the grimy and streaming faces of the toiling villagers.

"Was she burnt?" he said in a firm though husky voice, and stepping into the illuminated area. The rector came to him, and took him aside. "Is she burnt?" repeated Manston.

"She is dead: but thank God, she was spared the horrid agony of burning," the rector said solemnly; "the roof and gable fell in upon her, and crushed her. Instant death must have followed."

"Why was she here?" said Manston.

"From what we can hurriedly collect, it seems that she found the door of your house locked, and concluded that you had retired, the fact being that your servant Mrs. Crickett had gone out to supper. She then came back to the inn and went to bed."

"Where's the landlord?" said Manston.

Mr. Springrove came up, walking feebly, and wrapped in a cloak, and corroborated the evidence given by the rector.

"Did she look ill, or annoyed, when she came?" said the steward.

"I can't say: I didn't see; but I think . . ."

"What do you think?"

"She was much put out about something."

"My not meeting her, naturally," murmured the other, lost in reverie. He turned his back on Springrove and the rector, and retired from the shining light.

Everything had been done that could be done with the limited means at their disposal. The whole row of houses was destroyed, and each presented itself as one stage of a series, progressing from smoking ruins at the end where the inn had stood, to a partly flaming mass—glowing as none but wood embers will glow—at the other.

A feature in the decline of town fires was noticeably absent here; steam. There was present what is not observable in towns; incandescence.

The heat, and the smarting effect upon their eyes of the strong smoke from the burning oak and deal, had at last driven the villagers back from the road in front of the houses, and they now stood in groups in the churchyard, the surface of which, raised by the interments of generations, stood four or five feet above the level of the road, and almost even with the top of the low wall, dividing one from the other.

The headstones stood forth whitely against the dark grass and yews, their brightness being repeated on the white smock-frocks of some of the labourers, and in a mellower, ruddier form on their faces and hands, on those of the grinning gargoyles, and on other salient stonework of the weather-beaten church in the background.

The rector had decided that, under the distressing circumstances of the case, there would be no sacrilege in placing in the church, for the night, the pieces of furniture and utensils which had been saved from the several houses. There was no other place of safety for them, and they accordingly were gathered there.

§ 6. *Half-past twelve to one, a.m.*

Manston, when he retired to meditate, had walked round the church-yard, and now entered the opened door of the building.

He mechanically pursued his way round the piers into his own seat in the north aisle. The lower atmosphere of this spot was shaded by its own wall from the shine which streamed in over the window sills on the same side. The only light burning inside the church was a small tallow candle, standing in the font, in the opposite aisle of the building to that in which Manston had sat down, and near where the furniture was piled. The candle's mild rays were overpowered by the ruddier light from the ruins, making the weak flame to appear like the moon by day.

Sitting there he saw Farmer Springrove enter the door, followed by his son Edward, still carrying his travelling-bag in his hand. They were speaking of the sad death of Mrs. Manston, but the subject was relinquished for that of the houses burnt.

This row of houses, running from the inn eastward, had been built under the following circumstances.

Fifty years before this date, the spot upon which the cottages afterwards stood was a blank strip, along the side of the village street, difficult to cultivate, on account of the outcrop thereon of a large bed of flints called locally a "launch."*

The Aldclyffe then in possession of the estate conceived the idea that a row of cottages would be an improvement to the spot, and accordingly granted leases of portions to several respectable inhabitants. Each lessee was to be subject to the payment of a merely nominal rent for the whole term of lives,* on condition that he built his own cottage, and delivered it up intact at the end of the term.

Those who had built had, one by one, relinquished their indentures, either by sale or barter, to Farmer Springrove's father. New lives were added in some cases, by payment of a sum to the lord of the manor, etc., and all the leases were now held by the farmer himself, as one of the chief provisions for his old age.

The steward had become interested in the following conversation.

"Try not to be so depressed, father, they are all insured."

The words came from Edward, in an anxious tone.

"You mistake, Edward, they are not insured," returned the old man gloomily.

"Not?" the son asked.

"Not one!" said the farmer.

"In the Helmet Fire Office, surely?"

"They were insured there every one. Six months ago the office, which had been raising the premiums on thatched premises higher for some years, gave up insuring them altogether, as two or three other fire offices had done previously, on account, they said, of the uncertainty and greatness of the risk of thatch undetached. Ever since then I have been continually intending to go to another office, but have never gone. Who expects a fire?"

"Do you remember the terms of the leases?" said Edward, still more uneasily.

"No, not particularly," said his father, absently.

"Where are they?"

"In the bureau there, that's why I tried to save it first, among other things."

"Well, we must see to that at once."

"What do you want?"

"The key."

They went into the south aisle, took the candle from the font, and then proceeded to open the bureau, which had been placed in a corner under the gallery. Both leant over upon the flap; Edward holding the candle, whilst his father took the pieces of parchment from one of the drawers, and spread the first out before him.

"You read it, Ted. I can't see without my glasses. This one will be sufficient. The terms of all are the same."

Edward took the parchment, and read quickly and indistinctly for some time; then aloud and slowly as follows:

"𝕬𝖓𝖉 *the said John Springrove, for himself, his heirs, executors, and administrators, doth covenant and agree with the said Gerald Fellcourt Aldclyffe, his heirs and assigns, that he, the said John Springrove, his heirs and assigns, during the said term, shall pay unto the said Gerald Fellcourt Aldclyffe, his heirs and assigns, the clear yearly rent of ten shillings and sixpence . . . . at the several times hereinbefore appointed for the payment thereof respectively.* And also *shall, and at all times during the said term, well and sufficiently repair, and keep the said Cottage or Dwelling-house and all other the premises, and all houses or buildings erected or to be erected thereupon, in good and proper repair in every respect without exception: and the said premises in such good repair, upon the determination of this demise, shall yield up unto the said Gerald Fellcourt Aldclyffe, his heirs and assigns."*

They closed the bureau and turned towards the door of the church without speaking.

Manston also had come forward out of the gloom. Notwithstanding the farmer's own troubles, an instinctive respect and generous sense of sympathy with the steward for his awful loss, caused the old man to step aside, that Manston might pass out without speaking to them if he chose to do so.

"Who is he?" whispered Edward to his father, as Manston approached.

"Mr. Manston, the steward."

Manston came near, and passed down the aisle on the side of the younger man. Their faces came almost close together: one large flame, which still lingered upon the ruins outside, threw long dancing shadows of each across the nave till they bent upwards against the aisle wall, and also illuminated their eyes, as each met those of the other. Edward had learnt, by a letter from home, of the steward's passion for Cytherea, and his mysterious repression of it, afterwards explained by his marriage. That marriage was now nought. Edward realised the man's newly acquired freedom, and felt an instinctive enmity towards him,—he would hardly own to himself why. The steward too, knew of Cytherea's attachment to Edward, and looked keenly and inscrutably at him.

§7. *One to two, a.m.*

Manston went homeward alone, his heart full of strange emotions. Entering the house and dismissing the woman to her own home, he at once proceeded upstairs to his bedroom.

Reasoning worldliness and infidelity, especially when allied with sensuousness, cannot repress on some extreme occasions the human instinct to pour out the soul to some Being or Personality, who in frigid moments is dismissed with the title of Chance, or at most Law. Manston was impiously and inhumanly, but honestly and unutterably, thankful for the recent catastrophe. Beside his bed, for the first time during a period of nearly twenty years, he fell down upon his knees in a passionate, outburst of feeling.

Many minutes passed before he arose. He walked to the window, and then seemed to remember for the first time that some action on his part was necessary in connection with the sad circumstance of the night.

Leaving the house at once, he went to the scene of the fire, arriving there in time to hear the rector making an arrangement with a certain number of men to watch the spot till morning. The ashes were still red-hot and flaming. Manston found nothing could be done towards searching them at that hour of the night. He turned homeward again, in the company of the rector, who had considerately persuaded him to retire from the scene for a while, and promised that as soon as a man could live amid the embers of the Three Tranters Inn, they should be carefully searched for the remains of his unfortunate wife.

Manston then went indoors, to wait for morning.

CHAPTER III

THE EVENTS OF FIVE DAYS

§ 1. *November the twenty-ninth*

The search was commenced at dawn, but a quarter past nine o'clock came without bringing any result. Manston partook of a little breakfast, and crossed the hollow of the park which intervened between the old and modern manor-houses, to ask for an interview with Miss Aldclyffe.

He met her midway. She was about to pay him a visit of condolence, and to place every man on the estate at his disposal, that the search for any relic of his dead and destroyed wife might not be delayed an instant.

He accompanied her back to the house. At first they conversed as if the death of the poor woman was an event which the husband must of necessity deeply lament; and when all under this head that social form seemed to require had been uttered, they spoke of the material damage done, and of the steps which had better be taken to remedy it.

It was not till both were shut inside her private room that she spoke to him in her blunt and cynical manner. A certain newness of bearing in him, peculiar to the present morning, had hitherto forbidden her this tone: the demeanour of the subject of her favouritism had altered, she could not tell in what way. He was entirely a changed man.

"Are you really sorry for your poor wife, Mr. Manston?" she said.

"Well, I am," he answered, shortly.

"But only as for any human being who has met with a violent death?"

He confessed it—"For she was not a good woman," he added.

"I should be sorry to say such a thing now the poor creature is dead," Miss Aldclyffe returned, reproachfully.

"Why?" he asked; "Why should I praise her if she doesn't deserve it? I say exactly what I have often admired Sterne for saying in one of his letters,—that neither reason nor scripture asks us to speak nothing but good of the dead.* And now, madam," he continued, after a short interval of thought, "I may, perhaps, hope that you will assist me, or rather not thwart me, in endeavouring to win the love of a young lady living about you, one in whom I am much interested already."

"Cytherea!"

"Yes, Cytherea."

"You have been loving Cytherea all the while?"

"Yes."

Surprise was a preface to much agitation in her, which caused her to rise from her seat, and pace to the side of the room. The steward quietly looked on and added, "I have been loving and still love her."

She came close up to him, wistfully contemplating his face, one hand moving indecisively at her side.

"And your secret marriage was, then, the true and only reason for that backwardness regarding the courtship of Cytherea, which, they tell me, has been the talk of the village; not your indifference to her attractions." Her voice had a tone of conviction in it, as well as of inquiry; but none of jealousy.

"Yes," he said; "and not a dishonourable one. What held me back was just that one thing—a sense of morality that perhaps, madam, you did not give me credit for." The latter words were spoken with a mien and tone of pride.

Miss Aldclyffe preserved silence.

"And now," he went on, "I may as well say a word in vindication of my conduct lately, at the risk, too, of offending you. My actual motive in submitting to your order that I should send for my late wife, and live with her, was not the mercenary policy of wishing to retain an office which brings me a higher income than any I have enjoyed before, but this unquenchable passion for Cytherea. Though I saw the weakness, folly, and even wickedness of it continually, it still forced me to try to continue near her, even as the husband of another woman."

He waited for her to speak: she did not.

"There's a great obstacle to my making any way in winning Miss Graye's love," he went on.

"Yes, Edward Springrove," she said, quietly. "I know it, I did once want to see them married; they have had a slight quarrel, and it will soon be made up again, unless—" she spoke as if she had only half attended to Manston's last statement.

"He is already engaged to be married to somebody else," said the steward.

"Pooh!" said she, "you mean to his cousin at Peakhill; that's nothing to help us; he's now come home to break it off."

"He must not break it off," said Manston, firmly and calmly.

His tone attracted her, startled her. Recovering herself, she said, haughtily, "Well, that's your affair, not mine. Though my wish has been to see her *your* wife, I can't do anything dishonourable to bring about such a result."

"But it must be *made* your affair," he said in a hard, steady voice, looking into her eyes, as if he saw there the whole panorama of her past.

One of the most difficult things to portray by written words is that peculiar mixture of moods expressed in a woman's countenance when, after having been sedulously engaged in establishing another's position, she suddenly suspects him of undermining her own.

It was thus that Miss Aldclyffe looked at the steward.

"You—know—something—of me?" she faltered.

"I know all," he said.

"Then curse that wife of yours! She wrote and said she wouldn't tell you!" she burst out. "Couldn't she keep her word for a day?" She reflected and then said, but no more as to a stranger, "I will not yield. I have committed no crime. I yielded to her threats in a moment of weakness, though I felt inclined to defy her at the time: it was chiefly because I was mystified as to how she got to know of it. Pooh! I will put up with threats no more. Oh, can you threaten me?" she added, softly, as if she had for the moment forgotten to whom she had been speaking.

"My love must be made your affair," he repeated, without taking his eyes from her.

An agony, which was not the agony of being discovered in a secret, obstructed her utterance for a time. "How can you turn upon me so when I schemed to get you here—schemed that you might win her till I found you were married. O, how can you! O! . . . O!" She wept; and the weeping of such a nature was as harrowing as the weeping of a man.

"Your getting me here, was bad policy as to your secret—the most absurd thing in the world," he said, not heeding her distress, "I knew all, except the identity of the individual long ago. Directly I found that my coming here was a contrived thing and not a matter of chance, it fixed my attention upon you at once. All that was required was the mere spark of life, to make of a bundle of perceptions an organic whole."

"Policy, how can you talk of policy. Think, do think! And how can you threaten me when you know—you know—that I would befriend you readily without a threat!"

"Yes, yes, I think you would," he said more kindly, "but your indifference for so many many years has made me doubt it."

"No, not indifference—'twas enforced silence: my father lived."

He took her hand, and held it gently.

*   *   *   *   *   *   *   *   *   *

"Now listen," he said, more quietly and humanly, when she had become calmer, "Springrove must marry the woman he's engaged to. You may make him, but only in one way."

"Well: but don't speak sternly, Æneas!"

"Do you know that his father has not been particularly thriving for the last two or three years?"

"I have heard something of it, once or twice, though his rents have been promptly paid, haven't they?"

"O yes; and do you know the terms of the leases of the houses which are burnt?" he said, explaining to her that by those terms, she might compel him even to rebuild every house. "The case is the clearest case of fire by negligence that I have ever known, in addition to that," he continued.

"I don't want them rebuilt; you know it was intended by my father, directly they fell in, to clear the site for a new entrance to the park?"

"Yes, but that doesn't affect the position, which is that Farmer Springrove is in your power to an extent which is very serious for him."

"I won't do it—'Tis a conspiracy."

"Won't you for me?" he said eagerly.

Miss Aldclyffe changed colour.

"I don't threaten now, I implore," he said.

"Because you might threaten if you chose," she mournfully answered. "But why be so—when your marriage with her was my own pet idea long before it was yours! What must I do?"

"Scarcely anything: simply this. When I have seen old Mr. Springrove, which I shall do in a day or two, and told him that he will be expected to rebuild the houses, do you see the young man. See him yourself, in order that the proposal made may not appear to be anything more than an impulse of your own. You or he will bring up the subject of the houses. To rebuild them would be a matter of at least six hundred pounds, and he will almost surely say that we are hard in insisting upon the extreme letter of the leases. Then tell him, that neither can you yourself think of compelling an old tenant like his father to any such painful extreme—there shall be no compulsion to build, simply a surrender of the leases. Then speak feelingly of his cousin, as a woman whom you respect and love, and whose secret you have learnt to be that she is heart-sick with hope deferred. Beg him to marry her, his betrothed and your friend, as some return for your consideration towards his father. Don't suggest too early a day for their marriage, or he will suspect you of some motive beyond womanly sympathy. Coax him to make a promise to her that she shall be his wife at the end of a twelvemonth, and get him on assenting to this, to write to Cytherea, entirely renouncing her."

"She has already asked him to do that."

"So much the better—and telling her too, that he is about to fulfil his long-standing promise to marry his cousin. If you think it worth while, you may say Cytherea was not indisposed to think of me before she knew I was married. I have at home a note she wrote me the first evening I saw her, which looks rather warm, and which I could show you. Trust me, he will give her up. When he is married to Adelaide Hinton, Cytherea will be induced to marry me—perhaps before; a woman's pride is soon wounded."

"And hadn't I better write to Mr. Nyttleton, and inquire more particularly what's the law upon the houses?"

"O no, there's no hurry for that. We know well enough how the case stands—quite well enough to talk in general terms about it. And I want the pressure to be put upon young Springrove before he goes away from home again."

She looked at him furtively, long, and sadly, as after speaking he became lost in thought, his eyes listlessly tracing the pattern of the carpet. "Yes, yes, she will be mine," he whispered, careless of Cytherea Aldclyffe's presence. At last he raised his eyes inquiringly.

"I will do my best, Æneas," she answered.

Talibus incusat.* Manston then left the house, and again went towards the blackened ruins, where men were still raking and probing.

§ 2. *From November the twenty-ninth to December the second*

The smouldering remnants of the Three Tranters Inn seemed to promise that, even when the searchers should light upon the remains of the unfortunate Mrs. Manston, very little would be discoverable.

Consisting so largely of the charcoal and ashes of hard dry oak and chestnut, intermingled with thatch, the interior of the heap was one glowing mass of embers, which on being stirred about emitted sparks and flame long after it was dead and black on the outside. It was persistently hoped, however, that some traces of the body would survive the effect of the hot coals, and after a search pursued uninterruptedly for thirty hours, under the direction of Manston himself, enough was found to set at rest any doubts of her fate.

The melancholy gleanings consisted of her watch, bunch of keys, a few coins, and two charred and blackened bones.

Two days later the official inquiry into the cause of her death was held at the Traveller's Rest Inn, before Mr. Floy, the coroner, and a jury of the chief inhabitants of the district. The little tavern—the only remaining one in the village—was crowded to excess by the neighbouring peasantry as well as their richer employers: all who could by any possibility obtain an hour's release from their duties being present as listeners.

The jury viewed the sad and infinitesimal remains, which were folded in a white cambric* cloth, and laid in the middle of a well-finished coffin lined with white silk, (by Manston's order), which stood in an adjoining room, the bulk of the coffin being completely filled in with carefully arranged flowers and evergreens—also the steward's own doing.

Abraham Brown, of Hoxton, London—an old white-headed man, without the ruddiness which makes white hairs so pleasing—was sworn, and deposed that he kept a lodging-house at an address he named. On a Saturday evening less than a month before the fire, a lady came to him, with very little luggage, and took the front room on the second floor. He did not inquire where she came from, as she paid a week in advance, but she gave her name as Mrs. Manston, referring him, if he wished for any guarantee of her respectability, to Mr. Manston, Knapwater Park, near Froominster. Here she lived for three weeks, rarely going out. She slept away from her lodgings one night during the time. At the end of that time, on the twenty-eighth of November, she left his house in a four-wheeled cab, about twelve o'clock in the day, telling the driver to take her to the Waterloo Station. She paid all her lodging expenses, and not having given notice the full week previous to her going away, offered to pay for the next, but he only took half. She wore a thick black veil, and grey waterproof cloak, when she left him, and her luggage was two boxes, one of plain deal, with black japanned clamps,* the other sewn up in canvas.

Joseph Chinney, porter at the Carriford-Road Station, deposed that he saw Mrs. Manston, dressed as the last witness had described, get out of a second-class carriage on the night of the twenty-eighth. She stood beside him whilst her luggage was taken from the van. The luggage, consisting of the clamped deal box and another covered with canvas, was placed in the cloak-room. She seemed at a loss at finding nobody there to meet her. She asked him for some person to accompany her, and carry her bag to Mr. Manston's house, Knapwater Park. He was just off duty at that time, and offered to go himself. The witness here repeated the conversation he had had with Mrs. Manston during their walk, and testified to having left her at the door of the Three Tranters Inn, Mr. Manston's house being closed.

Next Farmer Springrove was called. A murmur of surprise and commiseration passed round the crowded room when he stepped forward.

The events of the few preceding days had so worked upon his nervously thoughtful nature, that the blue orbits of his eyes, and the mere spot of scarlet to which the ruddiness of his cheeks had contracted seemed the result of a heavy sickness. A perfect silence pervaded the assembly when he spoke.

His statement was that he received Mrs. Manston at the threshold, and asked her to enter the parlour. She would not do so, and stood in the passage whilst the maid went upstairs to see that the room was in order. The maid came down to the middle landing of the staircase, when Mrs. Manston followed her up to the room. He did not speak ten words with her altogether.

Afterwards, whilst he was standing at the door listening for his son Edward's return, he saw her light extinguished, having first caught sight of her shadow moving about the room.

The Coroner. "Did her shadow appear to be that of a woman undressing?"

Springrove. "I cannot say, as I didn't take particular notice. It moved backwards and forwards: she might have been undressing or merely pacing up and down the room."

Mrs. Fitler the ostler's wife, and chambermaid, said that she preceded Mrs. Manston into the room, put down the candle and went out. Mrs. Manston scarcely spoke to her, except to ask her to bring a little brandy. Witness went and fetched it from the bar, brought it up, and put it on the dressing-table.

The Coroner. "Had Mrs. Manston begun to undress when you came back?"

"No, sir: she was sitting on the bed, with everything on, as when she came in."

"Did she begin to undress before you left?"

"Not exactly before I had left: but when I had closed the door, and was on the landing, I heard her boot drop on the floor, as it does sometimes when pulled off."

"Had her face appeared worn and sleepy?"

"I cannot say, as her bonnet and veil were still on when I left, for she seemed rather shy and ashamed to be seen at the Three Tranters at all."

"And did you hear or see any more of her?"

"No more, sir."

Mrs. Crickett, provisional servant* to Mr. Manston, said that in accordance with Mr. Manston's orders, everything had been made comfortable in the house for Mrs. Manston's expected return on Monday night. Mr. Manston told her that himself and Mrs. Manston would be home late, not till between eleven and twelve o'clock, and that supper was to be ready. Not expecting Mrs. Manston so early, she had gone out on a very important errand to Mrs. Leat's the post-mistress.

Mr. Manston deposed that in looking down the columns of *Bradshaw* he had mistaken the time of the train's arrival, and hence was not at the station when she came. The broken watch produced was his wife's—he knew it by a scratch on the inner plate, and by other signs. The bunch of keys belonged to her: two of them fitted the locks of her two boxes.

Mr. Flooks, agent to Lord Claydonfield at Chettlewood, said that Mr. Manston had pleaded as his excuse for leaving him rather early in the evening after their day's business had been settled, that he was going to meet his wife at Carriford-Road Station, where she was coming by the last train that night.

The surgeon said that the remains were those of a human being. The small fragment seemed a portion of one of the lumbar vertebræ*—the other the extreme end of the os femoris*—but they were both so far gone that it was impossible to say definitely whether they belonged to the body of a male or female. There was no moral doubt that they were a woman's. He did not believe that death resulted from burning by fire. He thought she was crushed by the fall of the west gable, which being of wood, as well as the floor, burnt after it had fallen, and consumed the body with it.

Two or three additional witnesses gave unimportant testimony.

The coroner summed up, and the jury without hesitation found that the deceased Mrs. Manston came by her death accidentally, through the burning of the Three Tranters Inn.

§ 3. *December the second. Afternoon*

When Mr. Springrove came from the door of the Traveller's Rest at the end of the inquiry, Manston walked by his side as far as the stile to the park, a distance of about a stone's throw.

"Ah, Mr. Springrove, this is a sad affair for everybody concerned."

"Everybody," said the old farmer, with deep sadness, "'tis quite a misery to me. I hardly know how I shall live through each day as it breaks. I think of the words, 'In the morning thou shalt say, Would God it were even! and at even thou shalt say, Would God it were morning! for the fear of thine heart wherewith thou shalt fear, and for the sight of thine eyes which thou shalt see'."* His voice became broken.

"Ah—true. I read Deuteronomy myself," said Manston.

"But my loss is as nothing to yours," the farmer continued.

"Nothing; but I can commiserate you. I should be worse than unfeeling if I didn't, although my own affliction is of so sad and solemn a kind. Indeed my own loss makes me more keenly alive to yours, different in nature as it is."

"What sum do you think would be required of me to put the houses in place again?"

"I have roughly thought six or seven hundred pounds."

"If the letter of the law is to be acted up to," said the old man with more agitation in his voice.

"Yes, exactly."

"Do you know enough of Miss Aldclyffe's mind to give me an idea of how she means to treat me?"

"Well, I am afraid I must tell you that though I know very little of her mind as a rule, in this matter I believe she will be rather peremptory; she might share to the extent of a sixth or an eighth perhaps, in consideration of her getting new lamps for old,* but I should hardly think more."

The steward stepped upon the stile, and Mr. Springrove went along the road with a bowed head and heavy footsteps towards his niece's cottage, in which, rather against the wish of Edward, they had temporarily taken refuge.

The additional weight of this knowledge soon made itself perceptible. Though indoors with Edward or Adelaide nearly the whole of the afternoon, nothing more than monosyllabic replies could be drawn from him. Edward continually discovered him looking fixedly at the wall or floor, quite unconscious of another's presence. At supper he ate just as usual, but quite mechanically, and with the same abstraction.

§ 4. *December the third*

The next morning he was in no better spirits. Afternoon came: his son was alarmed, and managed to draw from him an account of the conversation with the steward.

"Nonsense! he knows nothing about it," said Edward, vehemently. "I'll see Miss Aldclyffe myself. Now promise me, father, that you'll not believe till I come back, and tell you to believe it, that Miss Aldclyffe will do any such unjust thing."

Edward started at once for Knapwater House. He strode rapidly along the high road, till he reached a wicket* a few yards below the brow of Buckshead Hill, where a foot-path allowed of a short cut to the mansion. Here he leant down upon the bars for a few minutes, meditating as to the best manner of opening his speech, and surveying the scene before him in that absent mood which takes cognisance of little things without being conscious of them at the time, though they appear in the eye afterwards as vivid impressions.* It was a yellow, lustrous, late-autumn day, one of those days of the quarter when morning and evening seem to meet together without the intervention of a noon. The clear yellow sunlight had tempted forth Miss Aldclyffe herself, who was at this same time taking a walk in the direction of the village. As Springrove lingered he heard behind the plantation a woman's dress brushing along amid the prickly husks and leaves which had fallen into the path from the boughs of the chestnut trees. In another minute she stood in front of him.

He answered her casual greeting respectfully, and was about to request a few minutes' conversation with her, when she directly addressed him on the subject of the fire. "It is a sad misfortune for your father," she said, "and I hear that he has lately let his insurances expire?"

"He has madam, and you are probably aware that either by the general terms of his holding, or the same coupled with the origin of the fire, the disaster may involve the necessity of his rebuilding the whole row of houses, or else of becoming a creditor* to the estate, to the extent of some hundreds of pounds?"

She assented; "I have been thinking of it," she went on, and then repeated in substance the words put into her mouth by the steward. Some disturbance of thought might have been fancied as taking place in Springrove's mind during her statement, but before she had reached the end, his eyes were clear, and directed upon her.

"I don't accept your conditions of release,"* he said.

"They are not conditions exactly."

"Well, whatever they are not, they are very uncalled-for remarks."

"Not at all—the houses have been burnt by your family's negligence."

"I don't refer to the houses—you have of course the best of all rights to speak of that matter; but you, a stranger to me comparatively, have no right at all to volunteer opinions and wishes upon a very delicate subject, which concerns no living beings but Miss Graye, Miss Hinton, and myself."

Miss Aldclyffe, like a good many others in her position, had plainly not realised that a son of her tenant and inferior, could have become an educated man, who had learnt to feel his individuality, to view society from a Bohemian* stand-point, far outside the farming grade in Carriford parish, and that hence he had all a developed man's unorthodox opinion about the subordination of classes.* And fully conscious of the labyrinth into which he had wandered between his wish to behave honourably in the dilemma of his engagement to his cousin Adelaide, and the intensity of his love for Cytherea, Springrove was additionally sensitive to any allusion to the case. He had spoken to Miss Aldclyffe with considerable warmth.

And Miss Aldclyffe was not a woman likely to be far behind any second person in warming to a mood of defiance. It seemed as if she was prepared to put up with a cold refusal, but that her haughtiness resented a criticism of her conduct ending in a rebuke. By this, Manston's discreditable object, which had been made hers by compulsion only, was now adopted by choice. She flung herself into the work.

A fiery man in such a case would have relinquished persuasion and tried palpable force. A fiery woman added unscrupulousness and evolved daring strategy; and in her obstinacy, and to sustain herself as mistress, she descended to an action the meanness of which haunted her conscience to her dying hour.

"I don't quite see, Mr. Springrove," she said, "that I am altogether what you are pleased to call a stranger. I have known your family, at any rate, for a good many years, and I know Miss Graye particularly well, and her state of mind with regard to this matter."

Perplexed love makes us credulous and curious as old women. Edward was willing, he owned it to himself, to get at Cytherea's state of mind, even through so dangerous a medium.

"A letter I received from her," he said, with assumed coldness, "tells me clearly enough what Miss Graye's mind is."

"You think she still loves you? O, yes, of course you do—all men are like that."

"I have reason to." He could feign no further than the first speech.

"I should be interested in knowing what reason?" she said, with sarcastic archness.

Edward felt he was allowing her to do, in fractional parts, what he rebelled against when regarding it as a whole; but the fact that his antagonist had the presence of a queen, and features only in the early evening of their beauty, was not without its influence upon a keenly conscious man. Her bearing had charmed him into toleration, as Mary Stuart's charmed the indignant Puritan visitors.* He again answered her honestly.

"The best of reasons—the tone of her letter."

"Pooh, Mr. Springrove!"

"Not at all, Miss Aldclyffe! Miss Graye desired that we should be strangers to each other for the simple practical reason that intimacy could only make wretched complications worse, not from lack of love—love is only suppressed."

"Don't you know yet, that in thus putting aside a man, a woman's pity for the pain she inflicts gives her a kindness of tone which is often mistaken for suppressed love?" said Miss Aldclyffe, with soft insidiousness.

This was a translation of the ambiguity of Cytherea's tone which he had certainly never thought of; and he was too ingenuous not to own it.

"I had never thought of it," he said.

"And don't believe it?"

"Not unless there was some other evidence to support the view."

She paused a minute and then began hesitatingly,

"My intention was—what I did not dream of owning to you—my intention was to try to induce you to fulfil your promise to Miss Hinton not solely on her account and yours (though partly). I love Cytherea Graye with all my soul, and I want to see her happy even more than I do you. I did not mean to drag her name into the affair at all, but I am driven to say that she wrote that letter of dismissal to you—for it was a most pronounced dismissal—not on account of your engagement. She is old enough to know that engagements can be broken as easily as they can be made. She wrote it because she loved another man; very suddenly, and not with any idea or hope of marrying him, but none the less deeply."

"Who?"

"Mr. Manston."

"Good——! I can't listen to you for an instant, madam; why, she hadn't seen him!"

"She had; he came here the day before she wrote to you; and I could prove to you, if it were worth while, that on that day, she went voluntarily to his house, though not artfully or blamably; stayed for two hours playing and singing; that no sooner did she leave him than she went straight home, and wrote the letter* saying she should not see you again, entirely because she had seen him and fallen desperately in love with him—a perfectly natural thing for a young girl to do, considering that he's the handsomest man in the county. Why else should she not have written to you before?"

"Because I was such a—because she did not know of the connection between me and my cousin until then."

"I must think she did."

"On what ground?"

"On the strong ground of my having told her so, distinctly, the very first day she came to live with me."

"Well, what do you seek to impress upon me after all? This—that the day Miss Graye wrote to me, saying it was better we should part, coincided with the day she had seen a certain man——"

"A remarkably handsome and talented man."

"Yes, I admit that."

"And that it coincided with the hour just subsequent to her seeing him."

"Yes, just when she had seen him."

"And been to his house alone with him."

"It is nothing."

"And stayed there playing and singing with him."

"Admit that, too," he said; "an accident might have caused it."

"And at the same instant that she wrote your dismissal she wrote a letter referring to a secret appointment with him."

"Never, by God, madam! never!"

"What do you say, sir?"

"Never."

She sneered.

"There's no accounting for beliefs, and the whole history is a very trivial matter; but I am resolved to prove that a lady's word is truthful, though upon a matter which concerns neither you nor herself. You shall learn that she *did* write him a letter concerning an assignation—that is, if Mr. Manston still has it, and will be considerate enough to lend it me."

"But besides," continued Edward, "a married man to do what would cause a young girl to write a note of the kind you mention!"

She flushed a little.

"That I don't know anything about," she stammered. "But Cytherea didn't, of course, dream any more than I did, or others in the parish, that he was married."

"Of course she didn't."

"And I have reason to believe that he told her of the fact directly afterwards, that she might not compromise herself, or allow him to. It is notorious that he struggled honestly and hard against her attractions, and succeeded in hiding his feelings, if not in quenching them."

"We'll hope that he did."

"But circumstances are changed now."

"Very greatly changed," he murmured, abstractedly.

"You must remember," she added, more suasively, "that Miss Graye has a perfect right to do what she likes with her own—her heart, that is to say."

Her descent from irritation was caused by perceiving that Edward's faith was really disturbed by her strong assertions, and it gratified her.

Edward's thoughts flew to his father, and the object of his interview with her. Tongue-fencing* was utterly distasteful to him.

"I will not trouble you by remaining longer, madam," he remarked, gloomily; "our conversation has ended sadly for me."

"Don't think so," she said, "and don't be mistaken. I am older than you are, many years older, and I know many things."

Full of miserable doubt, and bitterly regretting that he had raised his father's expectations by anticipations impossible of fulfilment, Edward slowly wended his way into the village, and approached his cousin's house. The farmer was at the door looking eagerly for him. He had been waiting there for more than half-an-hour. His eye kindled quickly.

"Well, Ted, what does she say?" he asked, in the intensely sanguine tones which fall sadly upon a listener's ear, because, antecedently, they raise pictures of inevitable disappointment for the speaker, in some direction or another.

"Nothing for us to be alarmed at," said Edward, with a forced cheerfulness.

"But must we rebuild?"

"It seems we must, father."

The old man's eye swept the horizon, then he turned to go in, without making another observation. All light seemed extinguished in him again. When Edward went in he found his father with the bureau open, unfolding the leases with a shaking hand, folding them up again without reading them, then putting them in their niche only to remove them again.

Adelaide was in the room. She said thoughtfully to Edward, as she watched the farmer,—

"I hope it won't kill poor uncle, Edward. What should we do if anything were to happen to him? He is the only near relative you and I have in the world." It was perfectly true, and somehow Edward felt more bound up with her after that remark.

She continued, "And he was only saying so hopefully the day before the fire, that he wouldn't for the world let anyone else give me away to you when we are married."

For the first time a conscientious doubt arose in Edward's mind as to the justice of the course he was pursuing in resolving to refuse the alternative offered by Miss Aldclyffe. Could it be selfishness as well as independence? How much he had thought of his own heart, how little he had thought of his father's peace of mind!

The old man did not speak again till supper-time, when he began asking his son an endless number of hypothetical questions on what might induce Miss Aldclyffe to listen to kinder terms: speaking of her now not as an unfair woman, but as a Lachesis* or Fate whose course it behoved nobody to condemn. In his earnestness he once turned his eyes on Edward's face: their expression was woeful: the pupils were dilated and strange in aspect.

"If she will only agree to that!" he reiterated for the hundredth time, increasing the sadness of his listeners.

An aristocratic knocking came to the door, and Jane entered with a letter, addressed

"Mr. Edward Springrove,* Junior."

"Charles from Knapwater House brought it," she said.

"Miss Aldclyffe's writing," said Mr. Springrove, before Edward had recognised it himself. "Now 'tis all right! she's going to make an offer; she doesn't want the houses there, not she; they are going to make that the way into the park."

Edward opened the seal and glanced at the inside. He said, with a supreme effort of self-command,—

"It is only directed by Miss Aldclyffe, and refers to nothing connected with the fire. I wonder at her taking the trouble to send it to-night."

His father looked absently at him and turned away again.

Shortly afterwards they retired for the night. Alone in his bedroom Edward opened and read what he had not dared to refer to in their presence.

The envelope contained another envelope in Cytherea's handwriting, addressed to "—Manston, Esq., Old Manor House." Inside this was the note she had written to the steward after her detention in his house by the thunderstorm:—

> "Knapwater House,
> "*September 20th.*

"I find I cannot meet you at seven o'clock by the waterfall as I promised. The emotion I felt made me forgetful of realities.

> "C. Graye."

Miss Aldclyffe had not written a line, and, by the unvarying rule observable when words are not an absolute necessity, her silence seemed ten times as convincing as any expression of opinion could have been.

He then, step by step, recalled all the conversation on the subject of Cytherea's feelings that had passed between himself and Miss Aldclyffe in the afternoon, and by a confusion of thought, natural enough under the trying experience, concluded that because the lady was truthful in her portraiture of effects, she must necessarily be right in her assumption of causes. That is, he was convinced that Cytherea—the hitherto-believed faithful Cytherea—had, at any rate, looked with something more than indifference upon the extremely handsome face and form of Manston.

Did he blame her, as guilty of the impropriety of allowing herself to love him in the face of his not being free to return her love? No: never for a moment did he doubt that all had occurred in her old, innocent, impulsive way: that her heart was gone before she knew it—before she knew anything, beyond his existence, of the man to whom it had flown. Perhaps the very note enclosed to him was the result of first reflection. Manston he would unhesitatingly have called a scoundrel, but for one strikingly redeeming fact. It had been patent to the whole parish, and had come to Edward's own knowledge by that indirect channel, that Manston, as a married man, conscientiously avoided Cytherea after those first few days of his arrival during which her irresistibly beautiful and fatal glances had rested upon him—his upon her.

Taking from his coat a creased and pocket-worn envelope containing Cytherea's letter to himself, Springrove opened it and read it through. He was upbraided therein, and he was dismissed. It bore the date of the letter sent to Manston, and by containing within it the phrase, "All the day long I have been thinking," afforded justifiable ground for assuming that it was written subsequently to the other, (and in Edward's sight far sweeter one), to the steward.

But though he accused her of fickleness, he would not doubt the genuineness, of its kind, of her partiality for him at Creston. It was a short and shallow feeling: not genuine love:—

"Love is not love
"Which alters when it alteration finds."*

But it was not flirtation; a feeling had been born in her and had died. It would be well for his peace of mind if his love for her could flit away so softly, and leave so few traces behind.

Miss Aldclyffe had shown herself desperately concerned in the whole matter by the alacrity with which she had obtained the letter from Manston, and her labours to induce himself to marry his cousin. Taken in connection with her apparent interest in, if not love for Cytherea, her eagerness, too, could only be accounted for on the ground that Cytherea indeed loved the steward.

§ 5. *December the fourth*

Edward passed the night he scarcely knew how, tossing feverishly from side to side, the blood throbbing in his temples, and singing in his ears.*

As soon as day began to break he dressed himself. On going out upon the landing he found his father's bedroom door already open. Edward concluded that the old man had risen softly, as was his wont, and gone out into the fields to start the labourers.

But neither of the outer doors was unfastened.

He entered the front room, and found it empty. Then animated by a new idea, he went round to the little back parlour, in which the few wrecks saved from the fire were deposited, and looked in at the door. Here, near the window, the shutters of which had been opened half way, he saw his father leaning on the bureau, his elbows resting on the flap, his body nearly doubled, his hands clasping his forehead. Beside him were ghostly-looking square folds of parchment—the leases of the houses destroyed.

His father looked up when Edward entered, and wearily spoke to the young man as his face came into the faint light.

"Edward, why did you get up so early?"

"I was uneasy, and could not sleep."

The farmer turned again to the leases on the bureau, and seemed to become lost in reflection. In a minute or two, without lifting his eyes, he said,

"This is more than we can bear, Ted, more than we can bear! Ted, this will kill me. Not the loss only—the sense of my neglect about the insurance and everything. Borrow I never will. 'Tis all misery now. God help us—all misery now!"

Edward did not answer, continuing to look fixedly at the dreary daylight outside.

"Ted," the farmer went on, "This upset of beën burnt out o' home makes me very nervous and doubtful about everything. There's this troubles me besides—our liven here with your cousin, and fillen up her house. It must be very awkward for her. But she says she doesn't mind. Have you said anything to her lately about when you are going to marry her?"

"Nothing at all lately."

"Well perhaps you may as well, now we are so mixed in together. You know, no time has ever been mentioned to her at all, first or last, and I think it right that now, since she has waited so patiently and so long—you are almost called upon to say you are ready. It would simplify matters very much, if you were to walk up to church wi' her one of these mornings, get the thing done, and go on liven here as we are. If you don't I must get a house all the sooner. It would lighten my mind, too, about the two little freeholds* over the hill—not a morsel a-piece, divided as they were between her mother and me, but a tidy bit tied together again. Just think about it, will ye, Ted?"

He stopped from exhaustion produced by the intense concentration of his mind upon the weary subject, and looked anxiously at his son.

"Yes, I will," said Edward.

"But I am going to see Her of the Great House this morning," the farmer went on, his thoughts reverting to the old subject. "I must know the rights of the matter, the when and the where. I don't like seën her, but I'd rather talk to her than the steward. I wonder what she'll say to me."

The younger man knew exactly what she would say. If his father asked her what he was to do, and when, she would simply refer him to Manston: her character was not that of a woman who shrank from a proposition she had once laid down. If his father were to say to her that his son had at last resolved to marry his cousin within the year, and had given her a promise to that effect, she would say, "Mr. Springrove, the houses are burnt: we'll let them go: trouble no more about them."

His mind was already made up. He said calmly, "Father, when you are talking to Miss Aldclyffe, mention to her that I have asked Adelaide if she is willing to marry me next Christmas. She is interested in my union with Adelaide, and the news will be welcome to her."

"And yet she can be iron with reference to me and her property," the farmer murmured; "Very well, Ted, I'll tell her."

§ 6. *December the fifth*

Of the many contradictory particulars constituting a woman's heart, two had shown their vigorous contrast in Cytherea's bosom just at this time.

It was a dark morning, the morning after old Mr. Springrove's visit to Miss Aldclyffe, which had terminated as Edward had intended. Having risen an hour earlier than was usual with her, Cytherea sat at the window of an elegant little sitting-room on the ground floor, which had been appropriated to her by the kindness or whim of Miss Aldclyffe, that she might not be driven into that lady's presence against her will. She leant with her face on her hand, looking out into the gloomy grey air. A yellow glimmer from the flapping flame of the newly-lit fire fluttered on one side of her face and neck like a butterfly about to settle there, contrasting warmly with the other side of the same fair face, which received from the window the faint cold morning light, so weak that her shadow from the fire had a distinct outline on the window-shutter in spite of it. There the shadow danced like a demon, blue and grim.

The contradiction alluded to was that in spite of the decisive mood which two months earlier in the year had caused her to write a peremptory and final letter to Edward, she was now hoping for some answer other than the only possible one a man who, as she held, did not love her wildly, could send to such a communication. For a lover who did love wildly, she had left one little loophole in her otherwise straightforward epistle. Why she expected the letter on some morning of this particular week was, that hearing of his return to Carriford, she fondly assumed that he meant to ask for an interview before he left. Hence it was, too, that for the last few days, she had not been able to keep in bed later than the time of the postman's arrival.

The clock pointed to half-past seven. She saw the postman emerge from beneath the bare boughs of the park trees, come through the wicket, dive through the shrubbery, reappear on the lawn, stalk across it without reference to paths—as country postmen do—and come to the porch. She heard him fling the bag down on the seat, and turn away towards the village, without hindering himself for a single pace.

Then the butler opened the door, took up the bag, brought it in, and carried it up the staircase to place it on the slab by Miss Aldclyffe's dressing-room door. The whole proceeding had been depicted by sounds.

She had a presentiment that her letter was in the bag at last. She thought then in diminishing pulsations of confidence, "He asks to see me! perhaps he asks to see me: I hope he asks to see me."

A quarter to eight: Miss Aldclyffe's bell—rather earlier than usual. "She must have heard the post-bag brought," said the maiden, as, tired of the chilly prospect outside, she turned to the fire, and drew imaginative pictures of her future therein.

A tap came to the door, and the lady's maid entered. "Miss Aldclyffe is awake," she said; "and she asked if you were moving yet, miss."

"I'll run up to her," said Cytherea, and flitted off with the utterance of the words. "Very fortunate this," she thought; "I shall see what is in the bag this morning all the sooner."

She took it up from the side table, went into Miss Aldclyffe's bedroom, pulled up the blinds, and looked round upon the lady in bed, calculating the minutes that must elapse before she looked at her letters.

"Well, darling, how are you? I am glad you have come in to see me," said Miss Aldclyffe. "You can unlock the bag this morning, child, if you like," she continued, yawning factitiously.

"Strange!" Cytherea thought; "it seems as if she knew there was likely to be a letter for me."

From her bed Miss Aldclyffe watched the girl's face as she trem-blingly opened the post-bag and found there an envelope addressed to her in Edward's handwriting; one he had written the day before, after the decision he had come to on an impartial, and on that account torturing, survey of his own, his father's, his cousin Adelaide's, and what he believed to be, Cytherea's position.

The haughty mistress's soul sickened remorsefully within her, when she saw suddenly appear upon the speaking countenance of the young lady before her, a wan desolate look of agony.

The master-sentences of Edward's letter were these; "You speak truly. That we never meet again is the wisest and only proper course. That I regret the past as much as you do yourself, it is hardly neces-sary for me to say."

CHAPTER IV

THE EVENTS OF TEN MONTHS

§ 1. *December to April*

Week after week, month after month, the time had flown by. Christmas had passed: dreary winter with dark evenings had given place to more dreary winter with light evenings. Thaws had ended in rain, rain in wind, wind in dust. Showery days had come—the period of pink dawns and white sunsets: with the third week in April the cuckoo had appeared; with the fourth, the nightingale.

Edward Springrove was in London, attending to the duties of his new office, and it had become known throughout the neighbourhood of Carriford that the engagement between himself and Miss Adelaide Hinton would terminate in marriage at the end of the year.

The only occasion on which her lover of the idle delicious days at Creston watering-place had been seen by Cytherea after the time of the decisive correspondence, was once in Church, when he sat in front of her, and beside Miss Hinton.

The rencontre* was quite an accident. Springrove had come there in the full belief that Cytherea was away from home with Miss Aldclyffe; and he continued ignorant of her presence throughout the service.

It is at such moments as these, when a sensitive nature writhes under the conception that its most cherished emotions have been treated with contumely, that the sphere-descended Maid, Music, friend of Pleasure at other times, becomes a positive enemy—racking, bewildering, unrelenting.*

The congregation sang the first Psalm and came to the verse,

> "Like some fair tree which, fed by streams,
>   With timely fruit doth bend,
> He still shall flourish, and success
>   All his designs attend."*

Cytherea's lips did not move, nor did any sound escape her: but could she help singing the words in the depths of her, although the man to whom she applied them sat at her rival's side?

Perhaps the moral compensation for all a woman's petty cleverness under thriving conditions is the real nobility that lies in her extreme foolishness at these other times: her sheer inability to be simply just, her exercise of an illogical power entirely denied to men in general—the power not only of kissing, but of delighting to kiss the rod* by a punctilious observance of the self-immolating doctrines in the Sermon on the Mount.*

As for Edward—a little like other men of his temperament, to whom, it is somewhat humiliating to think, the aberrancy of a given love is in itself a recommendation,—his sentiment, as he looked over his cousin's book, was of a lower rank, Horatian rather than Psalmodic:*

> "O what has thou of her, of her
> Whose every look did love inspire;
> Whose every breathing fanned my fire,
> And stole me from myself away!"*

Then, without letting him see her, Cytherea slipt out of Church early, and went home, the tones of the organ still lingering in her ears as she tried bravely to kill a jealous thought that would nevertheless live: "My nature is one capable of more, far more, intense feeling than hers! She can't appreciate all the sides of him—she never will! He is more tangible to me even now, as a thought, than his presence itself is to her!" She was less noble then.

But she continually repressed her misery and bitterness of heart till the effort to do so showed signs of lessening. At length she even tried to hope that her lost lover and her rival would love one another very dearly.

The scene and the sentiment dropped into the past. Meanwhile, Manston continued visibly before her. He, though quiet and subdued in his bearing for a long time after the calamity of November, had not simulated a grief that he did not feel. At first his loss seemed so to absorb him—though as a startling change rather than as a heavy sorrow—that he paid Cytherea no attention whatever. His conduct was uniformly kind and respectful, but little more. Then, as the date of the catastrophe grew remoter, he began to wear a different aspect towards her. He always contrived to obliterate by his manner all recollection on her side that she was comparatively more dependent than himself—making much of her womanhood, nothing of her situation.* Prompt to aid her whenever occasion offered, and full of delightful *petits soins** at all times, he was not officious. In this way he irresistibly won for himself a position as her friend, and the more easily, in that he allowed not the faintest symptom of the old love to be apparent.

Matters stood thus in the middle of the spring, when the next move on his behalf was made by Miss Aldclyffe.

§ 2. *The third of May*

She led Cytherea to a summer-house called the Fane,* built in the private grounds about the mansion in the form of a Grecian temple: it overlooked the lake, the island on it, the trees, and their undisturbed reflection in the smooth still water. Here the old and young maid halted: here they stood, side by side, mentally imbibing the scene.

The month was May—the time, morning. Cuckoos, thrushes, blackbirds, and sparrows, gave forth a perfect confusion of song and twitter. The road was spotted white with the fallen leaves of apple-blossoms, and the sparkling grey dew still lingered on the grass and flowers.

Two swans floated into view in front of the women, and then crossed the water towards them.

"They seem to come to us without any will of their own—quite involuntarily—don't they?" said Cytherea, looking at the birds' graceful advance.

"Yes, but if you look narrowly you can see their hips just beneath the water, working with the greatest energy."

"I'd rather not see that, it spoils the idea of proud indifference to direction which we associate with a swan."

"It does; we'll have 'involuntarily.' Ah, now this reminds me of something."

"Of what?"

"Of a human being who involuntarily comes towards yourself."

Cytherea looked into Miss Aldclyffe's face; her eyes grew round as circles, and lines of wonderment came visibly upon her countenance. She had not once regarded Manston as a lover since his wife's sudden appearance and subsequent death. The death of a wife, and such a death, was an overwhelming matter in her ideas of things.

"Is it a man or woman?" she said, quite innocently.

"Mr. Manston," said Miss Aldclyffe, quietly.

"Mr. Manston attracted by me *now?*" said Cytherea, standing at gaze.

"Didn't you know it?"

"Certainly I did not. Why, his poor wife has only been dead six months."

"Of course he knows that. But loving is not done by months, or method, or rule, or nobody would ever have invented such a phrase as 'falling in love.' He does not want his love to be observed just yet, on the very account you mention; but conceal it as he may from himself and us, it exists definitely—and very intensely, I assure you."

"I suppose then, that if he can't help it, it is no harm of him," said Cytherea, naïvely, and beginning to ponder.

"Of course it isn't—you know that well enough. She was a great burden and trouble to him. This may become a great good to you both."

A rush of feeling at remembering that the same woman, before Manston's arrival, had just as frankly advocated Edward's claims, checked Cytherea's utterance for awhile.

"There, don't look at me like that, for Heaven's sake!" said Miss Aldclyffe. "You could almost kill a person by the force of reproach you can put into those eyes of yours, I verily believe."

Edward once in the young lady's thoughts, there was no getting rid of him. She wanted to be alone.

"Do you want me here?" she said.

"Now there, there; you want to be off, and have a good cry," said Miss Aldclyffe, taking her hand. "But you mustn't, my dear. There's nothing in the past for you to regret. Compare Mr. Manston's honourable conduct towards his wife and yourself, with Springrove towards his betrothed and yourself, and then see which appears the more worthy of your thoughts."

§3. *From the fourth of May to the twenty-first of June*

The next stage in Manston's advances towards her hand was a clearly defined courtship. She was sadly perplexed, and some contrivance was necessary on his part in order to meet with her. But it is next to impossible for an appreciative woman to have a positive repugnance towards an unusually handsome and talented man, even though she may not be inclined to love him. Hence Cytherea was not so alarmed at the sight of him as to render a meeting and conversation with her more than a matter of difficulty.

Coming and going from Church was his grand opportunity. Manston was very religious now. It is commonly said that no man was ever converted by argument, but there is a single one which will make any Laodicean in England, let him be once love-sick, wear prayer-books and become a zealous Episcopalian*—the argument that his sweetheart can be seen from his pew.

Manston introduced into his method a system of bewitching flattery, everywhere pervasive, yet too, so transitory and intangible, that, as in the case of the poet Wordsworth and the Wandering Voice,* though she felt it present, she could never find it. As a foil to heighten its effect, he occasionally spoke philosophically of the evanescence of female beauty—the worthlessness of mere appearance. "Handsome is that handsome does" he considered a proverb which should be written on the looking-glass of every woman in the land. "Your form, your motions, your heart have won me," he said, in a tone of playful sadness. "They are beautiful. But I see these things, and it comes into my mind that they are doomed, they are gliding to nothing as I look. Poor eyes, poor mouth, poor face, poor maiden! 'Where will her glories be in twenty years,' I say. 'Where will all of her be in a hundred?' Then I think it is cruel that you should bloom a day, and fade for ever and ever. It seems hard and sad that you will die, as ordinarily as I, and be buried; be food for roots and worms, be forgotten and come to earth, and grow up a mere blade of church-yard-grass and an ivy leaf.* Then, Miss Graye, when I see you are a Lovely Nothing, I pity you, and the love I feel then is better and sounder, larger, and more lasting than that I felt at the beginning." Again an ardent flash of his handsome eyes.

It was by this route that he ventured on an indirect declaration and offer of his hand.

She implied in the same indirect manner that she did not love him enough to accept it.

An actual refusal was more than he had expected. Cursing himself for what he called his egregious folly in making himself the slave of a mere lady's attendant, and for having given the parish, should they know of her refusal, a chance of sneering at him—certainly a ground

for thinking less of his standing than before—he went home to the
Old House, and walked indecisively up and down his back yard.
Turning aside, he leant his arms upon the edge of the rain-water-
butt standing in the corner, and looked into it. The reflection from
the smooth stagnant surface tinged his face with the greenish shades
of Correggio's nudes.* Staves of sunlight slanted down through the
still pool, lighting it up with wonderful distinctness. Hundreds of
thousands of minute living creatures sported and tumbled in its
depths with every contortion that gaiety could suggest; perfectly
happy, though consisting only of a head, or a tail, or at most a head
and a tail, and all doomed to die within the twenty-four hours.

"D——n my position! Why shouldn't I be happy through my
little day too? Let the parish sneer at my repulses, let it. I'll get her, if
I move heaven and earth to do it!"

Indeed, the inexperienced Cytherea had, towards Edward in the
first place, and Manston afterwards, unconsciously adopted bearings
that would have been the very tactics of a professional fisher of men*
who wished to have them each successively dangling at her heels. For
if any rule at all can be laid down in a matter which, for men collectively, is notoriously beyond regulation, it is that to snub a petted
man, and to pet a snubbed man, is the way to win in suits of both
kinds. Manston with Springrove's encouragement would have
become indifferent. Edward with Manston's repulses would have
sheered off at the outset, as he did afterwards. Her supreme indifference added fuel to Manston's ardour—it completely disarmed
his pride. The invulnerable Nobody seemed greater to him than a
susceptible Princess.

§ 4. *From the twenty-first of June to the end of July*

Cytherea had in the meantime received the following letter from her
brother. It was the first definite notification of the enlargement of
that cloud no bigger than a man's hand* which had for nearly a
twelvemonth hung before them in the distance, and which was soon
to give a colour to their whole sky from horizon to horizon.

"CRESTON. *Saturday*.

"DARLING SIS,

"I have delayed telling you for a long time of a little matter which though not one to be seriously alarmed about, is sufficiently vexing, and it would be unfair in me to keep it from you any longer. It is that for some time past I have again been distressed by that lameness which I first distinctly felt when we went to Lewborne Bay, and again when I left Knapwater that morning early. It is an unusual pain in my left leg, between the knee and the ankle. I had just found fresh symptoms of it when you were here for that half-hour about a month ago—when you said in fun that I began to move like an old man. I had a good mind to tell you then, but fancying it would go off in a few days, I thought it was not worth while. Since that time it has increased, but I am still able to work in the office, sitting on the stool. My great fear is that Mr. G. will have some outdoor measuring work for me to do soon, and that I shall be obliged to decline. However, we will hope for the best. How it came, what was its origin, or what it tends to, I cannot think. You shall hear again in a day or two, if it is no better. . . . .

"Your loving brother,
"OWEN."

This she answered, begging to know the worst, which she could bear, but suspense and anxiety never. In two days came another letter from him, of which the subjoined paragraph is a portion.

"I had quite decided to let you know the worst, and to assure you that it was the worst, before you wrote to ask it. And again I give you my word that I will conceal nothing—so that there will be no excuse whatever for your wearing yourself out with fears that I am worse than I say. This morning then, for the first time, I have been obliged to stay away from the office. Don't be frightened at this, dear Cytherea. Rest is all that is wanted, and by nursing myself now for a week, I may avoid a sickness of six months."

After a visit from her he wrote again,

"Dr. Chestman has seen me. He said that the ailment was some sort of rheumatism, and I am now undergoing proper treatment for its cure. My leg and foot have been placed in hot bran, liniments have been applied, and also severe friction with a pad. He says I shall be as right as ever in a very short time. Directly I am I shall run up by the train to see you. Don't trouble to come to me if Miss Aldclyffe grumbles again about your being away, for I am going on capitally. . . . . You shall hear again at the end of the week."

At the time mentioned came the following:

"I am sorry to tell you, because I know it will be so disheartening after my last letter, that I am not so well as I was then, and that there has been a sort of hitch in the proceedings. After I had been treated for rheumatism a few days longer, (in which treatment they pricked the place with a long needle several times,) I saw that Dr. Chestman was in doubt about something, and I requested that he would call in a brother professional man to see me as well. They consulted together and then told me that rheumatism was not the disease after all, but erysipelas.* They then began treating it differently, as became a different matter. Blisters, flour, and starch, seem to be the order of the day now—medicine, of course, besides.

"Mr. Gradfield has been in to inquire about me. He says he has been obliged to get a clerk in my place, which grieves me very much, though, of course, it could not be avoided."

A month passed away; throughout this period, Cytherea visited him as often as the limited time at her command would allow, and wore as cheerful a countenance as the womanly determination to do nothing which might depress him could enable her to wear. Another letter from him then told her these additional facts.

"The doctors find they are again on the wrong tack. They cannot make out what the disease is. O Cytherea! how I wish they knew! This suspense is wearing me out. Could not Miss Aldclyffe spare you for a day? Do come to me. We will talk about the best course then. I am sorry to complain, but I am worn out."

Cytherea went to Miss Aldclyffe, and told her of the melancholy turn her brother's illness had taken. Miss Aldclyffe at once said that Cytherea might go, and offered to do anything to assist her which lay in her power. Cytherea's eyes beamed gratitude as she turned to leave the room, and hasten to the station.

"Oh, Cytherea," said Miss Aldclyffe, calling her back; "just one word. Has Mr. Manston spoken to you lately?"

"Yes," said Cytherea, blushing timorously.

"He proposed?"

"Yes."

"And you refused him?"

"Yes."

"Tut, tut! Now listen to my advice," said Miss Aldclyffe,

emphatically, "and accept him before he changes his mind. The chance which he offers you of settling in life is one that may possibly, probably, not occur again. His position is good and secure, and the life of his wife would be a happy one. You may not be sure that you love him madly; but suppose you are not sure? My father used to say to me as a child when he was teaching me whist, 'When in doubt win the trick!' That advice is ten times as valuable to a woman on the subject of matrimony. In refusing a man there is always the risk that you may never get another offer."

"Why didn't you win the trick when you were a girl?" said Cytherea.

"Come, my lady Pert; I'm not the text," said Miss Aldclyffe, her face glowing like fire.

Cytherea laughed stealthily.

"I was about to say," resumed Miss Aldclyffe, severely, "that here is Mr. Manston waiting with the tenderest solicitude for you, and you overlooking it, as if it were altogether beneath you. Think how you might benefit your sick brother if you were Mrs. Manston. You will please me *very much* by giving him some encouragement. You understand me, dear?"

Cytherea was silent.

"And," said Miss Aldclyffe still more emphatically, "on your promising that you will accept him some time this year, I will take especial care of your brother. You are listening, Cytherea?"

"Yes," she whispered, leaving the room.

She went to Creston, passed the day with her brother, and returned to Knapwater wretched and full of foreboding. Owen had looked startlingly thin and pale—thinner and paler than ever she had seen him before. The brother and sister had that day decided that, notwithstanding the drain upon their slender resources, another medical man should see him. Time was everything.

Owen told her the result in his next letter.

"The three practitioners between them have at last hit the nail on the head, I hope. They probed the place and discovered that the secret lay in the bone. I underwent an operation for its removal three days ago, (after taking chloroform*) ... Thank God it is over. Though I am so weak, my spirits are rather better. I wonder when I shall be at work again? I asked the doctors how long it would be first. I said a month? They shook their heads. A year? I said. Not so long, they said. Six months? I inquired. They would not, or could not tell me. But never mind.

"Run down, when you have half a day to spare, for the hours drag on so drearily. O Cytherea you can't think how drearily!"

She went. Immediately on her departure, Miss Aldclyffe sent a note to the Old House, to Manston. On the maiden's return, tired and sick at heart as usual, she found Manston at the station awaiting her. He asked politely if he might accompany her to Knapwater. She tacitly acquiesced. During their walk he inquired the particulars of her brother's illness, and with an irresistible desire to pour out her trouble to some one, she told him of the length of time which must elapse before he could be strong again, and of the lack of comfort in a lodging-house.

Manston was silent awhile. Then he said impetuously: "Miss Graye, I will not mince matters—I love you—you know it. Stratagem they say is fair in love, and I am compelled to adopt it now. Forgive me, for I cannot help it. Consent to be my wife at any time that may suit you, any remote day you may name will satisfy me— and you shall find him well provided for."

For the first time in her life she truly dreaded the handsome man at her side who pleaded thus selfishly, and shrank from the hot voluptuous nature of his passion for her, which, disguise it as he might under a quiet and polished exterior, at times radiated forth with a scorching white heat. She perceived how animal was the love which bargained.

"I do not love you, Mr. Manston," she replied coldly.

§ 5. *From the first to the twenty-seventh of August*

The long sunny days of the later summer-time brought only the same dreary accounts from Creston, and saw Cytherea paying the same sad visits.

She grew perceptibly weaker, in body and in mind. Manston still persisted in his suit, but with more of his former indirectness, now that he saw how unexpectedly well she stood an open attack. His was the system of Dares at the Sicilian games:—*

> "He, like a captain who beleaguers round,
> Some strong-built castle on a rising ground,
> Views all the approaches with observing eyes,

This and that other part again he tries,
And more on industry than force relies."

Miss Aldclyffe made it appear more clearly than ever that aid to
Owen from herself depended entirely upon Cytherea's acceptance of
her steward. Hemmed in and distressed, Cytherea's answers to his
importunities grew less uniform; they were firm, or wavering, as
Owen's malady fluctuated. Had a register of her pitiful oscillations
been kept, it would have rivalled in pathos the diary wherein De
Quincey tabulates his combat with Opium*—perhaps as noticeable an
instance as any in which a thrilling dramatic power has been given to
mere numerals. Thus she wearily and monotonously lived through
the month, listening on Sundays to the well-known round of chapters narrating the history of Elijah and Elisha in famine and drought:*
on week days to buzzing flies in hot sunny rooms. "So like, so very
like, was day to day."* Extreme lassitude seemed all that the world
could show her.

Her state was in this wise, when one afternoon, having been with
her brother, she met the surgeon, and begged him to tell the actual
truth concerning Owen's condition.

The reply was that he feared that the first operation had not been
thorough: that although the wound had healed, another attempt
might still be necessary, unless nature were left to effect her own
cure. But the time such a self-healing proceeding would occupy
might be ruinous.

"How long would it be?" she said.

"It is impossible to say. A year or two, more or less."

"And suppose he submitted to another artificial extraction?"

"Then he might be well in four or six months."

Now the remainder of his and her possessions, together with a
sum he had borrowed, would not provide him with necessary comforts for half that time. To combat the misfortune, there were two
courses open: her becoming betrothed to Manston, or the sending
Owen to the County Hospital.

Thus terrified, driven into a corner, panting and fluttering about
for some loophole of escape, yet still shrinking from the idea of being
Manston's wife, the poor little bird endeavoured to find out from
Miss Aldclyffe whether it was likely Owen would be well treated in
the hospital.

"County Hospital!" said Miss Aldclyffe, "Why it is only another name for Slaughter House—in surgical cases at any rate. Certainly if anything about your body is snapt in two they do join you together in a fashion, but 'tis so askew and ugly, that you may as well be apart again." Then she terrified the inquiring and anxious maiden by relating horrid stories of how the legs and arms of poor people were cut off at a moment's notice, especially in cases where the restorative treatment was likely to be long and tedious.

"You know how willing I am to help you, Cytherea," she added, reproachfully. "You know it. Why are you so obstinate then? Why do you selfishly bar the clear, honourable, and only sisterly path which leads out of this difficulty? I cannot, on my conscience, countenance you: no, I cannot."

Manston once more repeated his offer; and once more she refused, but this time weakly, and with signs of an internal struggle. Manston's eye sparkled: what Lavater calls the boundary line between affection and appetite, never very distinct in him, was visibly obliterated.* Moreover he saw for the hundredth time in his life, that perseverance, if only systematic, was irresistible by womankind.

§ 6. *The twenty-seventh of August*

On going to Creston three days later, she found to her surprise that the steward had been there, had introduced himself, and had seen her brother. A few delicacies had been brought him also by the same hand. Owen spoke in warm terms of Manston and his free and unceremonious call, as he could not have refrained from doing of any person, of any kind, whose presence had served to help away the tedious hours of a long day, and who had, moreover, shown that sort of consideration for him which the accompanying basket implied—antecedent consideration, so telling upon all invalids—and which he so seldom experienced except from the hands of his sister.

How should he perceive, amid this tithe-paying of mint, and anise, and cummin,* the weightier matters which were left undone?

Again the steward met her at Carriford-Road Station on her return journey. Instead of being frigid as at the former meeting at the same place, she was embarrassed by a strife of thought, and murmured brokenly her thanks for what he had done. The same request that he might see her home was made.

He had perceived his error in making his kindness to Owen a conditional kindness, and had hastened to efface all recollection of it. "Though I let my offer on her brother's—my friend's—behalf, seem dependent on my lady's graciousness to me," he whispered wooingly in the course of their walk, "I could not conscientiously adhere to my statement; it was said with all the impulsive selfishness of love. Whether you choose to have me, or whether you don't, I love you too devotedly to be anything but kind to your brother" . . . . "Miss Graye, Cytherea, I will do anything," he continued earnestly, "to give you pleasure—indeed I will."

She saw on the one hand her poor and much loved Owen recovering from his illness and troubles by the disinterested kindness of the man beside her, on the other she drew him dying, wholly by reason of her self-enforced poverty. To marry this man was obviously the course of common sense, to refuse him was impolitic temerity. There was reason in this. But there was more behind than a hundred reasons—a woman's gratitude and her impulse to be kind.

The wavering of her mind was visible in her tell-tale face. He noticed it, and caught at the opportunity.

They were standing by the ruinous foundations of an old mill in the midst of a meadow. Between grey and half-overgrown stone-work—the only signs of masonry remaining—the water gurgled down from the old mill-pond to a lower level, under the cloak of rank broad leaves—the sensuous natures of the vegetable world. On the right hand the sun, resting on the horizon-line, streamed across the ground from below copper-coloured and lilac clouds, stretched out in flats beneath a sky of pale soft green. All dark objects on the earth that lay towards the sun were overspread by a purple haze, against which a swarm of wailing gnats shone forth luminously, rising upward and floating away like sparks of fire.

The stillness oppressed and reduced her to mere passivity. The only wish the humidity of the place left in her was to stand motion-less. The helpless flatness of the landscape gave her, as it gives all such temperaments, a sense of bare equality with, and no superiority to, a single entity under the sky.

He came so close that their clothes touched. "Will you try to love me? Do try to love me?" he said, in a whisper, taking her hand. He had never taken it before. She could feel his hand trembling exceed-ingly as it held hers in its clasp.

Considering his kindness to her brother, his love for herself, and Edward's fickleness, ought she to forbid him to do this? How truly pitiful it was to feel his hand tremble so—all for her! Should she withdraw her hand? She would think whether she would. Thinking, and hesitating, she looked as far as the autumnal haze on the marshy ground would allow her to see distinctly. There was the fragment of a hedge—all that remained of a wet old garden—standing in the middle of the mead, without a definite beginning or ending, purposeless and valueless. It was overgrown, and choked with mandrakes, and she could almost fancy she heard their shrieks* . . . . Should she withdraw her hand? No, she could not withdraw it now; it was too late, the act would not imply refusal. She felt as one in a boat without oars, drifting with closed eyes down a river—she knew not whither.

He gave her hand a gentle pressure, and relinquished it.

Then it seemed as if he were coming to the point again. No, he was not going to urge his suit that evening. Another respite.

§7. *The early part of September*

Saturday came, and she went on some trivial errand to the village post-office. It was a little grey cottage with a luxuriant jasmine encircling the doorway, and before going in Cytherea paused to admire this pleasing feature of the exterior. Hearing a step on the gravel behind the corner of the house, she resigned the jasmine and entered. Nobody was in the room. She could hear Mrs. Leat, the widow who acted as post-mistress, walking about over her head. Cytherea was going to the foot of the stairs to call Mrs. Leat, but before she had accomplished her object, another form stood at the half-open door. Manston came in.

"Both on the same errand," he said, gracefully.

"I will call her," said Cytherea, moving in haste to the foot of the stairs.

"One moment." He glided to her side. "Don't call her for a moment," he repeated.

But she had said, "Mrs. Leat!"

He seized Cytherea's hand, kissed it tenderly, and carefully replaced it by her side.

She had that morning determined to check his further advances, until she had thoroughly considered her position. The remonstrance was now on her tongue, but as accident would have it, before the word could be spoken, Mrs. Leat was stepping from the last stair to the floor, and no remonstrance came.

With the sublety which characterised him in all his dealings with her, he quickly concluded his own errand, bade her a good-bye, in the tones of which love was so garnished with pure politeness that it only showed its presence to herself, and left the house—putting it out of her power to refuse him her companionship homeward, or to object to his late action of kissing her hand.

The Friday of the next week brought another letter from her brother. In this he informed her that, in absolute grief lest he should distress her unnecessarily, he had some time earlier borrowed a few pounds. A week ago, he said, his creditor became importunate, but that on the day on which he wrote, the creditor had told him there was no hurry for a settlement, that "his *sister's suitor* had guaranteed the sum." "Is he Mr. Manston? tell me, Cytherea," said Owen.

He also mentioned that a wheeled chair had been anonymously hired for his especial use, though as yet he was hardly far enough advanced towards convalescence to avail himself of the luxury. "Is this Mr. Manston's doing?" he inquired.

She could dally with her perplexity, evade it, trust to time for guidance, no longer. The matter had come to a crisis: she must once and for all choose between the dictates of her understanding and those of her heart. She longed, till her soul seemed nigh to bursting, for her lost mother's return to earth, but for one minute, that she might have tender counsel to guide her through this, her great difficulty.

As for her heart, she half-fancied that it was not Edward's to quite the extent that it once had been; she thought him cruel in conducting himself towards her as he did at Creston, cruel afterwards in making so lightly of her. She knew he had stifled his love for her—was utterly lost to her. But for all that she could not help indulging in a woman's pleasure of recreating defunct agonies, and lacerating herself with them now and then.

"If I were rich," she thought, "I would give way to the luxury of being morbidly faithful to him for ever without his knowledge."

But she considered; in the first place she was a homeless dependent; and what did practical wisdom tell her to do under such desperate circumstances?

To provide herself with some place of refuge from poverty, and with means to aid her brother Owen. This was to be Mr. Manston's wife.

She did not love him.

But what was love without a home? Misery. What was a home without love? Alas, not much; but still a kind of home.

"Yes," she thought, "I am urged by my common sense to marry Mr. Manston."

Did anything nobler in her say so too?

With the death (to her) of Edward her heart's occupation was gone.* Was it necessary or even right for her to tend it and take care of it as she used to in the old time, when it was still a capable minister?

By a slight sacrifice here she could give happiness to at least two hearts whose emotional activities were still unwounded. She would do good to two men whose lives were far more important than hers.

"Yes," she said, again, "even Christianity urges me to marry Mr. Manston."

Directly Cytherea had persuaded herself that a kind of heroic self-abnegation had to do with the matter, she became much more content in the consideration of it. A wilful indifference to the future was what really prevailed in her, ill and worn out, as she was, by the perpetual harassments of her sad fortune, and she regarded this indifference, as gushing natures will under such circumstances, as genuine resignation and devotedness.

Manston met her again the following day: indeed there was no escaping him now. At the end of a short conversation between them, which took place in the hollow of the park by the waterfall, obscured on the outer side by the low hanging branches of the limes, she tacitly assented to his assumption of a privilege greater than any that had preceded it. He stooped and kissed her brow.

Before going to bed she wrote to Owen explaining the whole matter. It was too late in the evening for the postman's visit, and she placed the letter on the mantelpiece to send it the next day.

The morning (Sunday) brought a hurried postscript to Owen's letter of the day before.

"September 9th, 1865.

"DEAR CYTHEREA,

"I have received a frank and friendly letter from Mr. Manston explaining the position in which he stands now, and also that in which he hopes to stand towards you. Can't you love him? Why not? Try, for he is a good, and not only that but a talented man. Think of the weary and laborious future that awaits you if you continue for life in your present position, and do you see any way of escape from it except by marriage? I don't. Don't go against your heart, Cytherea, but be wise.

"Ever affectionately yours,
"OWEN."

She thought that probably he had replied to Mr. Manston in the same favouring mood. She had a conviction that that day would settle her doom. Yet

"So true a fool is love,"*

that even now she nourished a half-hope that something would happen at the last moment to thwart her deliberately-formed intentions, and favour the old emotion she was using all her strength to thrust down.

§ 8. *The tenth of September*

The Sunday was the thirteenth after Trinity,* and the afternoon service at Carriford was nearly over. The people were singing the Evening Hymn.*

Manston was at church as usual in his accustomed place, two seats forward from the large square pew occupied by Miss Aldclyffe and Cytherea.

The ordinary sadness of an autumnal evening-service seemed, in Cytherea's eyes, to be doubled on this particular occasion. She looked at all the people as they stood and sang, waving backwards and forwards like a forest of pines swayed by a gentle breeze; then at the village children singing too, their heads inclined to one side, their eyes listlessly tracing some crack in the old walls, or following the movement of a distant bough or bird with features petrified almost to painfulness. Then she looked at Manston; he was already regarding her with some purpose in his glance.

"It is coming this evening," she said in her mind. A minute later, at the end of the hymn, when the congregation began to move out,

Manston came down the aisle. He was opposite the end of her seat as she stepped from it, the remainder of their progress to the door being in contact with each other. Miss Aldclyffe had lingered behind.

"Don't let's hurry," he said, when Cytherea was about to enter the private path to the House as usual. "Would you mind turning down this way for a minute till Miss Aldclyffe has passed?"

She could not very well refuse now. They turned into a secluded path on their left, leading round through a thicket of laurels to the other gate of the churchyard, walking very slowly. By the time the further gate was reached, the church was closed. They met the sexton with the keys in his hand.

"We are going inside for a minute," said Manston to him, taking the keys unceremoniously. "I will bring them to you when we return."

The sexton nodded his assent, and Cytherea and Manston walked into the porch, and up the nave.

They did not speak a word during their progress, or in anyway interfere with the stillness and silence that prevailed everywhere around them. Everything in the place was the embodiment of decay: the fading red glare from the setting sun, which came in at the west window, emphasizing the end of the day and all its cheerful doings, the mildewed walls, the uneven paving-stones, the wormy poppy-heads, the sense of recent occupation, and the dank air of death which had gathered with the evening, would have made grave a lighter mood than Cytherea's was then.

"What sensations does the place impress you with?" she said at last, very sadly.

"I feel imperatively called upon to be honest, from very despair of achieving anything by stratagem in a world where the materials are such as these." He too spoke in a depressed voice, purposely or otherwise.

"I feel as if I were almost ashamed to be seen walking such a world," she murmured; "that's the effect it has upon me: but it does not induce me to be honest particularly."

He took her hand in both his, and looked down upon the lids of her eyes.

"I pity you sometimes," he said, more emphatically.

"I am pitiable perhaps: so are many people. Why do you pity me?"

"I think that you make yourself needlessly sad."

"Not needlessly."

"Yes, needlessly. Why should you be separated from your brother so much, when you might have him to stay with you till he is well?"

"That can't be," she said, turning away.

He went on, "I think the real and only good thing that can be done for him is to get him away from Creston awhile; and I have been wondering whether it could not be managed for him to come to my house to live for a few weeks. Only a quarter of a mile from you. How pleasant it would be!"

"It would."

He moved himself round immediately to the front of her, and held her hand more firmly, as he continued, "Cytherea, why do you say 'It would,' so entirely in the tone of abstract supposition? I want him there; I want him to be my brother too. Then make him so and be my wife! I cannot live without you—O Cytherea, my darling, my love—come and be my wife!"

His face bent closer and closer to hers, and the last words sank to a whisper as weak as the emotion inspiring it was strong.

She said firmly and distinctly, "Yes, I will."

"Next month?" he said on the instant, before taking breath.

"No; not next month."

"The next?"

"No."

"December? Christmas-day, say?"

"I don't mind."

"O you darling!" He was about to imprint a kiss upon her pale cold mouth, but she hastily covered it with her hand.

"Don't kiss me—at least where we are now!" she whispered imploringly.

"Why?"

"We are too near God."

He gave a sudden start, and his face flushed. She had spoken so emphatically that the words, "Near God," echoed back again through the hollow building from the far end of the chancel.

"What a thing to say!" he exclaimed; "surely a pure kiss is not inappropriate to the place!"

"No," she replied, with a swelling heart; "I don't know why I burst out so—I can't tell what has come over me! Will you forgive me?"

"How shall I say 'Yes' without judging you? How shall I say 'No' without losing the pleasure of saying 'Yes'?" He was himself again.

"I don't know," she absently murmured.

"I'll say Yes," he answered, daintily. "It is sweeter to fancy we are forgiven, than to think we have not sinned; and you shall have the sweetness without the need."

She did not reply, and they moved away. The church was nearly dark now, and melancholy in the extreme. She stood beside him while he locked the door, then took the arm he gave her, and wended her way out of the churchyard with him. Then they walked to the House together, but the great matter having been set at rest, she persisted in talking only on indifferent subjects.

"Christmas-day, then," he said, as they were parting at the end of the shrubbery.

"I meant Old Christmas-day,"* she said, evasively.

"H'm, people do not usually attach that meaning to the words?"

"No, but I should like it best if it could not be till then?" It seemed to be still her instinct to delay the marriage to the utmost.

"Very well, Love," he said gently. " 'Tis a fortnight longer still, but never mind. Old Christmas-day."

§ 9. *The eleventh of September*

"There. It will be on a Friday!"

She sat upon a little footstool gazing intently into the fire. It was the afternoon of the day following that of the steward's successful solicitation of her hand.

"I wonder if it would be proper in me to run across the park and tell him it is a Friday," she said to herself, rising to her feet, looking at her hat lying near, and then out of the window towards the Old House. Proper or not, she felt that she must at all hazards remove the disagreeable, though, as she herself owned, unfounded impression the coincidence had occasioned. She left the house directly, and went to search for him.

Manston was in the timber-yard, looking at the sawyers as they worked. Cytherea came up to him hesitatingly. Till within a distance of a few yards she had hurried forward with alacrity—now that the practical expression of his face became visible she wished almost she had never sought him on such an errand: in his business-mood he was perhaps very stern.

"It will be on a Friday," she said confusedly, and without any preface.

"Come this way!" said Manston, in the tone he used for workmen, not being able to alter at an instant's notice. He gave her his arm and led her back into the avenue, by which time he was lover again. "On a Friday, will it dearest? You do not mind Fridays* surely? That's nonsense."

"Not seriously mind them, exactly—but if it could be any other day?"

"Well let us say Old Christmas-eve then. Shall it be Old Christmas-eve?"

"Yes. Old Christmas-eve."

"Your word is solemn and irrevocable now?"

"Certainly, I have solemnly pledged my word; I should not have promised to marry you if I had not meant it. Don't think I should." She spoke the words with a dignified impressiveness.

"You must not be vexed at my remark, dearest. Can you think the worse of an ardent man, Cytherea, for showing some anxiety in love?"

"No: no." She could not say more. She was always ill at ease when he spoke of himself as a piece of human nature in that analytical way, and wanted to be out of his presence. The time of day, and the proximity of the House afforded her a means of escape. "I must be with Miss Aldclyffe now—will you excuse my hasty coming and going?" she said prettily. Before he had replied she had parted from him.

"Cytherea, was it Mr. Manston I saw you scudding away from in the avenue just now?" said Miss Aldclyffe, when Cytherea joined her.

"Yes."

" 'Yes.' Come, why don't you say more than that? I hate those taciturn 'Yeses' of yours. I tell you everything, and yet you are as close as wax with me."

"I parted from him because I wanted to come in."

"What a novel and important announcement! Well, is the day fixed?"

"Yes."

Miss Aldclyffe's face kindled into intense interest at once. "Is it indeed? When is it to be?"

"On Old Christmas-eve."

"Old Christmas-eve." Miss Aldclyffe drew Cytherea round to her front, and took a hand in each of her own. "And then you will be a bride!" she said slowly, looking with critical thoughtfulness upon the maiden's delicately rounded cheeks.

The normal area of the colour upon each of them decreased perceptibly after that slow and emphatic utterance by the elder lady.

Miss Aldclyffe continued impressively, "You did not say 'Old Christmas-eve' as a fiancée should have said the words: and you don't receive my remark with the warm excitement that foreshadows a bright future. . . . . How many weeks are there to the time?"

"I have not reckoned them."

"Not? Fancy a girl not counting the weeks! I find I must take the lead in this matter—you are so childish, or frightened, or stupid, or something, about it. Bring me my diary, and we will count them at once."

Cytherea silently fetched the book.

Miss Aldclyffe opened the diary at the page containing the almanac, and counted sixteen weeks, which brought her to the thirty-first of December—a Sunday. Cytherea stood by, looking on as if she had no appetite for the scene.

"Sixteen to the thirty-first. Then let me see, Monday will be the first of January, Tuesday the second, Wednesday third, Thursday fourth, Friday fifth—You have chosen a Friday, as I declare!"

"A Thursday, surely?" said Cytherea.

"No:—Old Christmas-day comes on a Saturday."

The perturbed little brain had reckoned wrong. "Well it must be a Friday," she murmured in a reverie.

"No: have it altered of course," said Miss Aldclyffe cheerfully. "There's nothing bad in Friday, but such a creature as you will be thinking about its being unlucky—in fact, I wouldn't choose a Friday myself to be married on, since all the other days are equally available."

"I shall not have it altered," said Cytherea firmly; "it has been altered once, already: I shall let it be."

CHAPTER V

THE EVENTS OF ONE DAY

§ 1. *The fifth of January. Before dawn*

We pass over the intervening weeks. The time of the story is thus advanced exactly three months and twenty-four days.

On the midnight preceding the morning which would make her the wife of a man whose presence fascinated her into involuntariness of bearing, and whom in absence she almost dreaded, Cytherea lay in her little bed, vainly endeavouring to sleep.

She had been looking back amid the years of her short though varied past, and thinking of the threshold upon which she stood. Days and months had dimmed the form of Edward Springrove like the gauzes of a vanishing stage-scene,* but his dying voice could still be heard faintly behind. That a soft small chord in her still vibrated true to his memory, she would not admit: that she did not approach Manston with feelings which could by any stretch of words be called hymeneal,* she calmly owned.

"Why do I marry him?" she said to herself. "Because Owen, dear Owen my brother, wishes me to marry him. Because Mr. Manston is and has been, uniformly kind to Owen, and to me. 'Act in obedience to the dictates of common sense,' Owen said, 'and dread the sharp sting of poverty. How many thousands of women like you marry every year for the same reason, to secure a home, and mere, ordinary, material comforts, which after all go far to make life endurable, even if not supremely happy.'

" 'Tis right I suppose, for him to say that. O if people only knew what a timidity and melancholy upon the subject of her future grows up in the heart of a friendless woman who is blown about like a reed shaken with the wind, as I am, they would not call this resignation of one's self by the name of scheming to get a husband. Scheme to marry? I'd rather scheme to die! I know I am not pleasing my heart; I know that if I only were concerned, I should like risking a single future. But why should I please my useless self overmuch, when by doing otherwise I please those who are more valuable than I?"

In the midst of desultory reflections like these, which alternated with surmises as to the inexplicable connexion that appeared to exist between her intended husband and Miss Aldclyffe, she heard dull noises outside the walls of the house, which she could not quite fancy to be caused by the wind. She seemed doomed to such disturbances at critical periods of her existence. "It is strange," she pondered, "that this my last night in Knapwater House, should be disturbed precisely as my first was, no occurrence of the kind having intervened."

As the minutes glided by the noise increased, sounding as if some one were beating the wall below her window with a bunch of switches. She would gladly have left her room and gone to stay with one of the maids, but they were without doubt all asleep.

The only person in the house likely to be awake, or who would have brains enough to comprehend her nervousness, was Miss Aldclyffe, but Cytherea never cared to go to Miss Aldclyffe's room, though she was always welcome there, and was often almost compelled to go against her will.

The oft-repeated noise of switches grew heavier upon the wall, and was now intermingled with creaks, and a rattling like the rattling of dice. The wind blew stronger; there came first a snapping, then a crash, and some portion of the mystery was revealed. It was the breaking off and fall of a branch from one of the large trees outside. The smacking against the wall, and the intermediate rattling, ceased from that time.

Well, it was the tree which had caused the noises. The unexplained matter was that neither of the trees ever touched the walls of the house during the highest wind, and that trees could not rattle like a man playing castanets, or shaking dice.

She thought "Is it the intention of Fate that something connected with these noises shall influence my future as in the last case of the kind?"

During the dilemma she fell into a troubled sleep, and dreamt that she was being whipped with dry bones suspended on strings, which rattled at every blow like those of a malefactor on a gibbet;* that she shifted and shrank and avoided every blow, and they fell then upon the wall to which she was tied. She could not see the face of the executioner for his mask, but his form was like Manston's.

"Thank Heaven!" she said, when she awoke and saw a faint

light struggling through her blind. "Now what were those noises?" To settle that question seemed more to her than the event of the day.

She pulled the blind aside and looked out. All was plain. The evening previous had closed in with a grey drizzle, borne upon a piercing air from the north, and now its effects were visible. The hoary drizzle still continued; but the trees and shrubs were laden with icicles to an extent such as she had never before witnessed. A shoot of the diameter of a pin's head was iced as thick as her finger: all the boughs in the park were bent almost to the earth with the immense weight of the glistening incumbrance: the walks were like a looking-glass. Many boughs had snapped beneath their burden, and lay in heaps upon the icy grass. Opposite her eye, on the nearest tree, was a fresh yellow scar, showing where the branch that had terrified her had been splintered from the trunk.

"I never could have believed it possible," she thought, surveying the bowed-down branches, "that trees would bend so far out of their true positions without breaking." By watching a twig she could see a drop collect upon it from the hoary fog, sink to the lowest point, and there become coagulated as the others had done.

"Or that I could so exactly have imitated them," she continued. "On this morning I am to be married—unless this is a scheme of the great Mother* to hinder a union of which she does not approve. Is it possible for my wedding to take place in the face of such weather as this?"

§ 2. *Morning*

Her brother Owen was staying with Manston at the Old House. Contrary to the opinion of the doctors, the wound had healed after the first surgical operation, and his leg was gradually acquiring strength, though he could only as yet get about on crutches, or ride, or be dragged in a chair.

Miss Aldclyffe had arranged that Cytherea should be married from Knapwater House, and not from her brother's lodgings at Creston, which was Cytherea's first idea. Owen, too, seemed to prefer the plan. The capricious old maid had latterly taken to the contemplation of the wedding with even greater warmth than had at first inspired her, and appeared determined to do everything in her power, consistent with her dignity, to render the adjuncts of the ceremony pleasing and complete.

But the weather seemed in flat contradiction of the whole proceeding. At eight o'clock the coachman crept up to the House almost upon his hands and knees, entered the kitchen, and stood with his back to the fire, panting from his exertions in pedestrianism.

The kitchen was by far the pleasantest apartment in Knapwater House on such a morning as this. The vast fire was the centre of the whole system, like a sun, and threw its warm rays upon the figures of the domestics, wheeling about it in true planetary style. A nervously-feeble imitation of its flicker was continually attempted by a family of polished metallic utensils standing in rows and groups against the walls opposite, the whole collection of shines nearly annihilating the weak daylight from outside. A step further in, and the nostrils were greeted by the scent of green herbs just gathered, and the eye by the plump form of the cook, wholesome, white aproned, and floury—looking as edible as the food she manipulated—her movements being supported and assisted by her satellites the kitchen and scullery maids. Minute recurrent sounds prevailed—the click of the smoke-jack,* the flap of the flames, and the light touches of the women's slippers upon the stone floor.

The coachman hemmed, spread his feet more firmly upon the hearthstone, and looked hard at a small plate in the extreme corner of the dresser.

"No wedden this mornen—that's my opinion. In fact, there can't be," he said, abruptly, as if the words were the mere torso of a many-membered thought that had existed complete in his head.

The kitchen-maid was toasting a slice of bread at the end of a very long toasting-fork which she held at arm's length towards the unapproachable fire, like the Flanconnade in fencing.*

"Bad out of doors, isn't it?" she said, with a look of commiseration for things in general.

"Bad? Not a liven soul gentle or simple can stand on level ground. As to getten up hill to the church 'tis perfect lunacy. And I speak of foot-passengers. As to horses and carriage, 'tis murder to think of 'em. I am going to send straight as a line into the breakfast-room, and say 'tis a closer* . . . . . Hullo,—here's Clerk Crickett and John Day a-comen! Now just look at 'em and picture a wedden if you can."

All eyes were turned to the window, from which the clerk and gardener were seen crossing the court, bowed and stooping like Bel and Nebo.*

"You'll have to go if it breaks all the horses' legs in the county," said the cook, turning from the spectacle, knocking open the oven door with the tongs, glancing critically in, and slamming it together with a clang.

"Oh, oh; why shall I?" asked the coachman, including in his auditory by a glance the clerk and gardener who had just entered.

"Because Mr. Manston is in the business. Did you ever know him to give up for weather of any kind, or for any other mortal thing in heaven or earth?"

"——Mornen so's,—such as it is!" interrupted Mr. Crickett, cheerily, coming forward to the blaze and warming one hand without looking at the fire. "Mr. Manston gie up for anything in heaven or earth, did you say? You might ha' cut it short by sayen 'to Miss Aldclyffe,' and leaven out heaven and earth as trifles. But it might be put off; putten off a thing isn't getten rid of a thing, if that thing is a woman: Oh no, no."

The coachman and gardener now naturally subsided into second-aries. The cook went on rather sharply, as she dribbled milk into the exact centre of a little crater of flour in a platter,

"It might be in this case: she's so indifferent."

"Dang my old sides! and so it might be. I have a bit of news—I thought there was something upon my tongue: but 'tis a secret, not a word mind, not a word. Why, Miss Hinton took a holiday yesterday."

"Yes?" inquired the cook, looking up with perplexed curiosity. "D'ye think that's all?"

"Don't be so three-cunning*—if it is all, deliver you from the evil of raising a woman's expectations wrongfully; I'll skimmer your pate* as sure as you cry Amen!"

"Well it isn't all. When I got home last night my wife said, 'Miss Hinton took a holiday this mornen,' says she (my wife, that is); 'walked over to Stintham Lane, met the comen man, and got married!' says she."

"Got married! what, Lord-a-mercy, did Springrove come?"

"Springrove, no—no—Springrove's nothen to do wi' it—'twas Farmer Bollens. They've been playing bo-peep for these two or three months seemingly. Whilst Master Teddy Springrove has been daddlen, and hawken, and spetten* about having her, she's quietly left him all forsook. Serve him right. I don't blame the little woman a bit."

"Farmer Bollens is old enough to be her father!"

"Ay, quite; and rich enough to be ten fathers. They say he's so rich, that he has business in every bank, and measures his money in half-pint cups."

"Lord, I wish it was me, don't I wish 'twas me!" said the scullery-maid.

"Yes, 'twas as neat a bit of stitchen as ever I heard of," continued the clerk, with a fixed eye, as if he were watching the process from a distance. "Not a soul knew anything about it, and my wife is the only one in our parish who knows it yet. Miss Hinton came back from the wedden, went to Mr. Manston, puffed herself out large and said she was Mrs. Bollens, but that if he wished, she had no objection to keep on the house till the regular time of given notice had expired, or till he could get another tenant."

"Just like her independence," said the cook.

"Well, independent or no, she's Mrs. Bollens now. Ah, I shall never forget once when I went by Farmer Bollens's garden—years ago now—years, when he was taken up ash-leaf taties.* A merry feller I was at that time, a very merry feller—for 'twas before I took orders,* and it didn't prick my conscience as 'twould now. 'Farmer,' says I, 'little taties seem to turn out small this year, don't 'em?' 'Oh, no, Crickett,' says he, 'some be fair-sized.' He's a dull man—Farmer Bollens is—he always was. However, that's neither here nor there, he's a-married to a sharp woman, and if I don't make a mistake she'll bring him a pretty good family, gie her time."

"Well, it don't matter; there's a Providence in it," said the scullery-maid. "God A'mighty always sends bread as well as children."

"But 'tis the bread to one house and the children to another. However, I think I can see my lady Hinton's reason for choosen yesterday to sickness-or-health-it.* Your young Miss, and that one, had crossed one another's path in regard to young Master Sprin-grove: and I expect that when Addy Hinton found Miss Graye wasn't caren to have en, she thought she'd be beforehand with her old enemy in marrying somebody else too. That's maids' logic all over, and maids' malice too."

Women who are bad enough to divide against themselves under a man's partiality, are good enough to instantly unite in a common cause against his attack.

"I'll just tell you one thing, then:" said the cook, shaking out her words to the time of a whisk she was beating eggs with. "Whatever maids' logic is and maids' malice too, if Cytherea Graye even now knows that young Springrove is free again, she'll fling over the steward as soon as look at him."

"No, no: not now," the coachman broke in like a moderator. "There's honour in that maid, if ever there was in one. No Miss Hinton's tricks in her. She'll stick to Manston."

"Pifh!"

"Don't let a word be said till the wedden is over, for heaven's sake," the clerk continued. "Miss Aldclyffe would fairly hang and quarter me, if my news broke off that there wedden at a last minute like this."

"Then you had better get your wife to bolt you in the closet for an hour or two, for you'll chatter it yourself to the whole boiling parish if she don't! 'Tis a poor womanly feller."

"You shouldn't ha' begun it, clerk. I knew how 'twould be," said the gardener soothingly, in a whisper to the clerk's mangled remains.

The clerk turned and smiled at the fire, and warmed his other hand.

§ 3. *Noon*

The weather gave way. In half an hour there began a rapid thaw. By ten o'clock the roads, though still dangerous, were practicable to the extent of the half-mile required by the people of Knapwater Park. One mass of heavy leaden cloud spread over the whole sky; the air began to feel damp and mild out of doors, though still cold and frosty within.

They reached the church and passed up the nave, the deep-coloured glass of the narrow windows rendering the gloom of the morning almost night itself inside the building. Then the ceremony began. The only warmth or spirit imported into it came from the bridegroom, who retained a vigorous—even Spenserian—bridal-mood* throughout the morning.

Cytherea was as firm as he at this critical moment, but as cold as the air surrounding her. The few persons forming the wedding-party were constrained in movement and tone, and from the nave of the church came occasional coughs, emitted by those who, in spite of the weather, had assembled to see the termination of Cytherea's existence as a single woman. Many poor people loved her. They pitied her success, why, they could not tell, except that it was because she seemed to stand more like a statue than Cytherea Graye.

Yet she was prettily and carefully dressed, a strange contradiction in a man's idea of things; a saddening, perplexing contradiction. Are there any points in which a difference of sex amounts to a difference of nature? Then this is surely one. Not so much, as it is commonly put, in regard to the amount of consideration given, but in the conception of the thing considered. A man emasculated by coxcombry may spend more time upon the arrangement of his clothes than any woman, but even then there is no fetichism* in his idea of them—they are still only a covering he uses for a time. But here was Cytherea, in the bottom of her heart almost indifferent to life, yet possessing an instinct with which her heart had nothing to do, the instinct to be particularly regardful of those sorry trifles, her robe, her flowers, her veil, and her gloves.

The irrevocable words were soon spoken—the indelible writing soon written—and they came out of the vestry. Candles had been necessary here to enable them to sign their names, and on their return to the church the light from the candles streamed from the small open door, and across the chancel to a black chestnut screen on the south side, dividing it from a small chapel or chantry, erected for the soul's peace of some Aldclyffe of the past. Through the openwork of this screen could now be seen illuminated, inside the chantry, the reclining figures of cross-legged knights, damp and green with age, and above them a huge classic monument, also inscribed to the Aldclyffe family, heavily sculptured in cadaverous marble.*

Leaning here—almost hanging to the monument—was Edward Springrove, or his spirit.

The weak daylight would never have revealed him, shaded as he was by the screen; but the unexpected rays of candlelight in the front showed him forth in startling relief to any and all of those whose eyes wandered in that direction. The sight was a sad one—sad beyond all description. His eyes were wild, their orbits leaden. His face was of a sickly paleness, his hair dry and disordered, his lips parted as if he

could get no breath. His figure was spectre-thin.* His actions seemed
beyond his own control.

Manston did not see him; Cytherea did. The healing effect upon
her heart of a year's silence—a year and a half's separation—was
undone in an instant. One of those strange revivals of passion by
mere sight—commoner in women than in men, and in oppressed
women commonest of all—had taken place in her—so transcend-
ently, that even to herself it seemed more like a new creation than a
revival.

Marrying for a home—what a mockery it was!

It may be said that the means most potent for re-kindling old love
in a maiden's heart are, to see her lover in laughter and good spirits
in her despite when the breach has been owing to a slight from
herself; when owing to a slight from him, to see him suffering for his
own fault. If he is happy in a clear conscience, she blames him; if he
is miserable because deeply to blame, she blames herself. The latter
was Cytherea's case now.

First, an agony of face told of the suppressed misery within her,
which presently could be suppressed no longer. When they were
coming out of the porch, there broke from her in a low plaintive
scream the words, "He's dying—dying! O God save us!" She began
to sink down, and would have fallen had not Manston caught her.
The chief bridesmaid applied her vinaigrette.*

"What did she say?" inquired Manston.

Owen was the only one to whom the words were intelligible, and
he was far too deeply impressed, or rather alarmed, to reply. She did
not faint, and soon began to recover her self-command. Owen took
advantage of the hindrance to step back to where the apparition had
been seen. He was enraged with Springrove for what he considered
an unwarrantable intrusion.

But Edward was not in the chantry. As he had come, so he had
gone, nobody could tell how or whither.

§ 4. *Afternoon*

It might almost have been believed that an impossibility had taken
place in Cytherea's idiosyncrasy,* and that her nature had changed.

The wedding-party returned to the house. As soon as he could
find an opportunity, Owen took his sister aside to speak privately

with her on what had happened. The expression of her face was hard, wild, and unreal—an expression he had never seen there before, and it disturbed him. He spoke to her severely and sadly.

"Cytherea," he said, "I know the cause of this emotion of yours. But remember this, there was no excuse for it. You should have been woman enough to control yourself. Remember whose wife you are, and don't think anything more of a mean-spirited fellow like Springrove; he had no business to come there as he did. You are altogether wrong, Cytherea, and I am vexed with you more than I can say— very vexed."

"Say ashamed of me at once," she bitterly answered.

"I am ashamed of you," he retorted angrily; "The mood has not left you yet, then?"

"Owen," she said, and paused. Her lip trembled; her eye told of sensations too deep for tears. "No, Owen, it has not left me; and I will be honest. I own now to you, without any disguise of words, what last night I did not own to myself, because I hardly knew of it. I love Edward Springrove with all my strength, and heart, and soul. You call me a wanton for it, don't you? I don't care, I have gone beyond caring for anything!" She looked stonily into his face, and made the speech calmly.

"Well, poor Cytherea, don't talk like that!" he said, alarmed at her manner.

"I thought that I did not love him at all," she went on, hysterically. "A year and half had passed since we met. I could go by the gate of his garden without thinking of him—look at his seat in church and not care. But I saw him this morning—dying because he loves me so—I know it is that! Can I help loving him too? No, I cannot, and I will love him, and I don't care! We have been separated somehow by some contrivance—I know we have. O, if I could only die!"

He held her in his arms. "Many a woman has gone to ruin* herself," he said, "and brought those who love her into disgrace, by acting upon such impulses as possess you now. I have a reputation to lose as well as you. It seems that do what I will by way of remedying the stains which fell upon us, it is all doomed to be undone again." His voice grew husky as he made the reply.

The right and only effective chord had been touched. Since she had seen Edward, she had thought only of herself and him. Owen— her name—position—future—had been as if they did not exist.

"I won't give way and become a disgrace to *you* at any rate," she said.

"Besides, your duty to society, and those about you requires that you should live with (at any rate) all the appearance of a good wife, and try to love your husband."

"Yes—my duty to society," she murmured. "But ah, Owen, it is difficult to adjust our outer and inner life with perfect honesty to all! Though it may be right to care more for the benefit of the many than for the indulgence of your own single self, when you consider that the many, and duty to them, only exist to you through your own existence, what can be said? What do our own acquaintances care about us? Not much. I think of mine. Mine will now (do they learn all the wicked frailty of my heart in this affair) look at me, smile sickly, and condemn me. And perhaps, far in time to come, when I am dead and gone, some other's accent, or some other's song, or thought, like an old one of mine, will carry them back to what I used to say, and hurt their hearts a little that they blamed me so soon. And they will pause just for an instant, and give a sigh to me, and think, 'Poor girl,' believing they do great justice to my memory by this. But they will never, never realize that it was my single opportunity of existence, as well as of doing my duty, which they are regarding; they will not feel that what to them is but a thought, easily held in those two words of pity, 'Poor girl,' was a whole life to me; as full of hours, minutes, and peculiar minutes, of hopes and dreads, smiles, whisperings, tears, as theirs: that it was my world, what is to them their world, and they in that life of mine, however much I cared for them, only as the thought I seem to them to be. Nobody can enter into another's nature truly, that's what is so grievous."

"Well, it cannot be helped," said Owen.

"But we must not stay here," she continued, starting up and going. "We shall be missed. I'll do my best, Owen—I will, indeed."

It had been decided that, on account of the wretched state of the roads, the newly married pair should not drive to the station till the latest hour in the afternoon at which they could get a train to take them to Southampton (their destination that night) by a reasonable time in the evening. They intended the next morning to cross to Havre, and thence to Paris—a place Cytherea had never visited—for their wedding tour.

The afternoon drew on. The packing was done. Cytherea was so restless that she could stay still nowhere. Miss Aldclyffe, who, though she took little part in the day's proceedings, was as it were instinctively conscious of all their movements, put down her charge's agitation for once as the natural result of the novel event, and Manston himself was as indulgent as could be wished.

At length Cytherea wandered alone into the conservatory. When in it, she thought she would run across to the hot-house in the outer garden, having in her heart a whimsical desire that she should also like to take a last look at the familiar flowers and luxuriant leaves collected there. She pulled on a pair of over-shoes, and thither she went. Not a soul was in or around the place. The gardener was making merry on Manston's and her account.

The happiness that a generous spirit derives from the belief that it exists in others is often greater than the primary happiness itself. The gardener thought, "How happy they are!" and the thought made him happier than they.

Coming out of the forcing-house again, she was on the point of returning in-doors, when a feeling that these moments of solitude would be her last of freedom induced her to prolong them a little, and she stood still, unheeding the wintry aspect of the curly leaved plants, the straw-covered beds, and the bare fruit-trees around her. The garden, no part of which was visible from the house, sloped down to a narrow river at the foot, dividing it from the meadows without.

A man was lingering along the public path on the other side of the river; she fancied she knew the form. Her resolutions, taken in the presence of Owen, did not fail her now. She hoped and prayed that it might not be one who had stolen her heart away, and still kept it. Why should he have re-appeared at all, when he had declared that he went out of her sight for ever?

She hastily hid herself in the lowest corner of the garden close to the river. A large dead tree, thickly robed in ivy, had been considerably depressed by its icy load of the morning, and hung low over the stream, which here ran slow and deep. The tree screened her from the eyes of any passer on the other side.

She waited timidly, and her timidity increased. She would not allow herself to see him—she would hear him pass, and then look to see if it had been Edward.

But, before she heard anything, she became aware of an object reflected in the water from under the tree, which hung over the river in such a way that, though hiding the actual path, and objects upon it, it permitted their reflected images to pass beneath its boughs. The reflected form was that of the man she had seen farther off, but being inverted, she could not definitely characterise him.

He was looking at the upper windows of the House—at hers—was it Edward, indeed? If so, he was probably thinking he would like to say one parting word. He came closer, gazed into the stream, and walked very slowly. She was almost certain that it was Edward. She kept more safely hidden. Conscience told her that she ought not to see him. But she suddenly asked herself a question; "Can it be possible that he sees my reflected image, as I see his? Of course he does!"

He was looking at her in the water.

She could not help herself now. She stepped forward just as he emerged from the other side of the tree and appeared erect before her. It was Edward Springrove,—till the inverted vision met his eye, dreaming no more of seeing his Cytherea there than of seeing the dead themselves.

"Cytherea!"

"Mr. Springrove," she returned, in a low voice, across the stream.

He was the first to speak again.

"Since we have met, I want to tell you something, before we become quite as strangers to each other."

"No—not now—I did not mean to speak—it is not right, Edward." She spoke hurriedly and turned away from him, beating the air with her hand.

"Not one common word of explanation?" he implored. "Don't think I am bad enough to try to lead you astray. Well, go—it is better."

Their eyes met again. She was nearly choked. O how she longed—and dreaded—to hear his explanation!

"What is it?" she said, desperately.

"It is that I did not come to the church this morning in order to distress you: I did not, Cytherea. It was to try to speak to you before you were—married."

He stepped closer, and went on, "You know what has taken place? Surely you do?—my cousin is married, and I am free."

"Married—and not to you?" Cytherea faltered, in a weak whisper.

"Yes, she was married yesterday! A rich man had appeared, and she jilted me. She said she never would have jilted a stranger, but that by jilting me, she only exercised the right everybody has of snubbing their own relations. But that's nothing now. I came to you to ask once more if . . . . But I was too late."

"But, Edward, what's that, what's that!" she cried, in an agony of reproach. "Why did you leave me to return to her? Why did you write me that cruel, cruel letter that nearly killed me!"

"Cytherea! Why, you had grown to love—like—Mr. Manston, and how could you be anything to me—or care for me? Surely I acted naturally?"

"O no—never! I loved you—only you—not him—always you!— till lately . . . . I try to love him now."

"But that can't be correct! Miss Aldclyffe told me that you wanted to hear no more of me—proved it to me!" said Edward.

"Never! she couldn't."

"She did, Cytherea. And she sent me a letter—a love-letter, you wrote to Mr. Manston."

"A love-letter I wrote?"

"Yes, a love-letter—you could not meet him just then, you said you were sorry, but the emotion you had felt with him made you forgetful of realities."

The strife of thought in the unhappy girl who listened to this distortion of her meaning could find no vent in words. And then there followed the slow revelation in return, bringing with it all the misery of an explanation which comes too late. The question whether Miss Aldclyffe was schemer or dupe was almost passed over by Cytherea, under the immediate oppressiveness of her despair in the sense that her position was irretrievable.

Not so Springrove. He saw through all the cunning half-mis-representations—worse than downright lies—which had just been sufficient to turn the scale both with him and with her; and from the bottom of his soul he cursed the woman and man who had brought all this agony upon him and his Love.

But he could not add more misery to the future of the poor child by revealing too much. The whole scheme she should never know.

"I was indifferent to my own future," Edward said, "and was urged to promise adherence to my engagement with my cousin Adelaide by Miss Aldclyffe: now you are married I cannot tell you how, but it was on account of my father. Being forbidden to think of you, what did I care about anything? My new thought that you still loved me was first raised by what my father said in the letter announcing my cousin's marriage. He said that although you were to be married on Old Christmas-day—that is to-morrow—he had noticed your appearance with pity: he thought you loved me still. It was enough for me—I came down by the earliest morning train, thinking I could see you some time to-day, the day, as I thought, before your marriage, hoping, but hardly daring to hope, that you might be induced to marry me. I hurried from the station; when I reached the bottom of Church Lane I saw idlers about the church, and the private gate leading to the House open. I ran into the church by the north door and saw you come out of the vestry; I was too late. I have now told you. I was compelled to tell you. O, my lost darling, now I shall live content—or die content!"

"I am to blame, Edward, I am," she said, mournfully; "I was taught to dread pauperism; my nights were made sleepless; there was continually reiterated in my ears till I believed it:—

> " 'The world and its ways have a certain worth,
> And to press a point where these oppose
> Were a simple policy.'*

"But I will say nothing about who influenced—who persuaded. The act is mine after all. Edward, I married to escape dependence for my bread upon the whim of Miss Aldclyffe, or others like her. It was clearly represented to me that dependence is bearable if we have another place which we can call home; but to be a dependent and to have no other spot for the heart to anchor upon—O it is mournful and harassing! . . . . But that without which all persuasion would have been as air, was added by my miserable conviction that you were false; that did it, that turned me! You were to be considered as nobody to me, and Mr. Manston was invariably kind. Well, the deed is done—I must abide by it. I shall never let him know that I do not love him—never. If things had only remained as they seemed to be, if you had really forgotten me and married another woman, I could have borne it better. I wish I did not know the truth as I know it now! But our life, what is it? Let us be brave, Edward, and live out our few remaining years with dignity. They will not be long. O I hope they will not be long! . . . . . Now, good-bye, good-bye!"

"I wish I could be near and touch you once, just once," said Springrove, in a voice which he vainly endeavoured to keep firm and clear.

They looked at the river, then into it; a shoal of minnows were floating over the sandy bottom, like the black dashes on miniver;* though narrow, the stream was deep, and there was no bridge.

"Cytherea, reach out your hand that I may just touch it with mine."

She stepped to the brink and stretched out her hand and fingers towards his, but not into them. The river was too wide.

"Never mind," said Cytherea, her voice broken by agitation, "I must be going. God bless and keep you, my Edward! God bless you!"

"I must touch you, I must press your hand," he said.

They came near—nearer—nearer still—their fingers met. There was a long firm clasp, so close and still that each hand could feel the other's pulse throbbing beside its own.

"My Cytherea! my stolen pet lamb!"

She glanced a mute farewell from her large perturbed eyes, turned, and ran up the garden without looking back. All was over between them. The river flowed on as quietly and obtusely as ever, and the minnows gathered again in their favourite spot as if they had never been disturbed.

Nobody indoors guessed from her countenance and bearing that her heart was near to breaking with the intensity of the misery which gnawed there. At these times a woman does not faint, or weep, or scream, as she will in the moment of sudden shocks. When lanced by a mental agony of such refined and special torture that it is indescribable by men's words, she moves among her acquaintances much as before, and contrives so to cast her actions in the old moulds that she is only considered to be rather duller than usual.

§ 5. *Half-past two to five o'clock, p.m.*

Owen accompanied the newly married couple to the railway-station, and in his anxiety to see the last of his sister, left the brougham* and stood upon his crutches whilst the train was starting.

When the husband and wife were about to enter the railway-carriage they saw one of the porters looking frequently and furtively at them. He was pale, and apparently very ill.

"Look at that poor sick man," said Cytherea, compassionately, "surely he ought not to be here."

"He's been very queer to-day, madam, very queer," another porter answered. "He do hardly hear when he's spoken to, and d' seem giddy, or as if something was on his mind. He's been like it for this month past, but nothing so bad as he is to-day."

"Poor thing."

She could not resist an innate desire to do some just thing on this most deceitful and wretched day of her life. Going up to him she gave him money, and told him to send to the old manor-house for wine or whatever he wanted.

The train moved off as the trembling man was murmuring his incoherent thanks. Owen waved his hand; Cytherea smiled back to him as if it were unknown to her that she wept all the while.

Owen was driven back to the Old House. But he could not rest in the lonely place. His conscience began to reproach him for having forced on the marriage of his sister with a little too much peremptoriness. Taking up his crutches he went out of doors and wandered about the muddy roads with no object in view save that of getting rid of time.

The clouds which had hung so low and densely during the day cleared from the west just now as the sun was setting, calling forth a weakly twitter from a few small birds. Owen crawled down the path to the waterfall, and lingered thereabout till the solitude of the place oppressed him, when he turned back and into the road to the village. He was sad; he said to himself,—

"If there is ever any meaning in those heavy feelings which are called presentiments—and I don't believe there is—there will be in mine to-day . . . . Poor little Cytherea!"

At that moment the last low rays of the sun touched the head and shoulders of a man who was approaching, and showed him up to Owen's view. It was old Mr. Springrove. They had grown familiar with each other by reason of Owen's visits to Knapwater during the past year. The farmer inquired how Owen's foot was progressing, and was glad to see him so nimble again.

"How is your son?" said Owen mechanically.

"He is at home, sitting by the fire," said the farmer, in a sad voice.

"This mornen he slipped indoors from God knows where, and there he sits and mopes, and thinks, and thinks, and presses his head so hard, that I can't help feelen for him."

"Is he married?" said Owen. Cytherea had feared to tell him of the interview in the garden.

"No. I can't quite understand how the matter rests. . . . Ah! Edward, too, who started with such promise; that he should now have become such a careless fellow—not a month in one place. There, Mr. Graye, I know what it is mainly owing to. If it hadn't been for that heart affair, he might have done——but the less said about him the better. I don't know what we should have done if Miss Aldclyffe had insisted upon the conditions of the leases. Your brother-in-law the steward had a hand in maken it light for us, I know, and I heartily thank him for it." He ceased speaking, and looked round at the sky.

"Have you heard o' what's happened?" he said suddenly; "I was just comen out to learn about it."

"I haven't heard of anything."

"It is something very serious, though I don't know what. All I know is what I heard a man call out by-now—that it very much concerns somebody who lives in the parish."

It seems singular enough, even to minds who have no dim beliefs in adumbration and presentiment, that at that moment not the shadow of a thought crossed Owen's mind that the somebody whom the matter concerned might be himself, or any belonging to him. The event about to transpire was as portentous to the woman whose welfare was more dear to him than his own, as any, short of death itself, could possibly be; and ever afterwards, when he considered the effect of the knowledge the next half-hour conveyed to his brain, even his practical good sense could not refrain from wonder that he should have walked toward the village, after hearing those words of the farmer, in so leisurely and unconcerned a way. "How unutterably mean must my intelligence have appeared to the eye of a foreseeing God," he frequently said in after time. "Columbus on the eve of his discovery of a world was not so contemptibly unaware."*

After a few additional words of commonplace, the farmer left him, and, as has been said, Owen proceeded slowly and indifferently towards the village.

The labouring men had just left work, and passed the park gate, which opened into the street as Owen came down towards it. They went along in a drift, earnestly talking, and were finally about to turn in at their respective doorways. But upon seeing him they looked significantly at one another, and paused. He came into the road, on that side of the village green which was opposite the row of cottages, and turned round to the right. When Owen turned, all eyes turned; one or two men went hurriedly indoors, and afterwards appeared at the doorstep with their wives, who also contemplated him, talking as they looked. They seemed uncertain how to act in some matter.

"If they want me, surely they will call me," he thought, wondering more and more. He could no longer doubt that he was connected with the subject of their discourse.

The first who approached him was a boy.

"What has occurred?" said Owen.

"Oh, a man ha' got crazy-religious,* and sent for the pa'son."

"Is that all?"

"Yes, sir. He wished he was dead, he said, and he's almost out of his mind wi' wishen it so much. That was before Mr. Raunham came."

"Who is he?" said Owen.

"Joseph Chinney, one of the railway-porters; he used to be night porter."

"Ah—the man who was ill this afternoon; by-the-way, he was told to come to the house for something, but he hasn't been. But has anything else happened—anything that concerns the wedding to-day?"

"No, sir."

Concluding that the connection which had seemed to be traced between himself and the event must in some way have arisen from Cytherea's friendliness towards the man, Owen turned about and went homewards in a much quieter frame of mind—yet scarcely satisfied with the solution. The route he had chosen led through the dairy-yard, and he opened the gate.

Five minutes before this point of time, Edward Springrove was looking over one of his father's fields at an outlying hamlet of three or four cottages some mile-and-a-half distant. A turnpike-gate was close by the gate of the field.

The carrier to Froominster came up as Edward stepped into the road, and jumped down from the van to pay toll. He recognised

Springrove. "This is a pretty set-to in your place, sir," he said. "You don't know about it, I suppose?"

"What?" said Springrove.

The carrier paid his dues, came up to Edward, and spoke ten words in a confidential whisper: then sprang upon the shafts of his vehicle, gave a clinching nod of significance to Springrove, and rattled away.

Edward turned pale with the intelligence. His first thought was, "Bring her home!"

The next—did Owen Graye know what had been discovered? He probably did by that time, but no risk of probability must be run by a woman he loved dearer than all the world besides. He would at any rate make perfectly sure that her brother was in possession of the knowledge, by telling it him with his own lips.

Off he ran in the direction of the old manor-house.

The path was across arable land, and was ploughed up with the rest of the field every autumn, after which it was trodden out afresh. The thaw had so loosened the soft earth, that lumps of stiff mud were lifted by his feet at every leap he took, and flung against him by his rapid motion, as it were doggedly impeding him, and increasing tenfold the customary effort of running.

But he ran on—up hill, and down hill, the same pace alike—like the shadow of a cloud. His nearest direction too, like Owen's, was through the dairy-barton,* and as Owen entered it he saw the figure of Edward rapidly descending the opposite hill, at a distance of two or three hundred yards. Owen advanced amid the cows.

The dairyman, who had hitherto been talking loudly on some absorbing subject to the maids and men milking around him, turned his face towards the head of the cow when Owen passed, and ceased speaking.

Owen approached him and said,

"A singular thing has happened, I hear. The man is not insane, I suppose?"

"Not he—he's sensible enough," said the dairyman, and paused. He was a man noisy with his associates—stolid and taciturn with strangers.

"Is it true that he is Chinney the railway-porter?"

"That's the man, sir." The maids and men sitting under the cows were all attentively listening to this discourse, milking irregularly, and softly directing the jets against the sides of the pail.

Owen could contain himself no longer, much as his mind dreaded anything of the nature of ridicule. "The people all seem to look at me, as if something seriously concerned me; is it this stupid matter, or what is it?"

"Surely sir, you know better than anybody else if such a strange thing concerns you."

"What strange thing?"

"Don't you know! His confessing to Parson Raunham."

"What did he confess; tell me."

"If you really ha'n't heard, 'tis this. He was as usual on duty at the station on the night of the fire last year, otherwise he wouldn't ha' known it."

"Known what? for God's sake tell, man."

But at this instant the two opposite gates of the dairy-yard, one on the east, the other on the west side, slammed almost simultaneously.

The rector from one, Springrove from the other, came striding across the barton.

Edward was nearest, and spoke first. He said in a low voice, "Your sister is not legally married! His first wife is still living! How it comes out I don't know!"

"O here you are at last, Mr. Graye, thank heaven!" said the rector, breathlessly. "I have been to the Old House and then to Miss Ald-clyffe's looking for you—something very extraordinary." He beckoned to Owen, afterwards included Springrove in his glance, and the three stepped aside together.

"A porter at the station. He was a curious nervous man. He had been in a strange state all day, but he wouldn't go home. Your sister was kind to him, it seems, this afternoon. When she and her husband had gone, he went on with his work, shifting luggage-vans. Well, he got in the way, as if he were quite lost to what was going on, and they sent him home at last. Then he wished to see me. I went directly. There was something on his mind, he said, and told it. About the time when the fire of last November twelvemonth was got under, whilst he was by himself in the porter's room, almost asleep, some-body came to the station and tried to open the door. He went out and found the person to be the lady he had accompanied to Carriford earlier in the evening, Mrs. Manston. She asked, when would be another train to London? The first the next morning, he told her, was at a quarter past six o' clock from Creston, but that it was express, and didn't stop at Carriford-Road—it didn't stop till it got to Froominster. 'How far is it to Froominster?' she said. 'Four miles,' he said. She thanked him, and went away up the line. In a short time she ran back and took out her purse. 'Don't on any account say a word in the village or anywhere that I have been here, or a single breath about me—I'm ashamed ever to have come.' He promised; she took out two sovereigns. 'Swear it on the testament in the waiting room,'* she said, 'and I'll pay you these.' He got the book, took an oath upon it, received the money, and she left him. He was off duty at half-past five. He has kept silence all through the intervening time till now, but lately the knowledge he possessed weighed heavily upon his conscience and weak mind. Yet the nearer came the wedding-day, the more he feared to tell. The actual marriage filled him with remorse. He says your sister's kindness afterwards was like a knife going through his heart. He thought he had ruined her."

"But whatever can be done? Why didn't he speak sooner!" cried Owen.

"He actually called at my house twice yesterday," the rector continued, "resolved, it seems, to unburden his mind. I was out both times—he left no message, and they say, he looked relieved that his object was defeated. Then he says he resolved to come to you at the Old House last night—started, reached the door, and dreaded to knock—and then went home again."

"Here will be a tale for the newsmongers of the county," said Owen, bitterly. "The idea of his not opening his mouth sooner—the criminality of the thing!"

"Ah that's the inconsistency of a weak nature. But now that it is put to us in this way, how much more probable it seems that she should have escaped than have been burnt—"

"You will of course go straight to Mr. Manston, and ask him what it all means?" Edward interrupted.

"Of course I shall! Manston has no right to carry off my sister unless he's her husband," said Owen, "I shall go and separate them."

"Certainly you will," said the rector.

"Where's the man?"

"In his cottage."

" 'Tis no use going to him, either. I must go off at once and overtake them—lay the case before Manston, and ask him for additional and certain proofs of his first wife's death. An up-train passes soon, I think."

"Where have they gone?" said Edward.

"To Paris—as far as Southampton this afternoon, to proceed tomorrow morning."

"Where in Southampton?"

"I really don't know—some hotel. I only have their Paris address. But I shall find them by making a few inquiries."

The rector had in the meantime been taking out his pocket-book, and now opened it at the first page, whereon it was his custom every month to gum a small railway time-table—cut from the local newspaper.

"The afternoon express is just gone," he said, holding open the page, "and the next train to Southampton passes at ten minutes to six o'clock. Now it wants—let me see—five-and-forty minutes to that time. Mr. Graye, my advice is that you come with me to the porter's cottage, where I will shortly write out the substance of what he has said, and get him to sign it. You will then have far better grounds for interfering between Mr. and Mrs. Manston than if you went to them with a mere hearsay story."

The suggestion seemed a good one. "Yes, there will be time before the train starts," said Owen.

Edward had been musing restlessly.

"Let me go to Southampton in your place, on account of your lameness?" he said suddenly to Graye.

"I am much obliged to you, but I think I can scarcely accept the offer," returned Owen coldly. "Mr. Manston is an honourable man, and I had much better see him myself."

"There is no doubt," said Mr. Raunham, "that the death of his wife was fully believed in by himself."

"None whatever," said Owen; "and the news must be broken to him, and the question of other proofs asked, in a friendly way. It would not do for Mr. Springrove to appear in the case at all." He still spoke rather coldly; the recollection of the attachment between his sister and Edward was not a pleasant one to him.

"You will never find them," said Edward. "You have never been to Southampton, and I know every house there."

"That makes little difference," said the rector, "he will have a cab. Certainly Mr. Graye is the proper man to go on the errand."

"Stay; I'll telegraph to ask them to meet me when I arrive at the terminus," said Owen; "that is, if their train has not already arrived."

Mr. Raunham pulled out his pocket-book again. "The two-thirty train reached Southampton a quarter of an hour ago," he said.

It was too late to catch them at the station. Nevertheless, the rector suggested that it would be worth while to direct a message to "all the respectable hotels in Southampton," on the chance of its finding them, and thus saving a deal of personal labour to Owen in searching about the place.

"I'll go and telegraph, whilst you return to the man," said Edward; an offer which was accepted. Graye and the rector then turned off in the direction of the porter's cottage.

Edward, to dispatch the message at once, hurriedly followed the road towards the station, still restlessly thinking. All Owen's proceedings were based on the assumption, natural under the circumstances, of Manston's good faith, and that he would readily acquiesce in any arrangement which should clear up the mystery. "But," thought Edward, "suppose—and Heaven forgive me, I cannot help supposing it—that Manston is not that honourable man, what will a young and inexperienced fellow like Owen do? Will he not be hood-winked by some specious story or another, framed to last till Manston gets tired of poor Cytherea? And then the disclosure of the truth will ruin and blacken both their futures irremediably."

However, he proceeded to execute his commission. This he put in the form of a simple request from Owen to Manston, that Manston would come to the Southampton platform and wait for Owen's arrival, as he valued his reputation. The message was directed as the rector had suggested, Edward guaranteeing to the clerk who sent it off that every expense connected with the search would be paid.

No sooner had the telegram been dispatched than his heart sank within him at the want of foresight shown in sending it. Had Manston, all the time, a knowledge that his first wife lived, the telegram would be a forewarning which might enable him to defeat Owen still more signally.

Whilst the machine was still giving off its multitudinous series of raps, Edward heard a powerful rush under the shed outside, followed by a long sonorous creak. It was a train of some sort, stealing softly into the station, and it was an up-train. There was the ring of a bell. It was certainly a passenger-train.

Yet the booking-office window was closed.

"Ho, ho, John, seventeen minutes after time, and only three stations up the line. The incline again?" The voice was the stationmaster's, and the reply seemed to come from the guard.

"Yes, the other side of the tunnel. The thaw has made it all in a perfect cloud of fog, and the rails are as slippery as glass. We had to bring them through the tunnel at twice."*

"Anybody else for the four-forty-five express?" the voice continued. The few passengers, having crossed over to the other side long before this time, had taken their places at once.

A conviction suddenly broke in upon Edward's mind; then a wish overwhelmed him. The conviction—as startling as it was sudden—was that Manston was a villain, who at some earlier time had discovered that his wife lived, and had bribed her to keep out of sight, that he might possess Cytherea. The wish was—to proceed at once by this very train that was starting, find Manston before he would expect from the words of the telegram (if he got it), that anybody from Carriford could be with him—charge him boldly with the crime, and trust to his consequent confusion (if he were guilty), for a solution of the extraordinary riddle, and the release of Cytherea!

The ticket-office had been locked up at the expiration of the time at which the train was due. Rushing out as the guard blew his whistle, Edward opened the door of a carriage and leapt in. The train moved along, and he was soon out of sight.

Springrove had long since passed that peculiar line which lies across the course of falling in love—if indeed it may not be called the initial itself of the complete passion—a longing to cherish; when the woman is shifted in a man's mind from the region of mere admiration to the region of warm fellowship. At this assumption of her nature, she changes to him in tone, hue, and expression. All about the loved one that said "Her" before, says "Us" now. Eyes that were to be subdued become eyes to be feared for: a brain that was to be probed by cynicism becomes a brain that is to be tenderly assisted: feet that were to be tested in the dance become feet that are not to be distressed: the once-criticised accent, manner, and dress, become the clients of a special pleader.

§ 6. *Five to eight o'clock, p.m.*

Now that he was fairly on the track, and had begun to cool down, Edward remembered that he had nothing to show—no legal authority whatever to question Manston, or interfere between him and Cytherea as husband and wife. He now saw the wisdom of the rector in obtaining a signed confession from the porter. The document would not be a death-bed confession—perhaps not worth anything legally—but it would be held by Owen, and he alone, as Cytherea's natural guardian, could separate them on the mere ground of an unproved probability, or what might perhaps be called the hallucination of an idiot. Edward himself, however, was as firmly convinced as the rector had been of the truth of the man's story, and paced backward and forward the solitary compartment as the train wound through the dark heathery plains, the mazy woods, and moaning coppices, as resolved as ever to pounce on Manston, and charge him with the crime during the critical interval between the reception of the telegram and the hour at which Owen's train would arrive— trusting to circumstances for what he should say and do afterwards, but making up his mind to be a ready second to Owen in any emergency that might arise.

At thirty-three minutes past seven he stood on the platform of the station at Southampton: a clear hour before the train containing Owen could possibly arrive.

Making a few inquiries here, but too impatient to pursue his investigation carefully and inductively, he went into the town.

At the expiration of another half-hour he had visited seven hotels and inns, large and small, asking the same questions at each, and always receiving the same reply—nobody of that name, or answering to that description, had been there. A boy from the telegraph-office had called, asking for the same persons, if they recollected rightly.

He reflected awhile, struck again by a painful thought that they might possibly have decided to cross the Channel by the night boat. Then he hastened off to another quarter of the town to pursue his inquiries among hotels of the more old-fashioned and quiet class. His stained and weary appearance obtained for him but a modicum of civility wherever he went, which made his task yet more difficult. He called at three several houses in this neighbourhood, with the

same result as before. He entered the door of the fourth house whilst
the clock of the nearest church was striking eight.

"Have a tall gentleman named Manston, and a young wife arrived
here this evening?" he asked again, in words which had grown odd to
his ears from very familiarity.

"A new-married couple, did you say?"

"They are, though I didn't say so."

"They have taken a sitting-room and bedroom, number thirteen."

"Are they indoors?"

"I don't know. Eliza!"

"Yes, m'm."

"See if number thirteen is in—that gentleman and his wife."

"Yes, m'm."

"Has any telegram come for them?" said Edward, when the maid
had gone on her errand.

"No—nothing that I know of."

"Somebody did come and ask if a Mr. and Mrs. Masters, or some
such name, were here this evening," said another voice from the back
of the bar-parlour.

"And did they get the message?"

"Of course they did not—they were not here—they didn't come
till half-an-hour after that. The man who made inquiries left no
message. I told them when they came that they, or a name something
like theirs, had been asked for, but they didn't seem to understand
why it should be, and so the matter dropped."

The chambermaid came back. "The gentleman is not in, but the
lady is—Who shall I say?"

"Nobody," said Edward. For it now became necessary to reflect
upon his method of proceeding. His object in finding their whereabouts—apart from the wish to assist Owen—had been to see
Manston, ask him flatly for an explanation, and confirm the request
of the message in the presence of Cytherea—so as to prevent the
possibility of the steward's palming off a story upon Cytherea, or
eluding her brother when he came. But here were two important
modifications of the expected condition of affairs. The telegram had
not been received, and Cytherea was in the house alone.

He hesitated as to the propriety of intruding upon her in Manston's absence. Besides, the women at the bottom of the stairs would
see him—his intrusion would seem odd—and Manston might

return at any moment. He certainly might call, and wait for Manston with the accusation upon his tongue, as he had intended. But it was a doubtful course. That idea had been based upon the assumption that Cytherea was not married. If the first wife were really dead after all—and he felt sick at the thought—Cytherea as the steward's wife might in after years—perhaps, at once—be subjected to indignity and cruelty on account of an old lover's interference now.

Yes, perhaps the announcement would come most properly and safely for her from her brother Owen, the time of whose arrival had almost expired.

But, on turning round, he saw that the staircase and passage were quite deserted. He and his errand had as completely died from the minds of the attendants as if they had never been. There was absolutely nothing between him and Cytherea's presence. Reason was powerless now; he must see her,—right or wrong, fair or unfair to Manston—offensive to her brother or no. His lips must be the first to tell the alarming story to her. Who loved her as he! He went back lightly through the hall, up the stairs, two at a time, and followed the corridor till he came to the door numbered thirteen.

He knocked softly: nobody answered.

There was no time to lose if he would speak to Cytherea before Manston came. He turned the handle of the door and looked in. The lamp on the table burned low, and showed writing materials open beside it; the chief light came from the fire, the direct rays of which were obscured by a sweet familiar outline of head and shoulders—still as precious to him as ever.

§ 7. *A quarter past eight o'clock, p.m.*

There is an attitude—approximatively called pensive—in which the soul of a human being, and especially of a woman, dominates outwardly and expresses its presence so strongly, that the intangible essence seems more apparent than the body itself. This was Cytherea's expression now. What old days and sunny eves at Creston Bay was she picturing? Her reverie had caused her not to notice his knock.

"Cytherea!" he said, softly.

She let drop her hand, and turned her head, evidently thinking that her visitor could be no other than Manston, yet puzzled at the voice.

There was no preface on Springrove's tongue; he forgot his position—hers—that he had come to ask quietly if Manston had other proofs of being a widower—everything—and jumped to a conclusion.

"You are not his wife, Cytherea—come away, he has a wife living!" he cried in an agitated whisper. "Owen will be here directly."

She started up, recognised the tidings first, the bearer of them afterwards. "Not his wife?—Oh what is it—what—who is living?" She awoke by degrees. "What must I do? Edward, it is you! Why did you come? where is Owen?"

"What has Manston shown you in proof of the death of his other wife? Tell me quick."

"Nothing—we have never spoken of the subject. Where is my brother Owen? I want him, I want him!"

"He is coming by-and-by. Come to the station to meet him—do," implored Springrove. "If Mr. Manston comes, he will keep you from me: I am nobody," he added, bitterly, feeling the reproach her words had faintly shadowed forth.

"Mr. Manston is only gone out to post a letter he has just written," she said, and without being distinctly cognizant of the action, she wildly looked for her bonnet and cloak, and began putting them on, but in the act of fastening them uttered a spasmodic cry.

"No, I'll not go out with you," she said, flinging the articles down again. Running to the door she flitted along the passage, and downstairs.

"Give me a private room—quite private," she said breathlessly to some one below.

"Number twelve is a single room, madam, and unoccupied," said some tongue in astonishment.

Without waiting for any person to show her into it, Cytherea hurried up stairs again, brushed through the corridor, entered the room specified, and closed the door. Edward heard her sob out:—

"Nobody but Owen shall speak to me: nobody!"

"He will be here directly," said Springrove, close against the panel, and then went towards the stairs. He had seen her; it was enough.

He descended, stepped into the street, and hastened to meet Owen at the railway-station.

As for the poor maiden who had received the news, she knew not what to think. She listened till the echo of Edward's footsteps had died away: then bowed her face upon the bed. Her sudden impulse had been to escape from sight. Her weariness after the unwonted strain, mental and bodily, which had been put upon her by the scenes she had passed through during the long day, rendered her much more timid and shaken by her position than she would naturally have been. She thought and thought of that single fact which had been told her—that the first Mrs. Manston was still living—till her brain seemed ready to burst its confinement with excess of throbbing. It was only natural that she should, by degrees, be unable to separate the discovery, which was matter of fact, from the suspicion of treachery on her husband's part, which was only matter of inference. And thus there arose in her a personal fear of him.

"Suppose he should come in now and murder me!" This at first mere frenzied supposition, grew by degrees to a definite horror of his presence, and especially of his intense gaze. Thus she raised herself to a heat of excitement, which was none the less real for being vented in no cry of any kind. No: she could not meet Manston's eye alone, she would only see him in her brother's company.

Almost delirious with this idea, she ran and locked the door to prevent all possibility of her intentions being nullified, or a look or word being flung at her by anybody whilst she knew not what she was.

§ 8. *Half-past eight o'clock, p.m.*

Then Cytherea felt her way amid the darkness of the room till she came to the head of the bed, where she searched for the bell-rope and gave it a pull. Her summons was speedily answered by the landlady herself, whose curiosity to know the meaning of these strange proceedings knew no bounds. The landlady attempted to turn the handle of the door. Cytherea kept the door locked. "Please tell Mr. Manston when he comes that I am ill," she said from the inside, "and that I cannot see him."

"Certainly I will, madam," said the landlady. "Won't you have a fire?"

"No thank you."

"Nor a light?"

"I don't want one, thank you."

"Nor anything?"

"Nothing."

The landlady withdrew, thinking her visitor half-insane.

Manston came in about five minutes later, and went at once up to the sitting-room, fully expecting to find his wife there. He looked round, rang, and was told the words Cytherea had said, that she was too ill to be seen.

"She is in number-twelve room," added the maid.

Manston was alarmed, and knocked at the door. "Cytherea?"

"I am unwell, I cannot see you," she said.

"Are you seriously ill, dearest? Surely not."

"No, not seriously."

"Let me come in, I will get a doctor."

"No, he can't see me either."

"She won't open the door, sir, not to nobody at all!" said the chamber-maid with wonder-waiting eyes.

"Hold your tongue, and be off!" said Manston with a snap.

The maid vanished.

"Come, Cytherea, this is foolish—indeed it is—not opening the door. . . . . I cannot comprehend what can be the matter with you. Nor can a doctor either, unless he sees you."

Her voice had trembled more and more at each answer she gave, but nothing could induce her to come out and confront him. Hating scenes, Manston went back to the sitting-room, greatly irritated and perplexed.

And there Cytherea from the adjoining room could hear him pacing up and down. She thought, "Suppose he insists upon seeing me—he probably may—and will burst open the door!" This notion increased, and she sank into a corner in a half-somnolent state, but with ears alive to the slightest sound. Reason could not overthrow the delirious fancy that outside her door stood Manston and all the people in the hotel, waiting to laugh her to scorn.

§9. *Half-past eight to eleven, p.m.*

In the meantime, Springrove was pacing up and down the arrival-platform of the railway station.

Half-past eight o'clock—the time at which Owen's train was due—had come, and passed, but no train appeared.

"When will the eight-thirty train be in?" he asked of a man who was sweeping the mud from the step.

"She is not expected yet this hour."

"How is that?"

"Christmas time you see, 'tis always so. People are running about to see their friends. The trains have been like it ever since Christmas-eve, and will be for another week yet."

Edward again went on walking and waiting under the draughty roof. He found it utterly impossible to leave the spot. His mind was so intent upon the importance of meeting with Owen, and informing him of Cytherea's whereabouts, that he could not but fancy Owen might leave the station unobserved if he turned his back, and become lost to him in the streets of the town.

The hour expired. Ten o'clock struck. "When will the train be in?" said Edward to the telegraph-clerk.

"In five-and-thirty minutes. She's now at L——. They have extra passengers, and the rails are bad to-day."

At last, at a quarter to eleven, the train came in.

The first to alight from it was Owen, looking pale and cold. He casually glanced round upon the nearly deserted platform, and was hurrying to the outlet, when his eyes fell upon Edward. At sight of his friend he was quite bewildered, and could not speak.

"Here I am, Mr. Graye," said Edward cheerfully. "I have seen Cytherea, and she has been waiting for you these two or three hours."

Owen took Edward's hand, pressed it, and looked at him in silence. Such was the concentration of his mind, that not till many minutes after did he think of inquiring how Springrove had contrived to be there before him.

§ 10. *Eleven o'clock, p.m.*

On their arrival at the door of the hotel, it was arranged between Springrove and Graye that the latter only should enter, Edward waiting outside. Owen had remembered continually what his friend had frequently overlooked, that there was yet a possibility of his sister being Manston's wife, and the recollection taught him to avoid any rashness in his proceedings which might lead to bitterness hereafter.

Entering the room, he found Manston sitting in the chair which had been occupied by Cytherea on Edward's visit, three hours' earlier. Before Owen had spoken, Manston arose, and stepping past him, closed the door. His face appeared harassed—much more troubled than the slight circumstance which had as yet come to his knowledge seemed to account for.

Manston could form no reason for Owen's presence, but intuitively linked it with Cytherea's seclusion. "Altogether this is most unseemly," he said, "whatever it may mean."

"Don't think there is meant anything unfriendly by my coming here," said Owen, earnestly; "but listen to this and think if I could do otherwise than come."

He took from his pocket the confession of Chinney the porter, as hastily written out by the vicar, and read it aloud. The aspects of Manston's face whilst he listened to the opening words were strange, dark, and mysterious enough to have justified suspicions that no deceit could be too complicated for the possessor of such impulses, had there not overridden them all, as the reading went on, a new and irrepressible expression—one unmistakably honest. It was that of unqualified amazement in the steward's mind at the news he heard. Owen looked up, and saw it. The sight only confirmed him in the belief he had held throughout, in antagonism to Edward's suspicions.

There could no longer be a shadow of doubt that if the first Mrs. Manston lived, her husband was ignorant of the fact. What he could have feared by his ghastly look at first, and now have ceased to fear, it was quite futile to conjecture.

"Now I do not for a moment doubt your complete ignorance of the whole matter; you cannot suppose for an instant that I do," said Owen when he had finished reading. "But is it not best for both that

Cytherea should come back with me till the matter is cleared up? In fact, under the circumstances, no other course is left open to me than to request it."

Whatever Manston's original feelings had been, all in him now gave way to irritation, and irritation to rage. He paced up and down the room till he had mastered it; then said in ordinary tones:—

"Certainly, I know no more than you and others know—it was a gratuitous unpleasantness in you to say you did not doubt me. Why should you, or anybody have doubted me?"

"Well, where is my sister?" said Owen.

"Locked in the next room."

His own answer reminded Manston that Cytherea must by some inscrutable means have had an inkling of the event.

Owen had gone to the door of Cytherea's room.

"Cytherea, darling—'tis Owen," he said, outside the door. A rustling of clothes, soft footsteps, and a voice saying from the inside, "Is it really you, Owen—is it really?"

"It is."

"O, will you take care of me!"

"Always."

She unlocked the door and retreated again. Manston came forward from the other room with a candle in his hand, as Owen pushed open the door.

Her frightened eyes were unnaturally large, and shone like stars in the darkness of the background, as the light fell upon them. She leapt up to Owen in one bound, her small taper fingers extended like the leaves of a lupine. Then she clasped her cold and trembling hands round his neck, and shivered.

The sight of her again kindled all Manston's passions into activity. "She shall not go with you," he said firmly, and stepping a pace or two closer, "unless you prove that she is not my wife; and you can't do it!"

"This is proof," said Owen, holding up the paper.

"No proof at all!" said Manston hotly. " 'Tis not a death-bed confession, and those are the only things of the kind held as good evidence."

"Send for a lawyer," Owen returned, "and let him tell us the proper course to adopt."

"Never mind the law—let me go with Owen!" cried Cytherea, still holding on to him. "You will let me go with him, won't you, sir?" she said, turning appealingly to Manston.

"We'll have it all right and square," said Manston, with more quietness. "I have no objection to your brother sending for a lawyer if he wants to."

It was getting on for twelve o'clock, but the proprietor of the hotel had not yet gone to bed on account of the mystery on the first floor, which was an occurrence unusual in the quiet family lodging. Owen looked over the bannisters, and saw him standing in the hall. It struck Graye that the wisest course would be to take the landlord to a certain extent into their confidence, appeal to his honour as a gentleman, and so on, in order to acquire the information he wanted, and also to prevent the episode of the evening from becoming a public piece of news. He called the landlord up to where they stood, and told him the main facts of the story.

The landlord was fortunately a quiet, prejudiced man, and a meditative smoker.

"I know the very man you want to see—the very man," he said, looking into the extreme centre of the candle flame. "Sharp as a needle and not over rich. Timms will put you all straight in no time—trust Timms for that."

"He's in bed by this time, for certain," said Owen.

"Never mind that—Timms knows me, I know him. He'll oblige me as a personal favour. Wait here a bit. Perhaps too he's up at some party or another—he's a nice jovial fellow, sharp as a needle too; mind you, sharp as a needle too."

He went down-stairs, put on his overcoat, and left the house, the three persons most concerned entering the room, and standing motionless, awkward, and silent in the midst of it. Cytherea pictured to herself the long weary minutes she would have to stand there, whilst a sleepy man could be prepared for consultation, till the constraint between them seemed unendurable to her—she could never last out the time. Owen was annoyed that Manston had not quietly arranged with him at once; Manston at Owen's homeliness of idea in proposing to send for an attorney, as if he would be a touchstone of infallible proof.

Reflection was cut short by the approach of footsteps, and in a few moments the proprietor of the hotel entered, introducing his friend. "Mr. Timms has not been in bed," he said; "he had just returned from dining with a few friends, so there's no trouble given. To save time I explained the matter as we came along."

It occurred to Owen and Manston both that they might get a misty exposition of the law from Mr. Timms at that moment of concluding dinner with a few friends.

"As far as I can see," said the lawyer, yawning, and turning his vision inward by main force, "it is quite a matter for private arrangement between the parties, whoever the parties are—at least at present. I speak more as a father than as a lawyer, it is true, but let the young lady stay with her father, or guardian, safe out of shame's way, until the mystery is sifted, whatever the mystery is. Should the evidence prove to be false, or trumped up by anybody to get her away from you, her husband, you may sue them for the damages accruing from the delay."

"Yes, yes," said Manston, who had completely recovered his self-possession and common sense, "let it all be settled by herself." Turning to Cytherea he whispered so softly that Owen did not hear the words,

"Do you wish to go back with your brother, dearest, and leave me here miserable, and lonely, or will you stay with me, your own husband?"

"I'll go back with Owen."

"Very well." He relinquished his coaxing tone, and went on sternly, "And remember this, Cytherea, I am as innocent of deception in this thing as you are yourself. Do you believe me?"

"I do," she said.

"I had no shadow of suspicion that my first wife lived. I don't think she does even now. Do you believe me?"

"I believe you," she said.

"And now, good evening," he continued, opening the door and politely intimating to the three men standing by that there was no further necessity for their remaining in his room. "In three days I shall claim her."

The lawyer and the hotel-keeper retired first. Owen, gathering up as much of his sister's clothing as lay about the room, took her upon his arm, and followed them. Edward, to whom she owed everything, who had been left standing in the street like a dog without a home, was utterly forgotten. Owen paid the landlord and the lawyer for the trouble he had occasioned them, looked to the packing, and went to the door.

A cab, which somewhat unaccountably was seen lingering in front of the house, was called up, and Cytherea's luggage put upon it.

"Do you know of any hotel near the station that is open for night arrivals?" Owen inquired of the driver.

"A place has been bespoken for you, sir, at the White Unicorn— and the gentleman wished me to give you this."

"Bespoken by Springrove, who ordered the cab, of course," said Owen to himself. By the light of the street-lamp he read these lines, hurriedly traced in pencil:—

"I have gone home by the mail-train. It is better for all parties that I should be out of the way. Tell Cytherea that I apologise for having caused her such unnecessary pain, as it seems I did—but it cannot be helped now.

"E. S."

Owen handed his sister into the vehicle, and told the cabman to drive on.

"Poor Springrove—I think we have served him rather badly," he said to Cytherea, repeating the words of the note to her.

A thrill of pleasure passed through her bosom as she listened to them. They were the genuine reproach of a lover to his mistress; the trifling coldness of her answer to him would have been noticed by no man who was only a friend. But, in entertaining that sweet thought, she had forgotten herself, and her position for the instant.

Was she still Manston's wife—that was the terrible supposition, and her future seemed still a possible misery to her. For, on account of the late jarring accident, a life with Manston which would otherwise have been only a sadness, must become a burden of unutterable sorrow.

Then she thought of the misrepresentation and scandal that would ensue if she were no wife. One cause for thankfulness accompanied the reflection; Edward knew the truth.

They soon reached the quiet old inn, which had been selected for them by the forethought of the man who loved her well. Here they installed themselves for the night, arranging to go to Creston by the first train the next day.

At this hour Edward Springrove was fast approaching his native county on the wheels of the night mail.

END OF VOL. II

VOLUME III

VOLUME III

CHAPTER I

THE EVENTS OF FIVE WEEKS

§ 1. *From the sixth to the thirteenth of January*

Manston had evidently resolved to do nothing in a hurry.

This much was plain, that his earnest desire and intention was to raise in Cytherea's bosom no feelings of permanent aversion to him. The instant after the first burst of disappointment had escaped him in the hotel at Southampton, he had seen how far better it would be to lose her presence for a week than her respect for ever.

"She shall be mine; I will claim the young thing yet," he insisted. And then he seemed to reason over methods for compassing that object, which, to all those who were in any degree acquainted with the recent event, appeared the least likely of possible contingencies.

He returned to Knapwater late the next day, and was preparing to call on Miss Aldclyffe, when the conclusion forced itself upon him that nothing would be gained by such a step. No; every action of his should be done openly—even religiously. At least, he called on the rector, and stated this to be his resolve.

"Certainly," said Mr. Raunham, "it is best to proceed candidly and fairly, or undue suspicion may fall on you. You should, in my opinion, take active steps at once."

"I will do the utmost that lies in my power to clear up the mystery, and silence the hubbub of gossip that has been set going about me. But what can I do? They say that the man who comes first in the chain of inquiry is not to be found—I mean the porter."

"I am sorry to say that he is not. When I returned from the station last night, after seeing Owen Graye off, I went again to the cottage where he has been lodging, to get more intelligence, as I thought. He was not there. He had gone out at dusk, saying he would be back soon. But he has not come back yet."

"I rather doubt if we shall see him again."

"Had I known of this, I would have done what in my flurry I did not think of doing—set a watch upon him. But why not advertise for your missing wife as a preliminary, consulting your solicitor in the meantime?"

"Advertise. I'll think about it," said Manston, lingering on the word as he pronounced it. "Yes, that seems a right thing—quite a right thing."

He went home and remained moodily indoors all the next day and the next—for nearly a week in short. Then, one evening at dusk, he went out with an uncertain air as to the direction of his walk, which resulted, however, in leading him again to the rectory.

He saw Mr. Raunham. "Have you done anything yet?" the rector inquired.

"No—I have not," said Manston, absently. "But I am going to set about it." He hesitated, as if ashamed of some weakness he was about to betray. "My object in calling was to ask if you had heard any tidings from Creston of my—Cytherea. You used to speak of her as one you were interested in."

There was, at any rate, real sadness in Manston's tone now, and the rector paused to weigh his words ere he replied.

"I have not heard directly from her," he said, gently. "But her brother has communicated with some people in the parish——"

"The Springroves, I suppose," said Manston, gloomily.

"Yes; and they tell me that she is very ill, and I am sorry to say, likely to be for some days."

"Surely, surely, I must go and see her!" Manston cried.

"I would advise you not to go," said Raunham. "But do this instead—be as quick as you can in making a movement towards ascertaining the truth as regards the existence of your wife. You see, Mr. Manston, an outstep* place like this is not like a city, and there is nobody to busy himself for the good of the community; whilst poor Cytherea and her brother are socially too dependent to be able to make much stir in the matter, which is a greater reason still why you should be disinterestedly prompt."

The steward murmured an assent. Still there was the same indecision!—not the indecision of weakness—the indecision of conscious perplexity.

On Manston's return from this interview at the rectory, he passed the door of the Traveller's Rest Inn. Finding he had no light for his cigar, and it being three-quarters of a mile to his residence in the park, he entered the tavern to get one. Nobody was in the outer portion of the front room where Manston stood, but a space round the fire was screened off from the remainder, and inside the high oak settle, forming a part of the screen, he heard voices conversing. The speakers had not noticed his footsteps, and continued their discourse.

One of the two he recognised as a well known night-poacher, the man who had met him with tidings of his wife's death on the evening of the conflagration. The other seemed to be a stranger following the same mode of life. The conversation was carried on in the emphatic and confidential tone of men who are slightly intoxicated.

What the steward heard was enough, and more than enough, to lead him to forget or to renounce his motive in entering. The effect upon him was strange and strong. His first object seemed to be to escape from the house again without being seen or heard.

Having accomplished this he went in at the park gate, and strode off under the trees to the Old House. There sitting down by the fire, and burying himself in reflection, he allowed the minutes to pass by unheeded. First the candle burnt down in its socket and stunk: he did not notice it. Then the fire went out: he did not see it. His feet grew cold; still he thought on.

It may be remarked that a lady, a year and a quarter before this time, had, under the same conditions—an unrestricted mental absorption—shown nearly the same peculiarities as this man evinced now. The lady was Miss Aldclyffe.

It was half-past twelve when Manston moved, as if he had come to a determination.

The first thing he did the next morning was to call at Knapwater House; where he found that Miss Aldclyffe was not well enough to see him. She had been ailing from slight internal haemorrhage ever since the confession of the porter Chinney. Apparently not much aggrieved at the denial, he shortly afterwards went to the railway station and took his departure for London, leaving a letter for Miss Aldclyffe, stating the reason of his journey thither—to recover traces of his missing wife.

During the remainder of the week paragraphs appeared in the local and other newspapers, drawing attention to the facts of this singular case. The writers, with scarcely an exception, dwelt forcibly upon a feature which had at first escaped the observation of the villagers, including Mr. Raunham,—that if the announcement of the man Chinney was true, it seemed extremely probable that Mrs. Manston left her watch and keys behind on purpose to blind people as to her escape; and that therefore she would not now let herself be discovered, unless a strong pressure were put upon her. The writers added that the police were on the track of the porter, who very possibly had absconded in the fear that his reticence was criminal, and that Mr. Manston, the husband, was with praiseworthy energy, making every effort to clear the whole matter up.

§ 2. *From the eighteenth to the end of January*

Five days from the time of his departure, Manston returned from London and Liverpool, looking very fatigued and thoughtful. He explained to the rector and other of his acquaintance that all the inquiries he had made at his wife's old lodgings and his own had been totally barren of results.

But he seemed inclined to push the affair to a clear conclusion now that he had commenced. After the lapse of another day or two he proceeded to fulfil his promise to the rector, and advertised for the missing woman in three of the London papers, the *Times*, the *Daily Telegraph*, and the *Standard*. The advertisement was a carefully considered and even attractive effusion, calculated to win the heart, or at least the understanding, of any woman who had a spark of her own nature left in her.

There was no answer.

Three days later he repeated the experiment; with the same result as before.

"I cannot try any further," said Manston speciously to the rector, his sole auditor throughout the proceedings. "Mr. Raunham, I'll tell you the truth plainly: I don't love her; I do love Cytherea, and the whole of this business of searching for the other woman goes altogether against me. I hope to God I shall never see her again."

"But you will do your duty at least?" said Mr. Raunham.

"I have done it," said Manston. "If ever a man on the face of this earth has done his duty towards an absent wife, I have towards her,—living or dead—at least," he added, correcting himself, "since I have lived at Knapwater. I neglected her before that time—I own that, as I have owned it before."

"I should, if I were you, adopt other means to get tidings of her if advertising fails, in spite of my feelings," said the rector, emphatically. "But at any rate try advertising once more. There's a satisfaction in having made any attempt three several times."

When Manston had left the study, the rector stood looking at the fire for a considerable length of time, lost in profound reflection. He went to his private diary, and after many pauses, which he varied only by dipping his pen, letting it dry, wiping it on his sleeve, and then dipping it again, he took the following note of events:—

"January 25.—Mr. Manston has just seen me for the third time, on the subject of his lost wife. There have been these peculiarities attending the three interviews,—

"The first. My visitor, whilst expressing by words his great anxiety to do everything for her recovery, showed plainly by his bearing that he was convinced he should never see her again.

"The second. He had left off feigning anxiety to do rightly by his first wife, and honestly asked after Cytherea's welfare.

"The third (and most remarkable). He seemed to have lost all consistency. Whilst expressing his love for Cytherea (which certainly is strong) and evincing the usual indifference to the first Mrs. Manston's fate, he was unable to conceal the intensity of his eagerness for me to advise him to *advertise again* for her."

A week after the second, the third advertisement was inserted. A paragraph was attached, which stated that this would be the last time the announcement would appear.

§ 3. *The first of February*

At this, the eleventh hour, the postman brought a letter for Manston, directed in a woman's hand.

A bachelor friend of the steward's, Mr. Dickson by name, who was somewhat of a chatterer—*plenus rimarum*,*—and who boasted of an endless string of acquaintances, had come over from Froominster the preceding day by invitation—an invitation which had been a pleasant surprise to Dickson himself, insomuch that Manston, as a rule, voted him a bore almost to his face. He had stayed over the night and was sitting at breakfast with his host when the important missive arrived.

Manston did not attempt to conceal the subject of the letter, or the name of the writer. First glancing the pages through, he read aloud as follows:—

" 'MY HUSBAND,

" 'I implore your forgiveness.

" 'During the last thirteen months I have repeated to myself a hundred times that you should never discover what I voluntarily tell you now, namely, that I am alive and in perfect health.

" 'I have seen all your advertisements. Nothing but your persistence has won me round. Surely, I thought, he *must* love me still. Why else should he try to win back a woman who, faithful unto death as she will be, can, in a social sense, aid him towards acquiring nothing?—rather the reverse, indeed.

" 'You yourself state my own mind—that the only grounds upon which we can meet and live together, with a reasonable hope of happiness, must be a mutual consent to bury in oblivion all past differences. I heartily and willingly forget everything—and forgive everything. You will do the same, as your actions show.

" 'There will be plenty of opportunity for me to explain the few facts relating to my escape on the night of the fire. I will only give the heads in this hurried note. I was grieved at your not coming to fetch me, more grieved at your absence from the station, most of all by your absence from home. On my journey to the inn I writhed under a passionate sense of wrong done me. When I had been shown to my room I waited and hoped for you till the landlord had gone upstairs to bed. I still found that you did not come, and then I finally made up my mind to leave. I had half undressed, but I put on my things again, forgetting my watch (and I suppose dropping my keys, though I am not sure where) in my hurry, and stepped out of the house. The——' "

"Well, that's a rum story," said Mr. Dickson, interrupting.

"What's a rum story?" said Manston, hastily, and flushing in the face.

"Forgetting her watch and dropping her keys in her hurry."

"I don't see anything particularly wonderful in it. Any woman might do such a thing."

"Any woman might if escaping from fire or shipwreck, or any such immediate danger. But it seems incomprehensible to me that any woman in her senses, who quietly decides to leave a house, should be so forgetful."

"All that is required to reconcile your seeming with her facts is to assume that she was not in her senses, for that's what she did plainly, or how could the things have been found there? Besides, she's truthful enough." He spoke eagerly and peremptorily.

"Yes, yes, I know that. I merely meant that it seemed rather odd."

"O yes." Manston read on,—

" '——and stepped out of the house. The rubbish-heap was burning up brightly, but the thought that the house was in danger did not strike me; I did not consider that it might be thatched.

" 'I idled in the lane behind the wood till the last down-train had come in, not being in a mood to face strangers. Whilst I was there the fire broke out, and this perplexed me still more. However, I was still determined not to stay in the place. I went to the railway station, which was now quiet, and inquired of the solitary man on duty there concerning the trains. It was not till I had left the man that I saw the effect the fire might have on my history. I considered also, though not in any detailed manner, that the event, by attracting the attention of the village to my former abode, might set people on my track should they doubt my death, and a sudden dread of having to go back again to Knapwater—a place which had seemed inimical to me from first to last—prompted me to run back and bribe the porter to secrecy. I then walked on to Froominster, lingering about the outskirts of the town till the morning train came in, when I proceeded by it to London, and then took these lodgings, where I have been supporting myself ever since by needlework, endeavouring to save enough money to pay my passage home to America, but making melancholy progress in my attempt. However, all that is changed— can I be otherwise than happy at it? Of course not. I am happy. Tell me what I am to do, and

" 'Believe me still to be
" 'Your faithful wife,
" 'EUNICE.

" 'My name here is (as before)

" 'MRS. RONDLEY, and my address,
" '79, Addington Street,
" 'Lambeth.' "

The name and address were written on a separate slip of paper.

"So it's to be all right at last then," said Manston's friend. "But after all there's another woman in the case. You don't seem very sorry for the little thing who is put to such distress by this turn of affairs? I wonder you can let her go so coolly."

The speaker was looking out between the mullions of the window—noticing that some of the lights were glazed in lozenges,* some in squares—as he said the words, otherwise he would have seen the passionate expression of agonized hopelessness that flitted across the steward's countenance when the remark was made. He did not see it, and Manston answered after a short interval. The way in which he spoke of the young girl who had believed herself his wife, whom, a few short days ago, he had openly idolised, and whom, in his secret heart, he idolised still, as far as such a form of love was compatible with his nature, showed, that from policy or otherwise, he meant to act up to the requirements of the position into which fate appeared determined to drive him.

"That's neither here nor there," he said; "It is a point of honour to do as I am doing, and there's an end of it."

"Yes. Only I thought you used not to care overmuch about your first bargain."

"I certainly did not at one time. One is apt to feel rather weary of wives when they are so devilish civil under all aspects, as she used to be. But anything for a change—Abigail is lost, but Michal is recovered.* would hardly believe it, but she seems in fancy to be quite another bride—in fact almost as if she had really risen from the dead, instead of having only done so virtually."

"You let the young pink one know that the other has come or is coming?"

"*Cui bono?*"* The steward meditated critically, showing a portion of his intensely white and regular teeth within the ruby lips.

"I cannot say anything to her that will do any good," he resumed. "It would be awkward—either seeing or communicating with her again. The best plan to adopt will be to let matters take their course—she'll find it all out soon enough."

Manston found himself alone a few minutes later. He buried his face in his hands, and murmured, "O my lost one—O my Cytherea! That it should come to this is hard for me! 'Tis now all darkness—'a land of darkness as darkness itself; and of the shadow of death without any order, and where the light is as darkness.'"*

Yes, the artificial bearing which this extraordinary man had adopted before strangers ever since he had overheard the conversation at the inn, left him now, and he mourned for Cytherea aloud.

§ 4. *The twelfth of February*

Knapwater Park is the picture—at eleven o'clock on a muddy, quiet, hazy, but bright morning—a morning without any blue sky, and without any shadows, the earth being enlivened and lit up rather by the spirit of an invisible sun than by its bodily presence.

The local Hunt had met for the day's sport on the open space of ground immediately in front of the steward's residence—called in the list of appointments, "Old House, Knapwater"—the meet being here once every season, for the pleasure of Miss Aldclyffe and her friends.

Leaning out from one of the first-floor windows, and surveying with the keenest interest the lively picture of red and black jackets,* rich-coloured horses, and sparkling bits and spurs, was the returned and long-lost woman, Mrs. Manston.

The eyes of those forming the brilliant group were occasionally turned towards her, showing plainly that her adventures were the subject of conversation equally with or more than the chances of the coming day. She did not flush beneath their scrutiny; on the contrary, she seemed rather to enjoy it, her eyes being kindled with a light of contented exultation, subdued to square with the circumstances of her matronly position.

She was, at the distance from which they surveyed her, an attractive woman—comely as the tents of Kedar.* But to a close observer it was palpable enough that God did not do all. Appearing at least seven years older than Cytherea, she was probably her senior by double the number, the artificial means employed to heighten the natural good appearance of her face being very cleverly applied. Her form was full and round, its voluptuous maturity standing out in strong contrast to the memory of Cytherea's lissom* girlishness.

It seems to be an almost universal rule that a woman who once has courted, or who eventually will court, the society of men on terms dangerous to her honour,* cannot refrain from flinging the meaning glance whenever the moment arrives in which the glance is strongly asked for, even if her life and whole future depended upon that moment's abstinence.

Had a cautious, uxorious husband seen in his wife's countenance what might now have been seen in this dark-eyed woman's as she caught a stray glance of flirtation from one or other of the red-jacketed gallants outside, he would have passed many days in an agony of restless jealousy and doubt. But Manston was not such a husband, and he was, moreover, calmly attending to his business at the other end of the manor.

The steward had fetched home his wife in the most matter-of-fact way a few days earlier, walking round the village with her the very next morning—at once putting an end, by this simple solution, to all the riddling inquiries and surmises that were rank in the village and its neighbourhood. Some men said that this woman was as far inferior to Cytherea as earth to heaven; others, older and sager, thought Manston better off with such a wife than he would have been with one of Cytherea's youthful impulses, and inexperience in household management. All felt their curiosity dying out of them. It was the same in Carriford as in other parts of the world—immediately circumstantial evidence became exchanged for direct, the loungers in court yawned, gave a final survey, and turned away to a subject which would afford more scope for speculation.

CHAPTER II

§ 1. *From the twelfth of February to the second of March*

Owen Graye's recovery from the illness that had incapacitated him for so long a time was, professionally, the dawn of a brighter prospect for him in every direction, though the change was at first very gradual, and his movements and efforts were little more than mechanical. With the lengthening of the days, and the revival of building operations for the forthcoming season, he saw himself, for the first time, on a road which, pursued with care, would probably lead to a comfortable income at some future day. But he was still very low down the hill as yet.

The first undertaking entrusted to him in the new year, commenced about a month after his return from Southampton. Mr. Gradfield had come back to him in the wake of his restored health, and offered him the superintendence, as clerk of works, of a new church, which was to be built at the village of Palchurch, ten or twelve miles north of Creston, and about half that distance from Carriford.

"I am now being paid at the rate of a hundred and twenty pounds a year,"* he said to his sister in a burst of thankfulness, "and you shall never, Cytherea, be at any tyrannous lady's beck and call again as long as I live. Never pine or think about what has happened, dear; it's no disgrace to you. Cheer up—you'll be somebody's happy wife yet."

He did not say Edward Springrove's, for greatly to his disappointment, a report had reached his ears that the friend to whom Cytherea owed so much had been about to pack up his things and sail for Australia. However, this was before the uncertainty concerning Mrs. Manston's existence had been dispersed by her return, a phenomenon that altered the cloudy relationship in which Cytherea had lately been standing towards her old lover, to one of distinctness; which result would have been delightful, but for circumstances about to be mentioned.

Cytherea was still pale from her recent illness, and still greatly dejected. Until the news of Mrs. Manston's return had reached them, she had kept herself closely shut up during the day-time, never venturing forth except at night. Sleeping and waking she had been in perpetual dread, lest she should still be claimed by a man whom, only a few weeks earlier, she had regarded in the light of a future husband with quiet assent, not unmixed with cheerfulness.

But the removal of the uneasiness in this direction—by Mrs. Manston's arrival, and her own consequent freedom—had been the imposition of pain in another. Utterly fictitious details of the finding of Cytherea and Manston had been invented and circulated,* unavoidably reaching her ears in the course of time. Thus the freedom brought no happiness, and it seemed well-nigh impossible that she could ever again show herself the sparkling creature she once had been,—

"Apt to entice a deity."*

On this account, and for the first time in his life, Owen made a point of concealing from her the real state of his feelings with regard to the unhappy transaction. He writhed in secret under the humiliation to which they had been subjected, till the resentment it gave rise to, and for which there was no vent, was sometimes beyond endurance; it induced a mood that did serious damage to the material and plodding perseverance necessary if he would secure permanently the comforts of a home for them.

They gave up their lodgings at Creston, and went to Palchurch as soon as the work commenced.

Here they were domiciled in one half of an old farm-house, standing close beneath the ivy-covered church tower (which was all that was to remain of the original structure). The long steep roof of this picturesque dwelling sloped nearly down to the ground, the old tiles that covered it being overgrown with rich olive-hued moss. New red tiles in twos and threes had been used for patching the holes wrought by decay, lighting up the whole harmonious surface with dots of brilliant scarlet.

The chief internal features of this snug abode were a wide fire-place, enormous cupboards, a brown settle,* and several sketches on the wood mantel, done in outline with the point of a hot poker—the subjects mainly consisting of old men walking painfully erect, with a curly-tailed dog behind.

After a week or two of residence in Palchurch, and rambles amid the quaint scenery circumscribing it, a tranquillity began to spread itself through the mind of the maiden, which Graye hoped would be a preface to her complete restoration. She felt ready and willing to live the whole remainder of her days in the retirement of their present quarters: she began to sing about the house in low tremulous snatches:—

> "—I said, if there's peace to be found in the world,—
> A heart that is humble may hope for it here."*

§ 2. *The third of March*

Her convalescence had arrived at this point on a certain evening towards the end of the winter, when Owen had come in from the building hard by, and was changing his muddy boots for slippers, previously to sitting down to toast and tea.

A prolonged, though quiet knocking came to the door.

The only person who ever knocked at their door in that way was the new vicar, the prime mover in the church-building. But he was that evening dining with the Squire.

Cytherea was uneasy at the sound—she did not know why, unless it was because her nerves were weakened by the sickness she had undergone. Instead of opening the door she ran out of the room, and upstairs.

"What nonsense, Cytherea," said her brother, going to the door.

Edward Springrove stood in the grey light outside.

"Capital—not gone to Australia, and not going, of course!" cried Owen. "What's the use of going to such a place as that—I never believed that you would."

"I am going back to London again to-morrow," said Springrove, "and I called to say a word before going. Where is . . . ?"

"She has just run upstairs. Come in—never mind scraping your shoes—we are regular cottagers now; stone floor, yawning chimney-corner, and all, you see."

"Mrs. Manston came," said Edward, awkwardly, when he had sat down in the chimney-corner by preference.

"Yes." At mention of one of his skeletons Owen lost his blitheness at once, and fell into a reverie.

"The history of her escape is very simple."

"Very."

"You know I always had wondered, when my father was telling any of the circumstances of the fire to me, how it could be that a woman should sleep so soundly as to be unaware of her horrid position till it was too late even to give shout or sound of any kind."

"Well, I think that would have been possible, considering her long wearisome journey. People have often been suffocated in their beds before they awake. But it was hardly likely a body would be completely burnt to ashes as this was assumed to be, though nobody seemed to see it at the time. And how positive the surgeon was, too, about those bits of bone. Why he should have been so, nobody can tell. I cannot help saying that if it has ever been possible to find pure stupidity incarnate, it was in that jury at Carriford. There existed in the mass the stupidity of twelve and not the penetration of one."

"Is she quite well?" said Springrove.

"Who?—O my sister, Cytherea. Thank you, nearly well, now. I'll call her."

"Wait one minute. I have a word to say to you."

Owen sat down again.

"You know, without my saying it, that I love Cytherea as dearly as ever . . . . I think she loves me, too,—does she really?"

There was in Owen enough of that worldly policy on the subject of matchmaking which naturally resides in the breasts of parents and guardians, to give him a certain caution in replying, and, younger as he was by five years than Edward, it had an odd effect.

"Well, she may possibly love you still," he said, as if rather in doubt as to the truth of his words.

Springrove's countenance instantly saddened: he had expected a simple "Yes," at the very least. He continued in a tone of greater depression.

"Supposing she does love me, would it be fair to you and to her if I made her an offer of marriage, with these dreary conditions attached,—that we live for a few years on the narrowest system, till a great debt, which all honour and duty require me to pay off, shall be paid? My father, by reason of the misfortune that befel him, is under a great obligation to Miss Aldclyffe. He is getting old, and losing his energies. I am attempting to work free of the burden. This makes my prospects gloomy enough at present.

"But consider again," he went on. "Cytherea has been left in a nameless and unsatisfactory, though innocent state,* by this unfortunate, and now void, marriage with Manston. A marriage with me, though under the—materially—untoward conditions I have mentioned, would make us happy; it would give her a *locus standi.** If she wished to be out of the sound of her misfortunes we would go to another part of England—emigrate—do anything."

"I'll call Cytherea," said Owen. "It is a matter which she alone can settle." He did not speak warmly. His pride could not endure the pity which Edward's visit and errand tacitly implied. Yet, in the other affair, his heart went with Edward; he was on the same beat for paying off old debts himself.

"Cythie, Mr. Springrove is here," he said, at the foot of the staircase.

His sister descended the creaking old steps with a faltering tread, and stood in the fire-light from the hearth. She extended her hand to Springrove, welcoming him by a mere motion of the lip, her eyes averted—a habit which had engendered itself in her since the beginning of her illness and defamation. Owen opened the door and went out—leaving the lovers alone. It was the first time they had met since the memorable night at Southampton.

"I will get a light," she said, with a little embarrassment.

"No—don't, please, Cytherea," said Edward, softly. "Come and sit down with me."

"O yes. I ought to have asked *you* to," she returned, timidly. "Everybody sits in the chimney-corner in this parish. You sit on that side. I'll sit here."

Two recesses—one on the right, one on the left hand—were cut in the inside of the fire-place, and here they sat down facing each other, on benches fitted to the recesses, the fire glowing on the hearth between their feet. Its ruddy light shone on the underslopes of their faces, and spread out over the floor of the room with the low horizontality of the setting sun, giving to every grain of sand and tumour in the paving a long shadow towards the door.

Edward looked at his pale Love through the thin azure twines of smoke that went up like ringlets between them, and invested her, as seen through its medium, with the shadowy appearance of a phantom. Nothing is so potent for coaxing back the lost eyes of a woman as a discreet silence in the man who has so lost them—and thus the patient Edward coaxed hers. After lingering on the hearth for half a minute, waiting in vain for another word from him, they were lifted into his face.

He was ready primed to receive them. "Cytherea, will you marry me?" he said.

He could not wait in his original position till the answer came. Stepping across the front of the fire to her own side of the chimney-corner, he reclined at her feet, and searched for her hand. She continued in silence awhile.

"Edward, I can never be anybody's wife," she then said, sadly, and with firmness.

"Think of it in every light," he pleaded; "the light of love, first. Then, when you have done that, see how wise a step it would be. I can only offer you poverty as yet, but I want—I do so long to secure you from the intrusion of that unpleasant past, which will often and always be thrust before you as long as you live the shrinking solitary life you do now—a life which purity chooses, it may be; but to the outside world it appears like the enforced loneliness of neglect and scorn— and tongues are busy inventing a reason for it which does not exist."

"I know all about it," she said, hastily; "and those are the grounds of my refusal. You and Owen know the whole truth—the two I love best on earth—and I am content. But the scandal* will be continually repeated, and I can never give anyone the opportunity of saying to you—that—your wife ..." She utterly broke down, and wept hysterically.

"Don't, my own darling!" he entreated. "Don't Cytherea!"

"Please to leave me—we will be friends, Edward—but don't press me—my mind is made up—I cannot—I will not marry you or any man under the present ambiguous circumstances—never will I—I have said it: never!"

They were both silent. He listlessly regarded the illuminated blackness overhead, where long flakes of soot floated from the sides and bars of the chimney-throat like tattered banners in ancient aisles; whilst through the square opening in the midst one or two bright stars looked down upon them from the grey March sky. The sight seemed to cheer him.

"At any rate, you will love me?" he murmured to her.

"Yes—always—for ever and for ever!"

He kissed her once, twice, three times, and arose to his feet, slowly withdrawing himself from her side towards the door. Cytherea remained with her gaze fixed on the fire. Edward went out grieving, but hope was not extinguished even now.

He smelt the fragrance of a cigar, and immediately afterwards saw a small red star of fire against the darkness of the hedge. Graye was pacing up and down the lane, smoking as he walked. Springrove told him the result of the interview.

"You are a good fellow, Edward," he said; "but I think my sister is right."

"I wish you would believe Manston a villain, as I do," said Springrove.

"It would be absurd of me to say that I like him now—family feeling prevents it, but I cannot in honesty say deliberately that he is a bad man."

Edward could keep the secret of Manston's coercion of Miss Ald-clyffe in the matter of the houses a secret no longer. He told Owen the whole story.

"That's one thing," he continued, "but not all. What do you think of this—I have discovered that he went to Creston post-office for a letter the day before the first advertisement for his wife appeared in the papers. One was there for him, and it was directed in his wife's handwriting, as I can prove. This was not till after the marriage with Cytherea, it is true, but if (as it seems to show), the advertising was a farce, there is a strong presumption that the rest of the piece was."

Owen was too astounded to speak. He dropped his cigar, and fixed his eyes upon his companion.

"Collusion!"

"Yes."

"With his first wife?"

"Yes—with his wife. I am firmly persuaded of it."

"What did you discover?"

"That he fetched from the post-office at Creston a letter from her the day before the first advertisement appeared."

Graye was lost in a long consideration. "Ah!" he said, "it would be difficult to prove anything of that sort now. The writing could not be sworn to, and if he is guilty the letter is destroyed."

"I have other suspicions——"

"Yes—as you said," interrupted Owen, who had not till now been able to form the complicated set of ideas necessary for picturing the position. "Yes, there is this to be remembered—Cytherea had been taken from him before that letter came—and his knowledge of his wife's existence could not have originated till after the wedding. I could have sworn he believed her dead then. His manner was unmistakable."

"Well, I have other suspicions," repeated Edward; "and if I only had the right—if I were her husband or brother, he should be convicted of bigamy* yet."

"The reproof was not needed," said Owen, with a little bitterness. "What can I do—a man with neither money nor friends—whilst Manston has Miss Aldclyffe and all her fortune to back him up? God only knows what lies between the mistress and her steward, but since this has transpired—if it is true—I can believe the connection to be even an unworthy one—a thing I certainly never so much as owned to myself before."

§ 3. *The fifth of March*

Edward's disclosure had the effect of directing Owen Graye's thoughts into an entirely new and uncommon channel.

On the Monday after Springrove's visit, Owen had walked to the top of a hill in the neighbourhood of Palchurch—a wild hill that had no name,* beside a barren down where it never looked like summer. In the intensity of his meditations on the ever-present subject, he sat down on a weather-beaten boundary-stone gazing towards the distant valleys—seeing only Manston's imagined form.

Had his defenceless sister been trifled with? that was the question which affected him. Her refusal of Edward as a husband was, he knew, dictated solely by a humiliated sense of inadequacy to him in repute, and had not been formed till since the slanderous tale accounting for her seclusion had been circulated. Was it not true, as Edward had hinted, that he, her brother, was neglecting his duty towards her in allowing Manston to thrive unquestioned, whilst she was hiding her head for no fault at all?

Was it possible that Manston was sensuous villain enough to have contemplated, at any moment before the marriage with Cytherea, the return of his first wife, when he should have grown weary of his new toy? Had he believed that, by a skilful manipulation of such circumstances as chance would throw in his way, he could escape all suspicion of having known that she lived? Only one fact within his own direct knowledge afforded the least ground for such a supposition. It was that, possessed by a woman only in the humble and unprotected station of a lady's hired companion, his sister's beauty, great as it was, might scarcely have been sufficient to induce a selfish man like Manston to make her his wife, unless he had foreseen the possibility of getting rid of her again.

"But for that stratagem of Manston's in relation to the Springroves," Owen thought, "Cythie might now have been the happy wife of Edward. True, that he influenced Miss Aldclyffe only rests on Edward's suspicions, but the grounds are good,—the probability is strong."

He went indoors and questioned Cytherea.

"On the night of the fire, who first said that Mrs. Manston was burnt?" he asked.

"I don't know who started the report."

"Was it Manston?"

"It was certainly not he. All doubt on the subject was removed before he came to the spot,—that I am certain of. Everybody knew that she did not escape *after* the house was on fire, and thus all overlooked the fact that she might have left before—of course that would have seemed such an improbable thing for anybody to do."

"Yes, until the porter's story of her irritation and doubt as to her course, made it natural."

"What settled the matter at the inquest," said Cytherea, "was Mr. Manston's evidence that the watch was his wife's."

"He was sure of that, wasn't he?"

"I believe he said he was certain of it."

"It might have been hers—left behind in her perturbation, as they say it was—impossible as that seems at first sight. Yes—on the whole, he might have believed in her death."

"I know by several proofs that then, and at least for some time after, he had no other thought than that she was dead. I now think that before the porter's confession he knew something about her—though not that she lived."

"Why do you?"

"From what he said to me on the evening of the wedding-day, when I had fastened myself in the room at the hotel, after Edward's visit. He must have suspected that I knew something, for he was irritated, and in a passion of uneasy doubt. He said 'You don't suppose my first wife is come to light again, madam, surely?' Directly he had let the remark slip out, he seemed anxious to withdraw it."

"That's odd," said Owen.

"I thought it very odd."

"Still, we must remember he might only have hit upon the thought by accident, in doubt as to your motive. Yes, the great point to discover remains the same as ever—did he doubt his first impression of her death *before* he married you. I can't help thinking he did, although he was so astounded at our news that night. Edward swears he did."

"It was perhaps only a short time before," said Cytherea; "when he could hardly recede from having me."

"Seasoning justice with mercy* as usual, Cytherea. 'Tis unfair to yourself to talk like that. If I could only bring him to ruin as a bigamist—supposing him to be one, I should die happy. That's what we must find out by fair means or foul—was he a wilful bigamist."

"It is no use trying Owen. You would have to employ a solicitor, and how can you do that?"

"I can't at all—I know that very well. But neither do I altogether wish to at present—a lawyer must have a case—facts to go upon, that means. Now they are scarce at present—as scarce as money is with us, and till we have found more money there is no hurry for a lawyer. Perhaps by the time we have the facts we shall have the money. The only thing we lose in working alone in this way, is time—not the issue: for the fruit that one mind matures in a twelvemonth forms a more perfectly organised whole than that of twelve minds in one month,* especially if the interests of the single one are vitally concerned, and those of the twelve are only hired. But there is not only my mind available—you are a shrewd woman Cythie, and Edward is an earnest ally. Then, if we really get a sure footing for a criminal prosecution, the crown will take up the case."

"I don't much care to press on in the matter," she murmured. "What good can it do us, Owen, after all?"

"Selfishly speaking, it will be this good—that all the facts of your journey to Southampton will become known, and the scandal will die. Besides, Manston will have to suffer—it's an act of justice to you and to other women, and to Edward Springrove."

He now thought it necessary to tell her of the real nature of the

Springroves' obligation to Miss Aldclyffe—and their nearly certain knowledge that Manston was the prime mover in effecting their embarrassment. Her face flushed as she listened.

"And now," he said, "our first undertaking is to find out where Mrs. Manston lived during the separation; next, when the first communication passed between them after the fire."

"If we only had Miss Aldclyffe's countenance and assistance as I used to have them," Cytherea returned, "how strong we should be. O, what power is it that he exercises over her, swaying her just as he wishes! She loves me now. Mrs. Morris in her letter said that Miss Aldclyffe prayed for me—yes, she heard her praying for me, and crying. Miss Aldclyffe did not mind an old friend like Mrs. Morris knowing it, either. Yet in opposition to this, notice her dead silence and inaction throughout this proceeding."

"It is a mystery; but never mind that now," said Owen impressively. "About where Mrs. Manston has been living. We must get this part of it first—learn the place of her stay in the early stage of their separation, during the period of Manston's arrival here and so on, for that was where she was first communicated with on the subject of coming to Knapwater, before the fire; and that address too was her point of departure when she came to her husband by stealth in the night—you know,—the time I visited you in the evening and went home early in the morning, and it was found that he had been visited too. Ah! couldn't we inquire of Mrs. Leat, who keeps the post-office at Carriford, if she remembers where the letters to Mrs. Manston were directed?"

"He never posted his letters to her in the parish—it was remarked at the time. I was thinking if something relating to her address might not be found in the report of the inquest in the *Froominster Chronicle* of the date. Some facts about the inquest were given in the papers to a certainty."

Her brother caught eagerly at the suggestion. "Who has a file of the *Chronicles*?" he said.

"Mr. Raunham used to file them," said Cytherea. "He was rather friendly-disposed towards me, too."

Owen could not on any consideration escape from his attendance at the church-building till Saturday evening; and thus it became necessary, unless they actually wasted time, that Cytherea herself should assist. "I act under your orders, Owen," she said.

CHAPTER III

THE EVENTS OF ONE WEEK

§ 1. *March the sixth*

The next morning the opening move of the game was made. Cytherea, under cover of a thick veil, walked to Froominster railway station and took the train for Carriford-Road. It was with a renewed sense of depression that she saw again the objects which had become familiar to her eye during her sojourn under Miss Aldclyffe's roof,—the outline of the hills, the meadow streams, the old park trees. She hastened by a lonely path to the rectory house, and asked if Mr. Raunham was at home.

Now the rector, though a solitary bachelor, was as gallant and courteous to womankind as an ancient Iberian;* and moreover, he was Cytherea's friend in particular, to an extent far greater than she had ever surmised. Rarely visiting his relative Miss Aldclyffe, except on parish matters, more rarely still being called upon by Miss Aldclyffe, Cytherea had learnt very little of him whilst she lived at Knapwater. The relationship was on the paternal side, and for this branch of her family the lady of the estate had never evinced much sympathy.

In looking back upon our line of descent it is an instinct with us to feel that all our vitality was drawn from the richer side of any unequal marriage in the chain.

Since the death of the old captain, the rector's bearing in Knapwater House had been almost that of a stranger, a circumstance which he himself was the last man in the world to regret. This polite indifference was so frigid on both sides, that the rector did not concern himself to preach at her, which was a great deal in a rector; and she did not take the trouble to think his sermons poor stuff, which in a cynical female was a great deal more.

Though barely fifty years of age, his hair was as white as snow, contrasting strangely with the redness of his skin, which was as fresh and healthy as a lad's. Cytherea's bright eyes, mutely and demurely glancing up at him Sunday after Sunday, had been the means of driving away many of the saturnine humours that creep into an empty heart during the hours of a solitary life; in this case, however, to supplant them, when she left his parish, by those others of a more aching nature which accompany an over full one. In short, he had been on the verge of feeling towards her that passion to which his dignified self-respect would not give its true name, even in the privacy of his own thought.

He received her kindly; but she was not disposed to be frank with him. He saw her wish to be reserved, and with genuine good taste and good nature made no comment whatever upon her request to be allowed to see the *Chronicle* for the year before the last. He placed the papers before her on his study table, with a timidity as great as her own, and then left her entirely to herself.

She turned them over till she came to the first heading connected with the subject of her search,—"Disastrous Fire and Loss of Life at Carriford."

The sight, and its calamitous bearing upon her own life, made her so dizzy that she could, for a while, hardly decipher the letters. Stifling recollection by an effort, she nerved herself to her work, and carefully read the column. The account reminded her of no other fact than was remembered already.

She turned on to the following week's report of the inquest. After a miserable perusal she could find no more pertaining to Mrs. Manston's address than this:—"ABRAHAM BROWN, of Hoxton,* London, at whose house the deceased woman had been living, deposed," &c.

Nobody else from London had attended the inquest.

She arose to depart, first sending a message of thanks to Mr. Raunham, who was out gardening.

He stuck his spade into the ground, and accompanied her to the gate.

"Can I help you in anything, Cytherea?" he said, using her christian name by an intuition that unpleasant memories might be revived if he called her Miss Graye after wishing her good-bye as Mrs. Manston after the wedding. Cytherea saw the motive and appreciated it, nevertheless replying evasively,—

"I only guess and fear."

He earnestly looked at her again.

"Promise me that if you want assistance, and you think I can give it, you will come to me."

"I will," she said.

The gate closed between them.

"You don't want me to help you in anything now, Cytherea?" he repeated.

If he had spoken what he felt, "I want very much to help you, Cytherea, and have been watching Manston on your account," she would gladly have accepted his offer. As it was she was perplexed, and raised her eyes to his, not so fearlessly as before her trouble, but as modestly, and with still enough brightness in them to do fearful execution* as she said over the gate,

"No, thank you."

She returned to Palchurch weary with her day's work. Owen's greeting was anxious:

"Well, Cytherea?"

She gave him the words from the report of the inquest, pencilled on a slip of paper.

"Now to find out the name of the street and number," Owen remarked.

"Owen," she said, "will you forgive me for what I am going to say? I don't think I can—indeed I don't think I can—take any further steps towards disentangling the mystery. I still think it a useless task, and it does not seem any duty of mine to be revenged upon Mr. Manston in any way." She added more gravely, "It is beneath my dignity as a woman to labour for this; I have felt it so all day."

"Very well," he said, somewhat shortly, "I shall work without you then. There's dignity in justice." He caught sight of her pale tired face, and the dilated eye which always appeared in her with weariness. "Darling," he continued, warmly, and kissing her, "you shall not work so hard again—you are worn out quite. But you must let me do as I like."

§2. *March the tenth*

On Saturday evening Graye hurried off to Froominster, and called at the house of the reporter to the *Chronicle*. The reporter was at home, and came out to Graye in the passage. Owen explained who and what he was, and asked the man if he would oblige him by turning to his notes of the inquest at Carriford in the December of the year preceding the last—just adding that a family entanglement, of which the reporter probably knew something, made him anxious to ascertain some additional details of the event, if any existed.

"Certainly" said the other, without hesitation; "though I am afraid I haven't much beyond what we printed at the time. Let me see—my old note-books are in my drawer at the office of the paper: if you will come with me I can refer to them there." His wife and family were at tea inside the room, and with the timidity of decent poverty everywhere, he seemed glad to get a stranger away from his domestic groove.

They crossed the street, entered the office, and went thence to an inner room. Here, after a short search, was found the book required. The precise address, not given in the condensed report that was printed, but written down by the reporter, was as follows:

"Abraham Brown, Lodging-house keeper, 41, Charles Square, Hoxton."

Owen copied it, and gave the reporter a small fee. "I want to keep this inquiry private for the present," he said, hesitatingly. "You will perhaps understand why, and oblige me."

The reporter promised. "News is shop with me," he said, "and to escape from handling it is my greatest social enjoyment."

It was evening, and the outer room of the publishing-office was lighted up with flaring jets of gas.* After making the above remark, the reporter came out from the inner apartment in Graye's company, answering an expression of obligation from Owen with the words that it was no trouble. At the moment of his speech, he closed behind him the door between the two rooms, still holding his note-book in his hand.

Before the counter of the front room stood a tall man, who was also speaking, when they emerged. He said to the youth in attendance, "I will take my paper for this week now I am here, so that you needn't post it to me."

The stranger then slightly turned his head, saw Owen, and recognised him. Owen passed out without recognising the other as Manston.

Manston then looked at the reporter, who, after walking to the door with Owen, had come back again to lock up his books. Manston did not need to be told that the shabby marble-covered* book which he carried in his hand, opening endways and interleaved with blotting-paper, was an old reporting book. He raised his eyes to the reporter's face, whose experience had not so schooled his features but that they betrayed a consciousness, to one half-initiated as the other was, that his late proceeding had been connected with events in the life of the steward. Manston said no more, but, taking his newspaper, followed Owen from the office, and disappeared in the gloom of the street.

Edward Springrove was now in London again, and on this same evening before leaving Froominster, Owen wrote a careful letter to him, stating therein all the facts that had come to his knowledge, and begging him, as he valued Cytherea, to make cautious inquiries. A tall man was standing under the lamp-post, about half-a-dozen yards above the post-office, when he dropped the letter into the box.

That same night too, for a reason connected with the rencounter with Owen Graye, the steward entertained the idea of rushing off suddenly to London by the mail-train, which left Froominster at ten o'clock. But remembering that letters posted after the hour at which Owen had obtained his information—whatever that was—could not be delivered in London till Monday morning, he changed his mind and went home to Knapwater. Making a confidential explanation to his wife, arrangements were set on foot for his departure by the mail* on Sunday night.

§3. *March the eleventh*

Starting for church the next morning several minutes earlier than was usual with him, the steward intentionally loitered along the road from the village till old Mr. Springrove overtook him. Manston spoke very civilly of the morning, and of the weather, asking how the farmer's barometer stood, and when it was probable that the wind might change. It was not in Mr. Springrove's nature—going to church as he was, too—to return anything but a civil answer to such civil questions, however his feelings might have been biassed by late events. The conversation was continued on terms of greater friendliness.

"You must be feeling settled again by this time, Mr. Springrove, after the rough turn out you had on that terrible night in November."

"Ay, but I don't know about feelen settled, either, Mr. Manston. The old window in the chimney-corner of the old house I shall never forget. No window in the chimney-corner where I am now, and I had been used to en for more than fifty years. Ted says 'tis a great loss to me, and he knows exactly what I feel."

"Your son is again in a good situation, I believe?" said Manston, imitating that inquisitiveness towards inferiors which passes for high breeding among the pinchbeck aristocracy* of country villages.

"Yes, sir. I hope he'll keep it, or do something else and stick to it."

"'Tis to be hoped he'll be steady now."

"He's always been that, I assure ye," said the old man, tartly.

"Yes—yes—I mean intellectually steady. Intellectual wild oats will thrive in a soil of the strictest morality."

"Intellectual gingerbread! Ted's steady enough—that's all I know about it."

"Of course—of course. Has he respectable lodgings? My own experience has shown me that that's a great thing to a young man living alone in London."

"Warwick Street, Charing Cross—that's where he is."

"Well, to be sure—strange! A very dear friend of mine used to live at number fifty-two in that very same street."

"Edward lives at number forty-nine—how very near being the same house," said the old farmer, pleased in spite of himself.

"Very," said Manston. "Well, I suppose we had better step along a little quicker, Mr. Springrove; the parson's bell has just begun."

"Number forty-nine," he murmured.

§4. *March the twelfth*

Edward received Owen's letter in due time, but on account of his daily engagements he could not attend to any request till the clock had struck five in the afternoon. Rushing then from his office in the Adelphi, he called a Hansom and proceeded to Hoxton. A few minutes later he knocked at the door of number forty-one, Charles Square, the old lodging of Mrs. Manston.

A tall man, who would have looked extremely handsome had he not been clumsily and closely wrapped up in garments that were much too elderly in style for his years, stood at the corner of the quiet square at the same instant, having, too, alighted from a cab that had been driven along Old Street in Edward's rear. He smiled confidently when Springrove knocked.

Nobody came to the door. Springrove knocked again.

This brought out two people—one at the door he had been knocking upon, the other from the next on the right.

"Is Mr. Brown at home?" said Springrove.

"No, sir."

"When will he be in?"

"Quite uncertain."

"Can you tell me where I may find him?"

"No. O here he is coming, sir. That's Mr. Brown."

Edward looked down the pavement in the direction pointed out by the woman, and saw a man approaching. He proceeded a few steps to meet him.

Edward was impatient, and to a certain extent still a countryman, who had not, after the manner of city men, subdued the natural impulse to speak out the ruling thought without preface. He said in a quiet tone to the stranger, "One word with you—do you remember a lady lodger of yours of the name of Mrs. Manston?"

Mr. Brown half-closed his eyes at Springrove, somewhat as if he were looking into a telescope at the wrong end.

"I have never let lodgings in my life," he said, after his survey.

"Didn't you attend an inquest a year and a half ago, at Carriford?"

"Never knew there was such a place in the world, sir; and as to lodgings, I have taken acres first and last during the last thirty years, but I have never let an inch."

"I suppose there is some mistake," Edward murmured, and turned away. He and Mr. Brown were now opposite the door next to the one he had knocked at. The woman who was still standing there had heard the inquiry and the result of it.

"I expect it is the other Mr. Brown, who used to live there, that you want, sir," she said, "The Mr. Brown that was inquired for the other day?"

"Very likely that is the man," said Edward, his interest reawakening.

"He couldn't make a do of lodging-letting here, and at last he went to Cornwall, where he came from, and where his brother still lived, who had often asked him to come home again. But there was little luck in the change; for after London they say he couldn't stand the rainy west winds they get there, and he died in the December following. Will you step into the passage?"

"That's unfortunate," said Edward, going in. "But perhaps you remember a Mrs. Manston living next door to you?"

"O yes," said the landlady, closing the door. "The lady who was supposed to have met with such a horrible fate, and was alive all the time. I saw her the other day."

"Since the fire at Carriford?"

"Yes. Her husband came to ask if Mr. Brown was still living here—just as you might. He seemed anxious about it; and then one evening, a week or fortnight afterwards, when he came again to make further inquiries, she was with him. But I did not speak to her—she stood back, as if she were shy. I was interested, however, for old Mr. Brown had told me all about her when he came back from the inquest."

"Did you know Mrs. Manston before she called the other day?"

"No. You see she was only Mr. Brown's lodger for two or three weeks, and I didn't know she was living there till she was near upon leaving again—we don't notice next-door people much here in London. I much regretted I had not known her when I heard what had happened. It led me and Mr. Brown to talk about her a great deal afterwards. I little thought I should see her alive after all."

"And when do you say they came here together?"

"I don't exactly remember the day—though I remember a very beautiful dream I had that same night—ah, I shall never forget it! Shoals of lodgers coming along the square with angels' wings and bright golden sovereigns in their hands wanting apartments at West End prices. They would not give any less; no, not if you——"

"Yes. Did Mrs. Manston leave anything, such as papers, when she left these lodgings originally?" said Edward, though his heart sank as he asked. He felt that he was outwitted. Manston and his wife had been there before him, clearing the ground of all traces.

"I have always said 'No' hitherto," replied the woman, "considering I could say no more if put upon my oath, as I expected to be. But speaking in a common everyday way now the occurrence is past, I believe a few things of some kind (though I doubt if they were papers) were left in a workbox she had, because she talked about it to Mr. Brown, and was rather angry at what occurred—you see she had a temper by all account, and so I didn't like to remind the lady of this workbox when she came the other day with her husband."

"And about the workbox?"

"Well, from what was casually dropped, I think Mrs. Manston had a few articles of furniture she didn't want, and when she was leaving they were put in a sale just by. Amongst her things were two workboxes very much alike. One of these she intended to sell, the other she didn't, and Mr. Brown, who collected the things together, took the wrong one to the sale."

"What was in it?"

"O nothing in particular, or of any value—some accounts, and her usual sewing materials I think—nothing more. She didn't take much trouble to get it back—she said the bills were worth nothing to her or anybody else, but that she should have liked to keep the box because her husband gave it her when they were first married, and if he found she had parted with it he would be vexed."

"Did Mrs. Manston, when she called recently with her husband, allude to this, or inquire for it, or did Mr. Manston?"

"No—and I rather wondered at it. But she seemed to have forgotten it—indeed she didn't make any inquiry at all, only standing behind him, listening to his; and he probably had never been told anything about it."

"Whose sale were these articles of hers taken to?"

"Who was the auctioneer? Mr. Halway. His place is the third turning from the end of that street you see there. Anybody will tell you the shop—his name is written up."

Edward went off to follow up this clue with a promptness which was dictated more by a dogged will to do his utmost than by a hope of doing much. When he was out of sight, the tall and cloaked man, who had watched him, came up to the woman's door, with an appearance of being in breathless haste.

"Has a gentleman been here inquiring about Mrs. Manston?"

"Yes: he's just gone."

"Dear me! I want him."

"He's gone to Mr. Halway's."

"I think I can give him some information upon the subject. Does he pay pretty liberally?"

"He gave me half-a-crown."

"That scale will do. I'm a poor man, and will see what my little contribution to his knowledge will fetch. But by-the-way, perhaps you told him all I know—where she lived before coming to live here?"

"I didn't know where she lived before coming here. O no—I only said what Mr. Brown had told me. He seemed a nice gentle young man, or I shouldn't have been so open as I was."

"I shall now about catch him at Mr. Halway's," said the man, and went away as hastily as he had come.

Edward in the meantime had reached the auction-room. He found some difficulty, on account of the inertness of those whose only inducement to an action is a mere wish from another, in getting the information he stood in need of, but it was at last accorded him. The auctioneer's book gave the name of Mrs. Higgins, 3, Canley Passage, as the purchaser of the lot which had included Mrs. Manston's workbox.

Thither Edward went, followed by the man. Four bell-pulls, one above the other like waistcoat buttons, appeared on the door-post. Edward seized the first he came to.

"Who did you want?"* said a thin voice from somewhere.

Edward looked above and around him: nobody was visible.

"Who did you want?" said the thin voice again.

He found now that the sound proceeded from below the grating covering the basement window. He dropped his glance through the bars, and saw a child's white face.

"Who did you want?" said the voice the third time, with precisely the same languid inflection.

"Mrs. Higgins," said Edward.

"Third bell up," said the face, and disappeared.

He pulled the third bell from the bottom, and was admitted by another child, the daughter of the woman he was in search of. He gave the little thing sixpence, and asked for her mamma. The child led him upstairs.

Mrs. Higgins was the wife of a carpenter who from want of employment one winter had decided to marry. Afterwards they both took to drink, and sank into desperate circumstances. A few chairs and a table were the chief articles of furniture in the third-floor back room which they occupied. A roll of baby-linen lay on the floor: beside it a pap-clogged spoon and an overturned tin pap-cup. Against the wall a Dutch clock* was fixed out of level, and ticked wildly in longs and shorts, its entrails hanging down beneath its white face and wiry hands, like the fæces of a Harpy; ("fœdissima ventris proluvies, uncæque manus, et pallida semper ora.")* A baby was crying against every chair-leg, the whole family of six or seven being small enough to be covered by a washing-tub. Mrs. Higgins sat helpless, clothed in a dress which had hooks and eyes in plenty, but never one opposite the other, thereby rendering the dress almost useless as a screen to the bosom. No workbox was visible anywhere.

It was a depressing picture of married life among the very poor of a city. Only for one short hour in the whole twenty-four did husband and wife taste genuine happiness. It was in the evening, when, after the sale of some necessary article of furniture, they were under the influence of a bottle of gin.

Of all the ingenious and cruel satires that from the beginning till now have been stuck like knives into womankind, surely there is not one so lacerating to them, and to us who love them, as the trite old fact, that the most wretched of men can, in the twinkling of an eye, find a wife ready to be more wretched still for the sake of his company.

Edward hastened to dispatch his errand.

Mrs. Higgins had lately pawned the workbox with other useless articles of lumber, she said. Edward bought the duplicate of her, and went downstairs to the pawnbroker's.

In the back division of a musty shop, amid the heterogeneous collection of articles and odours invariably crowding such places, he produced his ticket, and with a sense of satisfaction out of all proportion to the probable worth of his acquisition, took the box and carried it off under his arm. He attempted to lift the cover as he walked, but found it locked.

It was dusk when Springrove reached his lodging. Entering his small sitting-room, the front apartment on the ground floor, he struck a light, and proceeded to learn if any scrap or mark within or upon his purchase rendered it of moment to the business in hand. Breaking open the cover with a small chisel, and lifting the tray, he glanced eagerly beneath, and found—nothing.

He next discovered that a pocket or portfolio was formed on the underside of the cover. This he unfastened, and slipping his hand within, found that it really contained some substance. First he pulled out about a dozen tangled silk and cotton threads. Under them were a short household account, a dry moss-rosebud, and an old pair of carte-de-visite photographs.* One of these was a likeness of Mrs.

Manston—"Eunice" being written under it in ink,—the other of Manston himself.

He sat down dispirited. This was all the fruit of his task—not a single letter, date, or address of any kind to help him—and was it likely there would be?

However, thinking he would send the fragments, such as they were, to Graye, in order to satisfy him that he had done his best so far, he scribbled a line, and put all except the silk and cotton into an envelope. Looking at his watch he found it was then twenty minutes to seven; by affixing an extra stamp* he would be enabled to dispatch them by that evening's post. He hastily directed the packet, and ran with it at once to the post-office at Charing Cross.

On his return he took up the workbox again to examine it more leisurely. He then found there was also a small cavity in the tray under the pincushion, which was moveable by a bit of ribbon. Lifting this he uncovered a flattened sprig of myrtle, and a small scrap of crumpled paper. The paper contained a verse or two in a man's handwriting. He recognised it as Manston's, having seen notes and bills from him at his father's house. The stanza was of a complimentary character, descriptive of the lady who was now Manston's wife.

"EUNICE.*

"Whoso for hours or lengthy days
Shall catch her aspect's changeful rays,
Then turn away, can none recall
Beyond a galaxy of all
    In hazy portraiture;
Lit by the light of azure eyes,
Like summer days by summer skies,
Her sweet transitions seem to be
A kind of pictured melody,
    And not a set contour.
                    "Æ. M."

To shake, pull, and ransack the box till he had almost destroyed it was now his natural action. But it contained absolutely nothing more.

"Disappointed again," he said flinging down the box, the bit of paper, and the withered twig that had lain with it.

Yet valueless as the new acquisition was, on second thoughts he

considered that it would be worth while to make good the statement
in his late note to Graye—that he had sent everything the box contained except the sewing-thread. Thereupon he enclosed the verse
and myrtle-twig in another envelope, with a remark that he had
overlooked them in his first search, and put it on the table for the
next day's post.

In his hurry and concentration upon the matter that occupied
him, Springrove on entering his lodging and obtaining a light had
not waited to pull down the blind or close the shutters. Consequently
all that he had done had been visible from the street. But as on an
average not one person in five minutes passed along the quiet pavement at this time of the evening, the discovery of the omission did
not much concern his mind.

But the real state of the case was, that a tall man had stood against
the opposite wall and watched the whole of his proceeding. When
Edward came out and went to the Charing Cross post-office, the man
followed him and saw him drop the letter into the box. The stranger
did not further trouble himself to follow Springrove back to his
lodging again.

Manston now knew that there had been photographs of some kind
in his wife's workbox, and though he had not been near enough to
see them, he guessed whose they were. The least reflection told him
to whom they had been sent.

He paused a minute under the portico of the post-office, looking
at the two or three omnibuses stopping and starting in front of him.
Then he rushed along the Strand, through Holywell Street, and on
to Old Boswell Court. Kicking aside the shoeblacks who began to
importune him as he passed under the colonnade, he turned up the
narrow passage to the publishing-office of the Post-Office Directory.
He begged to be allowed to see the Directory of the South-west
counties of England for a moment.

The shopman immediately handed down the volume from a shelf,
and Manston retired with it to the window-bench. He turned to
the county, and then to the parish of Palchurch. At the end of the
historical and topographical description of the village he read,

"Postmistress—Mrs. Hurston. Letters received at 6.30 a.m. by
foot-post from Mundsbury."

Returning his thanks, he handed back the book and quitted the
office, thence pursuing his way to an obscure coffee-house by the

Strand, where he now partook of a light dinner. But rest seemed impossible with him. Some absorbing intention kept his body continually on the move. He paid his bill, took his bag in his hand, and went out to idle about the streets and over the river till the time should have arrived at which the night mail left the Waterloo Station, by which train he intended to return homeward.

There exists as it were an outer chamber to the mind, in which, when a man is occupied centrally with the most momentous question of his life, casual and trifling thoughts are just allowed to wander softly for an interval, before being banished altogether. Thus, amid his concentration did Manston receive perceptions of the individuals about him in the lively thoroughfare of the Strand: tall men looking insignificant: little men looking great and profound: lost women of miserable repute looking as happy as the days are long: wives, happy by assumption, looking careworn and miserable. Each and all were alike in this one respect, that they followed a solitary trail like the inwoven threads which form a banner, and all were equally unconscious of the significant whole they collectively showed forth.

At ten o'clock he turned into Lancaster Place, crossed the river, and entered the railway station, where he took his seat in the down mail-train, which bore him, and Edward Springrove's letter to Graye, far away from London.

CHAPTER IV

THE EVENTS OF ONE DAY

§ 1. *March the thirteenth. Three to six o'clock, a.m.*

They entered Mundsbury Station—the next but one to Froominster on the London side—in the dead, still time of early morning, the clock over the booking-office pointing to twenty-five minutes to three. Manston lingered on the platform and saw the mail-bags brought out, noticing, as a pertinent pastime, the many shabby blotches of wax from innumerable seals that had been set upon their mouths. The guard took them into a fly, and was driven down the road to the post-office.

It was a raw, damp, uncomfortable morning, though, as yet, little rain was falling. Manston drank a mouthful from his flask and walked at once away from the station. Avoiding Mundsbury by keeping in a lane which curved about its outskirts, he pursued his way through the gloom till he stood on the side of the town opposite to the railway station, at a distance from the last house in the street of about two hundred yards.

Here the turnpike-road into the country lay, the first part of its course being across a moor. Having surveyed the highway up and down to make sure of its bearing, Manston methodically set himself to walk backwards and forwards a stone's throw in each direction. Although the spring was temperate, the time of day, and the condition of suspense in which the steward found himself, caused a sensation of chilliness to pervade his frame in spite of the overcoat he wore. The drizzling rain increased, and drops from the trees at the wayside fell noisily upon the hard road beneath them, which reflected from its glassy surface the faint halo of light hanging over the lamps of the adjacent town.

Here he walked and lingered for two hours, without seeing or hearing a living soul. Then he heard the market-house clock strike five, and soon afterwards, quick hard footsteps smote upon the pavement of the street leading towards him. They were those of the postman for the Palchurch beat. He reached the bottom of the street, gave his bags a final hitch-up, stepped off the pavement, and struck out for the country with a brisk shuffle.

Manston then turned his back upon the town, and walked slowly on. In two minutes a flickering light shone upon his form, and the postman overtook him.

The new-comer was a short, stooping individual of above five-and-forty, laden on both sides with leather bags large and small, and carrying a little lantern strapped to his breast, which cast a tiny patch of light upon the road ahead.

"A tryen mornen for travellers!" the postman cried, in a cheerful voice, without turning his head or slackening his trot.

"It is, indeed," said Manston, stepping out abreast of him. "You have a long walk every day."

"Yes—a long walk—for though the distance is only sixteen miles on the straight—that is eight to the furthest place and eight back, what with the ins and outs to the gentlemen's houses, d' make two-and-twenty for my legs. Two-and-twenty miles a day, how many a year? I used to reckon it, but I never do now. I don't care to think o' my wear and tear, now d' begin to tell upon me."

Thus the conversation was begun, and the postman proceeded to narrate the different strange events that had marked his experience. Manston grew very friendly.

"Postman, I don't know what your custom is," he said, after a while; "but, between you and me, I always carry a drop of something warm in my pocket when I am out on such a morning as this. Try it." He handed the bottle of brandy.

"If you'll excuse me, please. I haven't took no stimmilents these five years."

" 'Tis never too late to mend."

"Against the regulations, I be afraid."

"Who'll know it?"

"That's true—nobody will know it. Still, honesty's the best policy."

"Ah—it is certainly. But, thank God, I've been able to get on without it yet. You'll surely drink with me?"

"Really, 'tis a'most too early for that sort o' thing—however, to oblige a friend, I don't object to the faintest shadder of a drop." The postman drank, and Manston did the same to a very slight degree. Five minutes later, when they came to a gate, the flask was pulled out again.

"Well done!" said the postman, beginning to feel its effect; "but, guide my soul, I be afraid 'twill hardly do!"

"Not unless 'tis well followed, like any other line you take up," said Manston. "Besides, there's a way of liking a drop of liquor, and of being good—even religious—at the same time."

"Ay, for some thimble-and-button* in-and-out* fellers; but I could never get into the knack o' it; not I."

"Well, you needn't be troubled; it isn't necessary for the higher class of mind to be religious—they have so much common sense that they can risk playing with fire."

"That hits me exactly."

"In fact, a man I know, who always had no other god but Me, and devoutly loved his neighbour's wife,* says now that believing is a mistake."

"Well, to be sure! However, believing in God is a mistake made by very few people, after all."

"A true remark."

"Not one Christian in our parish would walk half a mile in a rain like this to know whether the Scripture had concluded him under sin or grace."

"Nor in mine."

"Ah, you may depend upon it they'll do away wi' Providence altogether, afore long, although we've had him over us so many years."

"There's no knowing."

"And I suppose the Queen will be done away wi' then. A pretty concern that'll be! Nobody's head to put on your letters; and then your honest man who do pay his penny* will never be known from your scamp who don't. O 'tis a nation!"

"Warm the cockles of your heart, however. Here's the bottle waiting."

"I'll oblige you, my friend."

The drinking was repeated. The postman grew livelier as he went on, and at length favoured the steward with a song, Manston himself joining in the chorus.

"He flung his mallet against the wall,
Said, 'The Lord make churches and chapels to fall,
And there'll be work for tradesmen all!'
When Joan's ale was new,
My boys,
When Joan's ale was new."*

"You understand, friend," the postman added, "I was originally a mason by trade: no offence to you if you be a parson?"

"None at all," said Manston.

The rain now came down heavily, but they pursued their path with alacrity, the produce of the several fields between which the lane wended its way being indicated by the peculiar character of the sound emitted by the falling drops. Sometimes a soaking hiss proclaimed that they were passing by a pasture, then a patter would show that the rain fell upon some large-leafed root crop, then a paddling plash announced the naked arable, the low sound of the wind in their ears rising and falling with each pace they took.

Besides the small private bags of the county families, which were all locked, the postman bore the large general budget for the remaining inhabitants along his beat. At each village or hamlet they came to, the postman searched for the packet of letters destined for that place, and thrust it into an ordinary letter-hole cut in the door of the receiver's cottage—the village post-offices being mostly kept by old women who had not yet risen, though lights moving in other cottage windows showed that such people as carters, woodmen, and stablemen, had long been stirring.

The postman had by this time become markedly unsteady, but he still continued to be too conscious of his duties to suffer the steward to search the bag. Manston was perplexed, and at lonely points in the road cast his eyes keenly upon the short bowed figure of the man trotting through the mud by his side, as if he were half inclined to run a very great risk indeed.

It frequently happened that the houses of farmers, clergymen, &c., lay a short distance up or down a lane or path branching from the direct track of the postman's journey. To save time and distance, at the point of junction of some of these lanes with the main one, the gate-post was hollowed out to form a letter-box, in which the postman deposited his missives in the morning, looking in the box again in the evening to collect those placed there for the return post. Palchurch Vicarage and Farmstead, lying apart from the village, were unitedly served on this principle. This fact the steward now learnt by conversing with the postman, and the discovery relieved Manston greatly, making his intentions much clearer to himself than they had been in the earlier stages of his journey.

They had reached the outskirts of the village. Manston insisted

upon the flask being emptied before they proceeded further. This
was done, and they ascended the sandy hill from which branched the
lane leading to the church, the vicarage, and the farmhouse in which
Owen and Cytherea were living.

The postman paused, fumbled in his bag, took out by the light of
his lantern some half-dozen letters, and tried to sort them. He could
not perform the task.

"We be crippled disciples a b'lieve," he said, with a sigh and a
stagger.

"Not drunk, but market-merry,"* said Manston, cheerfully.

"Well done! If I ben't so weak that I can't see the clouds—much
less letters. Guide my soul, if so be anybody should tell the queen's
postmaster-general of me! The whole story will have to go through
Parliament House, and I shall be high-treasoned*—as safe as
houses—and be fined, and who'll pay for a poor martel! O 'tis a
world!"

"Trust in the Lord—he'll pay."

"He pay a b'lieve! why should he when he didn't drink the drink,
and the devil's a friend o' them who did? He pay a b'lieve! D'ye think
the man's a fool?"

"Well, well, I had no intention of hurting your feelings—but how
was I to know you were so sensitive?"

"True—you were not to know I was so sensitive. Here's a caddle*
wi' these letters! Guide my soul, what will Billy do!"*

Manston offered his services.

"They are to be divided," the man said.

"How?" said Manston.

"These, for the village, to be carried on into it: any for the vicarage
or vicarage-farm must be left in the box of the gate-post just here.
There's none for the vicarage-house this mornen, but I saw when I
started there was one for the clerk o' works at the new church. This
is it, isn't it?"

He held up a large envelope, directed in Edward Springrove's
handwriting,

"MR. OWEN GRAYE,
"CLERK OF WORKS,
"PALCHURCH,
"NEAR MUNDSBURY."

The letter-box was scooped in an oak gate-post about a foot square. There was no slit for inserting the letters, by reason of the opportunity such a lonely spot would have afforded mischievous peasant-boys of doing mischief had such been the case; but at the side was a small iron door, kept close by an iron reversible strap locked across it. One side of this strap was painted black, the other white, and white or black outwards implied respectively that there were letters inside, or none.

The postman had taken the key from his pocket and was attempting to insert it in the keyhole of the box. He touched one side, the other, above, below, but never made a straight hit.

"Let me unlock it," said Manston taking the key from the postman. He opened the box and reached out with his other hand for Owen's letter.

"No, no. Oh no—no," the postman said. "As—one of—Majesty's servants—care—Majesty's mails—duty—put letters—own hands." He slowly and solemnly placed the letter in the small cavity.

"Now lock it," he said, closing the door.

The steward placed the bar across, with the black side outwards, signifying "empty," and turned the key.

"You've put the wrong side outwards!" said the postman. " 'Tisn't empty."

"And dropped the key in the mud, so that I can't alter it," said the steward, letting something fall.

"What an awkward thing!"

"It is an awkward thing."

They both went searching in the mud, which their own trampling had reduced to the consistency of pap, the postman unstrapping his little lantern from his breast, and thrusting it about, close to the ground, the rain still drizzling down, and the dawn so tardy on account of the heavy clouds that daylight seemed delayed indefinitely. The rays of the lantern were rendered individually visible upon the thick mist, and seemed almost tangible as they passed off into it, after illuminating the faces and knees of the two stooping figures dripping with wet; the postman's cape and private bags, and the steward's valise, glistening as if they had been varnished.

"It fell on the grass," said the postman.

"No: it fell in the mud," said Manston. They searched again.

"I'm afraid we shan't find it by this light," said the steward at length, washing his muddy fingers in the wet grass of the bank.

"I'm afraid we shan't," said the other, standing up.

"I'll tell you what we had better do," said Manston. "I shall be back this way in an hour or so, and since it was all my fault, I'll look again, and shall be sure to find it in the daylight. And I'll hide the key here for you." He pointed to a spot behind the post. "It will be too late to turn the index then, as the people will have been here, so that the box had better stay as it is. The letter will only be delayed a day, and that will not be noticed: if it is, you can say you placed the iron the wrong way without knowing it, and all will be well."

This was agreed to by the postman as the best thing to be done under the circumstances, and the pair went on. They had passed the village and come to a cross-road, when the steward, telling his companion that their paths now diverged, turned off to the left towards Frominster.

No sooner was the postman out of sight and hearing than Manston stalked back to the vicarage letter-box by keeping inside a fence, and thus avoiding the village; arrived here, he took the key from his pocket, where it had been concealed all the time, and abstracted Owen's letter. This done he turned towards home, by the help of what he carried in his valise adjusting himself to his ordinary appearance as he neared the quarter in which he was known.

An hour and half's sharp walking brought him to his own door in Knapwater Park.

§ 2. *Eight o'clock, a.m.*

Seated in his private office he wetted the flap of the stolen letter, and waited patiently till the adhesive gum could be loosened. He took out Edward's note, the accounts, the rosebud, and the photographs, regarding them with the keenest interest and anxiety.

The note, the accounts, the rosebud, and his own photograph, he restored to their places again. The other photograph he took between his finger and thumb, and held it towards the bars of the grate. There he held it for half a minute or more, meditating.

"It is a great risk to run, even for such an end," he muttered.

Suddenly, impregnated with a bright idea, he jumped up and left the office for the front parlour. Taking up an album of portraits, which lay on the table, he searched for three or four likenesses of the lady who had so lately displaced Cytherea, which were interspersed among the rest of the collection, and carefully regarded them. They were taken in different attitudes and styles, and he compared each singly with that he held in his hand. One of them, the one most resembling that abstracted from the letter in general tone, size, and attitude, he selected from the rest, and returned with it to his office.

Pouring some water into a plate, he set the two portraits afloat upon it, and sitting down tried to read.

At the end of a quarter of an hour, after several ineffectual attempts, he found that each photograph would peel from the card on which it was mounted. This done, he threw into the fire the original likeness and the recent card, stuck upon the original card the recent likeness from the album, dried it before the fire, and placed it in the envelope with the other scraps.

The result he had obtained, then, was this: in the envelope were now two photographs, both having the same photographer's name on the back and consecutive numbers attached. At the bottom of the one which showed his own likeness, his own name was written down; on the other his wife's name was written; whilst the central feature, and whole matter to which this latter card and writing referred, the likeness of a lady mounted upon it, had been changed.

Mrs. Manston entered the room, and begged him to come to breakfast. He followed her, and they sat down. During the meal he told her what he had done, with scrupulous regard to every detail, and showed her the result.

"It is indeed a great risk to run," she said, sipping her tea.

"But it would be a greater not to do it."

"Yes."

The envelope was again fastened up as before, and Manston put it in his pocket and went out. Shortly afterwards he was seen on horseback riding in a direction skirting Froominster and towards Palchurch. Keeping to the fields, as well as he could, for the greater part of the way, he dropped into the road by the vicarage letter-box, and looking carefully about, to ascertain that no person was near, he restored the letter to its nook, placed the key in its hiding-place, as he had promised the postman, and again rode homewards by a roundabout way.

§ 3. *Afternoon*

The letter was brought to Owen Graye, the same afternoon, by one
of the vicar's servants who had been to the box with a duplicate key,
as usual, to leave letters for the evening post. The man found that the
index had told falsely that morning for the first time within his
recollection; but no particular attention was paid to the mistake, as it
was considered. The contents of the envelope were scrutinized by
Owen and flung aside as useless.

The next morning brought Springrove's second letter, the existence of which was unknown to Manston. The sight of Edward's
handwriting again raised the expectations of brother and sister, till
Owen had opened the envelope and pulled out the twig and verse.

"Nothing that's of the slightest use after all," he said to her, "we
are as far as ever from the merest shadow of legal proof that
would convict him of what I am morally certain he did, marry you,
suspecting, if not knowing, her to be alive all the time."

"What has Edward sent?" said Cytherea.

"An old amatory verse in Manston's writing. Fancy," he said,
bitterly, "this is the strain he addressed her in when they were
courting—as he did you, I suppose."

He handed her the verse and she read,

> " 'EUNICE.
>
> " 'Whoso for hours or lengthy days
> Shall catch her aspect's changeful rays,
> Then turn away, can none recall
> Beyond a galaxy of all
>   In hazy portraiture;
> Lit by the light of azure eyes,
> Like summer days by summer skies,
> Her sweet transitions seem to be
> A kind of pictured melody,
>   And not a set contour.
>   " 'Æ. M.' "

A strange expression had overspread Cytherea's countenance. It
rapidly increased to the most death-like anguish. She flung down the
paper, seized Owen's hand tremblingly, and covered her face.

"Cytherea! What is it, for Heaven's sake?"

"Owen—suppose—O you don't know what I think."

"What?"

" '*The light of azure eyes*'," she repeated with ashy lips.

"Well, 'the light of azure eyes'?" he said, astounded at her manner.

"Mrs. Morris said in her letter to me that her eyes are *black!*"

"H'm. Mrs. Morris must have made a mistake—nothing likelier."

"She didn't."

"They might be either in this photograph," said Owen, looking at the card bearing Mrs. Manston's name.

"Blue eyes would scarcely photograph so deep in tone as that," said Cytherea. "No, they seem black here, certainly."

"Well then, Manston must have blundered in writing his verses."

"But could he? Say a man in love may forget his own name, but not that he forgets the colour of his mistress's eyes. Besides, she would have seen the mistake when she read them, and have had it corrected."

"That's true, she would," mused Owen. "Then, Cytherea, it comes to this—you must have been misinformed by Mrs. Morris, since there is no other alternative."

"I suppose I must."

Her looks belied her words.

"What makes you so strange—ill?" said Owen again.

"I can't believe Mrs. Morris wrong."

"But look at this, Cytherea. If it is clear to us that the woman had blue eyes two years ago, she *must* have blue eyes now, whatever Mrs. Morris or anybody else may fancy. Anyone would think that Manston could change the colour of a woman's eyes, to hear you."

"Yes," she said, and paused.

"You say yes, as if he could," said Owen, impatiently.

"By changing the woman herself," she exclaimed. "Owen, don't you see the horrid—what I dread?—that the woman he lives with is not Mrs. Manston—that she was burnt after all—and that I am HIS WIFE!"

She tried to support a stoicism under the weight of this new trouble, but no! The unexpected revulsion of ideas was so overwhelming that she crept to him and leant against his breast.

Before reflecting any further upon the subject Graye led her upstairs and got her to lie down. Then he went to the window and stared out of it up the lane, vainly endeavouring to come to some conclusion upon the fantastic enigma that confronted him.

Cytherea's new view seemed incredible, yet it had such a hold upon her that it would be necessary to clear it away by positive proof before contemplation of her fear should have preyed too deeply upon her.

"Cytherea," he said, "this will not do. You must stay here alone all the afternoon whilst I go to Carriford. I shall know all when I return."

"No, no, don't go!" she implored.

"Soon, then, not directly." He saw her subtle reasoning—that it was folly to be wise.

Reflection still convinced him that good would come of persevering in his intention and dispelling his sister's idle fears. Anything was better than this absurd doubt in her mind. But he resolved to wait till Sunday, the first day on which he might reckon upon seeing Mrs. Manston without suspicion. In the meantime he wrote to Edward Springrove, requesting him to go again to Mrs. Manston's former lodging.

CHAPTER V

THE EVENTS OF THREE DAYS

§ 1. *March the eighteenth*

Sunday morning had come, and Owen was trudging over the six miles of hill and dale that lay between Palchurch and Carriford.

Edward Springrove's answer to the last letter, after expressing his amazement at the strange contradiction between the verses, and Mrs. Morris's letter, had been to the effect that he had again visited the neighbour of the dead Mr. Brown, and had received as near a description of Mrs. Manston as it was possible to get at second-hand, and by hearsay. She was a tall woman, wide at the shoulders, and full-bosomed, and she had a straight and rather large nose. The colour of her eyes the informant did not know, for she had only seen the lady in the street as she went in or out. This confusing remark was added. The woman had almost recognised Mrs. Manston when she had called with her husband lately, but she had kept her veil down. Her residence, before she came to Hoxton, was quite unknown to this next-door neighbour, and Edward could get no manner of clue to it from any other source.

Owen reached the church-door a few minutes before the bells began chiming. Nobody was yet in the church, and he walked round the aisles. From Cytherea's frequent description of how and where herself and others used to sit, he knew where to look for Manston's seat; and after two or three errors of examination he took up a prayer book in which was written "Eunice Manston." The book was nearly new, and the date of the writing about a month earlier. One point was at any rate established: that the woman living with Manston was presented to the world as no other than his lawful wife.

The quiet villagers of Carriford required no pew-opener in their place of worship: natives and indwellers* had their own seats, and strangers sat where they could. Graye took a seat in the nave, on the north side, close behind a pillar dividing it from the north aisle, which was completely allotted to Miss Aldclyffe, her farmers, and her retainers, Manston's pew being in the midst of them. Owen's position on the other side of the passage was a little in advance of

Manston's seat, and so situated that by leaning forward he could look directly into the face of any person sitting there, though, if he sat upright, he was wholly hidden from such a one by the intervening pillar.

Aiming to keep his presence unknown to Manston if possible, Owen sat without once turning his head, during the entrance of the congregation. A rustling of silk round by the north passage and into Manston's seat, told him that some female had entered there, and as it seemed from the accompaniment of heavier footsteps, Manston was with her.

Immediately upon rising up, he looked intently in that direction, and saw a lady standing at the end of the seat nearest himself. Portions of Manston's figure appeared on the other side of her. In two glances Graye read thus many of her characteristics, and in the following order.

She was a tall woman.

She was broad at the shoulders.

She was full-bosomed.

She was easily recognisable from the photograph; but nothing could be discerned of the colour of her eyes.

With a preoccupied mind he withdrew into his nook, and heard the service continued—only conscious of the fact that in opposition to the suspicion which one odd circumstance had bred in his sister concerning this woman, all ostensible and ordinary proofs and probabilities tended to the opposite conclusion. There sat the genuine original of the portrait—could he wish for more? Cytherea wished for more. Eunice Manston's eyes were blue, and it was necessary that this woman's eyes should be blue also.

Unskilled labour wastes in beating against the bars ten times the energy exerted by the practised hand in the effective direction. Owen felt this to be the case in his own and Edward's attempts to follow up the clue afforded them. Think as he might, he could not think of a crucial test in the matter absorbing him, which should possess the indispensable attribute—a capability of being applied privately, that in the event of its proving the lady to be the rightful owner of the name she used, he might recede without obloquy from an untenable position.

But to see Mrs. Manston's eyes from where he sat was impossible, and he could do nothing in the shape of a direct examination at present. Miss Aldclyffe had possibly recognised him, but Manston had not, and feeling that it was indispensable to keep the purport of his visit a secret from the steward, he thought it would be as well too to keep his presence in the village a secret from him, at any rate till the day was over.

At the first opening of the doors, Graye left the church and wandered away into the fields to ponder on another scheme. He could not call on Farmer Springrove, as he had intended, until this matter was set at rest. Two hours intervened between the morning and afternoon services.

This time had nearly expired before Owen had struck out any line as to his method of proceeding, or could decide to run the risk of calling at the Old House and asking to see Mrs. Manston pointblank. But he had drawn near the place, and was standing still in the public path, from which a partial view of the front of the building could be obtained, when the bells began chiming for afternoon service. Whilst Graye paused, two persons came from the front door of the half-hidden dwelling, whom he presently saw to be Manston and his wife.

Manston was wearing his old garden-hat, and carried one of the monthly magazines under his arm. Immediately they had passed the gateway he branched off and went over the hill in a direction away from the church, evidently intending to ramble along, and read as the humour moved him. The lady meanwhile turned in the other direction, and went along the church path.

Owen resolved to make something of this opportunity. He hurried along towards the church, doubled round a sharp angle, and came back upon the other path, by which Mrs. Manston must arrive.

In about three minutes she appeared in sight without a veil. He discovered, as she drew nearer, a difficulty which had not struck him at first—that it is not an easy matter to particularise the colour of a stranger's eyes in a merely casual encounter on a path out of doors. That Mrs. Manston must be brought close to him, and not only so, but to look closely at him, if his purpose were to be accomplished.

He adumbrated a plan. It might by chance be effectual: if otherwise, it would not reveal his intention to her.

When Mrs. Manston was within speaking distance, he went up to her and said,

"Will you kindly tell me which turning will take me to Froominster?"

"The second on the right," said Mrs. Manston.

Owen put on a blank look: he held his hand to his ear—conveying to the lady the idea that he was deaf.

She came closer and said more distinctly,

"The second turning on the right."

Owen flushed a little. He fancied he had beheld the revelation he was in search of. But had his eyes deceived him?

Once more he used the ruse, still drawing nearer, and intimating by a glance that the trouble he gave her was very distressing to him.

"How very deaf," she murmured. She exclaimed loudly,

"The second turning to the right."

She had advanced her face to within a foot of his own, and in speaking mouthed very emphatically, fixing her eyes intently upon his. And now his first suspicion was indubitably confirmed. Her eyes were as black as midnight.

All this feigning was most distasteful to Graye. The riddle having been solved, he unconsciously assumed his natural look before she had withdrawn her face. She found him to be peering at her as if he would read her very soul—expressing with his eyes the notification of which, apart from emotion, the eyes are more capable than any other—inquiry.

Her face changed its expression—then its colour. The natural tint of the lighter portions sank to an ashy grey: the pink of her cheeks grew purpler. It was the precise result which would remain after blood had left the face of one whose skin was dark, and artificially coated with pearl-powder and carmine.*

She turned her head and moved away, murmuring a hasty reply to Owen's farewell remark of "Good-day," and with a kind of nervous twitch lifting her hand and smoothing her hair, which was of a light brown colour.

"She wears false hair," he thought, "or has changed its colour artificially. Her true hair matched her eyes."

And now, in spite of what Mr. Brown's neighbours had said about nearly recognising Mrs. Manston on her recent visit—which might have meant anything or nothing; in spite of the photograph, and in spite of his previous incredulity: in consequence of the verse, of her silence and backwardness at the visit to Hoxton with Manston, and of her appearance and distress at the present moment, Graye had a conviction that the woman was an impostor.

What could be Manston's reason for such an astounding trick he could by no stretch of imagination divine.

He changed his direction as soon as the woman was out of sight, and plodded along the lanes homeward to Palchurch.

One new idea was suggested to him by his desire to allay Cytherea's dread of being claimed, and by the difficulty of believing that the first Mrs. Manston lost her life as supposed, notwithstanding the inquest and verdict. Was it possible that the real Mrs. Manston, who was known to be a Philadelphian by birth, had returned by the train to London, as the porter had said, and then left the country under an assumed name, to escape that worst kind of widowhood— the misery of being wedded to a fickle, faithless, and truant husband?

In her complicated distress at the news brought by her brother, Cytherea's thoughts at length reverted to her friend, the rector of Carriford. She told Owen of Mr. Raunham's warm-hearted behaviour towards herself, and of his strongly expressed wish to aid her.

"He is not only a good but a sensible man. We seem to want an old head on our side."

"And he is a magistrate,"* said Owen in a tone of concurrence. He thought too that no harm could come of confiding in the rector, but there was a difficulty in bringing about the confidence. He wished that his sister and himself might both be present at an interview with Mr. Raunham, yet it would be unwise for them to call on him together, in the sight of all the servants and parish of Carriford.

There could be no objection to their writing him a letter.

No sooner was the thought born than it was carried out. They wrote to him at once, asking him to have the goodness to give them some advice they sadly needed, and begging that he would accept their assurance that there was a real justification for the additional request they made—that instead of their calling upon him, he would any evening of the week come to their cottage at Palchurch.

§ 2. *March the twentieth. Six to nine o'clock, p.m.*

Two evenings later, to the total disarrangement of his dinner hour, Mr. Raunham appeared at Owen's door. His arrival was hailed with genuine gratitude. The horse was tied to the palings, and the rector ushered indoors and put into the easy chair.

Then Graye told him the whole story, reminding him that their first suspicions had been of a totally different nature, and that it was in endeavouring to obtain proof of their truth they had stumbled upon marks which had surprised them into these new uncertainties, thrice as marvellous as the first, yet more prominent.

Cytherea's heart was so full of anxiety that it superinduced a manner of confidence which was a death-blow to all formality. Mr. Raunham took her hand pityingly.

"It is a serious charge," he said, as a sort of original twig on which his thoughts might precipitate themselves.

"Assuming for a moment that such a substitution was rendered an easy matter by fortuitous events," he continued; "there is this consideration to be placed beside it—what earthly motive can Mr. Manston have had which would be sufficiently powerful to lead him to run such a very great risk? The most abandoned roué could not, at that particular crisis, have taken such a reckless step for the mere pleasure of a new companion."

Owen had seen that difficulty about the motive; Cytherea had not.

"Unfortunately for us," the rector resumed, "no more evidence is to be obtained from the porter Chinney. I suppose you know what went with him? He got to Liverpool and embarked, intending to work his way to America, but on the passage he fell overboard and was drowned. But there is no doubt of the truth of his confession—in fact, his conduct tends to prove it true, and no moral doubt of the fact that Mrs. Manston left Froominster by that morning's train. This being the case, then, why did she take no notice of the advertisement—I mean not necessarily a friendly notice, but from the information it afforded her have rendered it impossible that she should be personified without her own connivance?"

"I think that argument is overthrown," Graye said, "by my earliest assumption of her hatred of him, weariness of the chain which bound her to him, and a resolve to begin the world anew. Let's suppose she has married another man—somewhere abroad, say; she would be silent for her own sake."

"You've hit the only genuine possibility," said Mr. Raunham, tapping his finger upon his knee. "That would decidedly dispose of the second difficulty. But his motive would be as mysterious as ever."

Cytherea's pictured dreads would not allow her mind to follow their conversation. "She's burnt," she said. "O, yes; I fear—I fear she is!"

"I don't think we can seriously believe that now, after what has happened," said the rector.

Still straining her thought towards the worst, "Then, perhaps, the first Mrs. Manston was not his wife," she returned; "and then I should be his wife just the same, shouldn't I?"

"They were married safely enough," said Owen. "There is abundance of circumstantial evidence to prove that."

"Upon the whole," said Mr. Raunham, "I should advise your asking in a straightforward way for legal proof from the steward that the present woman is really his original wife—a thing which, to my mind, you should have done at the outset." He turned to Cytherea kindly, and asked her what made her give up her husband so unceremoniously.

She could not tell the rector of her aversion to Manston, and of her unquenched love for Edward.

"Your terrified state, no doubt," he said, answering for her, in the manner of those accustomed to the pulpit. "But into such a solemn compact as marriage, all-important considerations, both legally and morally, enter; it was your duty to have seen everything clearly proved. Doubtless Mr. Manston is prepared with proofs, but as it concerns nobody but yourself that her identity should be publicly established, (and by your absenteeism you act as if you were satisfied), he has not troubled to exhibit them. Nobody else has taken the trouble to prove what does not affect them in the least—that's the way of the world always. You, who should have required all things to be made clear, ran away."

"That was partly my doing," said Owen.

The same explanation—her want of love for Manston—applied here too, but she shunned the revelation.

"But never mind," added the rector; "it was all the greater credit to your womanhood, perhaps. I say, then, get your brother to write a line to Mr. Manston, saying you wish to be satisfied that all is legally clear, (in case you should want to marry again, for instance) and I have no doubt that you will be. Or if you would rather, I'll write myself?"

"Oh, no sir, no," pleaded Cytherea, beginning to blanch, and breathing quickly. "Please don't say anything. Let me live here with Owen. I am so afraid it will turn out that I shall have to go to Knapwater and be his wife, and I don't want to. Do conceal what we have told you. Let him continue his deception—it is much the best for me."

Mr. Raunham at length divined that her love for Manston, if it had ever existed, had transmuted itself into a very different feeling now.

"At any rate," he said, as he took his leave and mounted his mare, "I will see about it. Rest content, Miss Graye, and depend upon it that I will not lead you into difficulty."

"Conceal it," she still pleaded.

"We'll see—but of course I must do my duty."

"No—don't do your duty!" She looked up at him through the gloom, illuminating her own face and eyes with the candle she held.

"I will consider, then," said Mr. Raunham, sensibly moved. He turned his horse's head, bade them a warm adieu, and left the door.

The rector of Carriford trotted homewards under the cold and clear March sky, its countless stars fluttering like bright birds. He was unconscious of the scene. Recovering from the effect of Cytherea's voice and glance of entreaty, he laid the subject of the interview clearly before himself.

The suspicions of Cytherea and Owen were honest, and had foundation—that he must own.

Was he—a clergyman, magistrate, and conscientious man— justified in yielding to Cytherea's importunities to keep silence, because she dreaded the possibility of a return to Manston?

Was she wise in her request? Holding her present belief, and with no definite evidence either way, she could, for one thing, never conscientiously marry any one else.

Suppose that Cytherea were Manston's wife—*i.e.*, that the first wife was really burnt? The adultery of Manston would be proved, and Mr. Raunham thought, cruelty sufficient to bring the case within the meaning of the statute.*

Suppose the new woman was, as stated, Mr. Manston's restored wife? Cytherea was perfectly safe as a single woman whose marriage had been void.

And if it turned out that, though this woman was not Manston's wife, his wife was still living, as Owen had suggested, in America or elsewhere, Cytherea was safe.

The first supposition opened up the worst contingency. Was she really safe as Manston's wife?

Doubtful. But however that might be, the gentle, defenceless girl, whom it seemed nobody's business to help or defend, should be put in a track to proceed against this man. She had but one life, and the superciliousness with which all the world now regarded her, should be compensated for in some measure by the man whose carelessness—to set him in the best light—had caused it.

Mr. Raunham felt more and more positively that his duty must be done. An inquiry must be made into the matter.

Immediately on reaching home, he sat down and wrote a plain and friendly letter to Mr. Manston, and despatched it at once to him by hand. Then he flung himself back in his chair, and went on with his meditation.

Was there anything in the suspicion? There could be nothing, surely. Nothing is done by a clever man without a motive, and what conceivable motive could Manston have for such abnormal conduct? Corinthian that he was, who had preyed on virginity like St. George's dragon,* he would never have been absurd enough to venture on such a course for the possession alone of the woman—there was no reason for it—she was inferior to Cytherea in every respect, physical and mental.

On the other hand it seemed rather odd, when he analysed the action, that a woman who deliberately hid herself from her husband for more than a twelvemonth, should be brought back by a mere advertisement. In fact, the whole business had worked almost too smoothly and effectually for unpremeditated sequence. It was too much like the indiscriminate righting of everything at the end of an old play.

And there was that curious business of the keys and watch. Her way of accounting for their being left behind by forgetfulness, had always seemed to him rather forced. The only unforced explanation was that suggested by the newspaper writers—that she left them behind on purpose to blind people as to her escape, a motive which would have clashed with the possibility of her being fished back by an advertisement, as the present woman had been.

Again, there were the two charred bones.

He shuffled the books and papers in his study, and walked about the room, restlessly musing on the same subject. The parlour-maid entered.

"Can young Mr. Springrove from London see you to-night, sir?"

"Young Mr. Springrove?" said the rector, surprised.

"Yes, sir."

"Yes, of course he can see me. Tell him to come in."

Edward came so impatiently into the room, as to show that the few short moments his announcement had occupied had been irksome to him. He stood in the doorway with the same black bag in his hand, and the same old grey cloak on his shoulders, that he had worn fifteen months earlier when returning on the night of the fire. This appearance of his conveyed a true impression; he had become a stagnant man. But he was excited now.

"I have this moment come from London," he said, as the door was closed behind him.

The prophetic insight, which so strangely accompanies critical experiences, prompted Mr. Raunham's reply.

"About the Grayes and Manston?"

"Yes. That woman is not Mrs. Manston."

"Prove it."

"I can prove that she is somebody else—that her name is Anne Seaway."

"And are their suspicions true indeed!"

"And I can do what's more to the purpose at present."

"Suggest Manston's motive?"

"Only suggest it, remember. But my assumption fits so perfectly with the facts that have been secretly unearthed and conveyed to me, that I can hardly conceive of another."

There was in Edward's bearing that entire unconsciousness of himself which, natural to wild animals, only prevails in a sensitive man at moments of extreme intentness. The rector saw that he had no trivial story to communicate, whatever the story was.

"Sit down," said Mr. Raunham. "My mind has been on the stretch all the evening to form the slightest guess at such an object, and all to no purpose—entirely to no purpose. Have you said anything to Owen Graye?"

"Nothing—nor to anybody. I could not trust to the effect a letter might have upon yourself either: the intricacy of the case brings me to this interview."

Whilst Springrove had been speaking the two had sat down together. The conversation, hitherto distinct to every corner of the room, was carried on now in tones so low as to be scarcely audible to the interlocutors, and in phrases which hesitated to complete themselves. Three-quarters of an hour passed. Then Edward arose, came out of the rector's study and again flung his cloak around him. Instead of going thence homeward, he went first to the Carriford-Road Station with a telegram, having despatched which he proceeded to his father's house for the first time since his arrival in the village.

§ 3. *From nine to ten o'clock, p.m.*

The next presentation is the interior of the Old House on the evening of the preceding section. The steward was sitting by his parlour fire, and had been reading the letter arrived from the rectory. Opposite to him sat the woman known to the village and neighbourhood as Mrs. Manston.

"Things are looking desperate with us," he said gloomily. His gloom was not that of the hypochondriac, but the legitimate gloom which has its origin in a syllogism. As he uttered the words he handed the letter to her.

"I almost expected some such news as this," she replied, in a tone of much greater indifference. "I knew suspicion lurked in the eyes of that young man who stared at me so in the church path: I could have sworn it."

Manston did not answer for some time. His face was worn and haggard: latterly his head had not been carried so uprightly as of old. "If they prove you to be—who you are . . . . . Yes, if they do—" he murmured.

"They must not find that out," she said, in a positive voice, and looking at him. "But supposing they do, the trick does not seem to me to be so serious as to justify that wretched, miserable, horrible look of yours. It makes my flesh creep: it is perfectly deathlike."

He did not reply, and she continued, "If they say and prove that Eunice is indeed living,—and dear, you know she is, she is sure to come back."

This remark seemed to awaken and irritate him to speech. Again, as he had done a hundred times during their residence together, he categorised the events connected with the fire at the Three Tranters. He dwelt on every incident of that night's history, and endeavoured, with an anxiety which was extraordinary under the apparent circumstances, to prove that his wife must, by the very nature of things, have perished in the flames.

She arose from her seat, crossed the hearth-rug, and set herself to soothe him: then she whispered that she was still as unbelieving as ever. "Come, supposing she escaped—just supposing she escaped—where is she?" coaxed the lady.

"Why are you so curious continually?" said Manston.

"Because I am a woman and want to know. Now where is she?"

"In the Flying Isle of San Borandan."*

"Witty cruelty is the cruellest of any. Ah, well—if she is in England, she will come back."

"She is not in England."

"But she will come back?"

"No she won't . . . . Come madam," he said arousing himself, "I shall not answer any more questions."

"Ah—ah—ah—she is not dead." the woman murmured again poutingly.

"She is, I tell you."

"I don't think so, love."

"She was burnt, I tell you!" he exclaimed.

"Now to please me, admit the bare possibility of her being alive,—just the possibility."

"O yes—to please you I will admit that," he said quickly. "Yes I admit the possibility of her being alive, to please you."

She looked at him in utter perplexity. The words could only have been said in jest, and yet they seemed to savour of a tone the farthest remove from jesting. There was his face plain to her eyes, but no information of any kind was to be read there.

"It is only natural that I should be curious," she murmured pettishly, "if I resemble her as much as you say I do."

"You are handsomer," he said, "though you are about her own height, and size. But don't worry yourself. You must know that you are body and soul united with me, though you are but my housekeeper."

She bridled a little at the remark. "Wife," she said, "most

certainly wife, since you cannot dismiss me without losing your character and position, and incurring heavy penalties."

"I own it—it was well said, though mistakenly—very mistakenly."

"Don't riddle to me about mistakenly and such dark things. Now what was your motive, dearest,—in running the risk of having me here?"

"Your beauty," he said.

"She thanks you much for the compliment, but will not take it. Come what was your motive?"

"Your wit."

"No, no; not my wit. Wit would have made a wife of me by this time instead of what I am."

"Your virtue."

"Or virtue either."

"I tell you it was your beauty—really."

"But I cannot help seeing and hearing, and if what people say is true, I am not nearly so good-looking as Cytherea, and several years older."

The aspect of Manston's face at these words from her was so confirmatory of her hint, that his forced reply of "O no," tended to develop her chagrin.

"Mere liking, or love for me," she resumed, "would not have sprung up all of a sudden, as your pretended passion did. You had been to London several times between the time of the fire and your marriage with Cytherea—you had never visited me or thought of my existence or cared that I was out of a situation and poor. But the week after you married her and were separated from her, off you rush to make love to me—not first to me either, for you went to several places—"

"No, not several places."

"Yes, you told me so yourself—that you went first to the only lodging in which your wife had been known as Mrs. Manston, and when you found that the lodging-house keeper had gone away and died, and that nobody else in the street had any definite ideas as to your wife's personal appearance, you came and proposed the arrangement we carried out—that I should personate her. Your taking all this trouble shows that something more serious than love had to do with the matter."

"Humbug,—what trouble after all did I take? When I found

Cytherea would not stay with me after the wedding I was much put out at being left alone again. Was that unnatural?"

"No."

"And those favouring accidents you mention—that nobody knew my first wife—seemed an arrangement of Providence for our mutual benefit, and merely perfected a half-formed impulse—that I should call you my first wife to escape the scandal that would have arisen if you had come here as anything else."

"My love, that story won't do. If Mrs. Manston was burnt, Cytherea, whom you love better than me—could have been compelled to live with you as your lawful wife.* If she was not burnt, why should you run the risk of her turning up again at any moment and exposing your substitution of me, and ruining your name and prospects?"

"Why—because I might have loved you well enough to run the risk (assuming her not to be burnt, which I deny)."

"No—you would have run the risk the other way. You would rather have risked her finding you with Cytherea as a second wife, than with me as a personator of herself—the first one."

"You came easiest to hand—remember that."

"Not so very easy, either, considering the labour you took to teach me your first wife's history. All about how she was a native of Philadelphia. Then making me read up the guide-book to Philadelphia, and details of American life and manners, in case the birthplace and history of your wife, Eunice, should ever become known in this neighbourhood—unlikely as it was. Ah! and then about the handwriting of hers that I had to imitate, and the dying my hair, and rouging, to make the transformation complete? You mean to say that that was taking less trouble than there would have been in arranging events to make Cytherea believe herself your wife, and live with you?"

"You were a needy adventuress, who would dare anything for a new pleasure and an easy life—and I was fool enough to give in to you——"

"Good Heavens above!—did I ask you to insert those advertisements for your old wife, and to make me answer it as if I was she? Did I ask you to send me the letter for me to copy and send back to you when the third advertisement appeared—purporting to come from the long-lost wife, and giving a detailed history of her escape and subsequent life—all which you had invented yourself? You deluded me into loving you, and then enticed me here! Ah, and this is another thing. How did you know the real wife wouldn't answer it, and upset all your plans?"

"Because I knew she was burnt."

"Why didn't you force Cytherea to come back then? Now, my love, I have caught you, and you may just as well tell first as last, *what was your motive in having me here as your first wife?*"

"Silence!" he exclaimed.

She was silent for the space of two minutes, and then persisted in going on to mutter, "And why was it that Miss Aldclyffe allowed her favourite young lady, Cythie, to be overthrown and supplanted without an expostulation or any show of sympathy? Do you know I often think you exercise a secret power over Miss Aldclyffe. And she always shuns me as if I shared the power. A poor, ill-used creature like me sharing power, indeed."

"She thinks you are Mrs. Manston."

"That wouldn't make her avoid me."

"Yes it would," he exclaimed impatiently. "I wish I was dead— dead!" He had jumped up from his seat in uttering the words, and now walked wearily to the end of the room. Coming back more decisively, he looked in her face.

"We must leave this place if Raunham suspects what I think he does," he said. "The request of Cytherea and her brother may simply be for a satisfactory proof, to make her feel legally free—but it may mean more."

"What may it mean?"

"How should I know?"

"Well, well, never mind, old boy," she said, approaching him to make up the quarrel. "Don't be so alarmed—anybody would think that you were the woman and I the man.* Suppose they do find out what I am—we can go away from here and keep house as usual. People will say of you, 'His first wife was burnt to death' (or 'ran away to the Colonies' as the case may be), 'He married a second, and deserted her for Anne Seaway.' A very everyday case—nothing so horrible after all."

He made an impatient movement. "Whichever way we do it, *nobody must know that you are not my wife, Eunice.* And now I must think about arranging matters."

Manston then retired to his office, and shut himself up for the remainder of the evening.

CHAPTER VI

THE EVENTS OF A DAY AND NIGHT

§ 1. *March the twenty-first. Morning*

Next morning the steward went out as usual. He shortly told his companion Anne, that he had almost matured their scheme, and that they would enter upon the details of it when he came home at night. The fortunate fact that the rector's letter did not require an immediate answer would give him time to consider.

Anne Seaway then began her duties in the house. Besides daily superintending the cook and housemaid, one of these duties was, at rare intervals, to dust Manston's office with her own hands, a servant being supposed to disturb the books and papers unnecessarily.

She softly wandered from table to shelf with the duster in her hand, afterwards standing in the middle of the room, and glancing around to discover if any noteworthy collection of dust had still escaped her.

Her eye fell upon a faint layer which rested upon the ledge of an old-fashioned chestnut cabinet of French Renaissance workmanship, placed in a recess by the fireplace. At a height of about four feet from the floor the upper portion of the front receded, forming the ledge alluded to, on which opened, at each end, two small doors, the centre space between them being filled out by a panel of similar size, making the third of three squares.

The dust on the ledge was nearly on a level with the woman's eye, and though insignificant in quantity, showed itself distinctly on account of this obliquity of vision. Now opposite the central panel, concentric quarter-circles were traced in the deposited film, expressing to her that this panel too was a door like the others; that it had lately been opened, and had skimmed the dust with its lower edge.

At last, then, her curiosity was slightly rewarded. For the right of the matter was that Anne had been incited to this exploration of Manston's office rather by a wish to know the reason of his long seclusion here, after the arrival of the rector's letter, and their subsequent discourse, than by any immediate desire for cleanliness.

Still, there would have been nothing remarkable to Anne in this sight but for one recollection. Manston had once casually told her that each of the two side lockers included half the middle space, the panel of which did not open, and was only put in for symmetry.

It was possible that he had opened this compartment by candle-light the preceding night, or he would have seen the marks in the dust, and effaced them, that he might not be proved guilty of telling her an untruth.

She balanced herself on one foot and stood pondering. She considered that it was very vexing and unfair in him to refuse her all knowledge of his remaining secrets, under the peculiar circumstances of her connection with him. She went close to the cabinet. As there was no keyhole, the door must be capable of being opened by the unassisted hand.

The circles in the dust told her at which edge to apply her force. Here she pulled with the tips of her fingers, but the panel would not come forward.

She fetched a chair and looked over the top of the cabinet, but no bolt, knob, or spring was to be seen.

"O, never mind," she said, with indifference; "I'll ask him about it, and he will tell me." Down she came and turned away. Then looking back again she thought it was absurd such a trifle should puzzle her. She retraced her steps, and opened a drawer beneath the ledge of the cabinet, pushing in her hand and feeling about on the underside of the board.

Here she found a small round sinking, and pressed her finger into it. Nothing came of the pressure. She withdrew her hand and looked at the tip of her finger: it was marked with the impress of the circle, and in addition, a line ran across it diametrically.

"How stupid of me—it is the head of a screw." Whatever mysterious contrivance had originally existed for opening the puny cupboard of the cabinet, it had at some time been broken, and this rough substitute provided. Stimulated curiosity would not allow her to recede now. She fetched a turnscrew,* withdrew the screw, pulled the door open with a penknife, and found inside a cavity about ten inches square. The cavity contained,

Letters from different women, with unknown signatures, Christian names only; (surnames being despised in Paphos*).

Letters from his wife Eunice.

Letters from Anne herself, including that she wrote in answer to his advertisement.

A small pocket book.

Sundry scraps of paper.

The letters from the strange women with pet names she glanced carelessly through, and then put them aside. They were too similar to her own regretted delusion, and curiosity requires contrast to excite it.

The letters from his wife were next examined. They were dated back as far as Eunice's first meeting with Manston, and the early ones before their marriage contained the usual pretty effusions of women at such a period of their existence. Some little time after he had made her his wife, and when he had come to Knapwater, the series commenced again, and now their contents arrested her attention more forcibly. She closed the cabinet, carried the letters into the parlour, reclined herself on the sofa, and carefully perused them in the order of their dates.

"JOHN STREET, *October* 17th, 1864.

"MY DEAREST HUSBAND,

"I received your hurried line of yesterday, and was of course content with it. But why don't you tell me your exact address instead of that 'Post Office, Creston'? This matter is all a mystery to me, and I ought to be told every detail. I cannot fancy it is the same kind of occupation you have been used to hitherto. Your command that I am to stay here awhile until you can 'see how things look' and can arrange to send for me, I must necessarily abide by. But if, as you say, a married man would have been rejected by the person who engaged you, and that hence my existence must be kept a secret until you have secured your position, why did you think of going at all?

"The truth is, this keeping our marriage a secret is troublesome, vexing, and wearisome to me. I see the poorest woman in the street bearing her husband's name openly—living with him in the most matter-of-fact ease, and why shouldn't I? I wish I was back again in Liverpool.

"To-day I bought a grey waterproof cloak. I think it is a little too long for me, but it was cheap for one of such a quality. The weather is gusty and dreary, and till this morning I had hardly set foot outside the door since you left. Please do tell me when I am to come.

"Very affectionately yours,

"EUNICE."

"JOHN STREET, *October 25th*, 1864.

"MY DEAR HUSBAND,

"Why don't you write? Do you hate me? I have not had the heart to do anything this last week. That I, your wife, should be in this strait, and my husband well to do! I have been obliged to leave my first lodging for debt—among other things they charged me for a lot of brandy which I am quite sure I did not taste. Then I went to Camberwell and was found out by them. I went away privately from thence, and changed my name the second time. I am now Mrs. Rondley. But the new lodging was the wretchedest and dearest I ever set foot in, and I left it after being there only a day. I am now at No. 20 in the same street that you left me in originally. All last night the sash of my window rattled so dreadfully that I could not sleep, but I had not energy enough to get out of bed to stop it. This morning I have been walking—I don't know how far—but far enough to make my feet ache. I have been looking at the outside of two or three of the theatres, but they seem forbidding if I regard them with the eye of an actress in search of an engagement. Though you said I was to think no more of the stage I believe you would not care if you found me there. But I am not an actress by nature, and art will never make me one. I am too timid and retiring, I was intended for a cottager's wife. I certainly shall not try to go on the boards again whilst I am in this strange place. The idea of being brought on as far as London and then left here alone! Why didn't you leave me in Liverpool? Perhaps you thought I might have told somebody that my real name was Mrs. Manston. As if I had a living friend to whom I could impart it—no such good fortune! In fact my nearest friend is no nearer than what most people would call a stranger. But perhaps I ought to tell you that a week before I wrote my last letter to you, after wishing that my uncle and aunt in Philadelphia (the only near relatives I had) were still alive, I suddenly resolved to send a line to my cousin James, who I believe is still living in that neighbourhood. He has never seen me since we were babies together. I did not tell him of my marriage, because I thought you might not like it, and I gave my real maiden name, and an address at the Post-office here. But God knows if the letter will ever reach him.

"Do write me an answer, and send something.

"Your affectionate wife
"EUNICE."

"FRIDAY, *October* 28*th*.

"MY DEAR HUSBAND,

"The order for ten pounds has just come, and I am truly glad to get it. But why will you write so bitterly? Ah—well, if I had only had the money I should have been on my way to America by this time, so don't think I want to bore you of my own free-will. Who can you have met with at that new place? Remember I say this in no malignant tone, but certainly the facts go to prove that you have deserted me! You are inconstant—I know it. O why are you so? Now I have lost you I love you in spite of your neglect. I am weakly fond—that's my nature. I fear that upon the whole my life has been wasted. I know there is another woman supplanting me in your heart—yes, I know it. Come to me—do come.

"EUNICE."

"41, CHARLES SQUARE, HOXTON,
"*November* 19*th*.

"DEAR ÆNEAS,

"Here I am back again after my visit. Why should you have been so enraged at my finding your exact address? Any woman would have tried to do it,—you know she would have. And no woman would have lived under assumed names so long as I did. I repeat that I did not call myself Mrs. Manston until I came to this lodging at the beginning of this month—what could you expect?

"A helpless creature I, had not fortune favoured me unexpectedly. Banished as I was from your house at dawn, I did not suppose the indignity was about to lead to important results. But in crossing the park I overheard the conversation of a young man and woman who had also risen early. I believe her to be the girl who has won you away from me. Well, their conversation concerned you and Miss Aldclyffe, *very peculiarly*. The remarkable thing is that you yourself, without knowing it, told me of what, added to their conversation, completely reveals a secret to me that neither of you understand. Two negatives never made such a telling positive before. One clue more, and you would see it. A single consideration prevents my revealing it here—just one doubt as to whether your ignorance was real, and was not feigned to deceive me. Civility now, please.

"EUNICE."

"41, CHARLES SQUARE,
"Tuesday, November 22d.

"MY DARLING HUSBAND,

"Monday will suit me excellently for coming. I have acted exactly up to your instructions, and have sold my rubbish at the broker's in the next street. All this movement and bustle is delightful to me after the weeks of monotony I have endured. It is a relief to wish the place good-bye—London always has seemed so much more foreign to me than Liverpool. The mid-day train on Monday will do nicely for me. I shall be anxiously looking out for you Sunday night.

"I hope so much that you are not angry with me for writing to Miss Aldclyffe. You are not, dear, are you? Forgive me.

"Your loving wife,
"EUNICE."

This was the last of the letters from the wife to the husband. One other, in Mrs. Manston's handwriting and in the same packet, was differently addressed.

"THREE TRANTERS INN,
"CARRIFORD, NEAR FROOMINSTER,
"November 28th, 1864.

"DEAR COUSIN JAMES,

"Thank you indeed for answering my letter so promptly. When I called at the post-office yesterday I did not in the least think there would be one. But I must leave this subject. I write again at once, under the strangest and saddest conditions it is possible to conceive.

"I did not tell you in my last that I was a married woman. Don't blame me—it was my husband's influence. I hardly know where to begin my story. I had been living apart from him for a time—then he sent for me (this was last week) and I was glad to go to him. Then this is what he did. He promised to fetch me, and did not—leaving me to do the journey alone. He promised to meet me at the station here: he did not. I went on through the darkness to his house, and found his door locked and himself away from home. I have been obliged to come here, and I write to you in a strange room in a strange village inn! I choose the present moment to write to drive away my misery. Sorrow seems a sort of pleasure when you detail it on paper—poor pleasure though.

"But this is what I want to know—and I am ashamed to tell it. I would gladly do as you say, and come to you as a housekeeper, but I have not the money even for a steerage passage. James, do you want me badly enough—do you pity me enough to send it? I could manage to subsist in London upon the proceeds of my sale for another month or six weeks. Will you send it to the same address at the Post-office? But how do I know that you . . . . . .

Thus the letter ended. From creases in the paper it was plain that the writer, having got so far, had become dissatisfied with her production, and had crumpled it in her hand. Was it to write another, or not to write at all?

The next thing Anne Seaway perceived was that the fragmentary story she had coaxed out of Manston, to the effect that his wife had left England for America, might be truthful, according to two of these letters, corroborated by the evidence of the railway-porter.

And yet, at first, he had sworn in a passion that his wife was most certainly consumed in the fire.

If she had been burnt, this letter, written in her bedroom, and probably thrust into her pocket when she relinquished it, would have been burnt with her. Nothing was surer than that.

Why then did he say she was burnt, and never show Anne herself this letter?

The question suddenly raised a new and much stranger one—kindling a burst of amazement in her. How did Manston become possessed of this letter?

That fact of possession was certainly the most remarkable revelation of all in connection with this epistle, and perhaps had something to do with his reason for never showing it to her.

She knew by several proofs, that before his marriage with Cytherea, and up to the time of the porter's confession, Manston believed—honestly believed—that Cytherea would be his lawful wife, and hence of course, that his wife Eunice was dead.

So that no communication could possibly have passed between his wife and himself from the first moment that he believed her dead on the night of the fire, to the day of his wedding. And yet he had that letter.

How soon afterwards could they have communicated with each other?

The existence of the letter—as much as, or more than its contents—implying that Mrs. Manston was not burnt, his belief in that calamity must have terminated at the moment he obtained possession of the letter, if no earlier.

Was then the only solution to the riddle that Anne could discern, the true one?—that he had communicated with his wife somewhere about the commencement of Anne's residence with him, or at any time since?

It was the most unlikely thing on earth that a woman who had forsaken her husband should countenance his scheme to personify her,—whether she were in America, in London, or in the neighbourhood of Knapwater.

Then came the old and harassing question, what was Manston's real motive in risking his name on the deception he was practising as regarded Anne. It could not be, as he had always pretended, mere passion. Her thoughts had reverted to Mr. Raunham's letter, asking for proofs of her identity with the original Mrs. Manston. She could see no loophole of escape for the man who supported her. True, in her own estimation, the worst alternative was not so very bad after all—the getting the name of libertine, a possible appearance in the Divorce or some other Court of law, and a question of damages. Such an exposure might hinder his worldly progress for some time. Yet to him this alternative was, apparently, terrible as death itself.

She restored the letters to their hiding-place, scanned anew the other letters and memoranda, from which she could gain no fresh information, fastened up the cabinet, and left everything in its former condition.

Her mind was ill at ease. More than ever she wished that she had never seen Manston. Where the person suspected of mysterious moral obliquity is the possessor of great physical and intellectual attractions, the mere sense of incongruity adds an extra shudder to dread. The man's strange bearing terrified Anne as it had terrified Cytherea; for with all the woman Anne's faults, she had not descended to such depths of depravity as to willingly participate in crime. She had not even known that a living wife was being displaced till her arrival at Knapwater put retreat out of the question, and had looked upon personation simply as a mode of subsistence a degree

better than toiling in poverty and alone, after a bustling and
somewhat pampered life as housekeeper in a gay mansion.

> "—Non illa colo calathisve Minervæ
> Fœmineas assueta manus."*

§2. *Afternoon*

Mr. Raunham and Edward Springrove had by this time set in motion
a machinery which they hoped to find working out important results.

The rector was restless and full of meditation all the following
morning. It was plain, even to the servants about him, that Spring-
grove's communication wore a deeper complexion than any that had
been made to the old magistrate for many months or years past. The
fact was that having arrived at the stage of existence in which the
difficult intellectual feat of suspending one's judgment becomes possible, he was now putting it in practice, though not without the
penalty of watchful effort.

It was not till the afternoon that he determined to call on his
relative, Miss Aldclyffe, and cautiously probe her knowledge of the
subject occupying him so thoroughly. Cytherea, he knew, was still
beloved by this solitary woman. Miss Aldclyffe had made several
private inquiries concerning her old companion, and there was ever a
sadness in her tone when the young lady's name was mentioned,
which showed that from whatever cause the elder Cytherea's
renunciation of her favourite and namesake proceeded, it was not
from indifference to her fate.

"Have you ever had any reason for supposing your steward anything but an upright man?" he said to the lady.

"Never the slightest. Have you?" said she reservedly.

"Well—I have."

"What is it?"

"I can say nothing plainly because nothing is proved. But my
suspicions are very strong."

"Do you mean that he was rather cool towards his wife when they
were first married, and that it was unfair in him to leave her? I know
he was; but I think his recent conduct towards her has amply atoned
for the neglect."

He looked Miss Aldclyffe full in the face. It was plain that she spoke honestly. She had not the slightest notion that the woman who lived with the steward might be other than Mrs. Manston—much less that a greater matter might be behind.

"That's not it—I wish it was no more. My suspicion is, first, that the woman living at the Old House is not Mr. Manston's wife."

"Not—Mr. Manston's wife?"

"That is it."

Miss Aldclyffe looked blankly at the rector. "Not Mr. Manston's wife—who else can she be?" she said, simply.

"An improper woman* of the name of Anne Seaway."

Mr. Raunham had, in common with other people, noticed the extraordinary interest of Miss Aldclyffe in the well-being of her steward, and had endeavoured to account for it in various ways. The extent to which she was shaken by his information, whilst it proved that the understanding between herself and Manston did not make her a sharer of his secrets, also showed that the tie which bound her to him was still unbroken. Mr. Raunham had lately begun to doubt the latter fact, and now, on finding himself mistaken, regretted that he had not kept his own counsel in the matter. This it was too late to do, and he pushed on with his proofs. He gave Miss Aldclyffe in detail the grounds of his belief.

Before he had done, she recovered the cloak of reserve that she had adopted on his opening the subject.

"I might possibly be convinced that you were in the right, after such an elaborate argument," she replied, "were it not for one fact, which bears in the contrary direction so pointedly, that nothing but absolute proof can turn it. It is that there is no conceivable motive which could induce any sane man—leaving alone a man of Mr. Manston's clear-headedness and integrity—to venture upon such an extraordinary course of conduct;—no motive on earth."

"That was my own opinion till after the visit of a friend last night—a friend of mine and poor little Cytherea's."

"Ah—and Cytherea," said Miss Aldclyffe, catching at the idea raised by the name. "That he loved Cytherea—yes, and loves her now, wildly and devotedly, I am as positive as that I breathe. Cytherea is years younger than Mrs. Manston—as I shall call her—twice as sweet in disposition, three times as beautiful. Would he have given her up quietly and suddenly for a common p——.* Mr. Raunham,

your story is monstrous, and I don't believe it!" She glowed in her
earnestness.

The rector might now have advanced his second proposition—the
possible motive—but for reasons of his own he did not.

"Very well, madam. I only hope that facts will sustain you in your
belief. Ask him the question to his face, whether the woman is his
wife or no, and see how he receives it."

"I will to-morrow, most certainly," she said. "I always let these
things die of wholesome ventilation, as every fungus does."

But no sooner had the rector left her presence, than the grain of
mustard-seed he had sown grew to a tree.* Her impatience to set her
mind at rest could not brook a night's delay. It was with the utmost
difficulty that she could wait till evening arrived to screen her
movements. Immediately the sun had dropped behind the horizon,
and before it was quite dark, she wrapped her cloak around her,
softly left the house, and walked erect through the gloomy park in
the direction of the old manor-house.

The same minute saw two persons sit down in the rectory-house
to share the rector's usually solitary dinner. One was a man of common-place, middle-class appearance in all except his eyes. The other
was Edward Springrove.

The discovery of the carefully concealed letters rankled in the
mind of Anne Seaway. Her woman's nature insisted that Manston
had no right to keep all matters connected with his lost wife a secret
from herself. Perplexity had bred vexation; vexation, resentment;
curiosity had been continuous. The whole morning this resentment
and curiosity increased.

The steward said very little to his companion during their lunch-
eon at mid-day. He seemed reckless of appearances—almost indifferent to whatever fate awaited him. All his actions betrayed that
something portentous was impending, and still he explained nothing. By carefully observing every trifling action, as only a woman can
observe them, the thought at length dawned upon her that he was
going to run away secretly. She feared for herself; her knowledge of
law and justice was vague, and she fancied she might in some way be
made responsible for him.

In the afternoon he went out of the house again, and she watched
him turn away in the direction of Froominster. She felt a desire to go

to Froominster herself, and, after an interval of half an hour, followed him on foot—ostensibly to do some shopping.

One among her several trivial errands was to make a small purchase at the druggist's. Opposite the druggist's stood the County Bank. Looking out of the shop window, between the coloured bottles, she saw Manston come down the steps of the bank, in the act of withdrawing his hand from his pocket, and pulling his coat close over its mouth.

It is an almost universal habit with people when leaving a bank, to be carefully adjusting their pockets if they have been receiving money; if they have been paying it, their hands swing laxly.

The steward had in all likelihood been taking money—possibly on Miss Aldclyffe's account—that was continual with him. And he might have been removing his own, as a man would do who was intending to leave the country.

§ 3.   *From five to eight o'clock, p.m.*

Anne reached home again in time to preside over preparations for dinner. Manston came in half an hour later. The lamp was lighted, the shutters were closed, and they sat down together. He was pale and worn—almost haggard.

The meal passed off in almost unbroken silence. When preoccupation withstands the influence of a social meal with one pleasant companion, the mental scene must be surpassingly vivid. Just as she was rising a tap came to the door.

Before a maid could attend to the knock, Manston crossed the room and answered it himself. The visitor was Miss Aldclyffe.

Manston instantly came back and spoke to Anne in an undertone. "I should be glad if you could retire to your room for a short time."

"It is a dry, starlight evening," she replied. "I will go for a little walk if your object is merely a private conversation with Miss Aldclyffe."

"Very well, do; there's no accounting for tastes," he said. A few commonplaces then passed between her and Miss Aldclyffe, and Anne went upstairs to bonnet and cloak herself. She came down, opened the front door, and went out.

She looked around to realise the night. It was dark, mournful, and quiet. Then she stood still. From the moment that Manston had requested her absence, a strong and burning desire had prevailed in her to know the subject of Miss Aldclyffe's conversation with him. Simple curiosity was not entirely what inspired her. Her suspicions had been thoroughly aroused by the discovery of the morning. A conviction that her future depended on her power to combat a man who, in desperate circumstances, would be far from a friend to her, prompted a strategic movement to acquire the important secret that was in handling now. The woman thought and thought, and regarded the dull dark trees, anxiously debating how the thing could be done.

Stealthily re-opening the front door she entered the hall, and advancing and pausing alternately, came close to the door of the room in which Miss Aldclyffe and Manston conversed. Nothing could be heard through the keyhole or panels. At a great risk she softly turned the knob and opened the door to a width of about half an inch, performing the act so delicately that three minutes, at least, were occupied in completing it. At that instant Miss Aldclyffe said,—

"There's a draught somewhere. The door is ajar, I think."

Anne glided back under the staircase. Manston came forward and closed the door.

This chance was now cut off and she considered again.

The parlour, or sitting-room, in which the conference took place, had the window-shutters fixed on the outside of the window, as is usual in the back portions of old country-houses. The shutters were hinged one on each side of the opening, and met in the middle, where they were fastened by a bolt passing continuously through them and the wood mullion within, the bolt being secured on the inside by a pin, which was seldom inserted till Manston and herself were about to retire for the night; sometimes not at all.

If she returned to the door of the room she might be discovered at any moment, but could she listen at the window, which overlooked a part of the garden never visited after nightfall, she would be safe from disturbance. The idea was worth a trial.

She glided round to the window, took the head of the bolt between her finger and thumb, and softly screwed it round until it was entirely withdrawn from its position. The shutters remained as before, whilst, where the bolt had come out, was now a shining hole three-quarters of an inch in diameter, through which one might see into the middle of the room. She applied her eye to the orifice.

Miss Aldclyffe and Manston were both standing; Manston with his back to the window, his companion facing it. The lady's demeanour was severe, condemnatory, and haughty. No more was to be seen; Anne then turned sideways, leant with her shoulder against the shutters and placed her ear upon the hole.

"You know where," said Miss Aldclyffe. "And how could you, a man, act a double deceit like this?"

"Men do strange things sometimes."

"What was your reason—come?"

"A mere whim."

"I might even believe that, if the woman were handsomer than Cytherea, or if you had been married some time to Cytherea and had grown tired of her."

"And can't you believe it, too, under these conditions: that I married Cytherea, gave her up because I heard that my wife was alive, found that my wife would not come to live with me, and then, not to let any woman I love so well as Cytherea run any risk of being displaced and ruined in reputation, should my wife ever think fit to return, induced this woman to come to me, as being better than no companion at all?"

"I cannot believe it. Your love for Cytherea was not of such a kind as that excuse would imply. It was Cytherea or nobody with you. As an object of passion, you did not desire the company of this Anne Seaway at all, and certainly not so much as to madly risk your reputation by bringing her here in the way you have done. I am sure you didn't, Æneas."

"So am I," he said, bluntly.

Miss Aldclyffe uttered an exclamation of astonishment: the confession was like a blow in its suddenness. She began to reproach him bitterly, and with tears.

"How could you overthrow my plans, disgrace the only girl I ever had any respect for, by such inexplicable doings! . . . . That woman must leave this place—the country, perhaps. Heavens! the truth will leak out in a day or two!"

"She must do no such thing, and the truth must be stifled, somehow—nobody knows how. If I stay here, or on any spot of the civilised globe, as Æneas Manston, this woman must live with me as my wife, or I am damned past redemption!"

"I will not countenance your keeping her, whatever your motive may be."

"You must do something," he murmured. "You must. Yes, you must."

"I never will," she said. " 'Tis a criminal act."

He looked at her earnestly. "Will you not support me through this deception if my very life depends upon it? Will you not?"

"Nonsense! Life! It will be a scandal to you, but she must leave this place. It will out sooner or later, and the exposure had better come now."

Manston repeated gloomily the same words. "My life depends upon your supporting me—my very life."

He then came close to her, and spoke into her ear. Whilst he spoke he held her head to his mouth with both his hands. Strange expressions came over her face; the workings of her mouth were painful to observe. Still he held her and whispered on.

The only words that could be caught by Anne Seaway, confused as her hearing frequently was by the moan of the wind and the waterfall in her outer ear, were these of Miss Aldclyffe, in tones which absolutely quivered:—

"They have no money—what can they prove?"

The listener tasked herself to the utmost to catch his answer, but it was in vain. Of the remainder of the colloquy one fact alone was plain to Anne, and that only inductively—that Miss Aldclyffe, from what he had revealed to her, was going to scheme body and soul on Manston's behalf.

Miss Aldclyffe seemed now to have no further reason for remaining, yet she lingered awhile as if loth to leave him. When, finally, the crest-fallen and agitated lady made preparations for departure, Anne quickly inserted the bolt, ran round to the entrance archway, and down the steps into the park. Here she stood close to the trunk of a huge lime-tree, which absorbed her dark outline into its own.

In a few minutes she saw Manston, with Miss Aldclyffe leaning on his arm, cross the glade before her and proceed in the direction of the House. She watched them ascend the rise and advance, as two black spots, towards the mansion. The appearance of an oblong space of light in the dark mass of walls denoted that the door was opened. Miss Aldclyffe's outline became visible upon it, the door shut her in, and all was darkness again. The form of Manston returning alone arose from the gloom, and passed by Anne in her hiding-place.

Waiting outside a quarter of an hour longer, that no suspicion of any kind might be excited, Anne returned to the old manor-house.

§ 4. *From eight to eleven o'clock, p.m.*

Manston was very friendly that evening. It was evident to her, now that she was behind the scenes, that he was making desperate efforts to disguise the real state of his mind.

Her terror of him did not decrease. They sat down to supper, Manston still talking cheerfully. But what is keener than the eye of a mistrustful woman? A man's cunning is to it as was the armour of Sisera to the thin tent-nail.* She found, in spite of his adroitness, that he was attempting something more than a disguise of his feeling. He was trying to distract her attention, that he might be unobserved in some special movement of his hands.

What a moment it was for her then! The whole surface of her body became attentive. She allowed him no chance whatever. We know the duplicated condition at such times—when the existence divides itself into two, and the ostensibly innocent chatterer stands in front, like another person, to hide the timorous spy.

Manston played the same game, but more palpably. The meal was nearly over when he seemed possessed of a new idea of how his object might be accomplished. He tilted back his chair with a reflective air, and looked steadily at the clock standing against the wall opposite him. He said didactically,

"Few faces are capable of expressing more by dumb show than the face of a clock. You may see in it every variety of incentive—from the softest seductions to negligence to the strongest hints for action."

"Well, in what way?" she inquired. His drift was, as yet, quite unintelligible to her.

"Why, for instance: look at the cold methodical, unromantic, business-like air of all the right-angled positions of the hands. They make a man set about work in spite of himself. Then look at the piquant shyness of its face when the two hands are over each other. Several attitudes imply 'make ready.' The 'make ready' of ten minutes to twelve differs from the 'make ready' of ten minutes to one, as youth differs from age. 'Upward and onward,' says twenty-five minutes to eleven. Mid-day or midnight expresses distinctly 'It is done.' You surely have noticed that?"

"Yes, I have."

He continued with affected quaintness,—

"The easy dash of ten minutes past seven, the rakish recklessness of a quarter past, the drooping weariness of twenty-five minutes past, must have been observed by everybody."

"Whatever amount of truth there may be, there is a good deal of imagination in your fancy," she said.

He still contemplated the clock.

"Then again the general finish of the face has a great effect upon the eye. This old-fashioned brass-faced one we have here, with its arched top, half-moon slit for the day of the month, and ship rocking at the upper part, impresses me with the notion of its being an old cynic, elevating his brows, whose thoughts can be seen wavering between good and evil."

A thought now enlightened her: the clock was behind her and he wanted to get her back turned. She dreaded turning, yet, not to excite his suspicion that she was on her guard, she quickly looked behind her at the clock as he spoke, recovering her old position again instantly. The time had not been long enough for any action whatever on his part.

"Ah," he casually remarked, and at the same minute began to pour her out a glass of wine. "Speaking of the clock has reminded me that it must nearly want winding up. Remember that it is wound up to-night. Suppose you do it at once, my dear."

There was no possible way of evading the act. She resolutely turned to perform the operation: anything was better than that he should suspect her. It was an old-fashioned eight-day clock, of workmanship suited to the rest of the antique furniture that Manston had collected there, and ground heavily during winding.

Anne had given up all idea of being able to watch him during the interval, and the noise of the wheels prevented her learning anything by her ears. But, as she wound, she caught sight of his shadow on the wall at her right hand.

What was he doing?

He was in the very act of pouring something into her glass of wine.

He had completed the manœuvre before she had done winding. She methodically closed the clock-case and turned round again.

When she faced him he was sitting in his chair as before she had risen.

In a familiar scene which has hitherto been pleasant, it is difficult to realise that an added condition, which does not alter its aspect, can have made it terrible. The woman thought that his action must have been prompted by no other intent than that of poisoning her, and yet she could not instantly put on a fear of her position.

And before she had grasped these consequences, another supposition served to make her regard the first as unlikely, if not absurd. It was the act of a madman to take her life in a manner so easy of discovery, unless there were far more reason for the crime than any that Manston could possibly have.

Was it not merely his intention, in tampering with her wine, to make her sleep soundly that night? This was in harmony with her original suspicion, that he intended secretly to abscond. At any rate he was going to set about some stealthy proceeding, as to which she was to be kept in utter darkness. The difficulty now was to avoid drinking the wine.

By means of one pretext and another she put off taking her glass for nearly five minutes, but he eyed her too frequently to allow her to throw the potion under the grate. It became necessary to take one sip. This she did, and found an opportunity of absorbing it in her handkerchief.

Plainly he had no idea of her countermoves. The scheme seemed to him in proper train, and he turned to poke out the fire. She instantly seized the glass and poured its contents down her bosom. When he faced round again she was holding the glass to her lips, empty.

In due course he locked the doors and saw that the shutters were fastened. She attended to a few closing details of housewifery, and a few minutes later they retired for the night.

§ 5. *From eleven o'clock to midnight*

When Manston was persuaded, by the feigned heaviness of her breathing, that Anne Seaway was asleep, he softly arose, and dressed himself in the gloom.

With ears strained to their utmost she heard him complete this operation; then he took something from his pocket, put it in the drawer of the dressing-table, went to the door and down the stairs. She glided out of bed and looked in the drawer. He had only restored to its place a small phial she had seen there before. It was labelled "Battley's Solution of Opium."* She felt relieved that her life had not been attempted. That was to have been her sleeping-draught.

No time was to be lost if she meant to be a match for him. She followed him in her night-dress. When she reached the foot of the staircase he was in the office and had closed the door, under which a faint gleam showed that he had obtained a light.

She crept to the door, but could not venture to open it, however slightly. Placing her ear to the panel, she could hear him tearing up papers of some sort, and a brighter and quivering ray of light coming from the threshold an instant later, implied that he was burning them. By the slight noise of his footsteps on the uncarpeted floor, she at length imagined that he was approaching the door. She flitted upstairs again and crept into bed.

Manston returned to the bedroom close upon her heels, and entered it—again without a light. Standing motionless for an instant to assure himself that she still slept, he went to the drawer in which their ready-money was kept, and removed the casket that contained it. Anne's ear distinctly caught the rustle of notes, and the chink of gold as he handled it. Some he placed in his pocket, some he returned to its place.

He stood thinking, as it were weighing a possibility. While lingering thus, he noticed the reflected image of his own face in the glass— pale and spectre-like in its indistinctness. The sight seemed to be the feather which turned the balance of indecision: he drew a heavy breath, retired from the room, and passed downstairs. She heard him unbar the back-door and go out into the yard.

Feeling safe in a conclusion that he did not intend to return to the bedroom again, she arose, and hastily dressed herself. On going to the door of the apartment she found that he had locked it behind him. "A precaution—it can be no more," she muttered. Yet she was all the more perplexed and excited on this account. Had he been going to leave home immediately, he would scarcely have taken the trouble to lock her in, holding the belief that she was in a drugged sleep.

The lock shot into a box-staple,* so that there was no possibility of her pushing back the bolt. How should she follow him? Easily.

An inner closet opened from the bedroom: it was large, and had some time heretofore been used as a dressing or bath-room, but had been found inconvenient from having no other outlet to the landing. The window of this little room looked out upon the roof of the porch, which was flat and covered with lead. Anne took a pillow from the bed, gently opened the casement of the inner room, and stepped forth on the flat. There, leaning over the edge of the small parapet that ornamented the porch, she dropped the pillow upon the gravel path, and let herself down over the parapet by her hands till her toes swung about two feet from the ground. From this position she adroitly alighted upon the pillow, and stood in the path.

Since she had come indoors from her walk in the early part of the evening the moon had risen. But the thick clouds overspreading the whole landscape rendered the dim light pervasive and grey: it appeared as an attribute of the air.

Anne crept round to the back of the house, listening intently. The steward had had at least ten minutes start of her. She had waited here whilst one might count fifty, when she heard a movement in the out-house—a fragment once attached to the main building. This out-house was partitioned into an outer and an inner room, which had been a kitchen and a scullery before the connecting erections were pulled down, but they were now used respectively as a brewhouse and workshop, the only means of access to the latter being through the brewhouse. The outer door of this first apartment was usually fastened by a padlock on the exterior. It was now closed but not fastened. Manston was evidently in the outhouse.

She slightly moved the door. The interior of the brewhouse was wrapped in gloom, but a streak of light fell towards her in a line across the floor from the inner or workshop door, which was not quite closed. This light was unexpected, none having been visible through hole or crevice. Glancing in, the woman found that he had placed cloths and mats at the various apertures, and hung a sack at the window to prevent the egress of a single ray. She could also perceive from where she stood, that the bar of light fell across the brewing-copper just outside the inner door, and that upon it lay the key of her bedroom.

The illuminated interior of the workshop was also partly visible from her position, through the two half-open doors. Manston was engaged in emptying a large cupboard of the tools, gallipots,* and old iron it contained. When it was quite cleared he took a chisel, and with it began to withdraw the hooks and shoulder-nails holding the cupboard to the wall. All these being loosened, he extended his arms, lifted the cupboard bodily from the brackets under it, and deposited it on the floor beside him.

That portion of the wall which had been screened by the cupboard was now laid bare. This, it appeared, had been plastered more recently than the bulk of the outhouse. Manston loosened the plaster with some kind of tool, flinging the pieces into a basket as they fell. Having now stripped clear about two feet area of wall, he inserted a crowbar between the joints of the bricks beneath; softly wriggling it until several were loosened. There was now disclosed the mouth of an old oven, which was apparently contrived in the thickness of the wall, and having fallen into disuse, had been closed up with bricks in this manner. It was formed after the simple old-fashioned plan of oven-building—a mere oblate* cavity without a flue.

Manston now stretched his arm into the oven, dragged forth a heavy weight of great bulk, and let it slide to the ground. The woman who watched him could see the object plainly. It was a common corn-sack, nearly full, and was tied at the mouth in the usual way.

The steward had once or twice started up, as if he had heard sounds, and his motions now became more cat-like still. On a sudden he put out the light. Anne had made no noise, yet a foreign noise of some kind had certainly been made in the intervening portion of the house. She heard it. "One of the rats," she thought.

He seemed soon to recover from his alarm, but changed his tactics completely. He did not light his candle—going on with his work in the dark. She had only sounds to go by now, and, judging as well as she could from these, he was piling up the bricks which closed the oven's mouth as they had been before he disturbed them. The query that had not left her brain all the interval of her inspection—how should she get back into her bedroom again—now received a solution. Whilst he was replacing the cupboard, she would glide across the brewhouse, take the key from the top of the copper, run upstairs, unlock the door, and bring back the key again: if he returned to bed, which was unlikely, he would think the lock had failed to catch in the staple. This thought and intention, occupying such length of words, flashed upon her in an instant, and hardly disturbed her strong curiosity to stay and learn the meaning of his actions in the workshop.

Slipping sideways through the first door and closing it behind her, she advanced into the darkness towards the second, making every individual footfall with the greatest care, lest the fragments of rubbish on the floor should crackle beneath her tread. She soon stood close by the copper, and not more than a foot from the door of the room occupied by Manston himself, from which position she could distinctly hear him breathe between each exertion, although it was far too dark to discern anything of him.

To secure the key of her chamber was her first anxiety, and accordingly she cautiously reached out with her hand to where it lay.

Instead of touching it, her fingers came in contact with the foot of a human being.

She drooped faint in a cold sweat.

It was the foot either of a man or woman, standing on the brewing-copper where the key had lain. A warm foot, covered with a polished boot.

The startling discovery so terrified her that she could hardly repress a sound. She withdrew her hand with a motion like the flight of an arrow. Her touch was so light that the leather seemed to have been thick enough to keep the owner of the foot in entire ignorance of it, and the noise of Manston's scraping might have been quite sufficient to drown the slight rustle of her dress.

The person was obviously not the steward: he was still busy. It was somebody who, since the light had been extinguished, had taken advantage of the gloom, to come from some dark recess in the brewhouse and stand upon the brickwork of the copper.

The fear which had at first paralysed her lessened with the birth of a sense that fear now was utter failure: she was in a desperate position and must abide by the consequences. The motionless person on the copper was, equally with Manston, quite unconscious of her proximity, and she ventured to advance her hand again, feeling behind the feet, till she found the key. On its return to her side, her finger-tip skimmed the lower verge of a trousers-leg.

It was a man, then, who stood there. To go to the door just at this time was impolitic, and she shrank back into an inner corner to wait.

The comparative security from discovery that her new position ensured, resuscitated reason a little, and empowered her to form some logical inferences:

1. The man who stood on the copper had taken advantage of the darkness to get there, as she had to enter.

2. The man must have been hid in the outhouse before she reached the door.

3. He must be watching Manston with much calculation and system, and for purposes of his own.

She could now tell by the noises that Manston had completed his re-erection of the cupboard. She heard him replacing the articles it had contained—bottle by bottle, tool by tool,—after which he came into the brewhouse, went to the window, and pulled down the cloths covering it; but the window being rather small, this unveiling scarcely relieved the darkness of the interior.

He returned to the workshop, hoisted something to his back by a jerk, and felt about the room for some other article. Having found it he emerged from the inner door, crossed the brewhouse, and went into the yard. Directly he stepped out she could see his outline by the light of the clouded and weakly moon. The sack was slung at his back, and in his hand he carried a spade.

Anne now waited in her corner in breathless suspense for the proceedings of the other man. In about half-a-minute she heard him descend from the copper, and then the square opening of the doorway showed the outline of this other watcher passing through it likewise. The form was that of a broad-shouldered man enveloped in a long coat. He vanished after the steward.

The woman vented a sigh of relief, and moved forward to follow. Simultaneously, she discovered that the watcher whose foot she had touched was in his turn watched and followed also.

It was by a woman. Anne Seaway shrank backward again.

The unknown woman came forward from the further side of the yard, and pondered awhile in hesitation. Tall, dark, and closely wrapped, she stood up from the earth like a cypress. She moved, crossed the yard without producing the slightest disturbance by her footsteps, and went in the direction the others had taken.

Anne waited yet another minute—then in her turn noiselessly followed the last woman.

But so impressed was she with the sensation of people in hiding, that in coming out of the yard she turned her head to see if any person were following her in the same way. Nobody was visible, but she discerned, standing behind the angle of the stable, Manston's horse and gig, ready harnessed.

He did intend to fly after all, then, she thought. He must have placed the horse in readiness, in the interval between his leaving the house, and her exit by the window.

However, there was not time to weigh this branch of the night's events. She turned about again, and continued on the trail of the other three.

§ 6. *From midnight to half-past one, a.m.*

Intentness pervaded everything; Night herself seemed to have become a watcher.

The four persons proceeded across the glade, and into the park plantation, at equi-distances of about seventy yards. Here the ground, completely overhung by the foliage, was coated with a thick moss which was as soft as velvet beneath their feet. The first watcher, that is, the man walking immediately behind Manston, now fell back, when Manston's housekeeper, knowing the ground pretty well, dived circuitously among the trees and got directly behind the steward, who, encumbered with his load, had proceeded but slowly. The other woman seemed now to be about opposite to Anne, or a little in advance, but on Manston's other hand.

He reached a pit, midway between the waterfall and the engine-house. There he stopped, wiped his face, and listened.

Into this pit had drifted uncounted generations of withered leaves, half filling it. Oak, beech, and chestnut, rotten and brown alike, mingled themselves in one fibrous mass. Manston descended into the midst of them, placed his sack on the ground, and raking the leaves aside into a large heap, began digging. Anne softly drew nearer, crept into a bush, and turning her head to survey the rest, missed the man who had dropped behind, and whom we have called the first watcher. Concluding that he, too, had hidden himself, she turned her attention to the second watcher, the other woman, who had meanwhile advanced near to where Anne lay in hiding, and now seated herself behind a tree, still closer to the steward than was Anne Seaway.

Here and thus Anne remained concealed. The crunch of the

steward's spade, as it cut into the soft vegetable mould, was plainly perceptible to her ears, when the periodic cessations between the creaks of the engine concurred with a lull in the breeze, which otherwise brought the subdued roar of the cascade from the farther side of the bank that screened it. A large hole—some four or five feet deep—had been excavated by Manston in about twenty minutes. Into this he immediately placed the sack, and then began filling in the earth, and treading it down. Lastly, he carefully raked the whole mass of dead and dry leaves into the middle of the pit, burying the ground with them as they had buried it before.

For a hiding-place the spot was unequalled. The thick accumulation of leaves, which had not been disturbed for centuries, might not be disturbed again for centuries to come, whilst their lower layers still decayed and added to the mould beneath.

By the time this work was ended the sky had grown clearer, and Anne could now see distinctly the face of the other woman, stretching from behind the tree, seemingly forgetful of her position in her intense contemplation of the actions of the steward. Her countenance was white and motionless.

It was impossible that Manston should not soon notice her. At the completion of his labour he turned, and did so.

"Ho—you here!" he exclaimed.

"Don't think I am a spy upon you," she said, in an imploring whisper. Anne recognised the voice as Miss Aldclyffe's.

The trembling lady added hastily another remark, which was drowned in the recurring creak of the engine close at hand. The first watcher, if he had come no nearer than his original position, was too far off to hear any part of this dialogue, on account of the roar of the falling water, which could reach him unimpeded by the bank.

The remark of Miss Aldclyffe to Manston had plainly been concerning the first watcher; for Manston, with his spade in his hand, instantly rushed to where the man was concealed, and, before the latter could disengage himself from the boughs, the steward struck him on the head with the blade of the instrument. The man fell to the ground.

"Fly!" said Miss Aldclyffe to Manston. Manston vanished amidst the trees. Miss Aldclyffe went off in a contrary direction.

Anne Seaway was about to run away likewise, when she turned and looked at the fallen man. He lay on his face, motionless.

Many of these women who own to no moral code* show considerable magnanimity when they see people in trouble. To act rightly simply because it is one's duty is proper; but a good action which is the result of no law of reflection shines more than any.

She went up to him and gently turned him over, upon which he began to show signs of life. By her assistance he was soon able to stand upright.

He looked about him with a bewildered air, endeavouring to collect his ideas. "Who are you?" he said to the woman, mechanically.

It was bad policy now to attempt disguise.

"I am the supposed Mrs. Manston," she said. "Who are you?"

"I am the detective employed by Mr. Raunham to sift this mystery—which may be criminal." He stretched his limbs, pressed his head, and seemed gradually to awake to a sense of having been incautious in his utterance. "Never you mind who I am," he continued. "Well—it doesn't matter now, either—it will no longer be a secret."

He stooped for his hat and ran in the direction the steward had taken—coming back again after the lapse of a minute.

"It's only an aggravated assault, after all," he said, hastily, "until we have found out for certain what's buried here. It may be only a bag of building rubbish; but it may be more. Come and help me dig." He seized the spade with the awkwardness of a town man, and went into the pit, continuing a muttered discourse. "It's no use my running after him single-handed," he said. "He's ever so far off by this time. The best step is to see what is here."

It was far easier for the detective to re-open the hole than it had been for Manston to form it. The leaves were raked away, the loam thrown out, and the sack dragged forth.

"Hold this," he said to Anne, whose curiosity still kept her standing near. He turned on the light of a dark lantern he had brought, and gave it into her hand.

The string which bound the mouth of the sack was now cut. The detective laid the bag on its side, seized it by the bottom, and jerked forth the contents. A large package was disclosed, carefully wrapped up in impervious tarpaulin, also well tied.

He was on the point of pulling open the folds at one end, when a light-coloured thread of something, hanging on the outside, arrested his eye. He put his hand upon it; it felt stringy, and adhered to his fingers. "Hold the light close," he said.

She held it close. He raised his hand to the glass, and they both peered at an almost intangible filament he held between his finger and thumb. It was a long hair; the hair of a woman.

"God! I couldn't believe it—no, I couldn't believe it!" the detective whispered, horror-struck. "And I have lost the man for the present through my unbelief. Let's get into a sheltered place. . . . Now wait a minute whilst I prove it."

He thrust his hand into his waistcoat pocket, and withdrew thence a minute packet of brown paper. Spreading it out he disclosed, coiled in the middle, another long hair. It was the hair the clerk's wife had found on Manston's pillow nine days before the Carriford fire.

He held the two hairs to the light: they were both of a pale brown hue. He laid them parallel and stretched out his arms: they were of the same length to a nicety. The detective turned to Anne.

"It is the body of his first wife," he said, quietly. "He murdered her, as Mr. Springrove and the rector suspected—but how and when, God only knows."

"And I!" exclaimed Anne Seaway, a probable and natural sequence of events and motives explanatory of the whole crime—events and motives shadowed forth by the letter, Manston's possession of it, his renunciation of Cytherea, and instalment of herself—flashing upon her mind with the rapidity of lightning.

"Ah—I see," said the detective, standing unusually close to her: and a handcuff was on her wrist. "You must come with me, madam. Knowing as much about a secret murder as God knows, is a very suspicious thing: it doesn't make you a goddess—far from it." He directed the bull's-eye* into her face.

"Pooh—lead on," she said, scornfully, "and don't lose your principal actor for the sake of torturing a poor subordinate like me."

He loosened her hand, gave her his arm, and dragged her out of the grove, making her run beside him till they had reached the rectory. A light was burning here, and an auxiliary of the detective's awaiting him: a horse ready harnessed to a spring-cart was standing outside.

"You have come—I wish I had known that," the detective said to his assistant, hurriedly and angrily. "Well, we've blundered—he's gone—you should have been here, as I said! I was sold by that woman, Miss Aldclyffe—she watched me." He hastily gave directions in an undertone to this man. The concluding words were, "Go in to the rector—he's up. Detain Miss Aldclyffe. I, in the meantime, am driving to Froominster with this one, and for help. We shall be sure to have him when it gets light."

He assisted Anne into the vehicle, and drove off with her. As they went, the clear, dry road showed before them between the grassy quarters at each side, like a white riband, and made their progress easy. They came to Churchway Bower, where the highway was overhung by dense firs for some distance on both sides. It was totally dark here.

A smash: a rude shock. In the very midst of its length, at the point where the road began to drop down a hill, the detective drove against something with a jerk which nearly flung them both to the ground.

The man recovered himself, placed Anne on the seat, and reached out his hand. He found that the off-wheel of his gig was locked in that of another conveyance of some kind.

"Hoy!" said the officer.

Nobody answered.

"Hoy, you man asleep there!" he said again. No reply.

"Well, that's odd—this comes of the folly of travelling without gig-lamps because you expect the dawn." He jumped to the ground and turned on his lantern.

There was the gig which had obstructed him, standing in the middle of the road; a jaded horse harnessed to it, but no human being in or near the vehicle.

"Do you know whose gig this is?" he said to the woman.

"No," she said, sullenly. But she did recognise it as the steward's.

"I'll swear it's Manston's! Come I can hear it by your tone. However, you needn't say anything which may criminate you. What forethought the man must have had—how carefully he must have considered possible contingencies! Why he must have got the horse and gig ready before he began shifting the body."

He listened for a sound among the trees. None was to be heard but the occasional scamper of a rabbit over the withered leaves. He threw the light of his lantern through a gap in the hedge, but could see nothing beyond an impenetrable thicket. It was clear that Manston was not many yards off, but the question was how to find him. Nothing could be done by the detective just then, encumbered as he was by the horse and Anne. If he had entered the thicket on a search unaided, Manston might have stepped unobserved from behind a bush and murdered him with the greatest ease. Indeed there were such strong reasons for the exploit in Manston's circumstances at that moment that, without showing cowardice, his pursuer felt it hazardous to remain any longer where he stood.

He hastily tied the head of Manston's horse to the back of his own vehicle, that the steward might be deprived of the use of any means of escape other than his own legs, and drove on thus with his prisoner to Froominster. Arrived there, he lodged her in the police-station, and then took immediate steps for the capture of Manston.

CHAPTER VII

THE EVENTS OF THREE HOURS

§ 1. *March the twenty-third. Mid-day*

Thirty-six hours had elapsed since Manston's escape.

It was market-day at Froominster. The farmers outside and inside the corn-exchange looked at their samples of wheat, and poured them critically as usual from one palm to another, but they thought and spoke of Manston. Grocers serving behind their counters, instead of using their constant phrase "The next thing, please?" substituted, "Have you heard if he's caught?" Dairymen and drovers standing beside the sheep and cattle-pens, spread their legs firmly, readjusted their hats, thrust their hands into the lowest depths of their pockets, regarded the animals with the utmost keenness of which the eye was capable, and said, "Ay, ay, so's: they'll have him avore night."

Later in the day, Edward Springrove passed along the street hurriedly and anxiously. "Well, have you heard any more?" he said to an acquaintance who accosted him.

"They tracked him in this way," said the other young man. "A vagrant first told them that Manston had passed a rick at daybreak, under which this man was lying. They followed the track he pointed out and ultimately came to a stile. On the other side was a heap of half-hardened mud, scraped from the road. On the surface of the heap, where it had been smoothed by the shovel, was distinctly imprinted the form of a man's hand, the buttons of his waistcoat, and his watch-chain, showing that he had stumbled in hurrying over the stile, and fallen there. The pattern of the chain proved the man to have been Manston.* They followed on till they reached a ford crossed by stepping-stones—on the further bank were the same footmarks that had shown themselves beside the stile. The whole of this course had been in the direction of Creston. On they went, and the next clue was furnished them by a shepherd. He said that wherever a clear space three or four yards wide ran in a line through a flock of sheep lying about a ewe-lease,* it was a proof that somebody had passed there not more than half-an-hour earlier. At twelve o'clock that day he had noticed such a feature in his flock. Nothing more could be heard of him, and they got into Creston. The steam-packet* to the Channel Islands was to start at eleven last night; and they at once concluded that his hope was to get to France by way of Jersey and St. Malo,—his only chance, all the railway stations being watched.

"Well, they went to the boat: he was not on board then. They went again at half-past ten: he had not come. Two men now placed them-selves under the lamp immediately beside the gangway. Another stayed by the office door, and one or two more up East Street—the short cut to the pier. At a quarter to eleven the mail-bags were put on board. Whilst the attention of the idlers was directed to the mails, down East Street came a man as boldly as possible. The gait was Manston's, but not the clothes. He passed over to the shaded part of the street: heads were turned. I suppose this warned him, for he never emerged from the shadow. They watched and waited, but the steward did not re-appear. The alarm was raised—they searched the town high and low—no Manston. All this morning they have been searching, but there's not a sign of him anywhere. However, he has lost his last chance of getting across the Channel. It is reported that he has since changed clothes with a labourer."

During this narration, Edward, lost in thought, had let his eyes follow a shabby man in a smock-frock, but wearing light boots*—who was stalking down the street under a bundle of straw which overhung and concealed his head. It was a very ordinary circum-stance for a man with a bundle of straw on his shoulders and over-hanging his head, to go down the High Street of Froominster. Edward saw him cross the bridge which divided the town from the country, place his shaggy encumbrance by the side of the road, and leave it there.

Springrove now parted from his acquaintance, and went also in the direction of the bridge. As far as he could see stretched the turn-pike-road, and, while he was looking, he noticed a man to leap from the hedge at a point two hundred, or two hundred and fifty yards ahead, cross the road, and go through a wicket on the other side. This figure seemed like that of the man who had been carrying the bundle of straw. He looked at the straw: it still stood alone.

The subjoined facts sprang as it were into juxtaposition in his brain:—

Manston had been seen wearing the clothes of a labouring man—a brown smock-frock.

So had this man, who seemed other than a labourer, on second thoughts: and he had concealed his face by his bundle of straw with the greatest ease and naturalness.

The path the man had taken led to Palchurch, where Cytherea was living.

If Mrs. Manston was murdered, as some said, on the night of the fire, Cytherea was the steward's lawful wife.

Manston, at bay, and reckless of results, might rush to his wife, and harm her.

It was a horrible supposition for a man who loved Cytherea to entertain; but Springrove could not resist its influence. He started off for Palchurch.

§ 2. *One to two o'clock, p.m.*

On that self-same mid-day, whilst Edward was proceeding to Palchurch by the foot-path across the fields, Owen Graye had left the village and was riding along the turnpike-road to Froominster, that he might ascertain the exact truth of the strange rumour which had reached him concerning Manston. Not to disquiet his sister, he had said nothing to her of the matter.

She sat by the window, reading. From her position she could see up the lane for a distance of at least a hundred yards. Passers-by were so rare in this retired nook, that the eyes of those who dwelt by the way-side were invariably lifted to every one on the road, great and small, as to a novelty.

A man in a brown smock-frock turned the corner and came towards the house. It being market-day at Froominster, the village was nearly deserted, and more than this, the old farm-house in which Owen and his sister were staying, stood, as has been stated, apart from the body of cottages. The man did not look respectable: Cytherea arose and bolted the door.

Unfortunately he was near enough to see her cross the room. He advanced to the door, knocked, and receiving no answer, came to the window; he next pressed his face against the glass, peering in.

Cytherea's experience at that moment was probably as trying a one as ever fell to the lot of a gentle woman to endure. She recognised in the peering face that of the man she had married.

But not a movement was made by her, not a sound escaped her. Her fear was great; but had she known the truth—that the man outside, feeling he had nothing on earth to lose by any act, was in the last stage of recklessness, terrified nature must have given way.

"Cytherea," he said, "let me come in: I am your husband."

"No," she replied, still not realising the magnitude of her peril. "If you want to speak to us, wait till my brother comes."

"O, he's not at home? Cytherea, I can't live without you! All my sin has been because I love you so! Will you fly with me? I have money enough for us both—only come with me."

"Not now—not now."

"I am your husband I tell you, and I must come in."

"You cannot," she said, faintly. His words began to terrify her.

"I will, I say!" he exclaimed. "Will you let me in, I ask once more?"

"No—I will not," said Cytherea.

"Then I will let myself in!" he answered, resolutely. "I will, if I die for it!"

The windows were glazed in lattice panes of leadwork, hung in casements. He broke one of the panes with a stone, thrust his hand through the hole, unfastened the latch which held the casement close, and began opening the window.

Instantly the shutters flew together with a slam, and were barred with desperate quickness by Cytherea on the inside.

"D——n you!" he exclaimed.

He ran round to the back of the house. His impatience was greater now: he thrust his fist through the pantry window at one blow, and opened it in the same way as the former one had been opened, before the terror-stricken girl was aware that he had gone round. In an instant he stood in the pantry, advanced to the front room where she was, flung back the shutters, and held out his arms to embrace her.

In extremely trying moments of bodily or mental pain, Cytherea either flushed hot, or faded pale, according to the state of her constitution at the moment. Now she burned like fire from head to foot, and this preserved her consciousness.

Never before had the poor child's natural agility served her in such good stead as now. A heavy oblong table stood in the middle of the room. Round this table she flew, keeping it between herself and Manston, her large eyes wide open with terror, their dilated pupils constantly fixed upon Manston's, to read by his expression whether his next intention was to dart to the right or the left.

Even he, at that heated moment, could not endure the expression of unutterable agony which shone from that extraordinary gaze of hers. It had surely been given her by God as a means of defence. Manston continued his pursuit with a lowered eye.

The panting and maddened demon*—blind to everything but the capture of his wife—went with a rush under the table: she went over it like a bird. He went heavily over it: she flew under it, and was out at the other side.

> "One on her youth and pliant limbs relies,
> One on his sinews and his giant size."*

But his superior strength was sure to tire her down in the long run. She felt her weakness increasing with the quickness of her breath: she uttered a wild scream, which in its heartrending intensity, seemed to echo for miles.

At the same juncture her hair became unfastened, and rolled down about her shoulders. The least accident at such critical periods is sufficient to confuse the overwrought intelligence. She lost sight of his intended direction for one instant, and he immediately out-manœuvred her.

"At last! my Cytherea!" he cried, overturning the table, springing over it, seizing one of the long brown tresses, pulling her towards him, and clasping her round. She writhed downwards between his arms and breast, and fell fainting on the floor. For the first time his action was leisurely. He lifted her upon the sofa, exclaiming, "Rest there for a while, my frightened little bird!"

And then there was an end of his triumph. He felt himself clutched by the collar, and whizzed backwards with the force of a battering-ram against the fireplace. Springrove, wild, red, and breathless, had sprung in at the open window, and stood once more between man and wife.

Manston was on his legs again in an instant. A fiery glance on the one side, a glance of pitiless justice on the other, passed between them.

It was again the meeting in the vineyard of Naboth the Jezreelite:

"Hast thou found me, O mine enemy? And he answered, I have found thee: because thou hast sold thyself to work evil in the sight of the Lord."*

A desperate wrestle now began between the two men. Manston was the taller, but there was in Edward much hard tough muscle which the delicate flesh of the steward lacked. They flew together like the jaws of a gin.* In a minute they were both on the floor, rolling over and over, locked in each other's grasp as tightly as if they had been one organic being at war with itself—Edward trying to secure Manston's arms with a small thong he had drawn from his pocket, Manston trying to reach his knife.

Two characteristic noises pervaded the apartment through this momentous space of time. One was the sharp panting of the two combatants, so similar in each as to be undistinguishable: the other was the stroke of their heels and toes, as they smote the floor at every contortion of body or limbs.

Cytherea had not lost consciousness for more than thirty seconds. She had then leapt up without recognising that Edward was her deliverer, unfastened the door, and rushed out, screaming wildly, "Come! Help! O help!"

Three men stood not twenty yards off, looking perplexed. They dashed forward at her words. "Have you seen a shabby man with a smock-frock on lately?" they inquired. She pointed to the door, and ran on the same as before.

Manston, who had just loosened himself from Edward's grasp, seemed at this moment to renounce his intention of pushing the conflict to a desperate end. "I give it all up for life—dear life!" he cried with a hoarse laugh. "A reckless man has a dozen lives—see how I'll baffle you all yet!"

He rushed out of the house, but no further. The boast was his last. In one half-minute more he was helpless in the hands of his pursuers.

Edward staggered to his feet, and paused to recover breath. His thoughts had never forsaken Cytherea, and his first act now was to hasten up the lane after her. She had not gone far. He found her leaning upon a bank by the roadside, where she had flung herself down in sheer exhaustion. He ran up and lifted her in his arms, and thus aided she was enabled to stand upright—clinging to him.

What would Springrove have given to imprint a kiss upon her lips then!

They walked slowly towards the house. The distressing sensation of whose wife she was, could not entirely quench the resuscitated pleasure he felt at her grateful recognition of him, and her confiding seizure of his arm for support. He conveyed her carefully into the house.

A quarter of an hour later, whilst she was sitting in a partially-recovered, half-dozing state in an arm-chair, Edward beside her waiting anxiously till Graye should arrive, they saw a spring-cart pass the door. Old and dry mudsplashes from long-forgotten rains disfigured its wheels and sides; the varnish and paint had been scratched and dimmed; ornament had long been forgotten in a restless contemplation of use. Three men sat on the seat, the middle one being Manston. His hands were bound in front of him, his eyes were set directly forward, his countenance pallid, hard, and fixed.

Springrove had told Cytherea of Manston's crime in a few short words. He now said solemnly, "He is to die."

"And I cannot mourn for him," she replied with a shudder, leaning back and covering her face with her hands.

In the silence that followed the two short remarks, Springrove watched the cart round the corner, and heard the rattle of its wheels gradually dying away as it rolled in the direction of Froominster.

CHAPTER VIII

THE EVENTS OF EIGHTEEN HOURS

§ 1. *March the twenty-ninth. Noon*

Exactly seven days after Edward Springrove had seen the man with the bundle of straw walking down the streets of Froominster, old Farmer Springrove was standing on the edge of the same pavement, talking to his friend Farmer Baker.

There was a pause in their discourse. Mr. Springrove was looking down the street at some object which had attracted his attention. "Ah, 'tis what we shall all come to," he murmured.

The other looked in the same direction. "True, neighbour Springrove; true."

Two men, advancing one behind the other in the middle of the road, were what the farmers referred to. They were carpenters, and bore on their shoulders an empty coffin, covered by a thin black cloth.

"I always feel a satisfaction at being breasted* by such a sight as that," said Springrove, still regarding the men's sad burden. "I call it a sort of medicine."

"And it is medicine . . . I have not heard of anybody being ill up this way lately? D'seem as if the person died suddenly."

"May be so. Ah, Baker, we say sudden death, don't we. But there's no difference in their nature between sudden death, and death of any other sort. There's no such thing as a random snappen off of what was laid down to last longer. We only suddenly light upon an end—thoughtfully formed as any other—which has been existen at that very same point from the beginnen, though unseen by us to be so soon."*

"It is just a discovery to your own mind, and not an alteration in the Lord's."

"That's it. Unexpected is not as to the thing, but as to our sight."

"Now you'll hardly believe me, neighbour, but this little scene in front of us d'make me feel less anxious about pushen on wi' that threshen and winnowen next week, that I was speaken about. Why should we not stand still, says I to myself, and fling a quiet eye upon the Whys and the Wherefores, before the end of it all, and we d'go down into the moulderen place, and are forgotten?"

" 'Tis a feelen that will come. But 'twont bear looken into. There's a backward current in the world, and we must do our utmost to advance in order just to bide where we be. But, Baker, they are turnen in here with the coffin, look."

The two carpenters had borne their load into a lane close at hand. The farmers, in common with others, turned and watched them along the lane.

" 'Tis a man's coffin, and a tall man's, too," continued Farmer Springrove. "His was a fine frame, whoever he was."

"A very plain box for the poor soul—just the rough elm, you see." The corner of the cloth had blown aside.

"Yes, for a very poor man. Well, death's all the less insult to him. I have often thought how far the richer class sink into insignificance beside the poor on extreme occasions like this. Perhaps the greatest of all the reconcilers of a thoughtful mind to poverty—and I speak from experience—is the grand quietness it possesses him with when the uncertainty of his life shows itself more vividly than usual."

As Springrove finished speaking, the bearers of the coffin went across a gravelled square facing the end of the lane, and approached a grim and massive archway. They paused beneath it, rang a bell, and waited.

Over the archway was written in Egyptian capitals,

"COUNTY GAOL."

The small rectangular wicket, which was constructed in one of the two iron-studded doors, was opened from the inside. The men severally stepped over the threshold, the coffin dragged its melancholy length through the aperture, and both entered the court, and were covered from sight.

"Somebody in the gaol, then?"

"Yes, one of the prisoners," said a boy, scudding by at the moment, and who passed on whistling.

"Do you know the name of the man who is dead?" inquired Baker of a third bystander.

"Yes, 'tis all over town—surely you know, Mr. Springrove? Why Manston, Miss Aldclyffe's steward. He was found dead the first thing this morning. He had hung himself behind the door of his cell, in some way, by a handkerchief and some strips of his clothes. The turnkey* says his features were scarcely changed, and just caught the early sunlight shining in at the grating upon him. He has left a complete account of the murder, and all that led to it. So there's an end of him."

It was perfectly true: Manston was dead.

The previous day he had been allowed the use of writing materials, and had occupied himself for nearly seven hours in preparing the following confession.

"LAST WORDS."

"HAVING FOUND man's life to be a wretchedly conceived scheme, I renounce it, and to cause no further trouble, I write down the facts connected with my past proceedings.

"After thanking God, on first entering my house, on the night of the fire at Carriford, for my release from bondage to a woman I detested, I went, a second time, to the scene of the disaster, and, finding that nothing could be done by remaining there, shortly afterwards I returned home again in the company of Mr. Raunham.

"He parted from me at the steps of my porch, and went back towards the rectory. Whilst I still stood at the door, musing on my strange deliverance, I saw a figure advance from beneath the shadow of the park trees. It was the figure of a woman.

"When she came near, the twilight was sufficient to show me her attire: it was a cloak reaching to the bottom of her dress, and a thick veil covering her face. These features, together with her size and gait, aided also by a flash of perception as to the chain of events which had saved her life, told me that she was my wife Eunice.

"I gnashed my teeth in a frenzy of despair; I had lost Cytherea; I had gained one whose beauty had departed, whose utterance was complaint, whose mind was shallow, and who drank brandy every day. The revulsion of feeling was terrible. Providence, whom I had just thanked, seemed a mocking tormentor laughing at me. I felt like a madman.

"She came close—started at seeing me outside—then spoke to me. Her first words were reproof for what I had unintentionally done, and sounded as an earnest* of what I was to be cursed with as long as we both lived. I answered angrily; this tone of mine changed her complaints to irritation. She taunted me with a secret she had discovered, which concerned Miss Aldclyffe and myself. I was surprised to learn it—more surprised that she knew it, but concealed my feeling.

" 'How could you serve me so?' she said, her breath smelling of brandy even then. 'You love another woman—yes, you do. See how you drive me about! I have been to the station, intending to leave you for ever, and yet I come to try you once more.'

"An indescribable exasperation had sprung up in me as she talked—rage and regret were all in all. Scarcely knowing what I did, I furiously raised my hand and swung it round with my whole force to strike her. She turned quickly—and it was the poor creature's end. By her movement my hand came edgewise exactly in the nape of her neck—as men strike a hare to kill it. The effect staggered me with amazement. The blow must have disturbed the vertebræ: she fell at my feet, made a few movements, and uttered one low sound.

"I ran indoors for water and some wine; I came out and lanced her arm with my pen-knife.* But she lay still, and I found that she was dead.

"It was a long time before I could realise my horrible position.

"For several minutes I had no idea of attempting to escape the consequences of my deed. Then a light broke upon me. Had anybody seen her since she left the Three Tranters? Had they not, she was already believed by the parishioners to be dust and ashes. I should never be found out.

"Upon this I acted.

"The first question was how to dispose of the body. The impulse of the moment was to bury her at once in the pit between the engine-house and waterfall; but it struck me that I should not have time. It was now four o'clock, and the working men would soon be stirring about the place. I would put off burying her till the next night. I carried her indoors.

"In turning the outhouse into a workshop, earlier in the season, I found, when driving a nail into the wall for fixing a cupboard, that the wall sounded hollow. I examined it, and discovered behind the plaster an old oven which had long been disused, and was bricked up when the house was prepared for me.

"To unfix this cupboard and pull out the bricks was the work of a few minutes. Then, bearing in mind that I should have to remove the body again the next night, I placed it in a sack, pushed it into the oven, packed in the bricks, and replaced the cupboard.

"I then went to bed.

"In bed, I thought whether there were any very remote possibilities that might lead to the supposition that my wife was not consumed by the flames of the burning house. The thing which struck me most forcibly was this, that the searchers might think it odd that no remains whatever should be found.

"The clinching and triumphant deed would be to take the body and place it among the ruins of the destroyed house. But I could not do this, on account of the men who were watching against an outbreak of the fire. One remedy remained.

"I arose again, dressed myself, and went down to the outhouse. I must take down the cupboard again. I did take it down. I pulled out the bricks, pulled out the sack, pulled out the corpse, and took her keys from her pocket and the watch from her side.

"I then replaced everything as before.

"With these articles in my pocket I went out of the yard, and took my way through the withy copse to the churchyard, entering it from the back. Here I felt my way carefully along till I came to the nook where pieces of bones from newly-dug graves are sometimes piled behind the laurel bushes. I had been earnestly hoping to find a skull among these old bones; but though I had frequently seen one or two in the rubbish here, there was not one now. I then groped in the other corner with the same result—nowhere could I find a skull. Three or four fragments of leg and back-bones were all I could collect, and with these I was forced to be content.

"Taking them in my hand, I crossed the road, and got round behind the inn, where the couch-heap* was still smouldering. Keeping behind the hedge, I could see the heads of the three or four men who watched the spot.

"Standing in this place I took the bones, and threw them one by one over the hedge and over the men's heads into the smoking embers. When the bones had all been thrown, I threw the keys: last of all I threw the watch.

"I then returned home as I had gone, and went to bed once more, just as the dawn began to break. I exulted—'Cytherea is mine again!'

"At breakfast-time I thought, 'Suppose the cupboard should by some unlikely chance get moved to-day!'

"I went to the mason's yard hard by, while the men were at breakfast, and brought away a shovel-full of mortar. I took it into the outhouse, again shifted the cupboard, and plastered over the mouth of the oven behind. Simply pushing the cupboard back into its place, I waited for the next night that I might bury the body, though upon the whole it was in a tolerably safe hiding-place.

"When the night came, my nerves were in some way weaker than they had been on the previous night. I felt reluctant to touch the body. I went to the outhouse, but instead of opening the oven, I firmly drove in the shoulder-nails* that held the cupboard to the wall. 'I will bury her to-morrow night, however,' I thought.

"But the next night I was still more reluctant to touch her. And my reluctance increased, and there the body remained. The oven was, after all, never likely to be opened in my time.

"I married Cytherea Graye, and never did a bridegroom leave the church with a heart more full of love and happiness, and a brain more fixed on good intentions, than I did on that morning.

"When Cytherea's brother made his appearance at the hotel in Southampton, bearing his strange evidence of the porter's disclosure, I was staggered beyond expression. I thought they had found the body. 'Am I to be apprehended and to lose her even now?' I mourned. I saw my error, and instantly saw, too, that I must act externally like an honourable man.

"So at his request I yielded her up to him, and meditated on several schemes for enabling me to claim the woman I had a legal right to claim as my wife, without disclosing the reason why I knew myself to have it.

"I went home to Knapwater the next day, and for nearly a week lived in a state of indecision. I could not hit upon a scheme for proving my wife dead without compromising myself.

"Mr. Raunham hinted that I should take steps to discover her whereabouts by advertising. I had no energy for the farce.

"But one evening I chanced to enter the Travellers' Rest inn.

"Two notorious poachers were sitting in the settle, which screened my entrance. They were half-drunk—their conversation was carried on in the solemn and emphatic tone common to that stage of intoxication, and I myself was the subject of it.

"The following was the substance of their disjointed remarks.

"On the night of the great fire at Carriford, one of them was sent to meet me, and break the news of the death of my wife to me. This he did; but because I would not pay him for his news, he left me in a mood of vindictiveness. When the fire was over, he joined his comrade. The favourable hour of the night suggested to them the possibility of some unlawful gain before daylight came. My fowl-house stood in a tempting position, and still resenting his repulse during the evening, one of them proposed to operate upon my birds.* I was believed to have gone to the rectory with Mr. Raunham. The other was disinclined to go, and the first went off alone.

"It was now about three o'clock. He had advanced as far as the shrubbery, which grows near the north wall of the house, when he fancied he heard, above the rush of the waterfall, noises on the other side of the building. He described them in these words, 'Ghostly mouths talking*—then a fall—then a groan—then the rush of the water and creak of the engine as before.' Only one explanation occurred to him: the house was haunted. And, whether those of the living or the dead, voices of any kind were inimical to one who had come on such an errand. He stealthily crept home.

"His unlawful purpose in being behind the house led him to conceal his adventure. No suspicion of the truth entered his mind till the railway-porter had startled everybody by his strange announcement. Then he asked himself, had the horrifying sounds of that night been really an enactment in the flesh between me and my wife?

"The words of the other man were,—

" 'Why don't he try to find her if she's alive?'

" 'True,' said the first. 'Well, I don't forget what I heard, and if she don't turn up alive my mind will be as sure as a bible upon her murder, and the parson shall know it, though I do get six months on the treadmill for being where I was.'

" 'And if she should turn up alive?'

" 'Then I shall know that I am wrong, and believing myself a fool as well as a rogue, hold my tongue.'

"I glided out of the house in a cold sweat. The only pressure in heaven or earth which could have forced me to renounce Cytherea was now put upon me—the dread of a death upon the gallows.

"I sat all that night weaving strategy of various kinds. The only effectual remedy for my hazardous standing that I could see, was a simple one. It was to substitute another woman for my wife before the suspicions of that one easily-hoodwinked man extended further.

"The only difficulty was to find a practicable substitute.

"The one woman at all available for the purpose was a friendless, innocent creature, named Anne Seaway, whom I had known in my youth, and who had for some time been the housekeeper of a lady in London. On account of this lady's sudden death, Anne stood in rather a precarious position, as regarded her future subsistence. She was not the best kind of woman for the scheme; but there was no alternative. One quality of hers was valuable: she was not a talker. I went to London the very next day, called at the Hoxton lodging of my wife (the only place at which she had been known as Mrs. Manston), and found that no great difficulties stood in the way of a personation. And thus favouring circumstances determined my course. I visited Anne Seaway, made love to her, and propounded my plan.

*   *   *   *   *   *   *   *   *   *

"We lived quietly enough until the Sunday before my apprehension. Anne came home from church that morning, and told me of the suspicious way in which a young man had looked at her there. Nothing could be done beyond waiting the issue of events. Then the letter came from Raunham. For the first time in my life I was half-indifferent as to what fate awaited me. During the succeeding day I thought once or twice of running away, but could not quite make up my mind. At any rate it would be best to bury the body of my wife, I thought, for the oven might be opened at any time. I went to Froominster and made some arrangements. In the evening Miss Aldclyffe (who is united to me by a common secret which I have no right or wish to disclose) came to my house, and alarmed me still more. She said that she could tell by Mr. Raunham's manner that evening, that he kept back from her a suspicion of more importance even than the one he spoke of, and that strangers were in his house even then.

"I guessed what this further suspicion was, and resolved to enlighten her to a certain extent, and so secure her assistance. I said that I killed my wife by an accident on the night of the fire, dwelling upon the advantage to her of the death of the only woman who knew her secret.

"Her terror, and fears for my fate, led her to watch the rectory that evening. She saw the detective leave it, and followed him to my residence. This she told me hurriedly when I perceived her after digging my wife's grave in the plantation. She did not suspect what the sack contained.

"I am now about to pass into my normal condition. For people are almost always in their graves. When we survey the long race of men, it is strange and still more strange to find that they are mainly dead men, who have scarcely ever been otherwise.

"ÆNEAS MANSTON."

The steward's confession, aided by circumstantial evidence of various kinds, was the means of freeing both Anne Seaway and Miss Aldclyffe from all suspicion of complicity with the murderer.

§ 2. *Six o'clock p.m.*

It was evening—just at sunset—on the day of Manston's death.

In the little cottage at Palchurch was gathered a group consisting of Cytherea, her brother, Edward Springrove, and his father. They sat by the window conversing of the strange events which had just taken place. In Cytherea's eye there beamed a hopeful ray, though her face was as white as a lily.

Whilst they talked, looking out at the yellow evening light that coated the hedges, trees, and church tower, a brougham rolled round the corner of the lane, and came in full view. It reflected the rays of the sun in a flash from its polished panels as it turned the angle, the spokes of the wheels bristling in the same light like bayonets. The vehicle came nearer, and arrived opposite Owen's door, when the driver pulled the rein and gave a shout, and the panting and sweating horses stopped.

"Miss Aldclyffe's carriage!" they all exclaimed.

Owen went out. "Is Miss Graye at home?" said the man. "A note for her, and I am to wait for an answer."

Cytherea read in the handwriting of the rector of Carriford:—

"DEAR MISS GRAYE,

"Miss Aldclyffe is ill, though not dangerously. She continually repeats your name, and now wishes very much to see you. If you possibly can, come in the carriage.

"Very sincerely yours,
"JOHN RAUNHAM."

"How comes she ill?" Owen inquired of the coachman.

"She caught a violent cold by standing out of doors in the damp on the night the steward ran away. Ever since, till this morning, she complained of fulness and heat in the chest. This morning the maid ran in and told her suddenly that Manston had killed himself in gaol—she shrieked—broke a blood-vessel—and fell upon the floor.* Severe internal hæmorrhage continued for some time and then stopped. They say she is sure to get over it: but she herself says no. She has suffered from it before."

Cytherea was ready in a few moments, and entered the carriage.

§3. *Seven o'clock, p.m.*

Soft as was Cytherea's motion along the corridors of Knapwater House, the preternaturally keen intelligence of the suffering woman caught the maiden's well-known foot-fall. She entered the sick chamber with suspended breath.

In the room everything was so still, and sensation was as it were so rarefied by solicitude, that thinking seemed acting, and the lady's weak act of trying to live a silent wrestling with all the powers of the universe. Nobody was present but Mr. Raunham, the nurse having left the room on Cytherea's entry, and the physician and surgeon being engaged in a whispered conversation in a side chamber. Their patient had been pronounced out of danger.

Cytherea went to the bedside, and was instantly recognised. O what a change—Miss Aldclyffe dependent upon pillows! And yet not a forbidding change. With weakness had come softness of aspect: the haughtiness was extracted from the frail thin countenance, and a sweeter mild placidity had taken its place.

Miss Aldclyffe signified to Mr. Raunham that she would like to be alone with Cytherea.

"Cytherea?" she faintly whispered, the instant the door was closed.

Cytherea clasped the lady's weak hand, and sank beside her.

Miss Aldclyffe whispered again. "They say I am certain to live; but I know that I am certainly going to die."

"They know, I think, and hope."

"I know best, but we'll leave that. Cytherea—O Cytherea, can you forgive me!"

Her companion pressed her hand.

"But you don't know yet—you don't know yet," the invalid mur-mured. "It is forgiveness for that misrepresentation to Edward Springrove that I implore, and for putting such force upon him—that which caused all the train of your innumerable ills!"

"I know all—all. And I do forgive you. Not in a hasty impulse that is revoked when coolness comes, but deliberately and sincerely:—as I myself hope to be forgiven, I accord you my forgiveness now."

Tears streamed from Miss Aldclyffe's eyes, and mingled with those of her young companion, who could not restrain hers for sym-pathy. Expressions of strong attachment, interrupted by emotion, burst again and again from the broken-spirited woman.

"But you don't know my motive. O, if you only knew it, how you would pity me then!"

Cytherea did not break the pause which ensued, and the elder woman appeared now to nerve herself by a superhuman effort. She spoke on in a voice weak as a summer breeze, and full of intermis-sion, and yet there pervaded it a steadiness of intention that seemed to demand firm tones to bear it out worthily.

"Cytherea," she said, "listen to me before I die.

"A long time ago—more than thirty years ago—a young girl of seventeen was cruelly betrayed by her cousin, a wild officer of six and twenty . . . He went to India, and died.

"One night, when that miserable girl had just arrived home from Germany with her parents,* she took all the money she possessed, pinned it on an infant's bosom, together with a letter, stating, among other things, what she wished the child's christian name to be; wrapped up the little thing, and walked with it to Clapham. Here in a retired street she selected a house. She placed the child on the door-step and knocked at the door, then ran away and watched. They took it up and carried it indoors.

"Now that her poor baby was gone, the girl blamed herself bitterly for cruelty towards it, and wished she had adopted her parents' counsel to secretly hire a nurse. She longed to see it. She didn't know what to do. She wrote in an assumed name to the woman who had taken it in and asked her to meet the writer with the infant, at certain places she named. These were hotels or coffee-houses in Chelsea, Pimlico, or Hammersmith. The woman, being well paid, always came, and asked no questions. At one meeting—at an inn in

Hammersmith—she made her appearance without the child, and told the girl it was so ill that it would not live through the night. The news, and fatigue, brought on a fainting-fit. . . . ."

Miss Aldclyffe's sobs choked her utterance, and she became painfully agitated. Cytherea, pale and amazed at what she heard, wept for her, bent over her, and begged her not to go on speaking.

"Yes—I must," she cried between her sobs. "I will—I must go on! And I must tell yet more plainly! . . . . you must hear it before I am gone, Cytherea." The sympathising and astonished girl sat down again.

"The name of the woman who had taken the child was *Manston*. She was the widow of a schoolmaster. She said she had adopted the child of a relation.

"Only one man ever found out who the mother was. He was the keeper of the inn in which she fainted, and his silence she has purchased ever since.

"A twelvemonth passed—fifteen months—and the saddened girl met a man at her father's house. Ah, such a man! Inexperience now perceived what it was to be loved in spirit and in truth! But it was too late. Had he known her secret he would have cast her out. She withdrew from him by an effort, and pined.

"Years and years afterwards, when she became mistress of a fortune and estates by her father's death, she formed the weak scheme of having near the son whom, in her father's lifetime, she had been forbidden to recognise. Cytherea, you know who that weak woman is!

*   *   *   *   *   *   *   *   *   *

"By such toilsome labour as this I got him here as my steward. And I wanted to see him *your husband*, Cytherea! It was a sweet dream to me. . . . . Pity me—O pity me! To die unloved is more than I can bear! I loved your father, and I love him now."

That was the burden of Cytherea Aldclyffe.

"I suppose you must leave me again—you always leave me," she said, after holding the young woman's hand a long while in silence.

"No—indeed I'll stay always. Do you like me to stay?"

Miss Aldclyffe in the jaws of death was Miss Aldclyffe still, though the old fire had degenerated to mere phosphorescence now. "But you are your brother's housekeeper?"

"Yes."

"Well, of course you cannot stay with me on a sudden like this. . . . . Go home, or he will be at a loss for things. And to-morrow morning come again, won't you dearest, come again—we'll fetch you. But you mustn't stay now, and put Owen out. O no—it would be absurd." The absorbing concern about trifles of daily routine, which is so often seen in very sick people, was present here.

Cytherea promised to go home, and come the next morning to stay continuously.

"Stay till I die then, will you not? Yes till I die—I shan't die till to-morrow."

"We hope for your recovery—all of us."

"I know best. Come at six o'clock, darling."

"As soon as ever I can," returned Cytherea, tenderly.

"But six is too early—you will have to think of your brother's breakfast. Leave Palchurch at eight, will you?"

Cytherea consented to this. Miss Aldclyffe would never have known had her companion stayed in the house all night, but the honesty of Cytherea's nature rebelled against even the friendly deceit which such a proceeding would have involved.

An arrangement was come to whereby she was to be taken home in the pony-carriage instead of the brougham that fetched her. The carriage to put up at Palchurch farm for the night, and on that account be in readiness to bring her back earlier.

§ 4. *March the thirtieth. Daybreak*

The third and last instance of Cytherea's subjection to those periodic terrors of the night which had emphasised her connection with the Aldclyffe name and blood, transpired at the present date.

It was about four o'clock in the morning when Cytherea, though most probably dreaming, seemed to awake,—and instantly was transfixed by a sort of spell, that had in it more of awe than of affright. At the foot of her bed, looking her in the face with an expression of entreaty beyond the power of words to portray, was the form of Miss Aldclyffe—wan and distinct. No motion was perceptible in her; but longing—earnest longing—was written in every feature.

Cytherea believed she exercised her waking judgment as usual in thinking, without a shadow of doubt, that Miss Aldclyffe stood before her in flesh and blood. Reason was not sufficiently alert to lead Cytherea to ask herself how such a thing could have occurred.

"I would have remained with you,—why would you not allow me to!" Cytherea exclaimed. The spell was broken: she became broadly awake; and the figure vanished.

It was in the grey time of dawn. She trembled in a sweat of disquiet, and not being able to endure the thought of her brother being asleep, she went and tapped at his door.

"Owen!"

He was not a heavy sleeper, and it was verging upon his time to rise.

"What do you want, Cytherea?"

"I ought not to have left Knapwater last night. I wish I had not. I really think I will start at once. She wants me, I know."

"What time is it?"

"A few minutes past four."

"You had better not. Keep to the time agreed upon. Consider, we should have such a trouble in rousing the driver, and other things."

Upon the whole it seemed wiser not to act on a mere fancy. She went to bed again.

An hour later, when Owen was thinking of getting up, a knocking came to the front door. The next minute something touched the glass of Owen's window. He waited—the noise was repeated. A little gravel had been thrown against it to arouse him.

He crossed the room, pulled up the blind, and looked out. A solemn white face was gazing upwards from the road, expectantly straining to catch the first glimpse of a person within the panes. It was the face of a Knapwater man, sitting on horseback.

Owen saw his errand. There is an unmistakable look in the face of every man who brings tidings of death. Graye opened the window.

"Miss Aldclyffe . . . . .," said the messenger, and paused.

"Ah; and is she dead?"

"Yes—she is dead."

"When did she die?"

"At ten minutes past four, after another effusion. She knew best, you see, sir. I started directly, by the rector's orders."

EPILOGUE

Fifteen months have passed, and we are brought on to midsummer night,* one thousand eight hundred and sixty-seven.

The picture presented is the interior of the old belfry of Carriford Church, at ten o'clock in the evening.

Eight Carriford men and one stranger are gathered there, beneath the light of a flaring candle stuck on a piece of wood against the wall. The eight Carriford men are the well-known ringers of the eight fine-toned old bells in the key of F, which have been music to the ears of Carriford parish and the outlying districts for the last four hundred years. The stranger is an assistant, who has appeared from nobody knows where.

The eight natives—in their shirt-sleeves, and without hats—pull and catch frantically at the dancing bell-ropes, the locks of their hair waving in the breeze created by their quick motions: the stranger, who has the treble bell, does likewise, but in his right mind and coat. Their ever-changing shadows mingle on the wall in an endless variety of kaleidoscopic forms, and the eyes of all the nine are religiously fixed on a diagram like a large addition sum, which is chalked on the floor.

Vividly contrasting with the yellow light of the candle upon the four unplastered walls of the tower, and upon the faces and clothes of the men, is the scene discernible through the screen beneath the tower archway. At the extremity of the long mysterious avenue of the nave and chancel can be seen shafts of moonlight streaming in at the east window of the church—blue, phosphoric,* and ghostly.

A thorough renovation of the bell-ringing machinery and accessories had taken place in anticipation of an interesting event. New ropes had been provided; every bell had been carefully shifted from its carriage, and the pivots lubricated. Bright red "sallies"* of woollen texture—soft to the hands and easily caught—glowed on the ropes in place of the old ragged knots, all of which newness in small details only rendered more evident the irrepressible aspect of age in the mass surrounding them.

The triple-bob-major* was ended, and the ringers wiped their faces and rolled down their shirt-sleeves, previously to tucking away the ropes and leaving the place for the night.

"Piph—h—h—h! A good twenty minutes," said a man with a streaming face, and blowing out his breath—one of the pair who had taken the tenor bell.*

"Our friend here pulled proper well—that 'a did—seën he's but a stranger," said Clerk Crickett, who had just resigned the second rope, and addressing the man in the black coat.

" 'A did," said the rest.

"I enjoyed it much," said the man, modestly.

"What we should ha' done 'ithout ye, words can't tell. The man that d'belong by rights to that there bell is ill o' two gallons o' wold cider."

"And now so's," remarked the fifth ringer, its pertaining to the last allusion, "we'll finish this drop o' metheglin* and cider, and every man home-along straight as a line."

"Wi' all my heart," Clerk Crickett replied. "And the Lord send if I ha'n't done my duty by Master Teddy Springrove—that I have so."

"And the rest o' us," they said, as the cup was handed round.

"Ay, ay—in ringen—but I was spaken in a spiritual sense o' this mornen's business o' mine up by the chancel rails there. 'Twas very convenient to lug her here and marry her instead o' doen it at that twopenny-halfpenny town o' Cres'n. Very convenient."

"Very. There was a little fee for Master Crickett."

"Ah—well. Money's money—very much so,—very—I always have said it. But 'twas a pretty sight for the nation. 'A coloured up like any maid, that 'a did."

"Well enough 'a mid colour up. 'Tis no small matter for a man to play wi' fire."*

"Whatever it may be to a woman," said the clerk, absently.

"Thou'rt thinken o' thy wife, clerk," said Gad Weedy. "She'll play wi'it again* when thou'st get mildewed."

"Well—let her, God bless her; for I'm but a poor third man,* I. The Lord have mercy upon the fourth . . . . Ay, Teddy's got his own at last. What little white ears that maid hev to be sure! choose your wife as you d'choose your pig—a small ear and a small tale—that was always my joke when I was a merry feller, ah,—years agone now! But Teddy's got her. Poor chap, he was getten as thin as a hermit wi' grief,—so was she."

"May be she'll pick up again now."

"True—'tis nater's law, which no man shall gainsay.* Ah, well do I bear in mind what I said to Pa'son Raunham, about thy mother's family o' seven, Gad, the very first week of his comen here, when I was just in my prime. 'And how many daughters has that poor Weedy got, clerk?' he says. 'Six, sir,' says I, 'and every one of 'em has a brother!' 'Poor woman,' says he 'a dozen children!—give her this half-sovereign from me, clerk.' 'A laughed a good five minutes afterwards, when he found out my merry nater*—'a did. But there, 'tis over wi' me now. Enteren the Church is the ruin of a man's wit, for wit's nothen without a faint shadder o' sin."

"If so be Teddy and the lady had been kept apart for life, they'd both ha' died," said Gad emphatically.

"It went proper well," said the fifth bell-ringer. "They didn't flee off to Babylonish places*—not they." He struck up an attitude— "Here's Master Springrove standen so: here's the married woman standen likewise: here they d'walk across to Knapwater House: and there they d'bide in the chimley corner, hard and fast."

"Yes, 'twas a pretty wedden, and well attended," added the clerk. "Here was my lady herself—red as scarlet: here was Master Springrove, looken as if he half-wished he'd never a-come,—Ah, toads o'em!*—the men always do! The women do stand it best—the maid was in her glory. Though she was so shy, the glory shone plain through that shy skin. Ah, it did so's."

"Ay," said Gad, "and there was Tim Tankins and his fine journeyman carpenters, standen tiptoe and peepen in at the chancel winders. There was Dairyman Dodman waiten in his new spring-cart to see 'em come out—whip in hand—that 'a was. Then up comes two master tailors. Then there was Christopher Runt wi' his pickaxe and shovel. There was wimmen-folk and there was menfolk traypsen* up and down church'ard till they wore a path wi' traypsen so—letten the squallen children slip down through their arms and nearly skinnen o' em. And these were all over and above the gentry and Sunday-clothes folk inside. Well, I sid Mr. Graye dressed up quite the dand.* 'Well Mr. Graye,' says I, from the top o' church'ard wall, 'How's yerself?' Mr. Graye never spoke—he'd dressed away his hearen. Seize the man, I didn' want en to spak. Teddy hears it, and turns round: 'Right Gad!' says he, and laughed like a boy. There's more in Teddy."

"Well," said Clerk Crickett, turning to the man in black, "now you've been among us so long, and d'know us so well, won't ye tell us what ye d'come here for, and what your trade is?"

"I am no trade,"* said the thin man, smiling, "and I came to see the wickedness of the land."

"I said thou wast one o' the devil's brood wi' thy black clothes," replied a sturdy ringer, who had not spoken before.

"No, the truth is," said the thin man, retracting at this horrible translation, "I came for a walk because it is a fine evening."

"Now let's be off, neighbours," the clerk interrupted.

The candle was inverted in the socket, and the whole party stepped out into the churchyard. The moon was shining within a day or two of full, and just overlooked the three or four vast yews that stood on the south-east side of the church, and rose in unvaried and flat darkness against the illuminated atmosphere behind them.

"Good-night," the clerk said to his comrades, when the door was locked. "My nearest way is through the park."

"I suppose mine is too?" said the stranger. "I am going to the railway station."

"Of course—come on."

The two men went over a stile to the west, the remainder of the party going into the road on the opposite side.

"And so the romance has ended well," the clerk's companion remarked, as they brushed along through the grass. "But what is the truth of the story about the property?"

"Now look here, neighbour," said Clerk Crickett. "If so be you'll tell me what your line o' life is, and your purpose in comen here to-day, I'll tell you the truth about the wedden particulars."

"Very well—I will when you have done," said the other man.

" 'Tis a bargain; and this is the right o' the story. When Miss Aldclyffe's will was opened it was found to have been drawn up on the very day that Manston (her sly-gotten*) married Miss Cytherea Graye. And this is what that deep woman did. Deep? she was as deep as the North Star.* She bequeathed all her property, real and personal, to 'the wife of Æneas Manston' (with one exception): failen her life to her husband: failen his life to the hairs of his head—body I would say: failen them to her absolutely and her heirs for ever: failen these to Pa'son Raunham, and so on to the end o' the world. Now do you see the depth of her scheme? Why, although upon the surface it appeared her whole property was for Miss Cytherea, by the word '*wife*' beën used, and not Cytherea's name, whoever was the wife o' Manston would come in for't. Wasn't that rale depth? It was done, of course, that her son Æneas, under any circumstances, should be master o' the property, without folk known it was her son or suspecting anything, as they would if it had been left to en straightway."

"A clever arrangement. And what was the exception?"

"The payment of a legacy to her relative, Pa'son Raunham."

"And Miss Cytherea was now Manston's widow and only relative, and inherited all absolutely."

"True, she did. 'Well,' says she, 'I shan't have it,' (she didn't like the notion o'getten anything through Manston, naturally enough, pretty dear). She waived her right in favour o' Mr. Raunham. Now, if there's a man in the world that d'care nothen about land—I don't say there is, but *if* there is—'tis our pa'son. He's like a snail. He's a-growed so to the shape o' that there rectory that 'a wouldn' think o'leaven it even in name. ' 'Tis yours, Miss Graye,' says he. 'No, 'tis yours,' says she. 'Tisn' mine,' says he. The Crown had cast his eyes upon the case, thinken o' forfeiture by felony,* —but 'twas no such thing, and 'a gied it up too. Did you ever hear such a tale?—three people, a man and a woman, and a Crown—neither o' em in a mad-house—flingen an estate backwards and forwards like an apple or nut? Well, it ended in this way. Mr. Raunham took it: young Springrove was had as agent and steward, and put to live in Knapwater House, close here at hand—just as if 'twas his own. He d'do just what he d'like—Mr. Raunham never interferen—and hither to day he's brought his new wife Cytherea. And a settlement ha' been drawn up this very day, whereby their children, heirs, and cetrer, be to inherit after Mr. Raunham's death. Good fortune came at last. Her brother, too, is doen well. He came in first man in some architectural competition,* and is about to move to London. Here's the house, look. Stap out from these bushes, and you'll get a clear sight o't."

They emerged from the shrubbery, breaking off towards the lake, and down the south slope. When they arrived exactly opposite the centre of the mansion, they halted.

It was a magnificent picture of the English country-house. The whole of the severe regular front, with its columns and cornices, were built of a white smoothly-faced freestone, which appeared in the rays of the moon as pure as Pentelic marble.* The sole objects in the scene rivalling the fairness of the façade, were a dozen swans* floating upon the lake.

At this moment the central door at the top of the steps was opened, and two figures advanced into the light. Two contrasting figures were they. A young lithe woman in an airy fairy dress—Cytherea Springrove: a young man in black stereotype raiment—Edward, her husband.

They stood at the top of the steps together, looking at the moon, the water, and the general loveliness of the prospect.

"That's the married man and wife—there, I've illustrated my story by rale liven specimens," the clerk whispered.

"To be sure how close together they do stand! You couldn' slip a penny-piece between 'em—that you couldn'! Beautiful to see it, is'nt it—beautiful! . . . . But this is a private path and we won't let'em see us, as all the ringers be goen there to a supper and dance to-morrow night."

The speaker and his companion softly moved on, passed through the wicket, and into the coach-road. Arrived at the clerk's house at the farther boundary of the park, they paused to part.

"Now for your half o' the bargain," said Clerk Crickett. "What's your line o' life, and what d'ye come here for?"

"I'm the reporter to the *Froominster Chronicle*, and I come to pick up news. Good-night."

Meanwhile Edward and Cytherea, after lingering on the steps for several minutes, slowly descended the slope to the lake. The skiff was lying alongside.

"O Edward," said Cytherea, "you must do something that has just come into my head!"

"Well, dearest—I know."

"Yes—give me one half-minute's row on the lake here now, just as you did on Creston Bay three years ago."

He handed her into the boat, and almost noiselessly pulled off from shore. When they were halfway between the two margins of the lake, he paused and looked at her.

"Ah, darling, I remember exactly how I kissed you that first time," said Springrove. "You were there as you are now. I unshipped the sculls in this way. Then I turned round and sat beside you—in this way. Then I put my hand on the other side of your little neck—"

"I think it was just on my cheek, in this way."

"Ah, so it was. Then you moved that soft red mouth round to mine—"

"But dearest—you pressed it round if you remember; and of course I couldn't then help letting it come to your mouth without being unkind to you, and I wouldn't be that."

"And then I put my cheek against that cheek, and turned my two lips round upon those two lips, and kissed them——so."

THE END

APPENDIX 1

Hardy's Poems 'dissolved into' *Desperate Remedies*

In his 1912 addition to the Preface to *Desperate Remedies*, Hardy points out for the first time that the novel contains passages 'the same in substance with some in the *Wessex Poems* and others published many years later'. This, he explains, was his way of getting them into print after earlier rejection. He describes himself as taking relevant parts of their content and 'dissolving it into prose'. It is possible to identify some of the Wessex Poems that Hardy 'dissolved', and their texts are given below, along with references to passages in the novel that they relate to.[1]

1. *'The Heiress and the Architect'* (i. 98)

She sought the Studios, beckoning to her side
An arch-designer, for she planned to build.
He was of wise contrivance, deeply skilled
In every intervolve for high and wide—
    Well fit to be her guide.

      'Whatever it be,'
      Responded he,
With cold, clear voice, and cold, clear view,
'In true accord with prudent fashionings
For such vicissitudes as living brings,
And thwarting note the law of stable things,
    That will I do.'

'Shape me', she said, 'high halls with tracery
And open ogive-work, that scent and hue
Of buds, and travelling bees, may come in through,
The note of birds, and singings of the sea,
    For these are much to me.'

      'An idle whim!'
      Broke forth from him

---

[1] See P. Dalziel, 'Exploiting the *Poor Man*: The Genesis of Hardy's *Desperate Remedies*', *Journal of English and Gemanic Philology*, 94: 2 (1995), 228–31, and M. Millgate, *Thomas Hardy: His Career as a Novelist* (London: Bodley Head, 1971), 34 and 364. References are to volume and page of S. Hynes (ed.), *The Complete Poetical Works of Thomas Hardy* (Oxford: Clarendon Press, 1987), 2 vols.

Whom nought could warm to gallantries:
'Cede all these buds and birds, the zephyr's call,
And scents, and hues, and things that falter all,
And choose as best the close and surly wall,
     For winters freeze.'

'Then frame', she cried, 'wide fronts of crystal glass,
That I may show my laughter and my light—
Light like the sun's by day, the stars' by night—
Till rival heart-queens, envying, wail, "Alas,
     Her glory!" as they pass.'

     'O maid misled!'
     He sternly said
Whose facile foresight pierced her dire;
'Where shall abide the soul when, sick of glee,
It shrinks, and hides, and prays no eye may see?
Those house them best who house for secrecy,
     For you will tire.'

'A little chamber, then, with swan and dove
Ranged thickly, and engrailed with rare device
Of reds and purples, for a Paradise
Wherein my Love may greet me, I my Love,
     When he shall know thereof?'

     'This, too, is ill,'
     He answered still,
The man who swayed her like a shade.
'An hour will come when sight of such sweet nook
Would bring a bitterness too sharp to brook,
When brighter eyes have won away his look;
     For you will fade.'

Then said she faintly: 'O, contrive some way—
Some narrow winding turret, quite mine own,
To reach a loft where I may grieve alone!
It is a slight thing; hence do not, I pray,
     This last dear fancy slay!'

     'Such winding ways
     Fit not your days,'
Said he, the man of measuring eye;
'I must even fashion as the rule declares,
To wit: Give space (since life ends unawares)

To hale a conffined corpse adown the stairs;
For you will die.'

1867.

In *Desperate Remedies* Miss Aldclyffe tells Cytherea on her first night at
Knapwater House that she should beware trusting in Edward Springrove's fidelity over time:

You, as the weary weary years pass by will fade and fade—bright eyes will
fade—and you will perhaps then die early—true to him to your latest breath
and believing him to be true to the latest breath also; whilst he, in some gay
and busy spot far away from your last quiet nook, will have married some
dashing lady, and not purely oblivious of you, will long have ceased to regret
you. (I, Ch. 6.1)

2. *'She to Him II' (i. 19)*

Perhaps, long hence, when I have passed away,
Some other's feature, accent, thought like mine,
Will carry you back to what I used to say,
And bring some memory of your love's decline.

Then you may pause awhile and think, 'Poor jade!'
And yield a sigh to me—as ample due,
Not as the tittle of a debt unpaid
To one who could resign her all to you—

And thus reflecting, you will never see
That your thin thought, in two small words conveyed,
Was no such fleeting phantom-thought to me,
But the Whole Life wherein my part was played;
And you amid its fitful masquerade
A Thought—as I in your life seem to be!

1866.

In *Desperate Remedies*, after the wedding ceremony with Manston, Cytherea complains to her brother that her acquaintances cannot comprehend
how she experiences life:

And perhaps, far in time to come, when I am dead and gone, some other's
accent, or some other's song, or thought, like an old one of mine, will carry
them back to what I used to say, and hurt their hearts a little that they blamed
me so soon. And they will pause just for an instant, and give a sigh to me, and
think, 'Poor girl', believing they do great justice to my memory by this. But
they will never, never realize that it was my single opportunity of existence, as
well as of doing my duty, which they are regarding; they will not feel that what
to them is but a thought, easily held in those two words of pity, 'Poor girl', was

a whole life to me; as full of hours, minutes and peculiar minutes, of hopes and dreads, smiles, whisperings, tears, as theirs: that it was my world, what is to them their world, and they in that life of mine, however much I cared for them, only as the thought I seem to them to be. Nobody can enter into another's nature truly, that's what is so grievous. (II, Ch. 5.4)

3. 'Her Dilemma' (i. 16) (In —— church)

The two were silent in a sunless church,
Whose mildewed walls, uneven paving-stones,
And wasted carvings passed antique research;
And nothing broke the clock's dull monotones.

Leaning against a wormy poppy-head,
So wan and worn that he could scarcely stand,
—For he was soon to die,—he softly said,
'Tell me you love me!'—holding long her hand.

She would have given a world to breathe 'yes' truly,
So much his life seemed hanging on her mind,
And hence she lied, her heart persuaded throughly
'Twas worth her soul to be a moment kind.

But the sad need thereof, his nearing death,
So mocked humanity that she shamed to prize
A world conditioned thus, or care for breath
Where Nature such dilemmas could devise.

　　　　　　　　　　　　　　　　　　　1866.

This apparently is 'prosed' in the episode on Cytherea's wedding day also, when she sees her lover Springrove at the church:

The sight was a sad one—sad beyond all description. His eyes were wild, their orbits leaden. His face was of a sickly paleness, his hair dry and disordered, his lips parted as if he could get no breath. His figure was spectre thin. His actions seemed beyond his own control. (II, Ch. 5.3)

An earlier scene at the church when Cytherea agrees to marry Manston also contains phrases from the poem:

Everything in the place was the embodiment of decay: the fading red glare from the setting sun, which came in at the west window, emphasizing the end of the day and all its cheerful doings, the mildewed walls, the uneven paving stones, the wormy poppy heads . . . (II, Ch. 4.8)

4. *'She, to Him IV'* (*i. 20–1*)

This love puts all humanity from me;
I can but maledict her, pray her dead,
For giving love and getting love of thee—
Feeding a heart that else mine own had fed!

How much I love I know not, life not known,
Save as one unit I would add love by;
But this I know, my being is but thine own—
Fused from its separateness by ecstasy.

And thus I grasp thy amplitudes, of her
Ungrasped, though helped by night-regarding eyes;
Canst thou then hate me as an envier
Who see unrecked what I so dearly prize?
Believe me, Lost One, Love is lovelier
The more it shapes its moan in selfish-wise.

1866.

It has been suggested[2] that this poem's content lies behind the scene
where Cytherea sees Springrove in church with his fiancé, Adelaide Hinton, and suffers pangs of grief. She feels:

My nature is one capable of more, far more, intense feeling than hers! She
can't appreciate all the sides of him—she never will! He is more tangible to me
even now, as a thought, than his presence itself is to her! (II, Ch. 4.1)

---

[2] Dalziel, 'Exploiting the *Poor Man*', 229.

APPENDIX 2

Later Prefaces to the Novel

The following story, the first published by the author, was written nineteen years ago, at a time when he was feeling his way to a method. The principles observed in its composition are, no doubt, too exclusively those in which mystery, entanglement, surprise, and moral obliquity are depended on for exciting interest; but some of the scenes, and at least one of the characters, have been deemed not unworthy of a little longer preservation; and as they could hardly be reproduced in a fragmentary form the novel is reissued complete—the more readily that it has for some considerable time been reprinted and widely circulated in America.

January, 1889.

To the foregoing note I have only to add that, in the present edition of 'Desperate Remedies', some Wessex towns and other places that are common to the scenes of several of these stories have been called for the first time by the names under which they appear elsewhere, for the satisfaction of any reader who may care for consistency in such matters.

This is the only material change; for, as it happened that certain characteristics which provoked most discussion in my latest story were present in this my first—published in 1871, when there was no French name for them—it has seemed best to let them stand unaltered.

February, 1896.

The reader may discover, when turning over this sensational and strictly conventional narrative, that certain scattered reflections and sentiments therein are the same in substance with some in the *Wessex Poems* and others, published many years later. The explanation of such tautology is that the poems were written before the novel, but as the author could not get them printed, he incontinently used here whatever of their content came into his head as being apt for the purpose—after dissolving it into prose, never anticipating at that time that the poems would see the light.

T.H.
August, 1912.

EXPLANATORY NOTES

In drawing up the Notes I have consulted the editions of *Desperate Remedies* by
C. J. P. Beatty (London: Macmillan, 1975) and M. Rimmer (Harmondsworth:
Penguin, 1998). *The Life and Work of Thomas Hardy by Thomas Hardy*, ed.
Michael Millgate (London: Macmillan, 1984), is cited as '*Life*'.

1 [*Title-page, Epigraph*]: *Though a course . . . of reality*: from *The Monastery*
(1820), by Sir Walter Scott. The passage is misquoted in the first
edition of *Desperate Remedies* and corrected by later editions which
changed 'a course' to 'an unconnected course'.

VOLUME I

7 *Cytherea*: an alternative name for Aphrodite, the Greek goddess of love
and beauty. The name is linked to the island of Cythera where she is said
to have landed after being born from the sea-foam. It is shared by the two
central women in the narrative.

a young architect: like Hardy himself at this time and like the hero of *A
Pair of Blue Eyes* (1873). The early chapters of the novel in particular are
marked by precise architectural descriptions and terms.

had entered orders: been ordained as a clergyman in the Anglican Church.

beautiful and queenly: this Cytherea (or Aphrodite, goddess of love and
beauty), who later becomes Miss Aldclyffe, is both goddess (as here) and
wickedly manipulative (later).

8 *a kind of moral Gaza*: Gaza was a city which marked the limits of Canaan
on the coast. The phrase may mean 'the limits of his joy'.

9 *travelling . . . on account of delicate health*: a euphemistic way of concealing that the delicate health problem was an unwanted pregnancy. The
phrase 'a delicate condition/state of health' means 'being pregnant'.

11 *an antic*: grotesque theatrical representation. At this stage in his career
Hardy was undergoing a shaky transition to London life, and shows a
somewhat irrelevant scorn for the provinces.

12 *nullo cultu*: without training, a Latin phrase probably picked up from
Virgil.

13 *transom of masonry*: architectural term for cross-piece in a window which
is divided both horizontally and vertically.

14 *the ancient Tarentines . . . the State*: the Greek inhabitants of Tarentum, a
city in the south of Italy. During the Pyrrhic Wars the city fell to the
Romans in 272 BC. One story suggests that the idle and dissolute Tarentines failed to recognize what was happening when the Roman fleet sailed
into their harbour.

15 *escritoire*: writing-desk.

Laminæ: thin sheets.

bottomry security: the practice of funding a cargo-ship's voyage and accepting the vessel as security. If, as here, the vessel sinks, the investor loses everything.

brig: two-masted square-rigged ship.

16 *blindly you will love . . . a well-disciplined heart*: an allusion to *David Copperfield* (1850) by Charles Dickens. There Annie Strong, who is married to a much older husband, finally resists the temptation of succumbing to a younger man. She thanks her husband 'for having saved me from the first mistaken impulse of my undisciplined heart' (ch. 45). A 'well-disciplined heart' would make a practical choice of love object.

17 *a bill . . . in Chancery*: as in *Bleak House* (1853) by Dickens. The reference is to this division of the High Court which could give relief to a litigant where there was no remedy in common law.

pot-wallopers: originally (before 1832) the most impoverished grade of voter, but by this time a term of abuse meaning 'vulgarians'.

18 *breastpins of a sarcastic kind*: presumably a flight of fancy suggesting that, to the vulnerable Grayes, even fastenings of this kind suggest derision.

a humble under-clerk: becomes 'under-draughtsman' in 1896, as Edward Springrove's social status is raised by Hardy. See also note to p. 23. Throughout these early chapters the novel focuses on minute shades of social difference in class and shows great sensitivity to anything construable as snobbery.

19 *complete his articles*: complete his training to become a professional qualified architect.

21 *peasantry*: an unusually condescending term for Hardy to use, possibly triggered by social unease. His preferred term later is 'work folk'.

Creston: based on Weymouth, on the coast of Dorset.

22 *Point-blank grief*: sudden and unexpected grief.

23 *fourth finger*: finger on which the engagement ring is usually worn.

If he's a bold, dashing soldier . . . still poor: evidently a play on the children's game for predicting a future husband: 'soldier, sailor . . . rich man, poor man . . .'.

head clerk: this becomes in 1889 'head draughtsman'. 'Clerk' was essentially a term for a minor office-worker. In the context of architecture, 'draughtsman' implies a skilled creator of drawings, though in other contexts it may refer to a mere copyist. See note to p. 18.

24 *cock-sparrow*: a male sparrow, but used to refer to sparrow-like characteristics such as smallness.

25 *He is . . . humble origin*: again Hardy upgrades Springrove socially in 1889. The latter adds: 'He is a thorough artist, but a man of rather humble origin.' See also notes to pp. 23 and 18.

Grecian nose: one that is straight and continues the line of the forehead.

tout ensemble: 'whole appearance'.

26 *pap-and-daisy school of verse*: evidently verse which combined blandness with superficial prettiness or appeal.

Has she the temper, hair, and eyes I meant to have: these questions are those which Elfride puts to Knight in *A Pair of Blue Eyes* (ch. 18) when longing for his affection.

29 *elderly unmarried girls*: in 1889 this phrase is replaced by 'some among the passengers'. 'Girls' (as in 'factory girls' or 'match girls') could be used in a patronizing way of a group of lower-class women of any age. Here Hardy uses it disparagingly of spinsters or elderly virgins.

31 *clear spirit . . . last infirmity of noble mind*: the first of several references to 'Lycidas' by John Milton (1637), which Hardy would have read in Palgrave's *Golden Treasury* (see Introduction, p. xii). He likens Springrove, in his present position as a failed poet, to Edward King, the drowned would-be poet for whom Milton's elegy was written. Both are perceived by the narrator as unfortunate in their fates, despite their high-minded dedication to the search for poetic fame. This dedication is ironically described in the phrase quoted as a 'weakness'. Later Springrove makes the same allusion and Cytherea picks it up (note to p. 45). Hardy himself at this period wrote much poetry which he did not or could not publish.

consols: government securities, which are a safe but not very profitable form of investment.

32 *A tie . . . to unite us*: it was in March 1870, while writing this novel, that Hardy met and suddenly fell in love with Emma Gifford who copied part of the manuscript for him. This may have suggested the phrase.

paddle-boxes: the boat is evidently a paddle-steamer and these boxes are the casings for the paddle-wheels which propel it.

33 *with a hopeless sense of loss . . . no more*: the same image is used in *The Well-Beloved* (1897) to describe Pierston's reaction to the departure of the first object of his successive infatuations: 'I thought my Well-Beloved had gone for ever (being then in the unpractised condition of Adam at sight of the first sunset)' (Part I, ch. 7).

One hope is too like despair | For prudence to smother: from 'One word is too often profaned' (1821) by P. B. Shelley (1792–1822), printed in *The Golden Treasury*, which expresses the frustration of one who, like Springrove, 'can give not what men call love'. In Springrove's case this is because he is already engaged to Adelaide Hinton.

35 *the keeper of a gate-house*: level-crossing guardian.

pallet: a straw mattress or bed.

The Houses of Parliament were on fire: this fits in with the date of the events in the first chapter since the fire occurred on 16 October 1835.

The precision as to the date here has a point, since it provides a reason for the man to remember the timing of the visit of Miss Aldclyffe (under the alias of Jane Taylor) and her swoon at the news of the illness of her illegitimate child.

37 *soi-disant*: so-called.

the Ancient Mariner: in 'The Rime of the Ancient Mariner' by S. T. Coleridge (1798), the Mariner is under a compulsion to repeat to certain of those he meets his strange story of how, by killing an albatross, he caused the deaths of all his shipmates. The gateman seems to be under a similar compulsion to tell his dramatic story.

38 *do without them*: changed in 1896 to 'make use of their poor relations', possibly implying a change of practice in the years since *Desperate Remedies* was published in 1871.

Twenty-five shillings a week: *A Manual of Domestic Economy* in 1857 gave an average lower-middle-class salary as £150 p.a. Owen Graye's income here of £66 p.a. is well below that figure.

journeymen mechanics: manual workers employed by a master.

40 *rudder unshipped*: the steering mechanism is unfixed and the boat needs someone to steer it.

41 *He looked at her . . . life began*: from 'The Statue and the Bust' (1855) by Robert Browning (ll. 29–31). The lines are used to describe the moment at which a Florentine duke and the bride of one of his subjects fall in love. Their passion is frustrated by the woman's husband who keeps her shut up at home, from the window of which each day she catches one glimpse of her lover.

Arcadian innocence: a reference to Arcadia, the home of the god Pan, idealized as a setting for rural life in Virgil's *Eclogues*. Here it suggests a happiness based on youthful illusion.

cockle-shell: a small, frail boat.

43 *a smooth*: a smooth stretch of water.

Sweet, sweet Love . . . slain thus: an allusion to *The Princess* by Alfred Tennyson (1809–92), where it is used to refer to the slaying of love if men and women were not seen as diverse or different.

delivered the god: released the god Love, mentioned in the previous sentence as likely to be slain if Springrove ends the trip with Cytherea prematurely.

pine at him: look yearningly at him.

44 *They give their whole attention . . . conversation*: this suggestion that social skills are what win authors success may echo Hardy's feeling when his first novel, a social satire *The Poor Man and the Lady*, was rejected for publication, partly on the grounds that he did not know from the inside the upper-class society he was satirizing.

like Cato . . . fashion: Marcus Porcius Cato 'the Elder' or 'the Censor'

(234–149 BC). He applied himself from 184 BC to reforming the morals and extravagance of the Roman nobility with a proverbial severity. His ideal was to return to the moral simplicity of an agricultural state.

45 *Poetical days . . . past with me*: Hardy himself, from 1865 onward, wrote poetry constantly but kept it 'private' (*Life*, 51). It remained unpublished in his lifetime.

it doesn't matter to me now . . . 'thankless Muse' no longer: Springrove, like the narrator, aligns himself with the drowned and ill-fated poet memorialized in 'Lycidas' (see note to p. 31).

'sporting' with her: Cytherea picks up the allusion to 'Lycidas' in which, unlike Milton and King, some other poets 'sport with Amaryllis in the shade', i.e. dally with the pastoral shepherdesses. This is why, guessing her thoughts, Springrove refers to her as 'an Amaryllis'. She regards the term, a conventional name for a shepherdess in pastoral, as slighting if applied to her.

the fame of Christopher Wren . . . Pudding Lane: the Great Fire of London, which began at Pudding Lane in 1666, destroyed much of the city. Wren subsequently built some fifty new churches, including his masterpiece, St Paul's Cathedral.

46 *they are either famous or unknown*: this statement is also found in *An Indiscretion in the Life of an Heiress* (Part I, ch. 8), published in 1878 and based on Hardy's first unpublished novel.

47 *The bloom and the purple light*: a compressed version of a line from 'The Progress of Poesy' by Thomas Gray (1716–71), found in *The Golden Treasury*: 'O'er her warm cheek and rising bosom move | The bloom of young Desire and purple light of Love'. This is a description of 'Cytherea', goddess of love. Purple was the imperial colour, which hence developed the sense 'brilliant/splendid/magnificent', and it is used here to suggest the transforming effect of love and desire. Hardy's version is more discreet than Gray's in that he makes no reference to the 'rising bosom'.

48 *many a voice of one delight*: from 'Stanzas written in Dejection near Naples' (1818), by Shelley. The poem (found in *The Golden Treasury*) contrasts the beautiful and joyous sunlit seashore with the poet's misery.

49 *forgetting herself to marble like Melancholy herself*: an allusion to 'Il Penseroso' (1631–2), by John Milton, an address to Melancholy whom he pictures as 'Sober, steadfast, and demure'. He urges her to come to him and, lost in contemplation, 'Forget thyself to marble'. The poem is in *The Golden Treasury*.

Love is a sowre delight . . . life: from a sonnet by Thomas Watson (*c.*1557–92), in which a lover accuses first the god Love and then his own mistress of turning his love to misery.

50 *we desire as a blessing . . . given us as a curse*: we desire work which God inflicted on Adam as a punishment for his sin: 'In the sweat of thy face shalt thou eat bread, till thou return unto the ground' (Genesis 3: 19).

51 *leaden-eyed despairs*: in 'Ode to a Nightingale' (1820), John Keats contrasts the world of the nightingale with the misery of the world of men: 'Where but to think is to be full of sorrow | And leaden-eyed despairs'. The poem is in *The Golden Treasury*.

53 *good deed in a naughty world*: Portia, the lady turned lawyer in *The Merchant of Venice* (*c.*1596–8) by Shakespeare, says: 'That light we see is burning in my hall, | How far that little candle throws his beams! | So shines a good deed in a naughty world' (v. i. 89–91). 'Naughty' in the sixteenth century meant 'evil, wicked'.

54 *crimson-flock paper*: wallpaper made by sprinkling fine fragments of wool onto the paper then dyeing it.

the embrasure . . . window: window recess.

a Roman nose: a nose having a prominent upper part or bridge.

56 *Those who remember Greuze's 'Head of a Girl'*: a reference to a painting thought then to be by Jean-Baptiste Greuze (1725–1805), in the National Gallery. This pose, with head partly turned over the shoulder, had long been a favourite in portraits of women. Hardy writes that from 1865 to 1867 'His interest in painting led him to devote for many months, on every day the National Gallery was open, twenty minutes after lunch to an inspection of the masters hung there' (*Life*, 53).

fishers of men: a phrase used by Christ to two of his followers who were fishermen: 'I will make you fishers of men' (Matthew 4: 19), i.e. of men's souls. Here it is ironically used of women fishing for men. See also note to p. 209.

tyro . . . wheeling: she is no novice at changing her mind.

59 *a cubit higher*: an echo of Matthew 7: 27: 'Which of you by taking thought can add one cubit unto his stature?' A cubit was approximately the length of a forearm.

pony-carriage . . . spring-waggon . . . chaise: the use of the pony-carriage/chaise, a private carriage drawn by one or more horses, indicates a degree of politeness on Miss Aldclyffe's part. A spring-waggon was a strongly made vehicle, probably open-topped, which was suitable for carrying heavy goods. Another indication of Hardy's preoccupation with the treatment of a lower class by a higher.

turnpike road: a major (toll) road.

61 *about to style her Miss*: 'Miss' was a polite term meaning roughly 'the young lady of the family'. Cf. note to p. 63.

as solitary as Robinson Crusoe: Hardy greatly admired and frequently reread *Robinson Crusoe* (1719) by Daniel Defoe. The servant's allusion to the novel is possible, since it was one of the most widely read books amongst working-class people and was often used in voluntary schools. But the connection between Crusoe and loneliness had become almost proverbial by this time.

Dang it: euphemistic substitute for 'damn'.

The Lord must be a Tory at heart: changed in 1889 to '. . . a neglectful party at heart'. Hardy always claimed later to have no interest in party politics. This suggests an early interest, later erased.

62 *proud as a lucifer*: proud as a devil or Satan.

She hangs the chief baker . . . between 'em: an instance of Hardy's practice of making rustic speakers apply biblical stories or statements to everyday use. In Genesis 40 Pharaoh imprisons his chief butler or steward and his chief baker for offending him. According to the dreams which each of them has, Joseph rightly predicts that the steward will be freed and the baker hanged.

Knapwater House: based on Kingston Maurwood House, the estate where Hardy's father worked.

freestone: any fine-grained sandstone or limestone that can be sawn easily.

Greek classicism . . . Roman orders: the so-called 'Greek Revival' at the end of the eighteenth century led to a simpler form of neo-classical architecture than the more ornamental style of preceding years. In 1912 Hardy removed the word 'Greek' from the sentence. His dislike of the earlier eighteenth-century Palladian forms of architecture is again clear in the description of High-Place Hall in *The Mayor of Casterbridge*: 'It was Palladian, and like most architecture erected since the Gothic age was a compilation rather than a design' (ch. 21).

a pediment: a triangular architectural feature over a portico.

63 *ice-houses*: a structure, usually partly underground and with non-conducting thick walls, in which ice was stored in winter for use throughout the year.

we are all mistresses: Cytherea comments ironically on the fact that, as servants, she and the housekeeper are to be called Mistress—regardless of their marital status. In some families successive maidservants were even given the same first name as their predecessor by their employers.

64 *sleepers*: guests who stay overnight.

like another Blessed Damozel: in Dante Gabriel Rossetti's poem 'The Blessed Damozel' (1850), she leans 'From the gold bar of Heaven'. The allusion is an ironic reference to the contrast between her state and Cytherea's.

65 *no enemy but winter and cold weather*: an allusion to the song 'Under the Greenwood Tree' in Shakespeare's *As You Like It*. It is sung by one of the lords living in the Forest of Arden with the exiled Duke and it expresses pleasure at a life where there is 'No enemy | But winter and rough weather' (II. v. 7–8).

Three Tranters Inn: a 'tranter' is a man who does jobs with a horse and cart, a carrier.

67 *cabinet piano*: a tall type of upright piano invented by William Southwell in 1807. The strings were placed vertically and reached to the ground. The front was often filled with pleated silk.

67 *Mr. James Sparkman, an ingenious joiner*: an uncle of Hardy's, James Sparks (1805–74) was a furniture-maker and some have thought the name based on his. In 1889 the name was removed.

n'importe: Fr. 'No matter'.

69 *The sole object . . . passed over*: this harks back to the opening lines of the novel but was omitted in 1889. See Introduction, p. xxiii.

70 *chemisette*: an ornamental and detachable part-bodice, like a shirt-front.

Brussels net: a machine-made imitation of Brussels lace, which was a delicate and even-textured kind of lace and very costly.

71 *arabesque work*: flowing, low-relief decoration.

72 *as if she had been a jar of electricity*: similar uses of this image are found in *The Woodlanders*. Fitzpiers there tells Winterborne, 'people living insulated, as I do by the solitude of this place, get charged with emotive fluid like a Leyden jar with electric' (ch. 16). Another, similar allusion comes later from his mistress, Felice Charmond: 'Hintock has the curious effect of bottling up the emotions till one can no longer hold them; I am often obliged to fly away and discharge my sentiments somewhere, or I should die outright' (ch. 26).

73 *fuel to maintain its fires*: a quotation from 'The True Beauty' by Thomas Carew (1594/5–1640) where it is used to describe how a lover fuels his passions by gazing at his mistress's beauty. The poem is in *The Golden Treasury*. Its inappropriateness here is typical of Hardy's early labour to acquire a 'literary' language.

If it were a lady's: if it were the language of a woman of a superior class. Cytherea is becoming as touchy as the narrator on the subject of social class.

Possest beyond the Muse's painting: here means incensed beyond what the narrator can describe. From 'The Passions: An Ode for Music' (1850), by William Collins (1720–1856), found in *The Golden Treasury*. The line describes the passions stirred by music.

76 *the Landed Gentry*: from 1833 onwards what is now known as *Burke's Landed Gentry* was published. Its full title was *A Genealogical and Heraldic Dictionary of the Landed Gentry of Great Britain and Ireland*. J. Burke was the first editor.

79 *'Now kiss me', she said*: in 1912 Hardy added 'You seem as if you were my own, own child!' This and other changes (see notes to pp. 80 and 82) all suggest that by 1912 Hardy had begun to fear that this passage might be read as depicting a 'Sapphic' passion on the older woman's part. Hence the attempt to stress its motherly nature, justified by Miss Aldclyffe's love for Cytherea's father.

80 *can't help loving you*: 1912 adds 'But I am a lonely woman, and I want the sympathy of a pure girl like you, and so . . .'

to love and be loved by: 1912 changes to 'to care for and be cared for by'.

82 *were you ever kissed by a man*: Henry Knight, in Hardy's *A Pair of Blue Eyes* (1873), shares Miss Aldclyffe's wish for an untouched girl, and tells Elfride: 'I always meant to be the first comer in a woman's heart; fresh lips or none for me' (ch. 30).

I love you better: 1912 changes this to 'I love you more sincerely'.

84 *Love's passions . . . a wintry sky*: from Shelley's 'The Flight of Love' (1824) (found in *The Golden Treasury*), with minor variations. There are also quotations from this poem in *A Pair of Blue Eyes* (ch. III) and *An Indiscretion in the Life of an Heiress* (Part II, ch. 3). Shelley is one of the poets Hardy quotes most frequently in his novels, up to the very last.

86 *delicious*: 1912 has 'ecstatic', perhaps because the former term was felt to be overused.

88 *People say it means death*: a common superstition. Hardy records how Wessex, his dog, turned his bark of greeting to 'a piteous whine' when a favourite of his, William Watkins, called at Max Gate in 1925. The dog seemed ill at ease throughout the visit, and the Hardys later heard that Watkins had died suddenly an hour after leaving them (*Life*, 461).

90 *Probably nine-tenths of the gushing letters . . . upon them*: Hardy writes in a notebook in 1870 that 'Nine-tenths of the letters in which people speak unreservedly of their inmost feelings are written after ten at night' (R. H. Taylor, *The Personal Notebooks of Thomas Hardy* (London: Macmillan, 1979), 4).

91 *blotting-book*: a book of blotting paper used for drying the ink on letters.

92 *as the banquet-hall deserted*: another quotation from *The Golden Treasury*, taken from 'The Light of Other Days' by Thomas Moore (1779–1852). The poem recalls in a sentimental manner the past happinesses with loved ones now dead: 'I feel like one | Who treads alone | Some banquet hall deserted, | Whose lights are fled | Whose garlands dead, | And all but he departed!'

as Hallam says of Juliet . . . this love: this refers to the comments of the critic Henry Hallam (1777–1859) on Shakespeare's *Romeo and Juliet*: Juliet is 'a child whose intoxication in loving and being loved whirls away the little reason she may have possessed' (*Introduction to the Literature of Europe in the Fifteenth, Sixteenth and Seventeenth Centuries* (1837–9), ii. 392).

94 *Rustics in smock-frocks*: the distinctive garb of farm labourers. They were loose garments of coarse linen worn instead of coats and reaching to the calf.

99 *a cross roof*: a roof at right angles to the gables.

mullioned and transomed . . . lights: mullions are the vertical bars dividing windows into sections, and *transoms* are the cross bars. The small glass divisions they create are *lights*.

saw-pit: an excavation over which a frame is erected to take a large log of timber. This enables two men to use a saw to cut it, one man in the pit, one at ground level.

101 *the Field and the Builder*: professional magazines, founded in 1853 and 1842 respectively.

102 *Lincoln's-Inn-Fields*: one of four sets of buildings in London which have exclusive rights to the training and admission of British barristers. The others are the Inner Temple, the Middle Temple, and Gray's Inn.

104 *clubbists*: members of exclusive London clubs for men. The implication is that they are idle snobs by contrast with hard-working labourers.

Society of Architects: shortly after going to London in 1862 Hardy became a member of the Architectural Association, and in 1863 won an essay prize from the Royal Institute of British Architects.

105 *ÆNEAS MANSTON, Esq.*: Aeneas is the Trojan hero of Virgil's *Aeneid* who, after the fall of Troy, sailed to Italy where he became the founder of Rome. His mother was Aphrodite/Venus/Cytherea. Hence a link is shown between the first names of Manston and Miss Aldclyffe, his mother.

109 *He is a voluptuary with activity*: he is actively dissipated. Possibly Manston's effeminate appearance suggests that he is 'unmanly'.

111 *woman and woman, not woman and man*: a remark designed evidently to dispel sexual innuendo. Arguably it could do the reverse.

a carnal plot: changed in 1896 to 'an ungodly machinery', to remove sexual overtones. See note to p. 79.

Ah, were he now ... could chide: taken from the comic opera *The Duenna* (1775), by Richard Brinsley Sheridan (1751–1816). Donna Clara is at first angry with her lover for kissing her, but here changes her mind.

112 *a war of lilies and roses*: lilies and roses in such a context are a traditional convention in love poetry. 'Cherry Ripe' by Thomas Campion (1567–1620) begins: 'There is a garden in her face | Where roses and white lilies blow.'

A person who socially is nothing ... a great deal: this remark focuses on differences within the working classes, and Hardy's consciousness of them. He wrote as late as 1927 that there were 'two distinct castes' in country villages: 'one being the artisans, traders, "liviers" (owners of freeholds), and the manor-house upper servants; the other "work-folk", i.e. farm labourers ... The two castes rarely intermarried, and did not go to each other's house-gatherings, save exceptionally' (Michael Millgate, *Thomas Hardy: A Biography* (Oxford: Oxford University Press, 1982), 26).

116 *one who lived in Abraham's bosom all the year*: 'in Abraham's bosom' means 'with God', like the beggar who, in Luke 16, is carried to heaven while the rich glutton goes to hell. The phrase also occurs in Wordsworth's poem 'By the Sea', which ends with this address to a young girl:

'Thou liest in Abraham's bosom all the year | And worshipp'st at the Temple's inner shrine, | God being with thee when we know it not.'

118 *The railway had absorbed . . . the village*: the railway reached Dorchester by 1847, and the imaginary village described here is supposedly near that town.

119 *pommace*: pulp from apples after the juice has been squeezed out.

rammer: a rod with a block attached to one end.

I foresee too much; it means more than I thought: the implication here is that Springrove feels increasingly gloomy about his future as he ages. This contrasts with the exuberant predictions of the poem 'So Long!' by Walt Whitman (1819–92), from which this line comes. These predictions include 'justice triumphant' and 'uncompromising liberty and equality', even though the poet foresees his own death. Hardy writes in 1868, when trying to place *The Poor Man and the Lady*, that he also read a good many books 'including Whitman' (*Life*, 61).

parish clerk . . . Bowdlerized rake: a parish clerk was a lay official who assisted the clergyman with details connected with church services. 'Bowdlerized rake' is ambiguous. It may mean a dissipated man who conceals his sexual vices or—more probably here—a minor official who sees himself as an important religious figure. Thomas Bowdler (1754–1825) published an expurgated *Family Shakespeare* in 1818, hence 'to bowdlerize'.

grinder: a labourer who squeezes out the juice from the apples to make cider.

120 *to stop a footpath*: to block a right of way.

little green crabs: little, hard crab-apples.

hopper: an inverted pyramid or cone through which apples pass into the mill.

like St. Cecilia: like the patron saint of music.

121 *in the tenth commandment . . . 'Laws in our hearts we beseech thee'*: she also repeated the response to the first nine commandments after the tenth, for which the correct response ends 'and write all these thy laws in our hearts, we beseech thee' (Book of Common Prayer). Crickett is airing his skills.

stunpoll: blockhead.

Well, 't has been a power o' marvel . . . ends wi' 'Amazement': Crickett's interpretation of 'Amazement' to refer to the supposedly extraordinary fact of becoming his wife's third husband is wide of the mark. The marriage ceremony ends with an injunction to wives to obey their husbands as Sarah obeyed Abraham: 'whose daughters ye are as long as ye do well, and are not afraid with any amazement' (Book of Common Prayer).

122 *let the maid . . . she is a maid*: let such an unmarried girl be a vain young thing.

122   *The chimney-sweeper's daughter . . . deck her hair, O*: like the ballad which
      Crickett sings later called 'A New Song called the Curling of the Hair',
      there may be an allusion to pubic hair as well as head hair.

123   *pickthongs and griffins*: country names for types of apple.

      chimney-crook: chimney corner or nook.

      quean: probably here harridan rather than hussy. Certainly it is an abusive
      reference to Miss Aldclyffe.

125   *the cuckoo would cry*: this may mean that a mere bird's cry could startle
      her or (more probably) that the cuckoo's cry, being associated with adul-
      tery, would embarrass her.

126   *Livid grey shades, like those of the modern French artists*: presumably a
      reference to the artists whose paintings Hardy saw more than once in the
      International Exhibition of 1862 at South Kensington (the predecessor
      to the Victoria and Albert Museum). They were Théodore Rousseau,
      Charles Daubigny, Constant Troyon, Rosa Bonheur, and Jules Breton.
      The English visitors found the paintings drab: ' "Frenchmen", said one
      contemporary reviewer, "are addicted to looking at nature through a glass
      darkly; they paint in a low key and show their preference for sombre
      colours" ' (J. B. Bullen, *The Expressive Eye: Fiction and Perception in the
      Works of Thomas Hardy* (Oxford: Clarendon Press, 1986), 39).

128   *the vindictive determination of a Theomachist*: a Theomachist is one who
      fights against God; i.e. Manston is utterly ruthless.

      but to a woman . . . body: this idea that a woman feels through her clothes
      as with her body is one used in early novels by Hardy to create a sexual
      frisson if they are touched by a man. See *A Pair of Blue Eyes*, ch. 22.

      Ultima Thule: originally the name for an unknown land far to the north of
      Britain. By this time it means the outmost limit.

129   *Here, you see, they have . . . old outline still*: this visit by Cytherea to see the
      house provides Manston with an opportunity to work on her and for the
      narrator to include an architectural account of an Elizabethan house.

130   *from their teeth*: merely with their mouths (not from the heart).

132   *The varying strains . . . surface*: in Hardy's *An Indiscretion in the Life of an
      Heiress* Egbert Mayne is similarly affected by music at a performance of
      Handel's *Messiah* (1842), which he hears at a concert where he sees
      Geraldine Allenville: 'The varying strains shook and bent him to them-
      selves as a rippling brook shakes and bends a shadow' (Part II, ch. 2).

      the Pastoral Symphony: Beethoven's Sixth Symphony (1808), the 'Pas-
      toral', includes a section 'Joyous thanksgiving after the storm', which
      may well be the part referred to here.

134   *Like Beatrice accusing Dante from the chariot*: a reference to Dante's *Pur-
      gatorio*, cantos 30 and 31. Dante arrives near the limits of Purgatory, his
      guide Virgil disappears, and he sees the dead Beatrice descending from
      Paradise in a chariot. She rebukes him for the sinful life he has led since
      her death, brings him to repentance and shame, cleanses him in the River

Lethe, and ultimately leads him through Paradise. Her reproaches, like Cytherea's, still indicate great tenderness.

135 *The emotion I felt made me forgetful of realities*: this again resembles *An Indiscretion in the Life of an Heiress*, where Geraldine writes to Egbert after their meeting at the concert: 'It was when under the influence of much emotion, kindled in me by the power of the music, that I half assented to a meeting with you' (Part II, ch. 3).

VOLUME II

139 *precipitance of soul*: rashness of spirit. The phrase is taken from the sonnet 'To Burke' (1794), by S. T. Coleridge (1772–1834). Like many other quotations in this novel, it is applied in a totally different context from the original 'proud precipitance of soul', which refers to the rashly reactionary nature of some of the political views of Edmund Burke (1729–97) in relation to the French Revolution.

140 *Ingenium mulierum . . . ultro*: 'the ways of women. When you will, they won't: | And when you won't they're dying for you' (trans. C. Tait Ramage, *Beautiful Thoughts From Latin Authors* (Liverpool: Edward Howell, 1864), a work owned by Hardy). The origin of the Latin here is *Eunuchus* by Terence (183/193–159 BC).

144 *A woman shall compass a man*: Manston seems to use a biblical quotation to imply ironically that a woman can ruin a man, i.e. his wife can spoil any chance of obtaining Cytherea. In Jeremiah the reference is to Israel as a 'backsliding daughter' who must turn again from her faults (31: 22).

145 *a hybrid . . . supremacy*: Owen shares his sister's extreme sensitivity to the treatment given out by those who are 'superior' in rank to those they see as inferiors. The Grayes presumably feel it acutely because they have fallen down the social ladder since the death of their father. In 1889 this phrase was changed to 'a hybrid monster as to social position' and in 1896 to 'a hybrid monster in social position'. This represents a weakening of the tone of social sensitivity as Hardy's own position became established.

The tearful glimmer of the languid dawn: from 'A Dream of Fair Women' (1832), by Alfred Tennyson.

146 *the attitude of Imogen . . . Belarius*: in Shakespeare's play *Cymbeline*, Imogen the heroine is in disguise and fleeing from unjust accusations. She soliloquizes miserably as she enters the cave of Belarius, only to find that his supposed sons are her long-lost brothers (III. vi).

two disconnected events . . . distinct: early evidence of Hardy's preoccupation with coincidence. In 1871 he wrote in his notebook: 'Though a good deal is too strange to be believed, nothing is too strange to have happened' (Taylor, *Personal Notebooks*, 8).

148 *distanced*: outdistanced.

with a peculiar corner to her eye . . . behind her: in 1872 Hardy wrote that

he heard in Dorset the statement 'She can use the corners of her eyes as
well as we can use the middle' (Taylor, *Personal Notebooks*, 10).

150 *the pencil of Carlo Crivelli*: a Venetian painter (*c.*1430–95). Distinctive
features of his paintings are his use of sharp outlines and slender, spidery
hands of a Gothic kind. Hardy would have seen his work in the National
Gallery, which he frequented in the late 1860s. 'Pencil' could mean
'brush' at this time.

a nameless thing: an unchaste woman. From the earlier sense of 'nameless', i.e. illegitimate, a bastard.

stick a moral clock in her face: react as though morally sensitive by fake
facial expressions.

151 *Sodom . . . Gomorrah*: the two cities in Genesis which are destroyed
because of the inhabitants' sexual immorality and other evil practices:
'because the cry of Sodom and Gomorrah is great, and because their sin
is very grievous' (Gen. 28: 20).

153 *street dog*: ownerless dog.

restitution of rights: the remedy of the restitution of rights was open to
her. A husband's non-compliance with the decree was a ground for
obtaining maintenance.

156 *She is an American*: this probably carries disparaging overtones, as American women were generally thought to be bolder, less womanly, and more
proactive than English women. Compare the American Mrs Hurtle, Paul
Montague's ex-mistress in Trollope's *The Way We Live Now* (1875), who
pursues him to England to persuade him to marry her.

157 *Quos ego . . . failing heart*: from Virgil's *Aeneid* (i. 135) where the god
Neptune expresses his anger at the winds for interfering in his dominion
by enraging the waves: 'Audacious winds! from whence | This bold
attempt, this rebel insolence? | . . . Whom I—but first 'tis fit the billows
to restrain' (Dryden's trans.) The implication is that Miss Aldclyffe is
feigning the indignation of a superior but cannot sustain it. Hardy had
early access to Dryden's translation of the *Aeneid*, which his mother gave
him in 1848, and from 1856 to 1859 he read several books of Virgil in
Latin (*Life*, 21 and 32). He also uses the same phrase in ch. 8 of *The
Pursuit of the Well-Beloved* (1892).

the same law of natural selection: an allusion to *The Origin of Species*
(1859), by Charles Darwin (1809–82) which in 1871 he followed with its
application to humanity in *The Descent of Man*. In the latter Darwin
discusses at length the process of human sexual selection and argues for
the importance of beauty and sexual attractiveness, particularly in
women, for acquiring a mate. In men it is strength and vigour which
attracts, so here Manston is casting himself in a female role when priding
himself on the power of his physical beauty to attract women. Ideas like
Darwin's were already being floated before 1871.

158 *Like Curius . . . her who did*: Manius Curius Dentatus, famous in Roman

times for his simplicity and severity. As consul in 290 and 275 BC, he was successful in defeating the Samnites and also in the Pyrrhic Wars. When the Samnites tried to bribe him he replied that he preferred to rule those who possessed gold rather than to possess it himself. Hardy makes ironic use of this story, since Manston's attitude is far from the high-mindedness of Curius. His source may be *The History of Rome* by Thomas Arnold (1795–1842).

159 *at a broker's*: at a pawnbroker's shop.

161 *gig*: a light, two-wheeled, one-horse carriage.

Bradshaw: a time-table of all the trains running in Britain. The earliest edition was published in 1839 by George Bradshaw (1801–53).

162 *carpet-bag*: a travelling bag, originally made of carpet material.

164 *gentle or simple*: whether with the status of gentleman or without.

165 *a strange concurrence of phenomena*: see Introduction, p. xxiv.

168 *grave*: a trench for earthing up root vegetables.

mangel-wurzel: beet.

ostler: stableman or groom.

169 *barge-boards*: ornamental boards running along the edge of gables to conceal supporting beams and to protect against rain.

garden engine: a portable force-pump used for watering gardens.

Ring the bells backwards: a superstitious practice supposed to warn of danger or threatened evil. 'Backwards' means ringing the bells in a sequence from lowest to highest pitch instead of the reverse, which is usual. In fact there is nothing now to be done by way of raising the alarm as that has already been effected, though there is a danger of the fire spreading.

171 *The autumn wind, tameless, and swift, and proud*: from Shelley's 'Ode to the West Wind'. The poet likens himself in spirit to the wind, though 'changed and saved'. (The poem is included in *The Golden Treasury*.) Hardy simply uses it without a contrast to describe the wind that spread the fire almost exultantly.

the Old Hundred-and-Thirteenth Psalm: Hardy, like many others, was familiar with the Psalms, which would have been performed by his father and grandfather, both church musicians. Psalm 113 is 'An exhortation to praise God for his excellency and for his mercy'. Its jubilant tone perhaps accounts for its being one of the psalm tunes used for church chimes in this way. It was used, according to Emma Gifford (whom Hardy met at this time), in St Andrew's Church in Plymouth, where she grew up (Evelyn Hardy and Robert Gittings (eds.), *Emma Hardy, Some Recollections* (London: Oxford University Press, 1964), 6).

172 *the mathematical horizon*: the astronomical or real horizon, as distinct from the apparent natural or visible horizon.

173 *somebody wanting*: somebody he lacked.

173 *in spite of a fashion . . . difference of degree*: Hardy here challenges the view
     that women are a complementary species to men, from whom they neces-
     sarily have 'separate spheres' of activity and a separate nature. It is a view
     he does not sustain in this novel, but in his late work he does maintain
     this perspective.

     indefinable helpmate . . . flesh of a woman: this is the germ of the idea
     which becomes the framework for *The Pursuit of The Well-Beloved* (1892)
     and its later version, *The Well-Beloved* (1897). There the hero, Pearston/
     Pierston, pursues an imagined object of desire through a series of infatu-
     ations with different women throughout his life. The idea is ironically
     treated in these late texts, but here it is simply used.

     'Tis she . . . cloudy character: from 'Wishes for the Supposed Mistress' by
     Richard Crawshaw (1612/13–49). The preceding two stanzas are used by
     Hardy as an epigraph to the first part of *The Well-Beloved* (1897). The
     poem is found in *The Golden Treasury*.

     "hungry generations" . . . muser in a city: Hardy uses this phrase from
     Keats's 'Ode to a Nightingale' (1818) to indicate that poverty drove
     Springrove to ignore his love for Cytherea for a time: 'Thou wast not
     born for death, immortal Bird! | No hungry generations tread thee
     down.' The poem is found in *The Golden Treasury*.

176 *a concussion*: a blow.

     Such a Cushi . . . king: Cushi is sent in the biblical story to tell King David
     of the death of his beloved son, Absalom: 'And the King was much
     moved; and went up to the chamber over the gate, and wept; and as he
     went, thus he said "O my son Absalom! Would God I had died for thee,
     O Absalom, my son, my son!" ' (2 Samuel 18: 33). Hardy described this
     biblical chapter in 1887 as 'the finest example of its kind that I know,
     showing beyond its power and pathos the highest artistic cunning'
     (Harold Orel (ed.), *Thomas Hardy's Personal Writings* (London: Macmil-
     lan, 1967), 107).

178 *launch*: a West-country word used also to describe the flinty ground at
     Flintcomb-Ash in *Tess of the d'Urbervilles*, ch. 43, where it is spelt 'lan-
     chets/lynchets'.

     the whole term of lives: the duration of a lease for a period covering named
     lives means that Springrove is like Giles Winterborne in *The Wood-
     landers*, who loses several cottages when his father dies. Here the farmer
     loses the cottages which he thought would support him in his old age.
     Such leaseholders were called 'liviers', and Hardy's family were among
     them.

182 *Sterne . . . good of the dead*: from a letter by Laurence Sterne (1713–68),
     author of *Tristram Shandy*, to a critic who complained of his satirizing
     the dead in the novel: ' "You are not to speak anything of the dead, but
     what is good" Why so?—Who says so?—neither reason nor scripture.'

187 *Talibus incusat*: the reference is to a passage in Virgil's *Aeneid* describing
     an encounter between Aeneas and his mother, Venus, disguised as a

huntress. He resents her not appearing in her own form. Dryden's translation reads 'Against the Goddess these complaints he made . . .' (i. 140). The use of the Virgilian scene suggests a heroic stature for Manston and his mother.

cambric: fine white linen.

188 *black japanned clamps*: clasps lacquered in the Japanese style.

189 *provisional servant*: one who works on a casual or part-time basis.

190 *lumbar vertebrae*: the lower spine

os femoris: thigh-bone.

In the morning . . . thou shalt see: in the Bible, part of God's punishment threatened for those who break the Mosaic Law (Deuteronomy 28: 67).

191 *new lamps for old*: a phrase taken from the tale of Aladdin, who acquired a magic lamp containing a genie which fulfilled his wishes. A magician gets possession of the lamp in Aladdin's absence by offering a servant new lamps for old. Once again the quotation is used in a way at odds with its original context. It merely means that Miss Aldclyffe will get new cottages for the old ones which were burnt.

wicket: a small gate for foot passengers.

192 *in that absent mood . . . vivid impressions*: similar to a description of the lover Egbert Mayne in *An Indiscretion in the Life of an Heiress*, as he goes to get a marriage licence, 'in that state of mind which takes cognisance of little things, without at the time being conscious of them, though they return vividly upon the memory long after' (Part II, ch. 6).

creditor: this should be 'debtor', and it was changed to that reading in 1889.

conditions of release: conditions for being free of the requirements of the lease that the houses should be rebuilt.

193 *Bohemian*: unconventional.

like a good many others . . . subordination of classes: this is the view of a man who, unlike the Grayes, is aspiring to go up the social ladder. They are distressed because they have gone down and are, they think, badly treated by those who are really their social equals, not superiors.

194 *as Mary Stuart's . . . Puritan visitors*: Mary, Queen of Scots (1542–87) was a Roman Catholic and consequently was not favoured by her puritanical Protestant subjects. It is not known which meeting with Puritans is referred to.

195 *She had; he came here . . . wrote the letter*: this statement is not accurate, since Manston had been there three or four days before Cytherea went to see him. Miss Aldclyffe may be trying to produce an impression of dramatic love at first sight within a day of his arrival.

196 *Tongue-fencing*: debating.

197 *Lachesis*: one of the three Fates in Greek legend, who control the thread of life: Klotho 'the spinner', who holds the distaff; Lachesis, who draws

off the thread; and Atropos, who cuts it short. An early instance of Hardy's use of Fate, Destiny, Providence, and other names for a superior power as well as God.

197 *MR EDWARD SPRINGROVE*: 'Mr.' is a term then used for those who did not rank high enough to be called 'esquire' (as Manston is, below).

199 *Love is not love . . . alteration finds*: from Shakespeare's Sonnet 116: 'Let me not to the marriage of true minds | Admit impediments.' It is found in *The Golden Treasury*.

tossing feverishly . . . singing in his ears: this description of Edward is another evidently based on Egbert in *An Indiscretion in the Life of an Heiress*: 'turning restlessly from side to side, the blood throbbing in his temples and singing in his ears' (Part II, ch. 5).

200 *freeholds*: evidently, in addition to the cottages he has lost in the fire, Springrove owns two cottages outright, one his own and one inherited by Adelaide from her mother, who was the farmer's sister.

204 *rencontre*: meeting.

the sphere descended Maid . . . unrelenting: from 'The Passions: An Ode for Music', by William Collins (1721–59): 'O Music! sphere-descended maid; | Friend of Pleasure, Wisdom's Aid! | Why, goddess! Why to us denied | Layst thou thy ancient lyre aside?' The poem is found in *The Golden Treasury*.

Like some fair tree . . . his designs attend: the congregation is singing Psalm 1 from the metrical version of Nahum Tate (1652–1715), which celebrates the just man in God's sight. It is an ironic contrast to Springrove's feelings of misery. In *An Indiscretion in the Life of an Heiress* Geraldine quotes another version of this psalm to praise Egbert Mayne's relative success in London: 'Last Sunday, when we came to this in the Psalms, "And he shall be like a tree . . . it shall prosper", I thought, "That's Egbert in London" ' (Part II, ch. 1).

205 *her sheer inability . . . delighting to kiss the rod*: this captures the conventional view of 'woman': that she was, if womanly, naturally self-sacrificing. There are other comments in the novel that contradict this view (see Introduction, p. xx).

punctilious observance . . . Sermon on the Mount: the Sermon lists the seven 'beatitudes', including 'Blessed are the meek: for they shall inherit the earth' (Matthew 5: 5). This, presumably, is the part of the Sermon to which Cytherea adheres.

Horatian rather than Psalmodic: secular rather than sacred.

O what hast thou of her . . . from myself away: from a translation by Thomas Creech (1659–1700) of one of the *Odes* of Horace (65–8 BC), addressed to a woman 'grown old' (iv. 13). Hardy uses it to describe Springrove's feeling about his cousin, Adelaide, whom he once loved.

206 *He always contrived . . . her situation*: always wooing her as an equal, not an inferior in social rank.

petits soins: small courtesies.

the Fane: the Temple.

208 *any Laodicean ... zealous Episcopalian*: the Laodiceans were rebuked in the Book of Revelation for lacking religious fervour, being 'neither cold nor hot' (Rev. 2: 16). Such a one could be converted into an ardent supporter of the Church of England by the fact that his sweetheart could be seen at church. Two other characters in Hardy are 'Laodiceans', Gabriel Oak in *Far From the Madding Crowd* and Paula Power in *A Laodicean*.

Wordsworth and the Wandering Voice: an allusion to Wordsworth's 'To the Cuckoo': 'O blithe new-comer! I have heard, | I hear thee and rejoice. | O Cuckoo! Shall I call thee Bird, | Or but a wandering voice?' The poem (found in *The Golden Treasury*) expands on the poet's search for the bird that remains invisible.

Your form ... an ivy leaf: this speech reads like a lengthy parody of the group of Shakespearian sonnets that urge a lover to pass on his beauty to his descendants by marrying.

209 *the greenish shades of Correggio's nudes*: Antonio Allegri, an Italian painter (*c.*1489–1534), was named after the town in Emilia where he was born. His nudes were usually mythological figures, sensuously painted. There is another reference to Correggio's nudes in *An Indiscretion in the Life of an Heiress* (Part II, ch. 1), where Egbert sees a painting by him.

a professional fisher of men: see note to p. 56.

a cloud no bigger than a man's hand: 'Behold there ariseth a little cloud out of the sea, like a man's hand' (1 Kings 18: 44). It foretells a storm.

211 *erysipelas*: a fever accompanied by a deep red rash. Also known as St Anthony's Fire.

212 *chloroform*: the use of chloroform as an anaesthetic was initiated in 1847 by Sir James Young Simpson (1811–90). It became more popular after being used during the birth of Queen Victoria's ninth child in 1853.

213 *Dares at the Sicilian games ... more on industry than force relies*: another passage from Dryden's *Aeneid*, with two changes. Dryden reads: 'And like a captain' and 'that other part in vain'. See also *An Indiscretion in the Life of an Heiress* for its use in the epigraph to Part II, ch. 2, which describes Egbert's efforts in London.

214 *wherein De Quincey ... Opium*: refers to *Confessions of an English Opium Eater* (1822), by Thomas De Quincey (1785–1859). He became an addict in 1812. Opium was much used in the nineteenth century by those who wanted oblivion.

chapters ... famine and drought: refers to 1 Kings 18–19, which were part of the liturgy of the Church of England in late summer.

So like, so very like, was day to day: from 'Elegiac Stanzas Suggested by a Picture of Peele Castle' by Wordsworth, which recalls past happiness when 'So pure the sky, so sweet was the air! | So like, so very like was day to day!'

215 *Lavater . . . obliterated*: Johann Kaspar Lavater (1741–1801) was a Swiss theologian who played a key role in making acceptable the theory of physiognomy, connecting facial appearance and innate character. In a translation of one of his works the effect of a woman's beauty on a man is said to be that it reveals 'the boundary between appetite and affection' (Thomas Holcroft (trans.), *Essays on Physiognomy for the Promotion of Knowledge and Love of Mankind* (1789), vol. iii, ch. 12). In Manston's case this division is unclear. In 1889 the sentence was deleted, perhaps reflecting the diminishing acceptability of Lavater's theories.

tithe-paying . . . cummin: the narrator's views on Manston are evident from the biblical passage to which this refers: 'Woe unto you scribes and Pharisees, hypocrites! For ye pay tithe of mint and anise and cumin, and have omitted the weightier matters of the law, judgement, mercy and faith' (Matthew 23: 23).

217 *mandrakes . . . their shrieks*: plants of the genus mandragora which have thick fleshy forked roots that were thought to resemble a human body. They were reputed to utter deadly shrieks when torn up by the roots.

219 *her heart's occupation was gone*: a paraphrase of Othello's 'farewell to arms' which ends 'Farewell! Othello's occupation's gone' (III. iii. 361).

220 *So true a fool is love*: from Shakespeare's Sonnet 57: 'Being your slave, what should I do but tend | Upon the hours and times of your desire?' The final couplet is: 'So true a fool is love that in your will, | Though you do anything, he thinks no ill.' The poem is included in *The Golden Treasury*.

Trinity: the Sunday after Whit Sunday, observed as a feast day in honour of the Holy Trinity. The season of Trinity follows this and lasts until the fourth Sunday before Christmas.

the Evening Hymn: a hymn by Bishop Thomas Ken (1637–1711): 'Glory to thee, my God, this night.' Ken is referred to as 'the author of the Evening Hymn' in *Jude the Obscure*, Part II, ch. 1. See also Part I, ch. 1 of *An Indiscretion in the Life of an Heiress*, which begins: 'The congregation in Tollamore Church were singing the evening hymn, the people gently swaying backwards and forwards like trees in a soft breeze.'

223 *Old Christmas-day*: although Christmas Day was fixed as 25 December in 1752, the date fixed earlier, 6 January (or Epiphany), was still referred to in country districts as Old Christmas Day. It would give Cytherea a respite for twelve days more before her wedding.

224 *You do not mind Fridays*: Friday was regarded as a day of ill-omen. Hence 'Friday-faced'—sad-looking. The source may be a connection with the crucifixion of Christ on Good Friday.

226 *like the gauzes of a vanishing stage-scene*: like the painted backcloths of a play being withdrawn.

hymeneal: marriage-like, joyous, from Hymen, the Greek God of marriage.

227 *like those of a malefactor on a gibbet*: in 1856 Hardy had seen the execution of a murderer at Dorchester and, using a telescope from a nearby hill, he watched as 'the white figure dropped downwards, and the faint note of the town clock struck eight' (*Life*, 33).

228 *the great Mother*: Nature.

229 *the smoke-jack*: an apparatus for turning a roasting-spit.

the Flanconnade in fencing: a thrust onto the side or flank.

a closer: it clinches the question of whether the wedding can take place.

230 *stooping like Bel and Nebo*: false idols of Babylon which, in the Book of Isaiah, are said to be overcome by God (Isa 46: 1).

three-cunning: devious, roundabout.

skimmer your pate: 'cover your head with flour', or 'beat your head with a skimming ladle'.

daddlen, and hawken, and spetten: dawdling, coughing, and spitting, i.e. not clearly making up his mind.

231 *ash-leaf taties*: small-sized potatoes.

before I took orders: to take orders is to be ordained as a priest. So Crickett, who is merely a parish clerk, is again displaying his delusion about his importance in the church.

to sickness-or-health-it: to marry. A reference to the phrase 'to have and to hold . . . in sickness and in health', from the marriage service (Book of Common Prayer).

232 *even Spenserian—bridal-mood*: a reference to the two wedding hymns 'Epithalamion' (1595) and 'Prothalamion' (1596) by Edmund Spenser (1552–99). Both are sumptuous celebrations of marriage, and the second (included in *The Golden Treasury*), closes each stanza with the refrain: 'Against their bridal day, which was not long: | Sweet Thames run softly, till I end my song.'

233 *fetichism*: attributing life to inanimate things. This would fit the earlier comment that women see clothes as an extension of their bodies.

cadaverous marble: marble with corpse-like pallor.

234 *spectre-thin*: from Keats's 'Ode to a Nightingale' (1818): 'Where youth grows pale, and spectre-thin, and dies'. It is found in *The Golden Treasury*.

vinaigrette: small ornamental bottle of smelling-salts.

idiosyncrasy: physical constitution.

235 *gone to ruin*: fallen into the pit of prostitution.

240 *The world and its ways . . . simple policy*: another quotation from 'The Statue and the Bust' by Robert Browning (see note to p. 41). It comes from the section where the frustrated lovers decide to accept their separ-

ation in the mistaken belief that they may gain by it. There is another reference to the poem in *Jude the Obscure*, Part VI, ch. 4.

241 *miniver*: fur used as a lining or trimming on ceremonial robes, possibly ermine.

    brougham: one-horse, closed carriage with two or four wheels. A closed carriage was more luxurious than an open one.

243 *Columbus . . . contemptibly unaware*: this implies that even Christopher Columbus, who was looking for a route to the East Indies when he discovered America, was not so unaware of what was happening as Owen later recognized himself to have been at this time.

244 *ha' got crazy-religious*: has become a religious maniac.

245 *the dairy-barton*: cows' part of the farmyard.

247 *the testament in the waiting room*: from 1845 the British and Foreign Bible Society placed bibles in railway waiting-rooms and other public places to encourage the reading of Scripture. The first stations to be provided with bibles were those of the South-Western Railway.

250 *at twice*: in two goes. The train was divided so that the engine could pull the carriages through in two stages.

VOLUME III

266 *outstep*: out of the way, remote.

269 *plenus rimarum*: full of holes, that leaks secrets as in the *Eunuchus* of Terence: 'plenus rimarum sum: hac atque illac perfluo' ('I am full of holes; I leak at every point').

272 *some of . . . lozenges*: lozenges are four equal-sided figures with two acute and two obtuse angles.

    Abigail is lost, but Michal is recovered: these women were two of David's many wives (see 1 Samuel 25 and 2 Samuel 6). Michal was given by Saul to Phalti. There is no other similarity than this between their stories and that of Cytherea and Mrs Manston.

    Cui bono?: to what end, or purpose.

    a land of darkness . . . as darkness: taken from Job 10: 22.

273 *red and black jackets*: this was changed in 1889 to the socially correct, 'pink and black coats'. Though the jackets are red, they are referred to as 'hunting pink'. Another indication of Hardy's social sensibilities, since it indicates his awareness by 1889 of an earlier solecism.

    comely as the tents of Kedar: from the Song of Solomon 1: 5: 'I am black but comely, O ye daughters of Jerusalem, | As the tents of Kedar, as the curtains of Solomon.'

    lissom: supple, agile.

terms dangerous to her honour: on terms that threaten her reputation; terms that lay her open to the charge of sexual misconduct.

275 *a hundred and twenty pounds a year*: compare this with the twenty-five shillings a week he earns earlier (note to p. 38).

276 *Utterly fictitious details . . . circulated*: presumably that the marriage had already been consummated.

Apt to entice a deity: from 'Rosaline' by Thomas Lodge (1558–1625): 'Her lips are like two budded roses | Whom ranks of lilies neighbour nigh, | Within which bounds she balms encloses | Apt to entice a deity' (included in *The Golden Treasury*). Hardy copied the phrase 'apt to entice' into his *'Studies, Specimens &c.' Notebook*, ed. Pamela Dalziel and Michael Millgate (Oxford: Clarendon Press, 1994), 11.

a brown settle: a bench with high arms and back, usually set beside the fireplace

277 *I said, if there's peace . . . hope for it here*: from 'Ballad Stanzas' by Thomas Moore (1779–1852), describing the kind of unkissed girl that Miss Aldclyffe (like Knight in *A Pair of Blue Eyes*) wants: 'to know that I sigh'd upon innocent lips, | Which had never been sigh'd on by any but mine.'

279 *a nameless and unsatisfactory, though innocent state*: she is neither wife, widow, nor unmarried girl.

locus standi: status.

280 *the scandal*: the rumour of Cytherea's having consummated the bigamous marriage.

282 *convicted of bigamy*: Springrove believes that Manston knew all along that his wife was alive and had not been burnt to death in the fire. Therefore he thinks Manston knowingly went through a bigamous ceremony with Cytherea.

a wild hill that had no name: in *A Pair of Blue Eyes* 'the Cliff without a Name' is the site of Knight's dangerous fall from which Elfride rescues him (ch. 21).

284 *Seasoning justice with mercy*: from the court scene in Shakespeare's *The Merchant of Venice*, where Portia, disguised as a man, defends Antonio against Shylock: 'And earthly power doth then show likest God's | When mercy seasons justice' (IV. i. 191–2).

the fruit that one mind matures . . . twelve minds in one month: this implies that the jury who judged Manston's wife dead were foolishly wrong.

286 *courteous . . . as an ancient Iberian*: 'Iberian' here may be a reference to Spaniards and their elaborate politeness. It is possible Hardy has in mind *Don Quixote* by Cervantes (1547–1616) whose eponymous hero is fascinated by chivalric behaviour.

287 *Hoxton*: a poor area of London, just north of Shoreditch.

288 *to do fearful execution*: to stir up Raunham's strong feelings for her.

289 *jets of gas*: a practical form of electric light was not invented until 1879 by

Sir Joseph Wilson Swan in the UK and by Thomas Edison in the USA.

289 *marble-covered*: covered with variegated colours and patterns made to resemble marble.

290 *by the mail*: by the mail train.

291 *pinchbeck aristocracy*: spurious nobility ('pinchbeck' is an alloy of zinc and copper, used to imitate gold). Cf. Thackeray (1859): 'Those golden locks were only pinchbeck.'

295 *Who did you want?*: unusually in Hardy, he tried to indicate a Cockney accent in 1896 in the three repetitions of this sentence by changing 'want' to 'woant'. It is not clear what sound he wished to suggest.

Dutch clock: Dutch here has the earlier sense of 'German', referring to a type of cheap clock originally made in Germany, with exposed weights and wall-hung.

like the fæces of a Harpy; ('fædissima ventris proluvies . . . semper ora'): one of the very few references in Hardy's work to urban as opposed to rural poverty. The quotation is from Virgil's *Aeneid*: 'with Wombs obscene | Foul paunches, and with Ordure still unclean; | With Claws for hands, and Looks for ever lean' (iii. 216–18, trans. Dryden). The Harpies in Greek mythology are birds with the faces of women, who defile the food of Aeneas and his men.

296 *carte-de-visite photographs*: small photographs, which from the 1850s were affixed to visiting cards.

297 *By affixing an extra stamp*: this was a provision to enable early delivery of a late posting between 6 p.m. and 7 p.m. The extra stamp cost sixpence.

EUNICE: this has been described as 'Hardy's first published poem' (C. J. P. Beatty's edn., p. 401). But since it is written in the persona of Manston, it is presumably intended as trite, rather than personal to Hardy.

302 *some thimble-and-button*: a derogatory term implying a feeble character. An earlier phrase, 'thimble-and-bodkin' (thimble and needle) was applied disparagingly to Cromwell's army on the grounds that they were poorly equipped because their weapons were purchased with the small funds contributed by their impoverished supporters.

in-and-out: someone who is in and out of the workhouse.

no other god . . . his neighbour's wife: a reference to the First Commandment, adjuring worship only of the one, true God; and to the Tenth Commandment, forbidding the coveting of a neighbour's wife (Exodus 20).

who do pay his penny: a reference to the Penny Post, set up in 1840 for the whole of the UK so that all letters were charged at this single rate.

He flung his mallet . . . Joan's ale was new: from 'The Seven Trades' or 'Joan's Ale'. This is 'the mason's verse' from the country drinking-song.

304 *market-merry*: can mean market-fresh, but here seems to mean mildly drunk.

high-treasoned: charged with high treason.

caddle: muddle, tangle.

what will Billy do!: What shall I—the silly idiot that I am—do?

311 *indwellers*: residents who are not native to the place.

314 *with pearl-powder and carmine*: a whitening face powder and a form of rouge. Make-up was associated with prostitutes.

315 *magistrate*: a person not legally trained who acted as a judge in a minor court, as Hardy himself did later.

318 *adultery ... statute*: this refers to divorce law prior to 1857, when a woman could not divorce her husband on the grounds of adultery alone but needed some aggravating cause such as cruelty, bigamy, incest, or bestiality.

319 *Corinthian that he was ... like St. George's dragon*: Corinthians were by reputation licentious: 'It is reported commonly that there is fornication among you, . . .', 1 Corinthians 5: 1. St George slew a dragon given to devouring a virgin every day.

322 *In the Flying Isle of San Borandan*: a mythical island, sometimes called St Brendan's Isle. It was said to have been seen by sailors, including the legendary Irish saint Brendan. The implication is that she is dead.

324 *could have been compelled ... lawful wife*: Manston could have sued for the restitution of his conjugal rights.

325 *anybody would think that you were the woman and I the man*: an echo of the many ambivalent comments by the narrator on Manston's gender.

327 *turnscrew*: a screwdriver.

in Paphos: in the kingdom of love. Paphos is a city near the south-west coast of Cyprus where, in legend, Aphrodite was born from the sea-foam.

334 *Non illa ... assueta manus*: 'Unbred to spinning, in the Loom unskilled' (*Aeneid* vii. 805–6, Dryden's trans.).

335 *an improper woman*: a woman of loose sexual morality. See note to p. 351 below.

a common p——: prostitute.

336 *the grain of mustard-seed ... a tree*: the doubts Raunham has planted in her mind grow to huge proportions, like the mustard-seed, in Matthew 13: 31–3.

341 *A man's cunning ... tent-nail*: in Judges 4: 21 Jael, having lured the enemy general Sisera into her tent, hammered a nail into his head as he slept.

344 *Battley's Solution of Opium*: opium was freely available and widely used in patent medicines.

box-staple: staple on a doorpost into which the bolt of a lock was shot and which was shaped to cover the end of the bolt.

345 *gallipots*: medicine pots.

346 *oblate*: spherical in shape, with flattened ends.

351 *these women who own to no moral code*: because prostitutes were sexually immoral, it was assumed that they were immoral in all respects. It was relatively daring to give a prostitute a central role in the plot, and the narrator is careful to refer to her immorality frequently.

352 *bull's eye*: lantern, named after the thick circular glass in its side.

355 *The pattern . . . Manston*: from this point on there is a train of 'clues' to be followed suggesting careful detection, though it is not clear how the pattern of Manston's chain could have been recognized.

   ewe-lease: pasture for ewes.

356 *steam-packet*: a boat plying at regular intervals between two places.

   but wearing light boots: not the heavy boots of a labourer.

359 *demon*: changed in 1889 to 'desperado'.

   One on her youth . . . giant size: from Dryden's translation of the *Aeneid* (v. 570–1), which has 'his youth'. Hardy has changed it to fit Cytherea.

360 *It was again the meeting . . . the Lord*: this describes the meeting of the prophet Elijah with King Ahab, who has seized the vineyard of Naboth after the latter has been put to death at the command of the king's wife Jezebel. Elijah rebukes Ahab, who repents of his crime (1 Kings 21: 20).

   the jaws of a gin: the two sets of teeth in a gin-trap which snap closed about the prey's foot.

362 *at being breasted*: being faced or confronted.

   We only suddenly . . . so soon: the idea of a preordained death day, like a birthday except that it is unknown, occurs in *Tess of the d'Urbervilles*. She realizes that there is another day more important than her birthday: 'that of her own death . . . a day which lay sly and unseen among all the other days of the year, giving no sign or sound when she annually passed it over' (Phase II, ch. 15).

364 *turnkey*: warder, prison guard.

   an earnest: an indication.

365 *lanced . . . with my pen-knife*: i.e. 'letting blood' in an attempt to bring her out of a faint.

366 *couch-heap*: heap of grass weed.

367 *shoulder nails*: strong, peg-like nails.

368 *operate upon my birds*: steal them.

   Ghostly mouths talking: this was changed in 1912 to 'the ghost of wife nagging her man'.

371 *she shrieked . . . and fell upon the floor*: severe internal haemorrhage continued. This fatal event echoes what happens to Geraldine, the heroine of *An Indiscretion in the Life of an Heiress*: 'she fainted, and ruptured a blood-vessel internally and fell upon the floor' (II, ch. 7). When writing *An Indiscretion*, Hardy had actually taken advice from a distant relative who was a surgeon about how to explain a sudden death. The answer was

'Hemorrage of the lungs', so Hardy reused the idea in *Desperate Remedies* (Millgate, *Thomas Hardy*, 109).

372 *from Germany with her parents*: in 1896 this was changed to 'with her parents from Germany, where her baby had been born'.

376 *midsummer night*: 24th June. Presumably chosen to indicate that this, unlike the marriage to Manston, is to be a happy one.

phosphoric: phosphorescent.

sallies: woollen grips for the hands near the lower end of a bell-rope.

377 *triple-bob-major*: a peal of bells, in which the treble ('triple') bell follows a dodging course which is rung on eight bells.

tenor bell: the deepest (and therefore heaviest) bell in a peal.

metheglin: a spiced mead made from honey.

for a man to play wi' fire: referring to Cytherea's dealings with Manston.

She'll play wi'it again: she'll marry another man.

a poor third man: he is his wife's third husband.

378 *she'll pick up again ... gainsay*: the context here implies that picking up means putting on weight through pregnancy.

'A laughed ... my merry nater: the joke is that Weedy has six daughters and one son (who is brother to them all), while the parson assumed there were six brothers.

to Babylonish places: either 'decadent' or 'catholic' or both. Presumably continental Europe, where honeymoons were often taken.

Ah, toads o'em!: what wretched creatures they are!

traypsen: walking.

the dand: dandy.

379 *I am no trade*: I am not a workman.

her sly-gotten: illegitimate. Changed in 1896 to 'her love child'.

as deep as the North Star: the North or Pole Star is often referred to as a type of something very distant. This same description is also used of Paula Power in *A Laodicean*, who keeps her real feeling for Charlotte de Stancy to herself (Part I, ch. 5).

380 *forfeiture by felony*: presumably those acting for the Crown at first assumed that, as a murderer, Manston forfeited his right to benefit. But since his inheritance did not follow from his crime, they abandoned the case.

first man in some architectural competition: like Hardy himself: in 1863 he won a silver medal from the Royal Institute of British Architecture for an essay on a house of coloured bricks and terracotta; and a small money prize from the Architectural Association for a design for a 'Country Mansion'.

381 *as pure as Pentelic marble*: a famous white marble quarried near Athens.

a dozen swans: reminiscent of a line in Virgil's *Aeneid* (i. 543): 'Twelve Swans behold; in beauteous order move' (Dryden's trans.).

GLOSSARY

Note: Throughout the discussions of the rustic speakers, the modern English ending of verbs *-ing* appears as *-en*, e.g. *singen* = 'singing'.

'a he
a' I
afore before
a-growd grown
a'ter after
by-now just now
caddle muddle
carking painful, wretched
cetrer et cetera
cockle-shell small rowing boat
coorted wooed
couch couch grass
d' do
daddlen dawdling
en him
feller fellow
flee fly (verb)
grinden grinding
ha' have
ha'n't have not
hawken coughing
hev have
home-along homewards
id'n is not
'ill/'ll will/shall
lug drag (verb)
luggage train freight train
martel mortal; person
mid might (verb)
mi't might (verb)
m'm madam

naibour neighbour
nater nature
o' of
pa'son parson
pate head; noggin
prent print (noun)
quean a bold or ill-behaved woman
rale real
roof-tree main beam supporting the roof of a house
shadder shadow
sheenen shining
sid saw (verbal)
spak speak
spaken speaking
span distance from the tip of the thumb to the tip of the little finger when the hand is fully extended
spetten spitting
stimmilents stimulants
swaller swallow (verb)
tap roots main roots
taties potatoes
'tidn' it is not
turnscrew screwdriver
wi' with
winders windows
wold old
ye you

American Literature

British and Irish Literature

Children's Literature

Classics and Ancient Literature

Colonial Literature

Eastern Literature

European Literature

Gothic Literature

History

Medieval Literature

Oxford English Drama

Poetry

Philosophy

Politics

Religion

The Oxford Shakespeare

A complete list of Oxford World's Classics, including Authors in Context, Oxford English Drama, and the Oxford Shakespeare, is available in the UK from the Marketing Services Department, Oxford University Press, Great Clarendon Street, Oxford OX2 6DP, or visit the website at www.oup.com/uk/worldsclassics.

In the USA, visit www.oup.com/us/owc for a complete title list.

Oxford World's Classics are available from all good bookshops. In case of difficulty, customers in the UK should contact Oxford University Press Bookshop, 116 High Street, Oxford OX1 4BR.